JERUSALEM

A Tom Doherty Associates Book
New York

Jerusalem

CECELIA HOLLAND

JERUSALEM

Copyright © 1996 by Cecelia Holland

This book is printed on acid-free paper.

A Forge Book
Published by Tom Doherty Associates, Inc.
175 Fifth Avenue
New York, N.Y. 10010

Forge® is a registered trademark of Tom Doherty Associates, Inc.

Book design by Deborah Kerner

Library of Congress Cataloging-in-Publication Data

Holland, Cecelia.
    Jerusalem / Cecelia Holland.—1st ed.
        p.   cm.
    "A Tom Doherty Associates book."
    ISBN 0-312-85956-2 (acid-free paper)
    1. Jerusalem—History—Latin Kingdom, 1099–1244—Fiction.
    2. Crusades—Fiction.   I. Title.
    PS3558.O348J47   1996
    813'.54—dc20   95-38814
                                                                CIP

First edition: January 1996
Printed in the United States of America
0 9 8 7 6 5 4 3 2 1

For CHARLES N. BROWN,
the Wizard of Oakland

We have heard that a new order of chivalry has appeared on earth, and in that region which once He who came from on high visited in the flesh—a new sort of chivalry that tirelessly wages war both against flesh and blood and against the spiritual forces of evil.

—Saint Bernard

Non nobis, Domine, non nobis, sed Nomine Tuo da gloriam.

—Templar motto

Death is the master of life.

—PROVERB

halfway through the morning the second horse went lame also. Right away, riding double behind Mark, Rannulf could feel the hitch and stagger in the animal's stride, which grew worse with every step, until the horse pulled up and refused to move any more.

Rannulf slid down over its crupper to the ground. The other knight kept to his saddle; with a half-spoken oath he slammed his spurred heels savagely into the horse's flanks. The beast gave a long weary groan. Rannulf went off a few steps, looking around.

Bleached as an old bone under the piercing blue of the sky, the desert spread away from them, rising in the south to the black barren hills that the local people called Ibrahim's Anvil. To the north the road wandered off toward an uneven ridge, rippling in the heat. The horse sighed, exhausted, its eyes glazed.

Still in the saddle, Mark said, "This brute's finished." He pulled off his hat and wiped his face on his sleeve. "And so are we."

Rannulf said, "If we ride all night we'll reach Ascalon by dawn."

"Yes, but we have no horses. Although in your usual all-knowing way you probably haven't noticed."

"There's a caravanserai up ahead. We can walk there, find fresh mounts."

At that Mark doubled up the ends of his reins, swearing under his breath, and flogged the horse's neck and shoulder. Rannulf looked to the south again, wondering if the haze climbing across the sky were the dust of the oncoming Saracens. He did not think Saladin's army would move so fast as that. Mark's arm hung slack, the reins useless; then the horse folded at the knees and hocks and collapsed. With a yell the knight sprang clear.

Rannulf said, "We have to take the saddle."

"The hell with the saddle! There's a million sandpigs just beyond that hill!" Mark kicked the ground. His voice was shrill with fear and rage. "How far to this inn?"

"The saddle belongs to the Order." Rannulf stooped over the horse, which was still alive, and tugged the girths loose; the animal's belly heaved when his hand grazed it. The chances of finding horses at the caravanserai were not good, the chances of finding a saddle almost none.

Mark wheeled toward him. "Forget the saddle, Saint. I'll walk, but I'm not carrying anything I don't have to."

Rannulf's temper jumped, a spurt of heat behind his eyes; he crossed himself against it and faced Mark, but the other knight had seen the blessing and knew what it meant and backed off a few steps, his hands rising. "All right. All right." Stooping, he unbuckled the bridle and slipped it off the head of the dying horse, and Rannulf heaved the saddle up over his shoulder, and they walked away along the road.

The summer was over, and the worst heat had broken, but on this broad dry pan the sun cooked the air and the light shimmered like watery veils. Here and there, weeds tufted the thin sand crust of the plain. Paler than the land on either side, the road was not a single path but a zone hundreds of yards across of countless dimpled footprints, crisscrossing ruts and tracks, and ancient piles of dung. Standing stones lined its edge, along with piles of rocks, broken wheels and pack frames and useless rotten harness, and bones.

"How far to this inn?" Mark asked, again.

Rannulf shaded his eyes. "We may not have to go that far. Look." He pointed across the road. Out beyond the spotty row of stones and debris, a flag of dust trailed away toward the blue hills. Somebody was approaching the road from the east.

"Saracens," Mark said.

"I don't think so," Rannulf said. "They're ours."

"You can't see anything. You're guessing."

"No. Look where they're coming from. The only thing out there is Kerak. They're ours." Rannulf looked on ahead of the drifting dust, trying to figure where this approaching train would reach the road. "Come on," he said, and broke into a trot.

✦ Sibylla said, "I wish you would ride. You slow everything up." She checked her horse again, keeping to the pace of the cart.

Behind the plodding mules that pulled it, her cousin Alys sprawled on cushions, half-sitting, clutching the edge of the box with one plump hand, while the other beat constantly at the flies humming in the shade of the awning. "If you think this is comfortable, Sibylla, come and join me. But if I had to ride a horse, believe me, we would go even slower."

Sibylla gave a sigh. They had been travelling across the same blank countryside for two days; she itched to get to the end of it, to be somewhere else, anywhere else. The five knights riding in front of her lifted a haze of dust, which got into her eyes; she had told Guile, who commanded her escort, that she wanted something done about that, that they should ride behind her, and Guile had sneered at her and told her to go sit in the cart and keep the curtains closed.

"You shouldn't let him talk to you like that," Alys said.

"No, probably not," Sibylla said. She did not want to admit that she was afraid of Guile. Then up ahead of them, a shout sounded, and the knights crowded together in front of her and stopped.

Something was going on. The cart halted; Alys leaned forward, peering through the flies, and said, "What's that?" Sibylla reined her horse away from the cart, and rode off past the knights to the head of the caravan.

In front of the knights, Guile of Kerak had reined in his horse and drawn his sword. He was a burly man, older than she was; under the edge of his cap his hair shagged down bone-white to his shoulders. He called out, "Stand where you are!"

Sibylla reined in behind him, out of his range of vision, and looked where he was looking. Two men were walking toward them across the road. Ragged, dirty, bearded, they seemed like outlaws. At Guile's command, one stopped, but the other walked straight on, came up to the white-haired knight, and said, "I'm taking your horse. And I want another for my brother."

Sibylla tossed up her head, startled, and Guile gave a contemptuous laugh. "What? Get out of my way; I'll cut you down." He cocked his sword back over his shoulder.

The man in front of him made no move to his own sword, which hung in a black scabbard at his hip. He was carrying a saddle on his shoulder, and he dropped it to the ground, as if he had arrived home. Taking off his hat he wiped his streaming face on the sleeve of his jerkin. His black hair was cut short above his ears. Calmly he stared up at Guile, and said, "I am a Knight of the Jerusalem Temple, and I want your horse. Get off."

Behind Sibylla, a ripple of excitement went through the men of her escort. "A Templar. A Templar." Guile lowered his sword. Sibylla rode up closer, staring at the black-haired knight's chest, and now under the layers of grime she saw the red Cross splayed across his jerkin.

She swung around toward Guile, who was motionless beside her, his sword held across his saddlebow and his jaw bunched with coiled muscle, and she said, "Well? What are you waiting for? Give him your horse."

Guile glared at her. At her words the Templar who had hung back on the road limped up beside the black-haired man. He said, "Find out if they have anything to eat."

Sibylla rode in between them and Guile. "We will help you. I am the Princess Sibylla of Jerusalem, my father was King Amalric, and King Baudouin is my brother. Tell me how I can serve."

She expected some reverence, some proper respect, or at least a little gratitude, but the black-haired Templar never even looked at her. He spoke to the other knight. "Tell her she can get back to Kerak, or wherever she belongs, fast, and leave that cart here." Guile dismounted and the Templar went around her to take his reins. "Bring a horse also for my brother," he said to Guile. "Move! Now!"

Sibylla felt the heat rise in her face. She thought she had been courteous enough to a dirty nameless man on the road. The other Templar stepped forward, his face lifted to her, young, brown-bearded, his eyes amazingly blue above the mottled sunburn of his cheeks. "My Princess, please excuse Saint, here. His vow forbids him any commerce with women. Our mission is desperate. Saladin is coming north out of Egypt, with an army of thirty thousand men. We have to get to Ascalon, where he'll strike first."

She said, startled, "Saladin. But that's impossible." She turned around in her saddle, looking south, into the great barrier of the desert. "They have never attacked from Egypt."

"He's coming now," the brown man said. "And my brother here is right, my lady Princess. You have to get to safety, and the cart can't move fast enough."

"My cousin is—she doesn't ride," Sibylla said.

The black-haired man swung into Guile's saddle. "Tie her to the saddle." He kept his eyes averted from her, as if she were unfit to notice. A squire jogged up, leading another horse, and the brown-haired knight took the reins and mounted.

He said, "I suppose I'm still not going to get anything to eat?"

The black-haired man gave a low bad-tempered growl. Under him Guile's horse was already dancing, eager, pulling at the hard hand on its reins. Looking over his shoulder, the Templar stared at Guile, on foot still. The knight from Kerak was scowling all over his red face. The Templar said, "Bring the saddle to the Temple in Jerusalem." He put Guile's horse into a quick trot away down the road, with the other knight at his stirrup.

"Ugly brute," Sibylla said, under her breath.

She looked back into the south again, alarmed. If what the Templars said were true, and the Saracens were coming out of Egypt, the King-dom of Jerusalem lay naked before them: she knew all the Christian armies were far away to the north, near Homs and Aleppo. She had to get to Ascalon, to do whatever she could.

Guile had shortened his glare to focus on her. "Well. You heard him. Get your damned cousin out of the damned cart, and let's move."

"Yes," she said. "I think that's a very good idea, Guile." She rode back to the cart, to pack Alys onto a horse.

ell," Mark said, unnecessarily, "there they are." Rannulf pushed his helmet back off his forehead.

They sat their sweated horses on the rim of a steep brushy hill; before them the land fell in a long swoop down to the plain that stretched south and west toward Ascalon and the sea. Dust hung thick in the windless air, blurring the dun-green slopes of the hills. Through this churning brown haze the army of the Saracens moved along the low ground like a great river.

Here a wadi broke out of the hills onto the plain, a vast dry watercourse carved across the lowland. The van of Saladin's army had already crossed it. The rearguard was far out of sight to the south, probably still somewhere near the city of Ramleh, which the Saracens had looted and burned the night before. The enemy kept no order; they knew that for a hundred miles there was no Christian army large enough to face them; if they had noticed the little pack of Franks skulking through the hills between them and Jerusalem, they showed no interest. They moved in waves, long strings of camels, each heaped up with baggage and carrying a pannier on either side, in each pannier an axeman, or a lancer, or an archer. There were horse archers, too, Bedouin, like flights of gulls in their long white robes. Among them all, other soldiers ran on foot, begging rides; sometimes a rider would let them catch hold of a stirrup, and sweep them along a dozen strides through the air.

Mark said, "They'll be two days crossing the wadi, at least."

"Could be." Rannulf knew this place. The gulley was shallow and broad, no real problem, but the southern bank dropped off abruptly some ten or fifteen feet, and the Saracen army was piling up along the high edge, the horses and many of the camels balking at the plunge. Those coming up behind were spreading out to either side, so that now the whole southern bank of the wadi was packed with Saladin's soldiers. As Rannulf watched, part of the bank collapsed under the weight. A dozen horses slid down with the sand; their screams faintly reached his ears.

Mark said, "Here comes the King. What are you going to tell him? God, this is a disaster."

Rannulf shook his head, his gaze on the sprawl of men creeping over the plain. There were thousands of them, tens of thousands; he got tired of trying to count them. Between them and Jerusalem and the Tomb of Christ stood less than five hundred Franks, most of them not knights.

Hoofbeats clattered on the dry slope behind him, and he turned to watch the King of Jerusalem ride up, with the Master of the Jerusalem Temple, and the Bishop of Saint-George, bouncing along on his white donkey. At the top of the slope, side by side with the Templars, the young King drew rein, and looked out over the land to the south, and took in a sharp breath.

Rannulf watched him closely. The King interested him. Baudouin was seventeen years old; he had been king three years. Longer than he had been king, he had been a leper. The plague had eaten his face into a lumpy ruin, and his lips were pocked with sores. The brushed silk of his gold-embroidered surcoat and the golden circle of his crown decorated this dead flesh like gravegoods. For a long while he stared out at his enemies.

"God, God," he said, presently, "there are so many of them."

Beside him was the Master of the Templars in Jerusalem, Odo de Saint-Amand. Most of the Jerusalem chapter of the Temple had gone to fight in the north, the month before, but Odo had refused to go on Crusade because the King had not gone, and Odo de Saint-Amand would not disparage himself by following anyone of a lesser rank. Now he combed his long tawny beard with his fingers, studying the distant army of Saracens.

"There are a lot of them. Many are not true fighting men."

"They are not in good order," the King said. His voice was tight. His fist clenched before him, above the high pommel of his saddle. "I want to hit them, now, at once. I want to hurt them, right away, no matter what the cost."

At this, Mark straightened up, alarmed; his gaze went to Rannulf in a quick plea for help. "Sire. We have only a few hundred men. And if we fall, there's no hope for Jerusalem."

Rannulf was watching Baudouin, liking the fire that burned up so bright in the rotting body of the young King. The leper sat canted forward in his saddle, his back taut, his hand still clenched. In the dead clay of his face his eyes shone, brilliantly alive, his attention fixed on the enemy army. He said, "We have Jesus Christ. We have the True Cross."

Behind the King, the Bishop murmured, "Sire, the Templars know their work."

He meant to side with Mark, who was being rabbity, as usual, but on the King's other hand Odo gave a chuckle. "Some of us do, anyway." He turned to Rannulf. "What do you think?"

Rannulf said, "We can try something. They're too spread out, as the King said."

Odo said, "One hard charge in and out, hit them right on this side of the wadi, where they're coming up the bank. They wouldn't be ready. We could kill a few, scare a lot of them."

"Charge," the Bishop said, tightly. "Outnumbered as we are, that seems madness."

"Do it," the King said. He wheeled his horse around toward his lieutenants. "Go to the men—tell them if they love Jesus and the True Cross, then they must follow me now."

Odo wheeled his horse and rode off down the slope toward the handful of men waiting on the flat ground below. The King followed him, the Bishop at his heels, and Rannulf lifted his reins to go after. Mark glowered at him.

"You had to talk up. Odo wouldn't have said anything if you hadn't spoken for it." The young knight cast a quick glance after the King and turned back to Rannulf. Behind the iron nasal of his helmet his cheeks were red. "Shrive me."

Rannulf reined in; the other men had gotten on ahead of them, but they had a moment yet to do this. He nudged his horse around head to tail with Mark's, so that the two knights faced each other, knee to knee, stirrup to stirrup. Mark put up one hand to screen his face. His voice shook, low, intense, the words hasty.

"Forgive me, Jesus, for I have sinned. I have been greedy for food, for wine, and for women. I wanted praises. I lied. I put my will before God's will. My mind wandered during prayers. I envied those above me and despised those below. I took the name of my Lord God in vanity and rage. I shirked my duty. I was afraid to die." He paused a moment, sounding breathless. "That's all."

"Are you contrite?"

"I am heartily sorry for having offended God, deserving of all my love."

"Te absolvo," Rannulf said, and made the sign of the cross over Mark, and then crossed himself. Mark was clean, now. Rannulf wished he felt so clean. Down there, Odo was forming the King's little army into columns. The squires were riding up from the rearguard with the packhorses that carried the knights' fighting gear. The Bishop of Saint-George on his white donkey bore the standard of the Cross out in front of them all. Mark started to turn his horse, and Rannulf stretched one arm out to hold him.

"Shrive me."

Mark's eyes widened, and one eyebrow went up, but he knew better than to speak. Rannulf lifted his hand between them and turned his eyes away. "Forgive me, Lord Jesus, for I have sinned. I have lusted after a woman, I have done adultery with her in my heart." At that Mark turned his head, against the rules, and stared at him. Rannulf felt the weight of the look; he lowered his gaze.

"Are you contrite?"

He mumbled the formula.

Mark said, "Te absolvo."

Now Rannulf faced him, and Mark reached out and embraced him, and kissed his cheek. Side by side they rode down toward the little Crusader army, where Odo was ordering the other Templars.

These knights were not of the Jerusalem chapter. Three days before, as Saladin's army marched past Gaza, the eighteen knights of the garrison of the tower there slipped by along the coast and met the King's little army at Ascalon. They were Templars, which was what mattered. With Rannulf and Mark, they made up the whole of Odo's command. The Master walked his horse along their rank, looking them over, and as Rannulf and Mark rode in, he gave his orders in a clear voice.

"We don't have a standard, so you have to watch me. Keep moving. The trick here is not to let them lay their weight on us. Never let them outflank us. That means hold the line." He turned to Rannulf, who was putting on his helmet. "Rannulf Fitzwilliam will ride on the far right end. If I fall, he is Master."

Rannulf went along to the end of the rank; Mark pulled in on his left. "You got us into this," he said. He unhooked the shield hanging on his saddle and pulled the strap up over his head, the long kite-shaped wooden target braced on his left arm.

Rannulf slid into his shield. His back and neck were tingling, as always before he fought. The strap of the shield pressed against the familiar sore place on his shoulder. "God help us all." He laid his hand on the hilt of his sword. On his left Mark rode up even with him, the other knights beyond him in a solid wall, all the way to the Master.

Odo raised his arm, and the whole Templar rank rode forward, their horses head to head.

"Hold." Rannulf reined in. The young King was galloping up across his path.

On the slope before him, the Bishop of Saint-George had stopped his donkey, blocking the way of the little Christian army. Above his head he held high the standard of the Kingdom, a long pole wound with ribbons of gold, which bore on the top a reliquary with a piece of the True Cross. Gold and jewels covered this box, and the gold ribbons glistened in the sun, so that the Christians could see it from far off, and take heart. Now as the Franks began to move forward the King galloped up and leapt from his horse, and in front of everybody he flung himself down on the dusty ground where the shadow of the standard fell. He stretched his arms out and lay on the ground, making a cross of himself.

A gasp went up from all the men watching, and they pushed closer. Even Rannulf and the other Templars started forward. The King's voice rang out.

"Sweet Jesus, Son of God, I won't see them pass. Let me lay down my life here, to defend Jerusalem. In Thy Name, for Thy Glory—I beg you. If Saladin must pass, let me die standing in his way." He stood up again out of the dust. In the wreckage of his face his eyes glistened, bright and clear, streaming tears. "Thy Will be done!"

Then from all the tight-packed men who watched there went up a raw yell. "God wills it! Deus le vult!"

That cry raised the hackles at the nape of Rannulf's neck; he felt a sudden surge of power in his arms and shoulders, and his hand itched for his sword. His horse bounded under him. At the far end of the rank of knights, Odo raised his arm, and they all moved forward at a quick trot. The young King was galloping up over the hill, the Bishop on his heels. Behind them, the clamorous swarm of the other Christian men let out a roar.

"God wills it!"

Two strides behind the King, the Templars in their unbroken rank crossed over the brow of the hill and spurred into a gallop. Now the land sloped down, and they could see all the way to their enemies, the sprawling coils of the Saracen host, indistinct in their own dust, spread across the plain below. Rannulf pulled out his sword, the leather hilt filling his hand; with the familiar weight in his hand he wanted suddenly to strike, to give blows, and to kill. Mark surged up so close Rannulf's leg banged into the shoulder of his horse.

"Deus le vult!"

The shout rang out, high-pitched, and a hundred others joined it.

"Deus le vult!" Thin, it seemed, and faint in the dust-laden air. But they heard it, up ahead.

All along the bank of the wadi, there rose a wail of warning. At the sight of the Christians swooping in on them, the Saracens first in their path tried to scramble back out of the way, and the young King charged straight into their midst, the True Cross half a stride behind him, now, and just behind that, the massed weight of the Templars like a moving wall.

The Saracens gave way. Before the young King drove into their midst many were already turning to run. The braver ones stood and tried to fight, and the mailed knights on their massive horses smashed into them and rode straight over them. Above the crunch and jar rose the first piercing shrieks of the dying. Rannulf's body blazed; he lashed out with his sword, feeling himself alive all the way out to its tip.

In front of him, on the crumbling lip of the ravine, a hundred fluttering white robes tottered, staggering back into the faces of those still trying to climb up from below. Rannulf plunged into their midst, beating at whatever was closest to him. Mark galloped hard by his right side, the other Templars thundering along beyond. For a moment the sheer mass of the enemy slowed them, a tangle of horses and camels and men all struggling for foothold on the wadi's bank. A camel like a tower swung around to meet Rannulf, a warrior slung on either side; the man on the right cocked back a long-handled axe to strike, and the man on the left hefted his lance. Rannulf drove his horse straight into the camel. His shield rang under the blow of the axe. The lance came at him, and he shunted it off with his sword and in the same move struck, and the lancer toppled backwards out of his basket. The camel shrilled in terror. On its far side the Saracen axeman was clutching for the rein, his eyes popping in his dark face, his mouth agape.

Then suddenly man and camel both pitched away, falling through the ground, and under Rannulf's horse the ravine wall collapsed. Rannulf shoved his feet into his stirrups, and sat back hard, and his horse slid on its haunches down the bank of the wadi, sending up fountains of sand and dust.

The other Templars came down with him, holding their rank. Through the dust-laden air he saw Odo's arm lift, at the far end of the line, signalling another charge before they even reached the bottom of the slide. With a lurch Rannulf's horse got its hoofs on solid ground, and at a dead gallop he hurtled blindly forward through the boiling dust.

For a moment Rannulf saw nothing; then abruptly the dust cleared, and ahead of him stretched the flat sandy bed of the wadi. Hundreds of the Saracens were streaming away along it in a disorderly flight, most on foot. Rannulf leaned forward over his horse's shoulder and slashed at a body in a striped gown that ran away from him, two strides, screaming, and then vanished under the churning hoofs. A herd of loose horses stampeded ahead of him, casting up more dust. He could see nothing; he steered close to Mark, on his right, and when Mark swerved away, Rannulf spurred hard to keep up, to hold his end of the rank. They burst out of the cloud of dust into clear air again. Ahead of them, some of the Saracens were turning, were trying to stand together against the charging knights. They looked like Bedouin, they wore no armor, they carried only sticks and spears. From the Templar line a jubilant roar rose, raw-throated. Rannulf reined in his horse a little, shortening its stride; the rank surged up beside him, sweeping in on the waiting pack of the Saracens, and at the last moment he gave his horse its head and it shot forward, crashing into the huddled men before him. The Bedouin wheeled to flee, too late, and the Templars rode over their backs. For the first few strides Rannulf could not even use his sword. Then, ahead, through a curtain of drifting dust, he saw more of the Saracens standing fast.

Mark yelled. Rannulf heard his voice even through the din, and pressed closer to him. He could just make out the other Templars in their rank beyond him. He could not see what Odo was signalling. Before him a band of mounted archers packed the flat ground of the wadi, their horses dancing. In the glittering dusty air he saw the curved limbs of their bows. He crouched down in his saddle, covering up behind his shield. An arrow ticked off his helmet. Then suddenly more arrows rained down all around him.

The Templars did not break stride. In their mail, behind their shields, they rode invulnerable through the cascading arrows, and at a full gallop they hit the lighter Saracen horsemen and threw them backward almost to the bank of the wadi. A scimitar sliced at Rannulf's face, and he struck backhanded under it and felt flesh and bone give under his blade. His horse stumbled and caught itself. He breathed in a lungful of dust. Then abruptly they were breaking into the open again.

Far away down there, Odo's arm went up. Rannulf sat back in his saddle, bringing the horse down to a walk, and the reeling line of the Templars straggled to a stop with him and hastily pushed back into a tight rank. Beside him, Mark was gasping audibly for breath. Most of the other men looked whole and hale. Rannulf twisted in his saddle, looking around him.

The whole southern bank of the wadi seethed with Saracens scrambling up the side of the ravine. Bodies strewed the flat low ground, dead men, dead horses and camels. Rannulf saw no sign of the King or the True Cross. The other Christians he saw were chasing up and down the wadi, harrying anyone who would run.

A blow struck his arm, and he jumped halfway out of his saddle. Mark was staring at him. "Odo wants you," he said, and gestured.

Rannulf galloped down the line to where the Master waited, hunch-shouldered in his saddle, staring across the wadi. As Rannulf slid his horse to a stop, Odo pointed. "What's there?"

Down the wadi a little, the Saracens had kept some order; the top of the bank swarmed with bowmen, defending the sheer bank so that the men in the ravine below them could make their way up safely.

"That must be somebody important," Rannulf said. Among the bowmen there was a sudden flash of yellow. The Sultan's color. "Look. Mamelukes—see their helmets?" He pointed toward the distant glint of polished steel. "That's the Halka. The Sultan's guard."

Odo hissed between his teeth. "Let's take him!"

Rannulf grabbed his arm, holding him. "Not from below—get up on top of the bank, hit him from the side."

"Lead off," Odo said. Standing in his stirrups, he wheeled his arm. "Double column. Double column."

Rannulf swung back to his place in the line and at a short gallop headed down the wadi toward a place where they could scale the bank without opposition. His horse's neck bent double to the bit; with every stride it snorted. The other men followed him in pairs. Mark stayed even with him, all the while, still breathing hard; his helmet hid most of his face, but he rode stiff on one side. At the foot of the steep soft embankment Rannulf reached out and gripped his shoulder.

"Are you all right?"

The young knight's head jerked. "God's will be done," he said, his voice rasping.

Rannulf held onto him a moment longer. Mark seemed steady enough, and he was keeping in line, but he held his sword across his saddlebows and Rannulf had never seen him raise it. Before them stood the sloping bank of the wadi, riven and torn from the goings up and down, and they scrambled to the top.

Two hundred yards away the Saracen bowmen had seen them coming. They swung around, and the first dark bolts of their arrows slithered into the air, falling harmlessly short. Past the skittery archers, Rannulf saw more yellow robes, and the shining breastplates and pointed helmets of Mameluke officers. His heart leapt. Waiting for the order, he shortened rein, his battle-mad horse bounding like a deer and fighting for its head, while Odo wheeled the double column of the Templars into a single rank again.

Rannulf's gaze sharpened. The yellow robes were clustered together on the bank like a row of marigolds. Behind them, men on foot were hauling something ungainly up out of the wadi. A litter. Ribbons fluttered from its canopy. Rannulf let out a roar.

"Odo! That's the Sultan!"

At the far end of the line the Master shouted, "Take him!"

The Templars charged. The Sultan's yellow-robed guards faced them, their backs to the wadi, and to their own terrified men struggling up from below. The massed bowmen fired such a swarm of arrows that they threw a shadow over the sun. The Templars in their mail coats rode scatheless through the darts, and seeing them come relentlessly on the Saracens shrieked and flung their bows aside and ran away.

The armored Mamelukes did not run. Swords drawn, they crowded together between the oncoming Templars and the litter, and their high ululating warcries quavered out defiantly. Rannulf's reins, slippery with sweat, slid loose through his fingers; his horse bolted, carrying him a stride ahead of the other Templars, straight into the enemy. For an instant as the two armies clashed together, they stood each other straight up; the clash of their impact rang in Rannulf's ears like anvil music. Then his horse bounded forward, beating through the smaller Saracen mares, and Rannulf hacked down with his sword. With sweeping blows he cleaved through the yellow swarm toward the litter. A blow rang off his shield and he swung his left arm out, striking with the shield itself. Something crunched under the edge. Mark loomed up on his right, pushing forward; Rannulf could not see that he used his sword, but he was forcing his way on nonetheless, keeping the line, his shield up. Then directly in front of Rannulf was the litter, only a few yards on.

The bearers had thrown it down, and torn the silken curtains back. Frantically they were getting its passenger out and onto a white camel, rangy as a spider. Rannulf was half a stride ahead of the rest of the Templars, and two of the yellow-robed guards lunged forward to fend him off. His horse reared.

Surrounded by guards and servants, the man climbing out of the litter turned an instant; through the filthy air, the dust and the screams, he looked straight at Rannulf—a slight man, with an elegant black beard, piercing eyes. His turban fell off. He was bald as an onion. Ran-

nulf shrieked. He drove his spurs into his horse, fighting to reach that
smooth skull, to break it under his blade. The slight man hauled himself up the side of the white camel and fled away into a cloud of men.

Furious at this escape, Rannulf laid around him with his sword, bash-
ing at the wall of men and horses between him and the smooth skull he
wanted to crush. They yielded, but not fast enough; his horse reared
again, and the bald man was getting away. And now Odo was calling
him back.

He yelled. Everything in him wanted to go on, to chase down that
sleek skull, but the line was turning, and he turned with it. Odo led them
out onto the open plain and stopped and wheeled around, ready for another charge.

When Rannulf reined in, Mark was still next to him, but as soon as
the horses stopped, the young knight slid out of his saddle and hit the
ground like a sack of stones. Rannulf glanced over his shoulder. The
Saracens were spreading off across the plain, racing wildly away in a
dozen directions, yellow robes and all. Lifting one arm to Odo, he swung
out of his saddle and went down on one knee next to Mark.

On the trampled powdery ground Mark was clenched up in a hard
knot of pain, his arms and legs drawn to his body, and his breath bubbling through his teeth.

Odo rode up. "That was the Sultan, and we missed him."

"You pulled me off." Rannulf laid his hand against Mark's throat,
above the collar of his hauberk, and felt the life knocking there, fast and
light.

Odo said, "Stay with him. I'm going to find the King." At once he
was riding off, the others following. There were five fewer than when
they had started, but they had left dead Saracens all over the plain: a good
exchange. Rannulf wished he had caught that smooth domed skull
under the edge of his sword.

He stood up. Slipped the shield off his arm and hung it on his saddle, took the bit out of the horse's mouth, and untied the black-and-
white blanket from behind the cantle. The battle had moved on. From
the south the wind brought the cries and the clash of weapons, the
pounding of hoofs, and screaming. He gave a quick keen look around
for looters and knelt down by Mark.

"Can you get up?"

Mark muttered something too soft to hear. Rannulf knew how it was
with him by the wet sound of his breathing, but he had relaxed a little,
and Rannulf could straighten his legs out and wrap the blanket around

him. He put his hands on the younger man's helmet and drew it off, and with a sigh Mark laid down his head on the ground.

His face was green-white. His right arm was broken—had been broken, Rannulf knew, since the first charge. He had taken another obvious wound, too, deep in the thigh, but what was killing him was something else, something crushed in his chest, which Rannulf could not see.

"Don't leave me alone," Mark said. "Please don't leave me alone."

"I won't," Rannulf said. He folded up the corner of the blanket for Mark to rest his head on.

"We won," Mark said.

"So far." Rannulf gave another look around him. He had fought in other battles that had seemed won, until suddenly they reversed into a disaster. All up and down this side of the wadi he could see nothing moving, except a few stray horses trotting nervously along in the distance. He heard no more sounds of fighting. A few yards away, his exhausted horse stood nose to tail with Mark's. There was blood all over its shoulder and one leg was gashed open so that the white muscle sheath showed.

"I'm dying," Mark whispered.

Rannulf's head bobbed. He sat down cross-legged next to him. "God have mercy on us," he said, and took Mark's hand and held it. With the fighting gone by, his soul shrank; he felt small and frail, there beside the dying man. He was cold. The day was going down over the horizon, the sky still filthy with blown dust, and now the breeze picked up, coming in sweet off the sea, blowing away the stale dirty air. A shadow like a curved blade swept across the plain and over him, and he lifted his eyes; across the unfathomable sky a vulture cut a smooth arc on its motionless wings. Another swept in behind the first, and another. He tightened his fingers around Mark's hand, and for a moment there was nothing. Then the faint pressure of an answer. Mark was still alive. Rannulf settled down to wait with him.

Young King Baudouin let his horse pick its way along through the gathering dusk, his squires coming close on his heels. The heavy air stank like a shambles. The twilight was thick with gross noises, the crunch of jaws and the snapping of beaks, the flutterings and flappings of wings, the hoarse caws of carrion birds, too gorged to fly.

The whole great plain was scattered with bodies; he had ridden for miles, now, and he was still passing bodies.

He was only now beginning to understand how great a victory this was. All these dead were Saracens. All Saladin's huge army had broken here, on the banks of this wadi, under the hammer of a few hundred knights. God's knights. God had given him this victory, a token, a promise; if he kept faith, if he did not give up, God would sustain his Kingdom.

Ahead in the gloom, the wadi like a wound laid the plain open. Just short of the bank, a looter rushed down like a jackal on a fallen man. Then fled back, driven off. Down there, someone was not dead.

The King said, "Hold," and reined in, wary. The light had gone. All he could see was a shape in the darkness, someone sitting there on the plain, his back to him. He thought suddenly, from the look of him, that this was a Frank, and he rode forward, and then, even in the night, he saw what Frank it was.

Again, he said, "Hold," and put out his hand, keeping his squires where they were, and alone he rode down the last few yards to the man sitting there on the plain.

It was the Templar Rannulf, bareheaded, silent. Even when King Baudouin reined in his horse next to him, the knight paid no heed to him. Then Baudouin saw the other Templar lying there.

This man was dead, or seemed so. Wrapped in a piebald blanket he lay huddled on the ground. The King dismounted. Still Rannulf said nothing. He sat cross-legged; in his left hand, resting on his knee, he held the dead knight's hand. His eyes were wide and unblinking, fixed on the infinite distance.

Baudouin stooped, and reached out toward Mark, and then abruptly Rannulf moved; his free arm shot out, he caught the King by the wrist and held him back. "Don't touch him."

The King drew his hand back. "Is he still alive? Bring him to Ramleh. We can tend him there."

Rannulf shook his head. "He's finished."

"We can bury him there, with the honor he deserves."

"I will bury him in Jerusalem, where he belongs."

The King sank down on his heels, face to face with him, trying to make the Templar focus on him. "We won a wonderful victory here. The other Templars say you nearly took Saladin himself. I have need of you. Come to Ramleh."

"I am going to Jerusalem."

"I am your King."

"Jesus is my King," the Templar said, and Baudouin gave up. He straightened onto his feet, tired; when he turned to his horse, it took all his strength and will to mount. The wind keened, a whistle of a dirge, a warning of the battles yet to come. He wanted to stay here, to make company with these men, but they were not his, and he had to go where he could act. Swinging his horse's head around, he led his squires away toward Ramleh.

C H A P T E R   I I I

annulf Fitzwilliam had been born in the Cotentin, in Normandy, youngest son of a landless knight. The family lived in a remote castle on the coast, where the father was chatelain. His mother died when Rannulf was still a baby, and he could not remember her. He had grown up like a weed, learned to fight before he could walk, to take what he wanted by force, to trust no one.

He followed his brothers into the Angevin wars, and when they died, he avenged them with an ardor far surpassing any affection he had ever felt for them alive. Fighting was all he could do. His sword got him a place in King Henry's army; his inferior birth kept him from advancement in King Henry's court. He could not read, or write, or figure, or speak much Latin. He seldom went inside a church. He spent his idle time drinking and gambling and chasing women, and knew no other medicine than that: when he woke up with a headache after a night's debauch, he drank to cure it, and when one woman nearly got him killed, he went out and found another.

He felt the rottenness and wickedness of this life like a curse laid on him, and yet he clung to it. He loved the power in it. He would reck no limit to his will, he refused himself nothing he wanted, even when what he wanted revolted him.

While he was serving in the garrison of a fortress on the Breton border, he fell in love with a village woman and harrassed her until she fled into a convent, and then he attacked the convent. For this the Bishop excommunicated him. The King dismissed him. His comrades shunned him. He felt the doors of faith and light and hope slamming shut around him; he saw himself plunging headlong into Hell, but he could not stop; sometimes he even wanted to hurry, to get it over with.

One day, somewhat after the bell was rung on him, and the book closed, he came on a chapel in a little wood, and for once, perhaps because it was forbidden him, the idea overcame him to pray. He went inside, and knelt down at an altar of turf and sticks. Suddenly there was a young girl in the chapel with him, carrying an armload of flowers.

"Have you come here to be saved?" she asked him. She was all un-afraid of him, although he was forming the notion right then of rav-ishing her. "I'll show you how," she said, "but first you must be bound."

"Bind me, then," he said, with a laugh, believing nothing of it, only wanting her to come within his reach.

She came up to him, sweet and soft and fair, so close her breath touched his face. She took hold of his callused hands and laid them palm against palm, and then wound a chain of her daisies around his wrists, all solemn, as if by such a means she could actually bind a man like him.

He trembled with lust; he wanted to throw her down and violate her, to see her weep, to see the blood mottling her white thighs. The flow-ers shackled him like iron. The child ruled him like a king. She looked into his eyes and said, "Now you must ask God to save you." He knelt beside her and repeated the Credo with her, and for the first time he heeded the words; then he it was who wept; blinded by shame and guilt and terror and sorrow, he cried for hours. When he returned to him-self, the child had vanished.

He understood that he had one more chance. He rode into Rouen, to the Templar preceptory there, and offered himself to Jesus Christ. Three months later he was on his way to the Holy Land, sworn never to look at a woman again, and to fight only against the enemies of God.

That had been more than ten years ago. Now it seemed to him that he had always lived here, in the Temple, in Jerusalem.

Mark had been here only a year and a half. Mark would lie here for-ever.

Rannulf stood at the edge of the grave, looking down at the dead man, who was dressed in a clean white jerkin and wrapped in his black cloak. Only three other knights stood with him to watch as the priest in his green robes said the last blessing and sprinkled holy water. The rest of the chapter had gone north weeks before to make a show of crusading around the city of Homs and thus far only a few of them had come back.

After the usual words of the funeral, the Templars gathered together in a rite of their own. Linking arms around the grave in a mass embrace they leaned together, swayed back and forth, and called out to God to deliver them as He had delivered Mark. Finally, passing the shovel from hand to hand, they cast down the dirt on top of Mark's body. When he had done his turn Rannulf knelt down by the grave and tried to pray. He hated this, more than any other part of this life, the endless kneeling and mumbling the same words over and over. Sometimes he could not do it at all, but only crouched on the ground, head down, while black thoughts of murder and lust streamed through his mind. For

Mark's sake he forced himself through several paternosters. As he said the words the shovel grated and swung, and the dirt thudded into the grave, and the other knights went away, all but one.

This was German de Montoya, the Preceptor, who had just come back from Homs; being an officer, he did not wait very long before he cleared his throat, and said, "Excuse me for interrupting you, Saint."

"I'm done," Rannulf said, and got up onto his feet. The wet dirt clung to his jerkin where he had knelt on it. He thought of Mark lying in the middle of the dirt and shuddered.

German de Montoya crossed himself. "God save him. When he first came here I thought he would fall away, or run away—he seemed a worthless man."

Rannulf remembered Mark's courage in the battle; God would surely take him, who had given up his life following the True Cross. He stuck the shovel into the loose earth and started up the hillside. "We're all pretty damned worthless."

The Templar graveyard was on the steep thorny slope outside the blocked-up Golden Gate, above the Valley of Kidron. Across the plunging ravine in a dark thicket of bushes and vines was Gethsemane. The burden of this place lay on him like iron. On this ground where he walked God Himself might have walked, or Abraham, or Jesus. Even the sun seemed the shadow of some greater light, floating like a ghost in the clouded sky. The eastern wall of the city rose above them, ranks of stone blocks like coffins piled one on the other.

"God made us, and wants to save us; we cannot be utterly without worth," German said placidly. "I'd like to hear about your journey to Cairo."

German's black beard was striped with grey, an oddity among the Templars, where Rannulf at thirty-six was heavy in years. German owed his age to his office as master of the novices, the duties of which usually kept him out of battles. As they walked along the foot of the wall to the next open gate, Rannulf told him about the long ride into Egypt, and how he and Mark had lied and bribed their way around Cairo.

"And Saladin's in control there, you think," said German. They went along the narrow footpath to the gate at the corner of the wall, and thus into the great sprawling quarter that was the Temple Mount.

"Nobody moves except as he tells them," Rannulf said. "They have no heart any more for fighting, the Egyptians. It's pitiable. All they want to do is sell you things."

"I thought the Shi'ites would liefer die in bed with a dog than live at peace with a Sunni. Don't they miss their caliph?"

"If they do they don't dare say so. Half the mullahs have disappeared and the other half have their faces to the floor."

They were climbing up onto the great broad pavement of the Temple. This was the highest place in Jerusalem, and beyond the western fringe of palm trees the city rooftops spread down and away in cluttered ledges. In front of Rannulf, midway down the ancient terrace, the Templum Domini stood, round and faceted; near the top of its lead dome a few patches of gold leaf shone. It had been a Saracen church once, and the blue tiles that covered its walls inside were Saracen work. But on top of the dome was the Cross of Jesus Christ.

"You were gone a long while," German said. He led Rannulf along the western side of the pavement, where there were fewer people. There in the columned archways of an old arcade were the storerooms and workrooms of the Order. "We had an election. For Marshall. Your name got into it."

Rannulf grunted at him, startled, and loath to show it, or to look pleased. "Not for too long, I think."

"Not long at all. Gerard de Ridford won."

That made it easier: he laughed, and turned toward German. "And worth its weight in gold it was, too."

German's smile widened only slightly. "As you can imagine, after six months, that joke's lost its shine. He should do well enough; we need men like that at court, to manage things there."

"We don't need him," Rannulf said, looking away. The great pavement was cracked, and grass grew up through the cracks; he scuffed his boot through the spidery green stalks.

"Don't make trouble over it," German said. "We need to stand together, or at least appear so to the world."

This sounded like a warning. Rannulf made no answer; he hated Gerard de Ridford. He knew German was right.

They were walking through the middle of the Temple haram. He had heard it was King Herod who had built this place, the slayer of the Innocents. The broken columns that held up the arcade roof were carved with leaves like stone palm trees. Each archway held a workshop: the saddler's, the candlemaker's, the shoemaker's. In a place where the arcade opened into a little square the forge stood, cold now, smelling of stale charcoal. A black-and-white cat rolled on the sun-baked pavement. Rannulf stopped, looking around him.

The Saracens believed that once Jesus and Mohammed had stood face-to-face on this spot. Rannulf liked knowing that. This, not Holy Sepulcher, was the heart of his war, just as Jesus was his only officer.

It held him fast, this way of understanding. He felt pulled together again, thinking it; he felt better about Mark, who was home now, gone to rest. His spirits lifted. German went on ahead of him, toward the sprawling building at the edge of the pavement that was the Templar barracks, and Rannulf followed him.

CHAPTER IV

After the miracle of the battle of Ramleh, King Baudouin went to Ascalon and to Gaza, to see to the defenses of the south of the Kingdom; then, in the cool of the year, as Advent began, he travelled back to Jerusalem, on its inland hilltop. The great men of his kingdom, who had all spent the summer crusading in the north, were gathering for the holy time of Christmas, and the King knew better than to let them gather without him.

His mother and his sister held court at their palace of La Plaisance, on the western side of the city, where the air was sweetest and coolest. In the afternoons they received their guests in a gallery whose long southern windows even in winter let in a flood of light. With only a page and a knight, the King went quietly into this crowded hall; shy of his looks, he wore a hooded cloak, and for a while he was there without anyone noticing.

He saw his mother, Agnes de Courtenay, sitting on a Persian chair by the window. Her hair was stiff with henna. She wore a gown of layers of Gaza cloth, the bodice cut very tight and low, as if she were a young woman, and her face was painted to hide the seams of age. Beside her stood a French knight named Amalric de Lusignan, who was his mother's constant friend, and as the King went slowly among the bright silks and satins of the courtiers, he saw his mother reach out idly and stroke the Frenchman's leg, as if she were petting a lapdog.

In the giddy reel and flutter of the court, the young King stood watching this, and his soul cankered. He remembered the first charge at Ramleh. That had been as honest as a sword blade, to give his life into God's hands, and run headlong against the enemy. Here nothing was honest, not the laughter, not the piety, not the faces of the women or the promises of the men. He wished for the perfect clarity of that moment in the battle. Then someone noticed him.

"The King," the whisper ran, like the wind through the grass. "The King."

The great crowd hushed, not all at once but in waves that spread out through the long cold room with its showers of sunlight, and everyone turned to see him, and seeing him, the women sank down in submission and the men bowed deep. A swift rustle of half-voiced greetings died away. He looked around him at the bent backs and the faces concealed behind hands and fans, and lifted his eyes to his mother, across the hall.

She stood up, her hand raised to him. "Sire. My dear boy. Come to me. Welcome back to Jerusalem. Come, let us heap you up with praises for your glorious victory."

Quietly he said, "God's is the glory." He walked up through the stooped court, toward his mother's side.

As he came up beside her chair, Amalric de Lusignan moved back, giving him room; the King looked wide-eyed at him, and said, "Thank you, Father."

The constable's handsome face twitched, puzzled. "I beg your pardon, Sire."

"I grant it," Baudouin said. He nodded to his page. "Fetch me a chair." Turning his back on the constable, he sat down side by side with his mother.

She said, "You look much better, my dear boy." But leaning forward to greet him, she kept a good depth of the air between them, kissed at his face, held her hands above his, never touching. The paint on her cheeks was cracking. Her brilliant hair was a wig. She turned her head slightly toward Amalric, now standing directly behind her chair. "My friend, see that the King has refreshment."

Baudouin sat still a moment. His strength was uncertain; his hands and feet had been numb and cold all day, which made him feel sometimes as if he were disappearing, inch by inch, into a black void. Before his chair the courtiers were pushing in closer, trying to be recognized. He had to do that soon, begin to see them, to let them come forth and dangle their little ambitions in his face. He shut his eyes a moment, unwilling.

"Sire," Amalric murmured, and young Baudouin opened his eyes and took the warm cup of wine from him, with its breath of cloves and cinnamon.

Agnes said quietly, "My dear boy, I have a boon to ask you."

She always did. "Yes, Mother." He listened to her circuitous request for a minor position at court for one of her friends' friends' friends.

In the milling crowd before him, now, Raymond of Tripoli had appeared. The Count of Tripoli always reminded Baudouin of a gazelle, slight and agile, with prominent, intelligent eyes. He had been Regent during Baudouin's minority and still thought himself true King of Jerusalem. He was too great a man to pretend not to see, and Baudouin caught his eye and smiled and nodded.

The Count of Tripoli strode forward. "Sire. God bless you for your splendid victory. You're looking very well." He bowed as an afterthought. His dark eyes searched eagerly over Baudouin's face, assessing the progress of his illness, wondering when he was going to die and get out of the way. "Very well, indeed."

Baudouin sipped his wine, the taste faintly metallic on his tongue. "Thank you, Cousin."

Agnes called out, "My lord Count, I understand your wife has a wonderful new harper; you must command her to send him to me at once."

Raymond gave her a swift bow, a fixed and empty smile, and turned back to the King. "Sire, there is the issue still of that thirty thousand dinars."

Baudouin had owed this money to Raymond for a long while and had no intention of repaying it. In the crowd pushing and shoving around in front of his chair, all striving to be noticed, he saw the perfect antidote to the Count of Tripoli.

"My lord Marshall," he said, and smiled, and nodded. "Come forward, and let me congratulate you on your elevation."

The new Marshall of the Jerusalem Temple swooped forward into the King's presence like someone seizing territory. He was the opposite of Raymond of Tripoli, fleshy and strongly made, with a magnificent proud carriage. The severe robes of his Order made him look very fine: the great black cloak, the white robe with its Cross of red showed off his wide shoulders and heavy chest.

"Sire," he said. "I quake at the honor of conversing with the victor of Ramleh."

"Yes," Raymond said, pushing forward, his eyes sharp. "A great battle won without Templars."

"Oh," the King said mildly, "there were a few."

The Marshall glared full into Raymond's face, his sandy beard bristling; he wore his hair very long and sleek, for a man whose Rule required a close trim. He said, "Perhaps if you'd been there, we would have had no victory at all, my lord Count, but another of your customary disappointments."

Tripoli bridled up at this remark, and his face tightened over the bones, his jaw jutting. Baudouin sat back, letting them squabble. Locked in their beloved feud, they paid no attention to him. He felt himself running out of vigor, dying in pieces.

Then, down at the door, the crowd began to buzz and laugh and bow and call out greetings, and he knew that Sibylla had come in.

He raised his head, his heart suddenly eager. He had not seen her in almost a year. All across the room, he picked her at once out of the crowd. So, unsick, he might have looked: lively, slender, light in step, with heavy fair hair, and a face bright with laughter, beautiful by nature.

"She has to cover her head," his mother said. "She's a widow, not a maiden, what is she thinking of?" Indeed his sister wore her hair loose around her shoulders, bound in a token ribbon. She never heeded rules. She came toward the crowd, calling and waving to her friends. Baudouin had not seen her since her son was born. She had put off her widow's weeds at her churching, as if with the baby she was delivered also of her marriage vows, and then she had flown off to the sweet and violent court of her cousin, Stephanie of Kerak, who had been twice a widow, and knew how to defeat the attendant glooms.

Straight across the room, head high and eyes direct, she walked toward the young King, with her favorite companion, another cousin, Alys of Beersheba, and her page trailing after her, not keeping pace. Tripoli stepped back; the Marshall moved aside.

Baudouin remembered, abruptly, that she had not seen him in some time. He braced himself. She walked up toward him, and when she saw his face clearly she stopped, her eyes wide with shock.

"Bati, God's breath, you look awful."

Ready as he was, he flinched anyway. His mother gasped: "Oh, no, no, no!" and the men nearby muttered protests. Baudouin made himself smile.

"Bili, you're the same. You never change." He reached one gloved hand toward her. Maliciously: "Come, sweet Sister, give me a kiss."

"No," she said. She stepped back, putting her hands behind her back, like a child. "Never. Does it hurt? I'm terribly sorry. I pray for you every day, Bati, sometimes twice."

Behind her, the Lady Alys said, "Sire, you are always in our thoughts." Alys was wide and well-padded, and wore her gowns too small, so that she bulged, overstuffed. She bobbed down and up in a courtesy to him. "God save you, Sire."

"Thank you, Lady Alys."

His sister stepped up beside their mother's chair; the two women leaned together, pressing cheek to cheek in false kisses. In unison they trilled a "Hmmmm!" of insincere delight. Sibylla straightened, looked cooly past the King.

"My lord Cousin Tripoli."

"God bless you, Princess," said the Count of Tripoli.

"Bili," said the King, "let me present to you the new Marshall of the Temple of Jerusalem, Gerard de Ridford."

To his surprise, that caught his sister's interest. She turned her back on her mother, her wide blue eyes sweeping toward the black-and-white knight on Baudouin's left. "My lord Marshall."

Gerard de Ridford inclined his head. He had an easy way with women, having been a monk for only a short time, and for his own purposes, not God's. With a smile, he said, "I live to serve the Princess of Jerusalem."

Sibylla held out her hand to be kissed. "God's grace, sir, I am pleased to see not all the men of your Order are churls."

Baudouin blinked. He had played chess with her since the nursery, and he recognized one of her baited openings. The Marshall walked innocently in where she wanted him.

"Churls, my lady." He bowed over her ringed fingers with the practiced dip of a courtier, his pursed lips passing a few inches above her knuckles. "Pray God we do not have such a reputation universally."

"A month ago, before my brother's great victory at Ramleh, I met a Templar on the road, who was very rude to me."

The Marshall stood back. The red Cross blazed on the white breast of his robe, his smile blazed on his face. "But name him, lady! I shall see him properly chastised."

"Yes. Well, I'm not sure of his name. The man with him called him Saint, which I thought distinctly peculiar."

At that name the Marshall gave a sudden start. "Rannulf Fitzwilliam," he said, and his lips twisted; he turned away, his hand rising to his face.

Baudouin said, "Oh, really." He eyed his sister. "How was he rude to you, Bili?"

"He accosted us on the road, and took some horses." She shrugged. "I did not grudge him any of it, since he was a Templar, but gave freely, and yet he was mannerless about it."

Alys said, "He showed no respect for any of us, Sire, and for our station."

The Marshall, de Ridford, swung back toward the throne again, and made a deep bow to Sibylla. His voice rang hard with purpose. "Princess, I know the man; you called him a churl, and rightly. He is unfit even to kneel at your feet, and I shall rebuke him most severely for daring to approach you."

"Rebuke him. I like that. I shall witness it—command him here, now. I shall hear your rebuke, and his apology."

De Ridford propped his fist on his hip. "In the Temple, lady, as you probably know, we keep all such things privy to ourselves."

"Really," she said. She took a step backward, her skirt caught in her hand—Baudouin saw she wore blue silk slippers—and looked the knight over, leisurely, calculating. "But I want him brought here. Is he then really called Saint? That must be a joke; you'll make me privy to that, too. What did you say his name was?"

Their mother crowed. "Sir Marshall, you'd best yield now. She will have what she wants."

"His name is Rannulf Fitzwilliam," Baudouin said to his sister. "He served excellently well—before the battle and during it, and after, he was rude to me also, as it happens."

"Then bring him here," the Princess said, "and he can be doubly rebuked." She said that word with relish, rolling it in her mouth like a piece of apple.

De Ridford performed another bow; he was yielding to her at once. "Whatever the Princess commands of me, I shall do." He beckoned to a Templar sergeant waiting by the wall.

While this was going on, Sibylla's page brought a stool, and she sat down at her brother's feet, her hands clasped on her knee. Her hair hung in sleek curls over her shoulders. She frowned up at Baudouin. "Why did you call me up here out of Kerak? I was enjoying myself there. Now I'm planted down, day after day, with all these Frenchborn French who think they're better than we are."

"Well, they're all going home again," the King said, "and you'll be free of them. But not of me. You are my heir, Bili. I almost died, in the month before Ramleh. I caught a trembling fever, and I felt the hand of God on me. In any case, as you say, the other thing is getting worse. When I die, you have to be ready to rule, Bili, and I must teach you."

"God's teeth," his mother said. "You're wasting your efforts, Sire. She's just going to get married again."

"I don't want to be married again," Sibylla said. She waved off a page with a cup of wine and a tray of sweets. "And I will be Queen of Jerusalem."

Their mother gave a scoffing laugh. "Oh, and that is to be Queen of the Amazons, I suppose?"

Tripoli was watching them, only a few steps away, and the Templar Marshall, and a dozen others. The King said, "Mother, keep counsel. Bili, you are light-minded. The Kingdom will be yours, but it needs a king. Women cannot fight wars. And Saladin is—"

"You've beaten Saladin," Sibylla said, her voice sharp with insistence, almost chiding him, as if he had failed at his lessons. "With a hundred knights against fifty thousand Saracens, a mighty victory for the Cross. You'll beat him again, and again. We'll always beat them. God is on our side. Don't you believe that? What are you fighting for if not that?"

Her voice rose, as she spoke, ringing out so that the folk around them heard, and heeded. A little cheer went up. The King stared at her a while. Her skin was fine and smooth, her wide brow clear as Heaven, her eyes full of the courage of the untried. Finally he said, "We have to go on winning, again and again. But he only has to win once."

"God won't let you lose," she said.

He gave up trying to corrupt this purity. "You are to remain here in Jerusalem until we find you a suitable husband," he said. This made him feel suddenly old. He who would never embrace a woman, who would never marry and never have a child. "I'll see that you are properly entertained."

At that she made a face, signifying how little he knew of entertainment, proper or not. She lifted her laughing eyes to him. "Well, anyway, Bati, we'll be together more. You said you would teach me. I'd like that."

"Good," he said. He started to take hold of her hand. Before she could notice and recoil from him he reined in the gesture. He said, "Tell me what you did at Kerak," and she burst out laughing, and began in on a string of gossip, most of it frivolous and scandalous. Tripoli ambled up nearer the throne, his eyes sharp. The Lord of Kerak was another of his many enemies. While his sister chattered, Baudouin sat back, watching the men around him, and saw the Templar from Ramleh coming into the hall.

No herald announced him. Another of the Order accompanied him; Templars went everywhere in couple, if not in mass. This pair came side by side across the room, cutting purposefully as tracking dogs through the languid clutter of the court. The one on the left was the knight called Saint. His long jerkin was grey with dirt and ripped and torn along the hems; the sleeves were rolled above his elbows. He could have been a country plowboy, except for the sword slung at his hip and the heavy spurred boots on his feet. At his approach the Marshall's face closed, not smiling anymore, intent.

The King saw, suddenly, that his sister, not the Marshall, had been used here: the Marshall had contrived this, a new battle in an old war. The two knights stopped before him, ignoring everybody else. The

King glanced over and saw Raymond of Tripoli to one side, watching keenly.

De Ridford said, "Rannulf, the Princess Sibylla has charged you with misconduct toward her, on the road south of Ramleh; you are to apologize."

The knight set his hands on his belt. In a voice curt with temper, he said, "Did you call me all the way over here just for that?"

The Marshall's eyes narrowed. "I gave you an order."

For a moment they stared at one another. Then Rannulf Fitzwilliam cast a sweeping look around him, as if he only now noticed the other people in the room. His gaze found the King's and locked. He said, "I did what was necessary. If I caused the Princess any trouble I am sorry for it." His attention swiveled back to de Ridford. "May I go now?" There was a startling ring of contempt in his voice.

De Ridford said, "You are a pig, Rannulf. You stink." He turned with a bow to Sibylla. "Princess? Are you satisfied with this?"

Quiet on her stool, she lifted her eyebrows at him; she had realized she was playing someone else's game. Coolly, she said, "I am perfectly satisfied, my lord."

The Marshall straightened, facing the King. "And you, Sire?"

Baudouin leaned forward, seizing this opening. He spoke directly to the ragged Templar before him. "You met my sister on the road?" De Ridford took a step forward to intercept, and the King waved him back out of the way.

Rannulf Fitzwilliam stood with his head down, his hands behind him. "We had just lost our horses. We came on her and her escort and borrowed some of their horses." He flung a furious glance at de Ridford, who had drawn off to one side. "I meant her no disrespect."

Baudouin let out a gust of laughter. "I think you have very little respect for any of us, Saint, by God's truth."

The knight straightened up, meeting his eyes again. "For you, Sire," he said.

The compliment so pleased Baudouin that for a moment he could make no reply. Finally he said, "Well, I shall try to deserve it. At Ramleh and on the road to it you were a champion of Jesus Christ and my cause, and I see no reason that you should apologize. To me, or to my sister."

The knight seemed suddenly taller. His head bobbed. "Thank you, my lord."

"The King is gracious and generous." De Ridford pushed in between them, his voice sharp with raw anger; this had not gone as he desired.

"I am also insulted, and I am not so forgiving. Rannulf, take your sanctimonious stench back to the Temple, and I will deal with you there later."

"You called me here," Rannulf said. He turned, and with the other man at his side walked off across the hall.

De Ridford said, "I beg your pardons for this knight. We have a few of this sort of man, for whom the Temple is a last refuge."

The Count of Tripoli moved in closer to the throne. He said, "Bah. You are all so, except some wear silk over it. Your vow is poverty, chastity, and murder, and you do not God's will, but your own." He signed to a page, who brought him a cup of wine.

"Murder," de Ridford said. "At that art you are the adept, my lord, isn't that so?"

Tripoli rounded on him with another insult. Baudouin sat back, exhaling a weary sigh. He was beginning to think of his supper, and a draught of strong wine, and going to bed. His mother craned forward in her chair, her voice raised, to join the two men before him at their duel of words.

The voices bubbled up around him; he felt himself drowning in their little quarrels, their petty private schemes. At his feet his sister twisted around on her stool, and raised her face toward him. She reached out her hand to him, and he reached down and their hands touched. She had a great heart, his sister, and he would teach her. He would find a way through this yet. He sank down in his chair, waiting for a good moment to leave.

CHAPTER V

The Templars held their chapter meetings in the refectory, which had been a Saracen mosque before the Christians took Jerusalem, eighty years before. The hall was almost as tall as it was deep and smelled like a cave of damp stone and moss and bats. Two rows of octagonal columns held up its vaulted roof. On the walls hung battle trophies—lances and arrows, swords, shields, helmets, coats of mail. Lamps dangling on chains from the ceiling cast lanes of light through the shadowy depths of the great room.

The knights flooded into the hall in a noisy tide. Rannulf was very uneasy; he remembered de Ridford's threat against him. He went up to his place in the front rank of the brothers. It was the custom of the chapter that new men stood at the back, and moved up as those in front of them died. Rannulf had been standing in the front rank for more than six years.

The officers walked in, going up to the space at the front of the hall, where there was a stone table like an altar. Odo de Saint-Amand, the Master of Jerusalem, went first, and then German de Montoya, and Gilbert Erail who was Seneschal of the Order, and the draper and the commander, and last of them, swaggering like a king, came Gerard de Ridford.

He wheeled to stand with the other officers, behind the stone table, and for an instant he and Rannulf looked at each other. Rannulf lowered his eyes. His heart clenched like a fist in his chest.

Odo de Saint-Amand's voice rose in a harsh call. "God be with all here!"

The packed ranks of the Templars answered in one voice. "And our spirits with Him in life everlasting, world without end, amen!"

"Rannulf Fitzwilliam, come before me."

Rannulf drew a deep breath, and gathered himself; he went forward into the gap between the massed ranks of the knights and the single rank of the officers. Facing Odo, he bowed, and then stood with his hands clasped behind his back, saying nothing.

Odo hooked his fingers in his tangled yellow beard. "Gerard de Ridford, step forward."

The Marshall walked around the end of the table and stood opposite Rannulf. Odo's narrowed eyes shifted from one man to the other. "My lord Marshall! You have some charge against this knight."

The place hushed. The Marshall de Ridford swung around to face the gathered men.

"He is unfit for this company. He is an insolent pig, and all know it! The Princess herself complained to me about him, and when I called him to account for it, he gave neither the lady nor me any satisfaction. He held me up to ridicule before the King; he degrades us all."

Rannulf lowered his gaze to the floor and bit his teeth shut. He longed to draw his sword and thrust it into de Ridford's chest. Behind him, someone called, "Throw him out of the chapter!" Across the hall, men shouted out in agreement, a dozen voices, maybe more.

"Pig!"

"Baseborn dirt. He's halfway a sand-digger anyway!"

"Cast him out!" De Ridford cocked up one arm, punched the air. "Cleanse the Order of him—we shall all be the better off."

Now a whole chorus of voices rose, like hounds baying at the scent of blood. The Master looked at Rannulf, and said quietly, "Will you not defend yourself?"

"I swore an oath," Rannulf said, "to fight only the enemies of my Lord Jesus Christ, and I shall keep to it." He lifted his head long enough to cast a look like a burning brand at Gerard de Ridford, and then lowered his gaze again to the floor.

"Well said," came a rough bellow from across the room. "Well said, Saint!"

"Throw him out," someone else cried. "He'll turn the King himself against us!"

Now suddenly German de Montoya raised his voice. "This is unso. I went in couple with Rannulf to the court—the King heaped praises on him, and called him a champion of Jesus, for the way he fought at Ramleh."

"Ramleh," the murmur went, from lip to lip. "Ramleh."

Again the rough voice across the room spoke out. "Yes! Rannulf fought at Ramleh, while the rest of us were up north holding doors for people. God gave him the victory at Ramleh. God did not mind a saint."

That brought forth a ragged yell from the massed knights, and a piercing whistle rang out, and some of the men stamped their feet. Somebody cried, "Let them fight it out!"

"Combat!" First one voice, then several took up the cry. "Combat!" Half a dozen men began to stamp their feet on the floor, and rapidly the rhythm spread, booming deafeningly loud.

Odo de Saint-Amand roared, "Quiet!" The din died away at once. In this new silence the Master turned toward Rannulf. "What goes between the two of you that runs so rough? I will not tolerate a feud in the Temple. Settle this, with swords, or with a clasp of hands, but settle it, here and now."

The hall was hushed, not calm; all the knights stirred, eager, ready for blood. Rannulf raised his head.

"I cannot fight a man who wears the Cross." Reluctantly he turned toward the Marshall, and held out his hand. "I will lay down my end of this, if de Ridford will lay down his."

The Master thumped his palms together. "Yes—this is the right way of it." Around the hall, a general sigh went up, and the men relaxed, a little disappointed there would be no fighting. De Ridford stood staring at Rannulf, and at last he took the outstretched hand.

"Excellently done," the Master said. He went up to the knights, and laid his fingers on the knot of their handclasp. "Henceforth, be friends to one another, and face our common enemy together." With his free arm he made the sign of the Cross over them. "Now, go, and keep your vows, for Jesus Christ's sake."

Rannulf drew his hand from de Ridford's grasp and crossed himself. He went to his place in the line, and de Ridford backed off, rejoining the other officers. Odo stood watching them a moment, his head moving slowly from side to side, and then he went on with the chapter meeting.

The barracks hall where Rannulf slept was called the Crypt, because it lay against the northern wall of the building and was always cold. When he went into the hall, after Compline, every head in the crowded room swung toward him.

Some of them turned quickly away. More of them called out to him, and Richard le Mesne, across the room, lifted his fist in the air, and bellowed, "God wills it, Saint!" Rannulf went to his cot, against the wall under the window.

The room was full of men, standing by their narrow cots, getting ready for bed. Some stood pulling off their robes, and others were already lying down, and still others, stripped to their drawers, were gathered by the basin table in the corner, to wash their hands and faces. In the big stone-walled room the uproar was considerable. Rannulf sat on his cot, and began pulling his boots off.

German de Montoya came in the door. The Preceptor was well liked, even if he was an officer. As he went through the room, he spoke a few words to nearly everybody; he stopped in the middle of the room and talked to a young redheaded knight Rannulf did not know, and then the two of them came into the back of the room, toward Rannulf. They exchanged greetings, and then Rannulf said, "Thank you for speaking for me. You and Richard Bear kept them from throwing me out of the Order."

German shook his head. "This was not so serious as that. Odo saw that justice was done. You belong here, more than de Ridford. Everybody knows it." He gestured to the young knight standing just behind him. "I would make this man known to you—Stephen de l'Aigle is his name; he came to Jerusalem while you were in Egypt."

Rannulf stood up. German always had his favorites. "Well met, Sir Stephen."

The redheaded knight looked distantly at him. He had the polished look of a wellborn man. He said, "I am at your service, sir," in a voice that said he was not.

German nodded to him. "You can go, Stephen. Thank you."

"My lord," said the redheaded knight, and went off again. Rannulf sat down on the cot.

"Another of your mice."

German said, blandly, "What, you don't like him? His uncle is the Seneschal of France, and his mother's the sister of the Duke of Burgundy. You need some well-connected friends."

"He doesn't seem too friendly."

German shrugged that off. "He'll warm to you, once he comes to know you. As to de Ridford, keep a care for yourself. He's a man without truth, and a mere handshake won't bind him." He clapped Rannulf on the shoulder. "But you have more of us on your side than you know." He turned, and went away across the room; being an officer, he had his own quarters.

A sergeant had come in, and was trimming the lamps that hung along the walls of the room: all but one, which would burn until dawn, the Rule forbidding them to sleep in the dark. The din faded. In the cavern of the room the first low snores rose like cattle noises. Rannulf stood up, pulling off his jerkin and shirt, and wrapped himself in his blanket. Sitting down on the cot he bowed his head and pressed his palms together and tried to pray.

German was right: this thing with de Ridford was not settled, only pushed down under the surface. In the end, one of them would kill the other. Yet the Rule would not let him fight de Ridford, even to save himself.

He said his prayers, although he knew God would not help him; God gave him this test, to prove his virtue. Rannulf thought he had no virtue. He was a bad man, and sooner or later he would break, and get his hands on de Ridford's fat neck and bash his brains out.

Yet as he said the worn old words of the prayers, an unexpected peace stole over him. If some had spoken against him in the chapter, some had spoken for him. The war was greater than any man, and would take both of them eventually, him and de Ridford, and turn them into the same dust. He lifted his gaze, looking across the room, to the cot where Mark had slept. It was empty: by custom no man would sleep there until the next battle was fought, and the next Templar died. Rannulf said another prayer, this one for Mark, or perhaps to Mark. Crossed himself and lay down, to sleep until the bell for vigils rang.

O ne afternoon, Agnes de Courtenay held her court in the garden so that they could play with her grandson, named Bau-
doin, called Baudoinet to distinguish him from the King. She
insisted that Sibylla come sit down with her to greet her baby son, although she had seen him only seldom since he was born, and had no interest in him.

The baby was small and pale, with hair so fine and light it seemed
like nothing; all his clothes were embroidered in red and blue silk, and
gold tassels adorned his little shoes. When he saw his grandmother, he
crowed, and held out his arms to her, but when he saw his mother, he
cried.

Embarrassed, Sibylla lowered her hands to her lap. "What a greeting
is this?" The baby twisted around on Agnes' lap, looking for his wet
nurse, a Syrian woman whose equipment swelled enormous under her
gown, advertising her perfect fitness for her role. "He doesn't like me. His
own mother."

"You ran off to Kerak without him," her mother said. "You should
take him into your apartment, let him live with you." Agnes bent over
the baby, cooing. He reached up one sticky hand for her hair. In the line
of his face Sibylla was reminded of somebody else's face. She remembered, suddenly, how she had gotten this baby, the losing battles in the
dark.

"You keep him. He smells." She sniffed at the baby. He had betrayed
her, loving a fat native woman more than her who had borne him. She
would have a better son. She got up, and went across the lawn toward
the garden.

"You should be more of a mother to him," Agnes said. She gave the
baby to his nurse and came after her. "You should be more of a woman."
She shot a dagger of a look at her daughter.

Sibylla said, "You are enough of a woman for all of us, Mother." She
looked pointedly at the handsome young man waiting behind them on
the terrace.

Her mother ignored that. "Why do you want to be a man, Sibylla? Why is being what God made you not enough for you?"

"I am what God made me, my lady. Not what paint made me."

"Oh, ho, the child throws an insult."

Sibylla felt herself flushing; her mother knew her entirely too well; even when she knew she was being clever her mother made her feel foolish, and childish. She looked out over the garden, which was a favorite place of hers, although now in winter it lay fallow. The roses needed to be trimmed. There were weeds sprouting in the unturned soil.

Her mother pursued her. "Why do you like Baudouin d'Ibelin so much?"

Sibylla tossed her head, having expected this, and gave her mother a cool look. "What, isn't he young and handsome enough for you?"

"He's an Ibelin. Are you sleeping with him?"

She had expected this, too, but still she could not meet her mother's eyes. To deny it would be meaningless. "I need not answer that."

"Perhaps not. But remember, if you get pregnant, all your prospects turn a little dark. And what a man likes in a lover he may abhor in a wife."

"My lady, I mean to be more than a wife. I will be Queen of Jerusalem."

"Yes, and a queen must be pure as Holy Mother Mary." Agnes tapped her fingers on her knee; her nails were plated with gold sheaths. "Well, be careful. These things mean more than you think, and you can't change them; once torn never mended, as they say. I suited your father well enough, lover and wife, when no one expected him to become King, but the crown came to him, and then suddenly I was a scandal, and had to be put aside, so he could marry some Greek."

Sibylla said, "Father still loved you. Nothing changed." Sibylla had loved her father more than she ever loved any of her flirts; she wanted him to be noble, and blameless. But now, looking back, she saw the thing differently, suddenly, more toward her mother's view. "Father always said nothing had changed."

"The King still wanted me in his bed." Agnes' voice was bitter as thin beer. "Especially when he found out the little Greek would only endure him, like a board with a hole in it. And he still loved you. You and Baudouin, always. But I was not good enough to be Queen."

"With me, they have no choice," Sibylla said. "I shall be Queen, virgin or whore."

"Bah, you little fool, you assume too much. And you'd give it all to an Ibelin!"

Sibylla stooped and picked a bit of dead wood off a rose bush. This was part of her mother's endless squirrel-work, chewing off a little bit of this, and piling up a little bit of that, as if by a thousand tiny doings she accomplished something great. Baudouin d'Ibelin's brother Balian was married to Sibylla's father's second wife, the Greek board, Maria Comnena.

Her mother said, "What is the King telling you, when you attend his court like that? Or do you just play chess with him? Why must you always try to do what men do?"

"I listen. I did not know how much the King must do, or how hard it is." Sinking down on her heels, she pulled up a few stalky yellow lion's-teeth, and then stood, brushing the dirt off her fingers. She would ruin her hands at this work. "I am not trying to do what men do." What it was she wanted, she could not explain, even to herself. "You make being a woman so small and narrow, Mother, I want more than that."

"You are a selfish girl, Sibylla, and impious, too."

"Oh, heigh, ho, stand up on your pulpit, Mother; you've got the morals for it." She turned, looking for a page, and saw Baudouin d'Ibelin himself coming in the door.

He smiled at her, looking apologetic, since he was late; as always his looks delighted her, his smooth and even features, his wide shoulders and long legs. She thought, He is better than my mother's man, and felt a little guilty at the comparison. With a smile she went toward him.

"Come. I need your help, my garden is a ruin." She caught his hand and led him off to find some servants, to do the work for her.

⊕ God had betrayed Gerard de Ridford; God had given him a king's soul, without a king's station.

The Marshall of the Templars stood at the edge of the garden of the palace La Plaisance, where the Countess of Courtenay and her daughter held their merry, frivolous court. He watched Sibylla of Jerusalem, heiress to the crown of Godfrey de Bouillon and Baudouin le Bourg and Fulk of Anjou, and considered how he might make up for God's misjudgment.

The garden lay between the back of the palace and the curve of the city wall, a semicircle of pavement and grass, some beds of untilled weedy earth, a band of trees. The Countess sat in the shade at one end of the pavement, sending her hangers-on this way and that to fetch her things. A handsome young man leaned on the back of her chair and whispered in her ear, and another such loitered on the grass behind her.

De Ridford had already assessed the Countess' appetites and decided that way was too dear a path, and too unsteady.

The Princess was another matter.

She was not so much pretty, he thought, watching her, as she was lively. She seemed always to be moving, to be doing something. Today she had brought out a little flock of servants to dig and delve in the gardens, and to gather up the branches and leaves fallen from the cherry trees that lay between the garden and the wall. She drew a few of her friends into the work too, the fat girl who was always with her, and a tall knight with fair curling hair who was following Sibylla around faithfully and doing everything she said. The Princess wore a long blue gown. Under de Ridford's gaze she turned and waved to someone across the garden, and in the turning of her body and the raising of her hand was an unconscious grace that lifted him to a pure pleasure.

He watched her, patient, looking for his chance to reach her, to use her, this blithe and reckless girl who had what he wanted.

He had brought two sergeants with him from the Temple, to comply with the Rule; they stood idle in the corner, near the table where pages waited beside the ewers of wine, the trays of small delicacies. The Rule said also he was not to have to do with women, but he was here on the business of the Order, and these women held power; therefore, he could deal with them sinlessly. The Rule was no hindrance to him. He understood it deeply, looking past the cramped letter to the expansive purpose, he knew it better than the fools like Rannulf Fitzwilliam who clung to the vow like slaves.

The thought of Rannulf made him angry. He hated the churlish Norman knight, with a hatred that arose from a depth below words; he wanted to crack that mean piety and show it for the worthless thing it was, ashes and dust.

The nobles of Jerusalem drifted in and out of the court. Joscelin de Courtenay appeared, the Countess' brother, head of his family, a big bluff man, dressed in Russian fur. The Princess went up to greet him, both hands out, and got a loud kiss on the mouth. The Marshall drew closer to her. The fair young man following her everywhere was an Ibelin, by his badge, not the lord, perhaps his younger brother. The Ibelins were rivals of the Courtenays and this one looked uncomfortable here, even as he hovered around the Princess like a bee in a linden tree. Then Joscelin de Courtenay was nodding to de Ridford, and the Marshall went forward into the nobles' presence.

He inclined his head to the lord of the house. Not as much as he might have, had de Courtenay led a few more knights. "My lord Count." Joscelin still claimed the title of Edessa, his father's fief, lost twenty years and more to the Saracens. De Ridford faced him with the confidence of a man whose power was, if not hereditary, at least real.

Joscelin said, "Well? What does the Temple think Saladin will do next?"

De Ridford lifted one shoulder; he planted his fist on his hip. "It matters not, my lord, whatever it might be, we shall more than match it." He turned to the Countess, who was leering toothily at him from her chair. "My lady." Now, at last, he came to the Princess; he put on a smile for her, and bowed his head.

"Princess, you are the fairest flower in this garden."

Her eyes flashed. "It's wintertime. There are no flowers." He saw she had heard every compliment, every flattery, every fawning lie, at least twice.

He smiled again, liking her better. He said, "What a sensible woman you are. A gem among gems."

The young man behind her moved forward, his eyes sharp. Establishing possession. He said, "Sib, are we done here?" De Ridford, murmuring his leave, stepped back, and the girl turned and went off with the young Ibelin, tipped her head to look up at him, and laughed. Just behind de Ridford, her mother uttered an unwomanly oath.

Joscelin was saying, "Maybe Ramleh finished him." He was still talking about Saladin. He passed his winecup nervously from hand to hand. "You know how the Saracens are. His own people will throw him down, as soon as he shows a weakness."

"Yes," said Amalric de Lusignan, the Countess' favorite, just behind her chair. "We should attack them now, take Damascus, or at least Aleppo. We have the advantage now, or so it seems. My lord Count, with a bold move we could recover Edessa."

Joscelin's eyes widened with alarm. His hands closed tight on the winecup. He had a horror of bold moves. "The King is hardly in a condition to lead us against Edessa."

"The King," said the Countess roughly. "Why does he keep on trying? He should yield the throne. He should go into a monastery. How can he lead anybody? God's teeth, he looks like death in a white shroud." Her gaze drifted away, toward her daughter out under the trees, ordering the gardeners around. "Some people think of nothing but themselves."

Her favorite leaned across her chair, still talking fervently to Joscelin. "My lord, we need not wait on the King to lead us. We can mount our own raid." Amalric's tawny head turned, looking for de Ridford. "My lord Marshall, will you join us? How stands the Temple on such an issue?"

De Ridford laughed. "Such an issue as an assault on Damascus, or Aleppo, or Edessa? Try to be sure which, before you leave home. Talk to the Hospital. I suppose they have some extra men." In fact, in the tail of his eye, he saw the Master of the Knights of the Hospital coming into the garden. He bowed to the Countess. "By your leave, lady." He took himself out of the common air before he had to bow to anyone else he knew to be beneath him.

✦ Baudouin d'Ibelin bent and whispered into Sibylla's ear. "Let's go, while they're not looking."

She raised her head, and he kissed her. She laughed. He was forever grabbing her and kissing her. Now she eeled out of the closing circle of his arm and walked off a few strides, still watching the court. She loved being wanted; she disliked being held. "What? You want to go play with your hawks?"

He came up behind her; his hand stroked around her waist. "I want to go play with you." He was drawing her again into his confining embrace. Across the garden, among the silk skirts and coifs, her mother watched them like a sphinx.

Sibylla shrugged him off, uncomfortable under her mother's gaze. She put her hand on his arm. "What think you of my Uncle Joscelin?"

He lifted his head, looking at Joscelin as if he had just noticed him. "As of a good and true knight," he said, cautiously.

"As of a craven," she said.

"Oh, now, Sib." He laughed. He tweaked a long lock of her hair. "Prudent, that's the word." He laughed again. "You'll never die following Joscelin de Courtenay."

She wrinkled up her nose. "Craven," she said. He was her uncle, head of her family; if she was to be Queen she would need his support, and yet his support was worthless.

To be Queen. All her life, that had lain before her; and yet it had seemed always far before her, never to become real. Her brother was so obviously, so totally the King. She had thought, somehow, he would stop being sick. A miracle would happen. He was good, he was a hero, surely God would save him, one day, one day soon, they would walk into his court and find him clean again, as he had been, handsome and virile.

He was not getting well. Her fist clenched, thinking that, how unfair that was. How cruel it was. And someday soon she really would be Queen of Jerusalem. And that made everything different.

She looked at the other people in the garden, judging their usefulness to her.

There was her mother, of course, and all her mother's clients, holding every office in the Kingdom. Agnes was still staring at her across the bare brown grass of the garden. Sibylla smiled at her, and lifted up her lover's hand and kissed it; her mother's face flattened like a snake's.

Her mother was on her side. Of course the Countess thought it was Agnes de Courtenay's side.

Then, as she was weighing these matters, the chamberlain came in and brayed out an announcement, and through the door from the gallery walked the Count of Tripoli.

Not on her side. The greatest baron in the Kingdom, he had served as regent, when her brother was a child, and she remembered still how Tripoli had struggled to keep control, when her brother at fourteen became of major age—how Baudouin had needed every threat and plea and law to force Tripoli out of power. The Count came into the garden in the middle of a swarm of his attendants, enlarging him, so that he passed through the court like a great disturbance. His brown velvet coat was threadbare. He wore no jewels. It was said he never spent money, only loaned it. He went toward her mother, to give her greeting.

Beside Sibylla, Baudouin d'Ibelin said, "What has you so gripped? I just asked you if you wanted some wine. You see, they are bringing out something fresh."

She said, "I'm watching Cousin Tripoli. I'm wondering how to deal with him."

"Oh, Sibylla, now, don't worry about such things." He put his mouth to her ear, his arm around her waist again. "When we are married, I'll handle all that. You can leave Tripoli to me."

"Go bring me a cup of wine," she said.

She watched him go, tall, fair, handsome, boring. She knew already she would never marry him. But he was useful in goading her mother. The Countess was deep in talk with Tripoli; Sibylla looked around the garden again, measuring people. Then, at the far end of the pavement, away from everybody else, she saw Gerard de Ridford.

The Templar Marshall was staring across the garden at Tripoli, his face a rictus of malice; he looked as if he wanted his teeth locked in Tripoli's neck.

She lowered her eyes, masking a sudden surge of interest. Her Ibelin was back, with a cup in each hand. A page trailed after him with a tray of sweetmeats. She said, "I have forgotten why this Flemish Templar de Ridford so hates my Cousin Tripoli."

Baudouin laughed. "The de Botrun wedding, remember?"

"Oh, yes." She wanted to look at de Ridford again but she did not; she looked into the cup, full of the strong dark wine. She remembered the story now: Tripoli had promised de Ridford an heiress, and then had given her to someone else. "He was no monk, then. When did he become a Templar?"

"After that. Come on, now, Sib, let's not talk about these things, let's get away from here. Your mother is needling me with her eyes."

"I'm waiting for my brother," she said. But she knew he wasn't coming; it was too late in the afternoon now. Which meant he was sick. She wrenched her hand from the Ibelin's grasp and went off a few steps. She gave a harsh look at Tripoli, who had the gall to be healthy. Then, feeling the pressure of another's gaze on her, she turned her head, and briefly her eyes met Gerard de Ridford's.

He turned his head away. Yet clearly he had been watching her. She stared steadily at him, the prerogative of a Queen. Judging his value. He led two hundred knights, the best fighters in Outremer. He hated Tripoli, which put him on her side. She turned away from him, and faced Baudouin d'Ibelin scowling at her.

"Are you listening to me at all? I said: if you want to see the King, let's go there." He jerked up one hand in exasperation.

"Very good idea," she said. She had to think about all this anyway. "Send a page for my cloak, and command us some horses."

CHAPTER VII

The Temple lived by the monastic Rule; they slept and woke, prayed and ate, did their chores and rode their patrols, according to the ringing of church bells. Now the bells were ringing for Tierce, and like everybody else Stephen de l'Aigle went up to the refectory and got in line to go in for dinner, one of two hundred men, all alike.

All alike, and yet he was alone among them; they were all strangers to him. He had been in Jerusalem for more than a month, and still, even the men he had arrived here with were only names and faces to him. He felt unnecessary here, unknown and unconnected.

So he was glad when German de Montoya came up to him, smiling, and joined him in the line, although German's interest also put him on his guard.

"Well met, Stephen," the Preceptor said. "Have you been assigned to a patrol yet?"

"Not yet, sir," Stephen said. "I've just been working with my horses, and getting my gear in order."

German pulled on his moustache. He had shrewd pale eyes, and a constant smile. "Well, let me see what I can do about getting you some orders," he said, and then another knight tramped up to them.

This knight ignored Stephen, and spoke without preliminary to German. "I just got a message from the Under City. There's a caravan in from Cairo. Come down there with me."

Stephen drew back, affronted. It was the black-haired knight who had gotten himself hauled up in front of the chapter meeting. Stephen had forgotten his name. He understood why so many men hated him; he was dirty and coarse, and Norman besides. German said, "I can't go anywhere, I have the Lord's work with my novices. Take Bear, or Felx."

"They are on patrol," the black-haired knight said. "You'll give me up to sin. I need somebody to go with me; who else is there?"

German looked regretful, and paused a moment; then the bell inside the refectory began to ring. They were serving the dinner. He said, "No, I'm hungry. Here. Take Stephen."

"What?" the black-haired knight said. Stephen jerked his head up, startled. The line began to move past them, into the hall.

German blocked the way, smiled from one to the other of them, and spoke to the black-haired knight. "Take him. He is new to Jerusalem. You can show him her many wonders."

Stephen said, "My lord, I have not eaten yet today." He looked with alarm at the black-haired knight, who was watching him glumly.

"He'll teach you to forage," German said to Stephen. "Go. I order it. I promise you, you will find much to think on."

"I don't like to think," Stephen said. The black-haired knight had turned and walked away, long-striding, as if he would happily leave Stephen behind him. "Thinking's too much trouble." He broke into a trot for a few steps to catch up.

The Norman said nothing, but took him across the haram, going back down to the stable.

This was in an old quarry, lying under one corner of the pavement; the knights went up and down by a flight of steps carved into the raw stone. At their foot the stairs curved around a corner, and the rock wall of the pavement opened up in a vast irregular space, stretching back far beneath the Temple Mount itself. This great space had begun as a natural cave, but the walls had been mined for limestone blocks like those of which the Temple Mount itself was built, and as they cut out the rock the quarrymen had propped the ceiling up with great vaults and columns and pushed the space far back into the hillside. The knights called this the Stables of Solomon, and kept their horses here. The horses were tethered in fours to the forest of the columns. The whole vast shadowy cavern rustled with their stamping and champing and nickering.

The knights saddled their horses and rode out to the city. In the street the sun was bright enough to dazzle Stephen, and he put his hand up to shade his eyes. Above them rose the Temple Mount. The domed top of the refectory cast its curved shadow halfway across the street. They turned left along the foot of the western edge of the pavement, a tremendous facing of dressed stone blocks, sprouting tufts of wild greens like hair.

Stephen said, suddenly, "I always thought the streets of Jerusalem were paved with gold. When I first got here I was very disappointed."

The Norman laughed. He gave Stephen a quick look. They turned down into the street. On either side were the walls of gardens. Along the top of the wall on the right side a string of arches ran like stone lace. They went along in a steady stream of people, mostly on foot, porters with loads on their backs, merchants, and vendors. Coming up the street some pilgrims passed them. The pilgrims wore sackcloth; as they went along they sobbed and prayed and pounded themselves with their fists like madmen. In the narrow street, Stephen let his horse drop back a little, behind the other knight, and rode along gawking, his rein slack, watching everything. They passed through the arch of a gate, and the sound of their horses' hoofs changed, hollow in the dark.

Beyond was a broad marketplace, one end covered with a high arched roof, and the other open to the sky. The shops were in arcades along the sides, and among the crowds of people there were the litters of noblewomen, and many splendid riding horses. Beyond it, on the corner, loomed up the first head-heavy tower of the citadel of Jerusalem, where the King lived.

Beyond that, the two Templars came to David's Gate, the main way through the city wall, which was a double portal with its iron portcullis cranked up like a set trap. The sentry sitting on the stairs waved them through, past the rows of people waiting to pay the tolls.

Outside the gate, the sunbleached hillside tipped steeply downward. Stephen caught up and rode side by side with the other knight along the narrow white gash of the road. They skirted a wedge-shaped pit, its walls straight and unnaturally even; rubble half-filled it. Another quarry. The ground was littered with bits of blue tile. Stephen twisted in his saddle to look around him.

On the spur of the ridge above them the city stood honey-colored against the blue glare of the sky. Beyond the rooftops he could see the domes of the Temple, and off to the left the open-topped dome of the Church of the Holy Sepulcher. There were other spires and domes he did not recognize, all tucked inside the yellow wall.

Below the wall, the steep hillside, veined with footpaths, fell away like a skirt. Graves covered it, flat stones in the earth, stone boxes, fancy little corpse-houses with pointed roofs. Between the graves, he saw other buried things. A doorway, its jambs buckled, its lintel crushed down to its threshold. A solitary wall. A column sticking halfway out of the ground. Five steps of a staircase that went nowhere.

He blurted out, "There are cities under this one."

The black-haired knight glanced at him. "This is the oldest place in the world," he said. He sounded proud of it as if he had built it himself.

"Some of it has fallen down so many times nobody can get it to stand up anymore."

The road had flattened out again, and ahead the houses piled against each other like driftwood. Not the palaces and great houses of the city, couched in gardens behind their walls; these were hovels and shacks, set shoulder to shoulder, their stained faces overgrown with weeds and grass. In the windows, in the doorways, everywhere in the street, were the people, women at the well, men on a corner, a shoemaker with his hammer tapping, a tinker with his hammer tapping, crowds of little boys, a woman at a loom in a small courtyard, a stray goat eating flowers off a window sill. Someone shrieked, "Al-Wali!" Ahead, the street opened out into a wide dusty marketplace.

This place was longer than it was wide, and wider at one end than at the other, where there was a cistern and a fountain. All along the edge were little tents and awnings, patched and striped, gaudy under their dirt, that shaded the wooden stalls of a bazaar. Here there were no litters, and very few riding horses. Crowds of people four and five deep pushed toward the arrays of vegetables and drawn chickens. On either corner, as the street entered the marketplace, filthy beggars clustered, their hands out, their voices singsong.

The Norman knight rode into this place as if he belonged here. From all around people screamed and yelled and waved at him; he paid no heed to any of it. He led Stephen across the suk to the fountain, and there drew rein and swung down out of his saddle, and little naked boys swarmed in from all sides, fighting to hold his horse.

Stephen squawked. "You're handing your horse over to a dirty brown brat who can't even speak French?"

The black-haired knight gave him a sideways glance. While the boys fought over his reins he took a leather purse out of the front of his jerkin, fished out a copper and tossed it to the boy who had won control of the reins.

The sight of the money caught Stephen with another scathing question halfway out of his throat; he blinked, dazed, trapped between outrages. The Norman tucked the pouch inside his jerkin again.

"Get down, Mouse, what are you, afraid of the streets?" He started off across the marketplace. Stephen sat a moment longer on his horse, looking around him, and the black-haired knight frowned back over his shoulder, and walked into the crowd.

Stephen bounded down from his horse. The boy grabbed his reins, and he went after the black-haired knight at a run, through the crowd.

"What is this?" he asked, when he caught him.

The other man shrugged. "Jerusalem."

Stephen jostled his arm. "Then what's that up there?" He pointed up behind him; on the steep slope above them the wall of the city notched the sky.

"Also Jerusalem." The black-haired knight swung to face him. "Everybody has his own Jerusalem. There's the High City, where only Christian people live. And this, the Under City, where everybody else lives."

"Then these people are Saracens."

"Some Saracens. Some Jews. Maronites. Jacobites."

"Why do we let them live here?"

The black-haired knight shrugged. "Because it's easier than trying to drive them out. They always come back, and they have their value. Come on, now, and be quiet."

He went off through the crowded suk. Behind the camels a row of stalls sold nuts in baskets, dates on trays, figs hung in strings from the uprights. Green heaps of limes, red pomegranates. The black-haired knight strolled along the row of counters, stopped, picked up a handful of dates, and spoke to the vendor, in a language not French, like a mixture of plainsong and spitting. The vendor bobbed up and down, smiling, and padded off into the back of the stall, which let into a tent.

Stephen said, "You talk their jabber."

The black-haired knight stuffed fruit into his mouth. "They don't speak French here, much." He spat out a date stone.

"Well, then, they should learn it. We are their lords."

The knight looked him over, cold. He spat again. "You're disappointing me, Mouse. This is not our Jerusalem." A short slender man in a cap was coming up to the stall. "Stay here, and keep your mouth shut." He went away down the lane between this stall and the next.

Stephen looked around uncertainly. All these people were staring at him, the vendors behind the counters, the crowd of shoppers. He felt too visible, as if he gave off colors. He was hungry. He remembered how the other knight had taken what he wanted from the stall. There was a large pile of pomegranates next to him; he had learned to eat pomegranates on Cyprus, on his way here. He reached out and took one and began to peel it.

After a while the black-haired knight came back. By then Stephen had eaten three pomegranates and some millet cakes. The knight led him on through the marketplace again, and almost at once another native man, in a long striped gown and a turban, came up and spoke urgently to him, and the black-haired knight listened and then took out his pouch of money and paid him some coins.

"What are you buying?" Stephen asked, when the man in the gown had gone.

"Gossip," the knight said. "News. Rumors." He handed a copper to Stephen. "See this? This is the good money."

The round coin was the size of his palm. Battered and dented as the metal was, yet the coin was finely made, the images sharp and clear on both sides, pretty as jewelry. The black-haired knight pointed to the man's profile looking across the metal circle. "This is a michael; it's Greek. That's the money everybody wants. The rest of the money is worth much less, some of it nothing."

Stephen held the coin with distaste. "Why are you telling me this? We aren't allowed to have money."

"It's the Order's, not mine," the knight said. He went on, across the marketplace; Stephen followed on his heels.

"I don't see that explains much of anything, does it? We are supposed to be poor."

The black-haired knight gave him another of his piercing, disdainful looks. "You know, you're right about one thing. You shouldn't try to think." He took the coin from Stephen and tossed it to the boy holding their horses.

Stephen recoiled from the barb, but the strangeness of the suk kept him cool. The black-haired knight knew his way around here; Stephen could endure a little insult.

"I'm sorry. I forgot your name," he said, when they were both in the saddle.

"A bad memory too? German's lost his eye. My name is Rannulf Fitzwilliam. Everybody calls me Saint." The Norman pointed across the marketplace with his chin. "That's the way home." Obediently Stephen started off through the crowd.

⊕ Midway through the afternoon the bells rang out Nones, and Stephen went down toward the practice yard, to work at the butts with his sword. When he came down the steps to the yard, there was already a knight at each of the six wooden posts set in the pavement, and he stopped at the foot of the steps and waited for his turn.

He heard someone come up behind him, and knew without looking that it was German de Montoya. The back of his neck prickled up. German's interest was getting too particular. Stephen said nothing, and kept his gaze in front of him.

The man at the nearest of the butts was Rannulf Fitzwilliam, the Norman; he stood square before the post, and hacked dutifully away at it, like a woodcutter. Behind Stephen, German said, "Rannulf is incapable of elegance."

Stephen said, "He's very strong off both wings."

"Yes, he gets the work done."

"Nonetheless I fail to see why you all call him Saint." Stephen turned to face the Preceptor. "He handles money, he's common as a serf, he has the manner and bearing of a bandit, he hardly seems a model of obedience. What makes him saintly?"

German was smiling at him from an infuriating pinnacle of understanding. "When you need to know, you'll find out. He took you into the Under City? What did you find there?"

"He went around the bazaar. People talked to him. He went to a house, and accosted somebody. A native."

"A sandpig," German murmured.

Disquieted, Stephen looked around, to see if anybody was watching; here on the steps they were sheltered somewhat from open view. Rannulf had left the practice yard. After a moment German laid his hand on Stephen's upper arm.

"I'm sorry. You think I'm spying. Well, perhaps I am." His hand remained on Stephen's arm, his fingers gently pressing the curve of the muscle. "But Rannulf is our master spy. He learns everything, somehow. He knows everything first." His fingertips stroked the inside of Stephen's elbow.

Stephen turned, violently, and thrust German off. Unruffled, smiling, the older man drew back his hand.

"I like you very much, Stephen."

"I came to the Order," Stephen said, "as a penance. I was caught in bed with my cousin. My male cousin." He stared defiantly into German's eyes, wanting to see him wince, or quail, or at least stop smiling. "I mean to leave my sin behind me."

German nodded. "My story is much the same. Only it was my family priest." One hand moved in a short, throwaway gesture. "It's only one sin."

"The Order requires us to be chaste," Stephen said.

"The Order requires us to avoid women." German's hand rose again; leisurely, confident, he drew his fingertips down the front of Stephen's robe. "Something I've never had any trouble doing."

Stephen's mouth was dry; he felt the old heat rising in his loins. His body was betraying him again. He jerked his gaze from German's, turning his look out across the practice yard.

"What about Rannulf?"

German's hand slid down to his side again. "Rannulf is a saint, remember?" His voice was flat.

Stephen collected himself. "If Rannulf can be chaste, so can I be."

German shook his head. "You are young, Stephen. And very handsome."

Stephen flushed. Steadfastly he looked away across the practice yard, fighting off a climbing surge of lust. To be touched again. To be kissed, to be loved again. He would say yes. He would do it. Before he could speak German was moving off. Stephen realized, with a sour regret, that he had resisted temptation. With an oath he went on down to the practice yard, to take his turn at the post.

Before Vespers, German de Montoya went into the Temple of the Lord, to say some prayers; he walked across the ambulatory and through the opposite archway into the circular nave of the church. Kneeling down, he crossed himself, put his hands together, and asked God either to give him Stephen de l'Aigle, or let him stop wanting him.

The deep gloom of the church purged his eyes clear. Above him the dome rose away toward Heaven, dim and light as a cloud. Beneath it lay the omphalos, the center of the universe, the great Rock of Moriah, its rumpled surface half-drowned in the lamplight shining in through the archways of the ambulatory. German thought of Father Abraham, who had brought his only son to this place to die, and crossed himself again.

Abruptly he realized that someone else was there; he turned his head, and saw Rannulf Fitzwilliam, sitting on his heels at the edge of the Rock, a third of the way around.

"Well, Rannulf," he said. "You've stabbed me in the back. What did you say to Stephen de l'Aigle?"

Rannulf said, "Not much. Why?"

"Some of your insufferable sanctimony seems to have leaked into him."

Rannulf had a wide, thin-lipped mouth, unpleasant even smiling. He smiled now. "Believe me, it was nothing I said. He's turning you down, is he? I thought you never missed."

German grunted at him. "What, are you jealous? I'll get him." He knew how to seduce Stephen; the very game of it tempted him, as much as the young French knight's arrogant beauty. He turned forward again, bowing his head, waiting through a sudden wave of guilt. "See how the shadows pool on the rock, like blood. Was this not a place of sacrifice?"

"The sandpigs think Mohammed came here to go to Heaven. And that the Rock tried to follow, and the Angel Gabriel had to hold it down." Rannulf pointed with his chin to a spot somewhere indefinitely before him. "There's the mark of the Angel's hand, that dent."

"How come you to know things like that?" German shook his head, voluble speaking thus of something unimportant. Not wanting to speak his thoughts he spoke thoughtlessly. "You're just like them, Saint. You're nothing but a sandpig yourself."

In the cold gloom he heard an echo of his own words, and said, at once, "I'm sorry. I meant no offense."

Rannulf grunted at him, offended. "Whatever you want, German."

"Ah, but what I want is this boy."

"You said he isn't taking. Unless you're going to tie him down and rape him, I think your problem's solved." He turned his head, looking in the opposite direction. "We are all sworn to love each other."

German laughed. "Oh, yes, as you love Gerard de Ridford."

"Well," Rannulf said, "some things are impossible."

"You keep to your sins, then; I'll keep to mine." German got to his feet; he had work to do before Vespers. "I shall confess to you," he said. "When the need arises." Rannulf would keep the confession to himself. If German's sin—the sin German was contemplating—came out in a chapter meeting, he would be in serious trouble. Behind him, in the ambulatory, a voice called; the sergeants were coming in to tend the lamps, and to make ready for the Vespers Mass. He went out to the sunlight, leaving Rannulf there in the sanctuary alone.

CHAPTER VIII

The winter was the fighting season; during the summer, the heat and drought and lack of forage kept the men at home. So the summer after Ramleh was quiet. Then, at the Feast of the Conception, in September, the Master of the Templars went to the King and told him that Saladin was gathering his armies again, and that the likely point of his attack would be the great new castle Chastelet, which the King was building at Jacob's Ford on the Jordan River north of Lake Tiberias.

"Then I shall summon my knights," the King said, "and hold myself ready. We should strengthen the garrison at Chastelet."

Odo de Saint-Amand, the Master, said, "We have already sent fifty of our brothers there, Sire, under the command of the Marshall, Gerard de Ridford."

Odo de Saint-Amand had brought some ten knights with him into the King's hall, to make his presence greater. In the front rank of this honor guard, Rannulf stood, his hands locked on the hilt of his sword, and his thoughts savage.

He had got word of the Sultan's intentions through his informants in the suk; he had taken the news into the chapter meeting, and there, in front of everybody, with the help of half of them, Gerard de Ridford had stood up like an emperor and taken Rannulf's campaign away from him. Now the Marshall rode off to Jacob's Ford, and Rannulf stood nameless among the ordinary men, waiting to be told what to do.

In the chapter meeting, he had lost his temper, roared at de Ridford and Odo, half-drawn his sword. Stalked off, humiliated, into the shadows at the back of the refectory, until the Master called him forward again to repent in front of everybody. His hands still shook. He gripped his sword hilt until his knuckles hurt. Beside him, German de Montoya shot a sideways glance at him.

The King was saying, "We shall send to the Count of Tripoli, to make him aware of this, and beg his help."

German murmured, "Is that the Princess?"

Unmindful in his sulky fury, Rannulf lifted his eyes, and made the mistake of looking at her. He lowered his gaze at once. "Yes."

Slender in a blue gown, her hair down around her shoulders like a maid's. German was saying, "I wonder what she is doing here. Hardly a place for a woman." Rannulf grunted at him. He did not look at her again; he kept his gaze pinned to the flagstone floor. But suddenly his defeat in the chapter meeting mattered somewhat less.

He had seen her only twice, and only for a moment. He fought the urge to lift his eyes now, and gorge on her.

The King was saying, "We shall send to Kerak, also, and make him aware of this."

"Small good that will do," German muttered.

"You talk too much," Rannulf said.

"Stop licking your wounds. De Ridford can't do anything until the rest of us get there anyway."

"You're an officer," Rannulf said. "You don't know what you're talking about." He shut his eyes.

"What are you doing now?" German laughed. "Are you praying? The audience is over." Turning, side by side, the knights lined up to follow the Master out of the hall. Rannulf kept his head down, his gaze lowered to the floor.

"You know I'm coming with you on this campaign," German said, as they left.

"Why, so you can show off for your little French mouse?"

German shrugged. "I need to get out in the field now and then. I miss the march. Come along, now, keep moving."

The Countess of Courtenay said, "I think this is utterest folly, Sibylla."

"Yes, so you've said several times now." Sibylla helped her mother up into the litter. The courtyard was full of baggage and servants loading baggage. The men were going off to war, and all the women of the court were leaving for the safety of Ascalon, or Acre, or one of the other cities on the coast. Agnes settled herself in the litter, throwing cushions out of the way. Sibylla leaned on the side of it, watching.

"If somehow you fell into the hands of the Saracens, you know," Agnes said, "you would be better off dead."

"We will not lose Jerusalem," Sibylla said. "But if by some chance the inconceivable happens and I do get in the way of a horde of screaming Mohammedans, Mother, I promise you I will fall on my sword."

Her mother's face contorted with impatience. "Ah, girl. You can't walk one pace in step with me, can you?"

"You're about to spend two days in a litter," Sibylla said. "To avoid that I would marry a whole harem of Saracens. There is Baudouinet." Across the crowded courtyard her son had just come out of the palace, holding the hand of his nurse.

Her mother lurched forward, craning her neck, and called and waved her hand. The child would travel with her. Sibylla started off, out of the way of this grandmotherly excess, and her mother put out her hand to stop her, and faced her again.

"If you change your mind, come to me at Ascalon. And if you must reach me privily, there is a merchant in the Under City named Abu Hamid, who can have a message to me. But beware, he works also for the Templars." She twisted around again, calling out to the little prince, her arms reaching toward him; even through the crowd noise Sibylla heard the little boy's shriek of welcome to her.

Sibylla moved off, back toward the palace. From the steps Alys called to her. "Sibylla, come tell me what to pack!" They were moving over their little household to her brother's citadel. Now that her mother was going, Sibylla felt as free as air; she could go around with her hair down, wear men's clothes, walk barefoot. Say whatever she wanted, think whatever she wanted. She even skipped, going up the steps to Alys.

✦ The fall rains began. Then after a week of heavy storms, the dormitory bell roused Stephen from a deep sleep, and he got up, with all the rest, and heard the orders sending them first to Mass, and then to Jacob's Ford.

In the armory, in a crowd, in a hurry, he put on his hauberk, and lifted his helmet and shield down from the wall. His palms were sweating. His throat was dry; he kept coughing. Around him were some of the other men who had arrived here with him: other men going to their first battles as Templars. His head hooded in double-linked chain mail, Hilaire de Bretagne grinned tightly at him.

"I guess Rannulf Fitzwilliam's spies were right, hah?"

Stephen said, "What do you know of Rannulf's spies?" He followed Hilaire to the armory door; it was still dark outside. Two by two, their column was forming on the pavement, with German commanding them.

They went into the stable for their horses, and lined up in columns again in the street; while they were waiting to be ordered out, servants from the kitchen walked down along the rows of mounted men and gave them each a loaf of bread and a full skin of wine. German rode past them, looking them all over.

"On the march," German said, "the rule is silence."

Pedro de Varegas gave a huff of a laugh. "Yes, such as at supper." Suppers in the refectory were uproarious, in spite of the Rule.

German overheard him, and turned his head, frowning. "No, not like supper—this is a march, fool," and thereafter Pedro said nothing. By daybreak, one double column among many, they were riding out through David's Gate.

They struck out east and north through the hills turned momentarily green from the rains, the wind blustery and raw at their backs. The rain stopped. The day grew warmer. From the folds of the treeless hillsides there rose drifts of fog like cool smoke. In this monotonous country it seemed they went nowhere, stride after stride.

Stephen rode with Hilaire beside him, Pedro de Varegas in front of him, but he went separated from them by a cushion of fears and doubts. He had fought before only in melees. Ahead of him was his first battle. He had always imagined himself galloping into this affray with a flaming sword in his hand and a fiery courage in his heart. Now that it was actually about to happen he was halfway wetting his pants and he hadn't even seen the enemy yet.

That night they camped on a hilltop, looking down toward the Jordan River. Encased in the heavy clinking mail shirt, his sword beside him under the blanket, Stephen could not sleep; he lay listening to the trampling and shouting of other armies moving in to join them. This went on all through the night, and when the grey dawn leaked in through the clouds, he saw, amazed, that the Christian camp had grown overnight into a minor city, teeming over the slopes as far as he could see.

In silence, the Templars rose and broke their camp, and in a light rain, they formed their columns again and led the way down toward the river, its braided streams running sloppy and brown along its wide sandy bed. As they dropped down the long slope the rain stopped. Like the other men around him Stephen took off his cloak and rolled it up and lashed it to the cantle of his saddle.

As he twisted around to do this, he looked back over the rest of the Frankish army straggling along the bare hillside after them, in no order, a noisy tide. Neat and purposeful in their double columns, the Templars were already well out in front of everybody else. Out where they would take the first blow. Sinking down into his saddle, Stephen flung a wild glance out at the slopes around them.

His stomach hurt. He had to shit, but he could not leave the march. He cursed himself for a wretched coward. The march was endless. His rumpbones hurt. His insides were turning to sand. Then at noon they rode around the foot of a spur of rock, and came suddenly on Jacob's Ford.

Here the river ran wide and shallow across ledges of the sandy rock. The castle rose from an outcrop above the water, its building stone the same color as the land around it, the curtain wall climbing sheer out of the dust, the great keep standing square against the sky, and all around it in zigs and zags the lines of half-built walls.

As the Templars rode down toward this heap of stone there rose a wild buzzing, like bees swarming out of the desert. Suddenly Stephen realized that the dark mass shifting along the curtain wall was a cheering crowd, and that the buzzing came from them. He swung his gaze toward the river, and past the river, and past the castle, looking for the enemy, but there was no enemy. Only, the whole horizon had faded into a rising cloud of dust.

His heart leapt with a bounding hope. He stood in his stirrups, trying to make out the source of the dust. The army behind him let out a roar, until all over the slope behind him, men were cheering and whooping. Ahead of Stephen in the column, Hilaire twisted around in his saddle.

His face shone. "They've run!" He flung his arm out, pointing across the river. "The sandpigs saw us coming and they ran away!"

Stephen gave a half-dazed laugh. Down on the curtain wall of the castle, two long blue banners unfurled suddenly, and the men carrying them began to run up and down on the wall to make the silk flutter and flap. People waved their arms, jumped, and screamed, while behind Stephen, the army resounded with yells of triumph.

Stephen settled down into his saddle again. He fought off an overwhelming sense of relief. But he had never really been afraid. Hastily he recrafted his memory. He had just been eager for the fight. He was a Templar. The sandpigs had run from him, run from the very sight of him, from the whispered word of his coming. He was a Templar. Highheaded, silent, fearless as any other of God's heroes, and certainly not saddle-sore, he rode down into Chastelet.

There will be stables for four hundred horses, storerooms deep enough to keep a thousand men for a year, cisterns and wells, gardens, even its own salt mine," German said. "I'll walk around it with you tomorrow; you should see the whole castle." They were coming up the ramp to the foot of the great square keep; ahead of them more knights were waiting to be let into the hall. German's voice was rich with pride. "The King ordered her built, but Chastelet belongs to the Order. A Templar drew the plans, and Templars are raising the stones, and when it is done, Templars alone will serve in the garrison."

Stephen said, "It's easy to see how important it is."

From this rise he looked out to the east, across the curtain wall, over the glittering transparent braids of the river. Beyond the overflowing Jordan lay the desert, flat and brown as a stretched hide. The roads that crossed the ford fanned out across it, paler than the untrodden sand, all rays focussing here, where this castle stood, as if God had taken a rule, and drawn arrows.

German said, "Out there, though you cannot see it, is the great highway that leads down ultimately to Mecca and to Cairo. During the time of the Muslims' pilgrimage, folk throng along it thick as a city street sometimes."

Stephen said, "The sandpigs go on pilgrimage? What—to devil shrines?" He laughed.

German smiled at him. "No, to Mecca." His face smoothed out with amusement. "Such is your thought; they worship the devil?"

Stephen gave an uncertain shrug. "Whatever they worship, it's not the one true God. What's the difference?"

Still smiling, the Preceptor looked away, and Stephen thought he saw him give a little shake of his head. A rough heat harshened the young knight's neck and cheeks; he felt tricked, caught in the jigs in the Rule that sometimes held and sometimes didn't. Suddenly he wished himself away from here.

But German was turning back to him, still overstuffed with passion for this castle. "This will be first of a string of fortresses along the river, from Jacob's Ford here down to the Sea of Salt. We'll hold this highway in a fist of stone and iron, and dominate the whole of the Ultrajordain with a handful of men." He nodded to Stephen. "You might serve in one of these garrisons. Become the commander here, serve nobly, and you could guarantee election as Master in Jerusalem!"

"Me," Stephen said. "I can't be Master." But he was pleased at it; he wondered for the first time why he should not rise, and smiled, and German smiled back at him.

They climbed steep steps into the castle keep. All the stones were still sharp-edged and chalky, so fresh were they from the quarries; the air smelled like lime. Out a window midway up the stairs, Stephen looked out over a half-finished terrace, where in an angle of two walls several courses of stonework formed the base of a tower. More stones lay around the terrace in heaps, with hods and trays for mixing mortar, and scattered tools. Sitting on one end of the unfinished circular wall was a wine jug. The workmen had gone, off celebrating the defeat of Saladin. On German's heels, Stephen went into the hall, to another celebration.

The air was abruptly warmer, lighter, abuzz with voices. Startled, he looked around him, past the little groups of men talking and laughing. It was as if he had walked in a single step from the harsh desert into a splendid French palace. The chamber stretched away like a church, impressively large, the stone walls faced with wood, the ceiling supported on barrel vaults. His feet sank into a luxurious softness, and he looked down, and saw Turkish carpets covering the floor. The tall iron standards that held the lamps were tipped with ferrules of silver; the lamps themselves were made of silver and gold. On one long wall, a great arras hung, showing somebody's martyrdom, all stuck with arrows— Saint Sebastian, he remembered now. A row of silk banners hung above the hearth, festooned with golden tassles.

"There's the King," German said.

Stephen followed the older man down the room. The Preceptor greeted other knights, nodded, smiled, knew everybody. A tall beardless man rushed forward and seized his hand. "God's blood, Sir German, I have never seen the like of it. Before the first ten of you had come over the hill, the Saracens were flying like chickens."

German said, "God is good. Have you met—" He introduced Stephen, and they went through the little ritual of greetings and names and connections. German said, "Sir Stephen's uncle is the Seneschal of France."

"Excellent," said the beardless man, and shook his hand again. "Excellent." He bowed himself away, toward someone else.

"Why do you always mention that?" Stephen asked.

The older man shrugged, his face bland. "Your grandfather was a close friend of King Louis, wasn't he?"

Stephen frowned at him. "They were friends. I remember the King being a cold bore, frankly, who went to Mass too much. Every time he came, we had to sing psalms all day."

German's face crinkled into ready laughter. "Good. Remember that, that's a very good story. There, over there, that's Humphrey de Toron; you should meet him, too, eventually. See who's hounding the King."

Stephen looked around. Near the end of the hall, a low dais of polished wood had been set up, and some heavy chairs set on it; in front of the chairs stood Gerard de Ridford, talking and gesturing over a smaller man, not a Templar, in a long lavish coat of purple silk.

De Ridford held Stephen's gaze. The Marshall had a way of carrying himself that caught the eye; for a moment, in fact, he thought German meant the Marshall when he spoke of the King, as if it were a sarcastic nickname, like Saint. Then the man in the purple coat turned to face them.

"Sir German, welcome, please join us."

Stephen jerked back. The face before him was a monster's, swollen shapeless, the flesh thick and coarse and puckered; there was a wound below one hideous eye. Stephen gasped, shocked stupid.

The eyes blinked. "You have my leave," the King said, and turned back to de Ridford.

Stephen went off a few feet; he knew he had just destroyed himself at this court, and he had given a terrible offense; surely he would be ordered out of the castle, maybe thrown out of the Order. German came up beside him.

"Well, that was something of a disaster. What's the matter with you? You didn't know?"

"I'm sorry," Stephen said, in agony. "I'm sorry."

"Well, you should be, but never mind. Come along, we'll try it again."

"What?" Stephen cast a glance around, toward the purple coat, before which de Ridford strutted and postured. People did not seem to be staring at him. Yet he felt the tingling pressure of a thousand watching eyes. "He'll dismiss me."

"No, he won't," German said. "He'll forget. He has no more thought for himself than an angel. He gave you leave for your sake, not his. Are you steady, now?"

"German, I can't. After what I just did—"

"Keep your courtesy this time," German said, and pulled him forward.

De Ridford was leaning over the young King, his voice booming. "Sire, you should have Templars all around you, always, a wall against your enemies."

"I'd rather not be inside walls," the King said, mildly, and nodded to German; a little late, Stephen realized he and German were performing a rescue. "Well, Preceptor, what are you doing out here in the wastelands? I thought you never left the Temple."

German bowed. "Sire, even the saints and virgins must one day leave Jerusalem, and I am neither of those. May I introduce—" He turned, saying Stephen's name.

Stephen stepped forward, cold to his fingertips, with a bow that kept his gaze lowered. The King said, "Welcome to you, Sir Stephen. God bless your career in the Order."

"Thank you, Sire." He could not look up, he could not bear to see that horror of a face, to meet the eyes of one he had offended. De Ridford rushed back into his campaign.

"Sire, I mark that neither Tripoli nor Kerak has come to join us. I pray God will strengthen their loyalty."

The King's voice was mild. "Tripoli is in his wife's castle at Tiberias, waiting to see what happens. Kerak is in the Ultrajordain, well-armed and ready, and will come if we need him." He was moving, climbing up into the nearer of the big chairs; two pages leapt forward to put cushions by him, and to bring him a cup of wine. Stephen thought how it would be, to look so horrible that no one could endure the sight of him.

De Ridford said, "Yet with their armies we could make an attack now on Saladin that might ruin him for good and all." He was pushing closer to the King, who turned again to German.

"Saladin probably hears much the same thing. We are marching out tomorrow to try to chase him down and when we catch him we will see what can be done. Do you play chess, Sir German?"

There was a small uncomfortable silence. Then German said, "Sire, I regret, we are forbidden to play chess."

The King gave a short, explosive grunt of mirth. "Not with chessmen, anyway. But the colors are apt. What a grim life you lead." His gaze rose, scanning the hall. "On the other hand, the setting is magnificent."

German said, "There were some who thought the theme of the arras should have been Christ driving the money changers out of the Temple."

At that, the King burst out laughing, and Stephen, looking at him, thought him not so hideous after all. German's ease with him, in this place, impressed Stephen; he felt a sudden rush of affection toward the Preceptor, who belonged among all these great men, and who brought Stephen among them as well. Then behind them, an old man appeared, flanked by six knights, and all the Templars were dismissed.

Together, they went a few steps back up the hall. German said to de Ridford, "He is not warm to this idea of yours we should stand guard over him; leave off with it."

De Ridford sneered at him. "You'll tell me what to do, Preceptor!" With a swagger he went off toward the arras, where the Master Odo stood in a crowd of lesser men.

Stephen looked back at the greybeard, standing stiffly over the King, haranguing him as steadily as de Ridford had. "Who is that?"

"Humphrey de Toron," German said. "A very great baron." He was staring after de Ridford, his brows folded into a frown. Stephen watched the King; two young men in short jackets, long hair, and earrings sauntered down the hall toward the dais, and the King deftly exchanged Humphrey de Toron for these newcomers. The pages hurried around setting up a chessboard.

German said, "The Ibelins. The younger one is to marry the Princess Sibylla."

"Really," Stephen said. "Which, the one with the fine, fine backside?"

German laughed. "No, that's Balian. The taller one is the Princess'."

"Well, then, she can have him," Stephen murmured. He followed German on across the room. He decided he liked this place. To command such a castle would make a man great as a king. Fondly he looked around at the oiled cedar walls and the arras; he felt almost as if they really were his.

✦ Rannulf was glad of the silence of the march. Against the work, the constant riding, the hunger and thirst and sleeping in his hauberk on the ground, he laid the hard edge of his temper, and the one ground against the other, and he got a certain kind of peace from that.

Because de Ridford hated him, he led the first column of the vanguard, which was the most dangerous. That suited him very well. Riding at the point, he could move where he willed, go as fast as he wanted, and he drew the rest after him, first to catch Saladin's army and then to keep pace with it.

From Jacob's Ford the armies rode south, following the course of the river. Saladin's force had swung off toward Damascus, and then turned back again, and for a while the Franks and the Saracens rode along nearly parallel to each other, between them the thin green ribbon of the Jordan. Then they passed by Lake Tiberias, which was the same Sea of Galilee that Jesus had walked on, and Rannulf lost contact with the Sultan's army.

The Count of Tripoli joined them, with fifty knights and a hundred men-at-arms. He and de Ridford argued over every move, every step. The Franks swung west, and crossed the Litani River, flooded from the recent rains, where it broke from its chasm in the hills and gushed out onto the plain. The King and his nobles held up on the northern bank of the river, while the Templars picked a way over the marshy plain and rode into the steep pass leading over the hills to the east.

The rain had let up and the sky had suddenly cleared of clouds and the sunlight blasted the raw red earth of the hillside. Grit and red mud and pebbles, freshly washed down from the heights, half-buried the goat track that mounted into the pass. The air was heavy and ripe, like turned earth. There was no wind.

First of them all, Rannulf rode at a hard trot up into the saddle of the pass; the sun blazed in his eyes. From the height, he looked out over a broad valley, steaming after the rain. Sheets of standing water still lay like silver on the flat ground below, and all along the dark lowlands were Saracen horsemen by the thousand.

Rannulf set his teeth together. The rest of his column was waiting just behind him, and he sent two of them back for the officers. He shaded his eyes with his hand. The Saracens down there were moving steadily toward him, gathering on the road leading into this same pass; he wondered if they had seen him yet. With a clatter of hoofs, the Master of Jerusalem and the Marshall and the other officers swept in around him.

De Ridford cried out. "So they haven't escaped!"

"This isn't the whole of Saladin's army." The Master turned to Rannulf. "What do you make of this?"

Rannulf pointed with his chin down at the dark swarm of horsemen. "The green turbans are Turkish bowmen. Those, over there, on the big horses, those are lancers, Kurds, Saladin's own people, they're good fighters. You're right, this certainly isn't the main army. It might be a vanguard."

Gerard de Ridford said, "Sound the attack. We have the high ground."

Rannulf snorted at him. "There are two hundred of us. Some thousands of them."

"We'll smash them in a single charge. Like at Ramleh." De Ridford's voice rang, strident. He wheeled around and glared down at the Saracens and his chest heaved.

Rannulf said, "They're much closer together and much readier than they were at Ramleh. This line will yield in the middle and come around each flank and surround us."

De Ridford swung toward him, leading with his jutting jaw, and smiled. "What! The hero quails? There were only a few hundred men at Ramleh, too, weren't there? Why don't you show us how you did it there?"

Rannulf's whole body clenched, and the heat rose in his cheeks; with the Saracens there before him he wanted only to strike this other Christian knight. He crossed himself against the devil in him. "God wills it," he said. His voice shook. He turned to the Master. "If you order the charge, lord, I will charge. But if you do it you are a damned fool."

De Ridford swelled like a poisonous toad. The Master chuckled. "What, Rannulf—however de Ridford wants it, you want it opposite? We'll just give them a push, now. They've run from us before. They will again. We must not let them take this pass." He lifted his arm. "Form ranks."

Rannulf aimed his gaze down the slope toward the valley below. The host on the gleaming plain had seen them, was moving, orderly, compact, to meet them. He felt the warnings in every nerve in his body, a tingle in his skin, a pulse down his spine, something coiling in his gut. He wheeled his horse around to go back to his place in line.

"Hold," de Ridford said, and charged up across his path. The Marshall rode a tall stallion with a great white blaze down its face, and four white socks: he always took a horse with a lot of white on it. Beyond him, on the slope leading up to the pass, the rest of the Templars were breaking out of their columns, a brief boil of activity that swiftly froze into three long ranks across the road. A horn blew. De Ridford's face was flushed red as a grape. He had his helmet cradled in his arm. He said, "Rannulf, take the end of the front rank. The right end."

The Master twisted in his saddle, and his look swept from de Ridford to Rannulf and back to de Ridford, but he said nothing. De Ridford said, "Or are you afraid?"

Rannulf laughed. He had no answer for de Ridford and gave him none, but turned, and galloped away across the break of the slope, where the road came out of the pass, and the Templars were gathered for their charge.

There the sergeants were rushing around with shields and extra horses. Rannulf found a sergeant and got his shield, and went around to take his place at the right end of the front line.

The man on his left gave a faint cheer of relief. "The dead man's end. And welcome to it, brother."

"Just keep your shield up," Rannulf said, "and ride to the right."

He slung the strap of his shield over his shoulder. He was sweating already under his mail. For a moment his chest tightened, and his breath stuck. His horse would not stand still, but trod forward two steps, backward two steps, shaking its head against the bit; with one hand he managed it and with the other got his helmet onto his head. The man on his right turned to him again, a boy whose fair downy beard scarcely covered his cheeks.

"Are we going to charge? What's the order?"

"God wills it," Rannulf said. "That's the order." He hitched his shield up on his left arm, and then the horns were blowing.

All together, knee to knee, the knights swung forward, and the clatter of their horses' hoofs on the hard ground was like the roll of drums. With the slope before them they flowed at once into a gallop. Rannulf's belly churned. Out here on the far end he had to ride harder than the others, stay up half a stride in front, hit the Saracens first of all of them. His whole body felt too large for his skin, every nerve painfully taut.

He drew the weight of his sword into his hand, iron for his arm, fire for his gut. His horse carried him down over the summit of the pass. Now he could see the whole wide valley below him. The Saracens were a solid mass on the plain, their ranks picked out with green banners. Someone cried, "God wills it!" in a high quavering voice. Then his horse reached full stride, with all the other horses, and the horns blasted.

Swinging into the charge, he spurred his horse on, surging out across the open slope, and then up from his left, where they had been lurking all the while, half a thousand Kurds came thundering straight toward him.

The sudden sight of them galloping at him from the side brought a raw yell out of his throat. The Saracens had set a trap for them, and the Templars had ridden straight into it. He clamped his legs tight around his horse to hold it steady, and wheeled toward the enemy. The downfaced boy galloped on his left, beyond him, a solid wall of Templars, the whole line rotating around to face this unexpected attack, but the Kurds were sweeping down at them like a scythe.

The fluting Arab warcry trilled out through the dust. Rannulf held his horse back, the pivot for the rest of the line, and two Kurds converged on him. He sat deep in his saddle and braced his feet in his stirrups and charged his horse between them.

Their lances swung toward his chest. One iron point skidded off his shield and he struck the other aside with his sword. The Kurd on his left galloped straight on by; the Kurd on his right slowed, cocking back his lance to strike again; then the charging Templar line overtook him, and he went down under their driving hoofs.

Ahead the enemy rank rose up in a barrier of shields and lances. Dust rose in clouds, blinding, throat-clogging, billowing yellow through the air. Rannulf's horse slowed, blocked by more horses. A Kurdish lancer jittered along in front of him, trying to get a safe angle; when he got on Rannulf's quarter he gave Rannulf the good angle, and the Templar lunged in and struck the Saracen rider down. To Rannulf's left the down-faced boy was still fighting, his shield too low, his sword too high, and then a hedge of lances closed over him and he was gone. Rannulf slashed after him, trying to catch up with the rest of the line.

There was no Templar line, only masses of Kurds around him.

On his blind side a lance struck his shield square on and drove it back into his body and nearly lifted him out of the saddle. He shuddered it off. He lost a stirrup. With his knees he clung to his horse. Three men crowded at him at once, flailing blows at him so fast and heavy he could barely fend them off. He felt the sky redden. Felt the angel close above him. His horse screamed and reared and went over backward.

Sliding free, he landed on the ground on all fours, his sword still in his hand and his shield still on his arm, and had a moment, while they swarmed after the horse, to collect himself. He flung off the encumbering shield and darted out into the open. The air was so thick with dust he could hardly see, and his lungs and throat burned; before him in the haze a form loomed, a tiny horse, an archer in a green turban perched on its back. The second wave of the Saracen attack had reached him.

Rannulf leapt up from the ground, and the little horse shied violently backward. He grabbed its bridle with his left hand and with his sword struck across its withers at the bowman, point on, jab and jab and jab, and each time the sword bit flesh, and then once more and the green turban plunged away over the horse's rump. An arrow sank into Rannulf's arm. Another slapped off his helmet. He vaulted onto the tiny horse and swung blindly around, looking for Templars, and seeing only the enemy.

Get out of here.

Like a voice speaking in his mind this order sounded, clear and cool. He obeyed it instantly, a command from God. He booted the little horse into a gallop; it carried him heavily, but it carried him, it had the good heart of most Arab horses. Grimly he struggled uphill, toward the clear blue sky.

In the third rank of the Templars, with Hilaire on his left and Pedro on his right, Stephen charged across the slope; his gaze was pinned to the back of the man in front of him, his guts felt like running water, his ears roared as if he were under the ocean. The forward surge of men and horses swept him on, and then suddenly the whole momentum of the charge shifted. Abruptly everybody was turning, swinging to the left, and he heard horns blaring and saw the black-and-white standards bobbing in the dusty air, and then he heard rather than saw the enemy attack.

They screamed, the Saracens, like women, or like demons. They crashed into the unready Templars, and armor crunched, horses shrilled, bodies thudded together. Ahead of Stephen the orderly black-and-white line vanished into a clutter of heaving backs and lashing arms. He drove his horse on, and then before him was a Saracen on a horse, aiming a lance straight at Stephen's heart.

He shrieked. Wildly he flailed away with his sword, trying to hide behind his shield; when he had the shield up where it did him any good, he couldn't see at all. On his left, hunched like a gnome behind his own target, Pedro was beating at the air with his sword, and Stephen remembered their training and pushed sideways to cover Pedro's flank, and then from the little Spaniard's other side a spear struck Pedro so hard it bore him up in a fountain of blood out of his saddle and into Stephen's lap.

Stephen was screaming; his throat was raw, but he couldn't even hear himself for the racket around him. Pedro's body sprawled across him, getting in his way, and the lance came at him; he never saw the man wielding it, only the long three-winged blade and the haft all covered with blood, Pedro's blood, and that he remembered forever. He struck at the lance with his sword, and missed, and then the lance caught Pedro again, and jerked him away into the morass, the din, the chaos.

He swung toward Hilaire, and saw an empty saddle there.

His horse wheeled around, needing no order from its rider, and clambered back up the slope. Another lancer came at Stephen, and while their horses strode side by side for several paces, the two men struck at each other, hitting nothing; then the lancer swung away. Stephen's horse stumbled and he lurched forward up against the pommel of his saddle. Another rider galloped up beside him.

He recoiled, yanking his sword back to strike, and the rider shrieked at him—he heard nothing, but saw the mouth open in the grizzled beard—and he realized it was German.

He jerked his sword down, swung his shield around, fell in beside German as he had been drilled to do; suddenly he felt stronger, safer. German led him on, up the slope, toward a dozen men, Saracens and Templars, fighting back and forth across the trail.

"God wills it!"

The Saracens saw them coming, and peeled off. The Templars swung around and fit into German's line. They scrambled up the steep slope toward the pass. There, on the height, German turned, one arm raised, and drew the twenty-odd men who had followed him around in a long rank. Stephen looked back, and his breath left him in a yell.

The dust hung over the long decline like a filthy fog, but even through the haze he could see the bodies that lay there, twisted and trampled bodies, as far as he could see. And far down there, at the foot of the slope, he could make out vast packs of Saracens, moving steadily toward him. His belly knotted, his mouth gone dry, and his heart fluttered.

German bawled, "Rannulf! Rannulf!"

Up out of the dust a little horse labored, Rannulf on its back; seeing the other Templars, he swerved to join them, and rode in among them; his face was painted with yellow dust. A moment later, another of the knights of the Jerusalem chapter galloped up beside him—Richard le Mesne, whom they all called Bear.

German reached out and gripped Rannulf's arm. "What's this?"

Rannulf had taken an arrow through the forearm, just below the cuff of his hauberk. The knight looked down, as if he had just noticed it, and flexed his hand. His head swiveled toward the plain.

"They are coming."

"Yes." German took hold of Rannulf's arm in one hand and the shaft of the arrow in the other. "Can we stand them off here, on this ground?"

"How many men do we have?" Rannulf turned back toward the Templars gathered around him. For a moment his eyes met Stephen's, without recognition, only counting him. "Maybe. But if we fail here—" German thrust the arrow on through the meat of his arm until the head came out the other side.

Rannulf gasped, and buckled forward from the waist, his mouth open. German broke off the arrowhead and drew the shaft back out of the wound. A squirt of blood followed it; Stephen turned his eyes away, sick.

"Aaaaagh." Rannulf clutched his arm to his chest, his body still curled forward. The Preceptor sniffed the arrowhead and then the shaft of the arrow.

"It smells clean. You're lucky."

Rannulf gave his head a shake. "God give me no such luck again. We can't stay here." Spittle drooled from the corner of his mouth. He shook his head again. "Get back to the King."

"I agree," German said. "I'll take command, since I seem to be the only officer. You ride on the right." He tossed down the pieces of the arrow. To Stephen, he said, "Ride by me." Stephen swung up beside him, grateful for the order. Straightening, Rannulf picked the little Arab horse up on the bit and galloped around to the far end of the Templar rank.

Stephen looked back over his shoulder again. The dust was lifting. The fighting had stopped. The white surcoats of the dead men littered the slope like scattered feathers. His belly hurt. Down there was Pedro. Hilaire. Now nameless white scud on the hillside. Behind his eyes a throbbing blind panic began, a desperate will to get as far from here as possible. With German on his right and a stranger on his left he trotted across the pass and back toward the Litani River, going faster with every step.

The Count of Tripoli said, "I'm getting out of here." He was staring across the swampy lowland toward the pass to the east. "The river is still rising, and the sun is going down. Sire, you should withdraw us all back to the far side of the river."

King Baudouin looked back over his shoulder. The Litani rolled along behind them in a broad boiling tide, brown as bean porridge, its surface streaked with white scum. Upstream the hills closed down sheer around it; downstream, the river spread out to cover the whole narrow plain. The King turned, and looked up at the pass again.

The sun had gone down behind the peaks. The foot of the hill was deep in shadow. He knew Tripoli was right.

He said, "The Templars are still out there. We can't abandon them."

Tripoli said, "Let the Templars take care of themselves." He swung his horse around, toward his men, gathered on the soggy ground behind him.

The King was staring at the pass; he thought he saw some riders up there, but he could not make out who they were. He turned to Tripoli again, to ask him, but the Count was riding toward his men. Baudouin pressed his lips together and turned his back. Let Tripoli take care of himself, then.

Some of the other nobles sat their horses a little way up the plain from the river, watching the pass; old Humphrey de Toron was among them, the constable of the Kingdom, and the King's uncle, Joscelin de Courtenay. Baudouin rode up to join them, peering toward the pass again.

"Up there." He reined his horse over to Humphrey de Toron, who had been his father's closest friend. "Can you see? What's going on up there?"

The old man shook his head. "It doesn't look good." He cast a look behind him, at the river, and shook his head again.

Among the other men with him were Balian d'Ibelin and his brother, Sibylla's knight. Balian called out, "Sire, we should cross back to the other side of the river, before the night falls."

"No," the King cried, and flung out his hand. Now he could see what men those were that flew down toward him from the pass. "There are the Templars. What are they doing? Where are the rest of them?"

Humphrey stood in his stirrups, squinting across the valley. Balian's head swiveled; his brother said, "Where? I don't see anybody." And then Balian himself seized a horn and put it to his lips.

The King's horse bounded at the sudden shriek of the horn. Baudouin rode forward a few steps, the horse snorting and sidestepping under him. The oncoming knights all wore white surcoats; certainly they were Templars, but there were far fewer of them than had ridden over the pass in the other direction. Above them, the hammock of the pass was empty a moment.

Then, all along it, through the last true sunlight, a surging wave of Saracens crested the horizon, brimmed over, flooded down the slope, and behind them came more, and more, an endless tide.

The King let out a yell. Behind him, Balian's horn sounded its three shrill notes, again and again. All along the river, the Frankish army was wheeling around to answer that call. A raw shout went up from a thousand throats. The King loosed his horse; first of all of them, he charged out to the support of the Templars.

Humphrey de Toron in his black armor raced up on his left, Balian d'Ibelin on his bay horse pressed in on his right. The King did not draw his sword, and he had no shield; his arms were shaking, and he could barely close his hands on the reins, much less wield a weapon. His legs hung like stones from his knees. He felt the thundering of the horses' hoofs like something beating against his body. He splashed across the marshy ground, and then the land tipped steeply up, and his horse began to work hard.

Above him on the slope, the retreating Templars slowed. With the oncoming Franks to bolster them, they swerved around, facing uphill again, to meet the Saracens rushing down the slope toward them all like an unrolling wave. The King gave a cry, lost in the myriad cries of his men: "God wills it!" Then the two armies slammed together.

The impact almost knocked him from his horse. Around him men were fighting hand to hand, the rip and clash of steel ringing in his ears, and the screams of the dying. He reined his horse hard to one side to avoid a charging Turk, and from his right old Humphrey de Toron flung himself forward and bore the enemy down. For a moment in the furious tangle of men the King saw nothing, save fragments and flashes of color, and heard only a volcanic roaring; his horse staggered; a blow across his ribs nearly flung him from the saddle. Then suddenly his horse wheeled and galloped off, and between him and the Saracens, an open space appeared, as the Christian army shrank back toward the plain, and the Saracen army shrank back toward the heights.

A horn blew, up there in the pass, over and over, an alien command. The King gasped for breath and gripped his saddle with both hands. In the midst of a hundred other horses, his horse carried him back another twenty yards. There, again, he turned, and saw the distance between his men and the Saracens grown wider than a bowshot. The fighting had stopped.

He wiped one numbed hand over his face. Turning, he looked for old Humphrey, for Balian, for his uncle Joscelin, and instead came face to face with German de Montoya, the Templar Preceptor.

"What happened?" His voice was hoarse. "Why did they give up?"

"They haven't given up," German said. "They think they've won." He leaned over and spat on the ground. "They think we're trapped here, what with the river down there. They can wait. By tomorrow morning, they'll have brought up the rest of their army, and they'll finish us off then."

King Baudouin clenched his teeth. He threw off the craven weakness in him that wanted to cry and run. God would help him, if he kept heart. The Saracens had given him a space, at least, a chance. But just a little space. The sun was gone. The sky was lusterless, like paper. Like the skin of his hands, when he took his gloves off. "Come with me," he said, and with the reins wrapped around his wrists he rode along the

front of his army, German at his flank, until he found Baudouin
d'Ibelin and his brother Balian, slumped in their saddles, and staring into
the east, where the first night hung dark and empty behind the hills.

"Where is Humphrey de Toron?"

Balian swung toward him. "He went down. Didn't you see him,
Sire? He was right in front of you."

His brother whispered, "God, God, we are in it now. Look at this."

German de Montoya said, "We have to try to get back across the
river." Behind him, silent, a handful of Templars formed a ragged double column. Rannulf Fitzwilliam was among them, riding on a ridicu-
lously small horse.

Baudouin was looking for the rest of his nobles. "What happened to
Count Tripoli?"

"Gone." Balian shook his head. "He and his men swam for it, while
we were fighting up there."

"Damn him," somebody said, under his breath.

Baudouin looked back, toward the river; there was no sign of Tripoli
on the far bank. He had not waited. He had run for cover, as soon as he
was safe. The King wrestled down his temper. Yet he knew Tripoli was
right; they should have crossed this river long before, and if the rest of
the army had been fools he should not have to make himself as much
of a fool to prove his honor. Now the river was rising, a relentless surge.
Baudouin watched a crooked branch course swiftly down through the
current. His body felt useless and insensible as mud. Looking down he
saw the first damp curl of water lapping at his horse's hoofs.

One of the Templars said, "We can't stay here. The river is coming
up fast, between it and the Saracens we'll be wiped out by daybreak."

Balian d'Ibelin said, "Go upriver, maybe we can get by that way."

The King straightened. He had to make a decision; he had to save
this army, somehow, and he had no idea what to do. He crossed himself. God would help him. In the saddle of the pass, a white blob was
just breaking into sight: the brim of the rising moon. He blinked, his
vision flooded. For a long time he saw only blurs and darkness.

He said, "We have to cross the river."

"Sire," Balian said, "we'll all drown. My brother is right, we should
go along the river, either up or down."

The King was shivering. He lifted his reins, swinging his horse
around. "Let those who will, follow you. Those who will follow me,
come along."

He did not look to see if any came; he trotted his horse back toward
the river, glinting now in the moonlight, rumbling and growling as it

hurtled powerfully along. When his horse's hoofs began to splash up the water, he stopped and looked around.

Many of the men had come after him. All up and down the river, in the dark, the Frankish knights moved cautiously forward. Off to the King's left, a man bellowed, like a warcry, and rushed at the river as if at an enemy, that he could bowl down by force. Swiftly a dozen others joined him. In the deepening gloom it was hard to see them. They splattered out through the shallows, casting up sheets of water into the moonlight. At first the river seemed meek enough, hardly above the horses' knees, and seeing this, half the men watching shouted and plunged after the leaders. Then midway to the far edge of the water, the first of the riders slid off into the deep.

The King could see nothing of it, only hear the splashing, the terrified neighing of the horses, but the men around him shrieked, and some called out, "This way! Swim back!" and others: "Go on—keep going!" Then a wail of dismay rose from all around.

The King reached out to the man beside him and clutched his arm; it was German de Montoya. "What is it? Are they getting across?"

The Templar stared fixedly into the moonlight. His calm seemed like madness. "The river runs wild, in the middle—some of the horses are swept away. The stronger ones are swimming through it."

"Have them hold onto one another," the King said. "Keep them moving. Is there a better place?" His voice squeaked.

The knight shrugged. "How to find it, in the dark?" He lifted his voice. "Brothers, to me! Form a chain. Rannulf!"

"Here."

"Can we cross here?"

"As well as anywhere," Rannulf said. "And a lot sooner."

The King could not at first see him; then he saw that the Norman knight had dismounted from his horse, on German's far side, and was stripping off his surcoat. The King looked back toward the river. Most of the knights had fallen back, giving up the attempt to cross; as he watched, a horn blew. Balian's horn, he guessed. The great mass of mounted men veered off and started at a trot up the river. The King turned back to the Templars.

German said, "Where's your horse?"

"Done in," Rannulf said, muffled. Now he was wrestling off his mail. The other Templars waited, silent, in a semi-circle just beyond him. There were only a few of them, a dozen at most. The King looked around them again.

Most of his army had ridden off and left him, following Balian down the river. He dragged in a deep breath and looked quickly out toward the lapping, rolling water. His spirit quailed; he thought of going after Balian.

German was snapping orders, forming the Templars into a column. He leaned over Rannulf and said, "What are you doing with your mail, you donkey? Come on, we have to move."

Half-naked, Rannulf pulled his sword belt around him. "If I have to swim, I'm not doing it in a mail coat."

"I'd rather drown than go without armor like a serf." German turned to the King. "Sire, ride behind me. Keep this fool here in the lee of your horse. Saint, see that he gets to the other side."

The King said, "Rannulf, take hold of my stirrup."

The knight came up beside him. German de Montoya called out, and the rest of the Templars moved at a trot, splashing into the shallow water. With Rannulf at his knee the King rode along just behind German. His horse went easily through shin-deep water. The Templar column did not follow him, but rode up on his left, making a barrier between him and the thrust of the current. He could tell by the plunging sound of the hoofs that the water was getting deeper. He clutched his reins and his saddle pommel. But they were almost halfway across. In a sudden, panicky will to get this done with, he kicked his horse on toward the other side.

Somebody yelled, and the water lapped up over his horse's shoulder, thrusting and banging at the King's knees, and Rannulf was clinging to the horse's mane and swimming.

The King's fingers stiffened, losing their grip. His vision tricked him, showed him only a random swirl of water and moonlight, the furling of a horse's mane, an arm suddenly thrust up into the air. In front of him the white oblong of German's surcoat bobbed in the moonlight, and the King fixed his gaze on that, pushing forward ahead of him.

His horse lurched and began to swim, sinking deeper into the water. Suddenly the balance was different, unsteady, and he was too high, he was tipping sideways out of the saddle. Ahead of him, German was a white shape against the leaping silver of the river. German swayed and seemed to grow taller, and then German was gone.

The King blinked, trying to get that white shape back again. Much smaller, darker, the blob of the horse's head knifed through the glinting water. Dizzy, the leper slid sideways out of his saddle, the reins sliding through his frozen hands.

Rannulf caught him. Wedged against the horse's side, the King sank into the river up to his armpits, his back jammed against Rannulf's chest, Rannulf's arms on either side of him clinging to the saddle. Baudouin flailed uselessly with his legs. Water splashed into his mouth. He flung his right arm across his saddle and jammed his stiffened fingers under the far stirrup leather. He could see nothing, hear only the roar and gurgle of the river. The horse was swimming. Halfhanging on the saddle, he floated along between the knight and the horse.

"Help me." A voice, gasping in his ear. Blindly he thrust out his left arm, and wrapped it tight around the knight's shaggy head, and held on.

The river ruled them. The current hauled them along in a giddy swoop. For a moment they sailed along in the open, and then they were swept into a tangle of branches. The King pressed his face against his shoulder to protect his eyes. His left arm was kinked tight around Rannulf's neck. His knee struck ground. The horse dragged him through branches that crackled and stabbed at him. He was out of the river. He realized, a little late, that he could let go, and he let go, and dropped onto dry ground on his hands and knees.

Another body draped over his. A rough hand on his hair. "Not a bad swim, little boy."

Baudouin lifted his head, dazed. "Where—where are the rest?" Around him was only the silver glare of the moonlight, the black shadow of the riverbank.

"I don't know," Rannulf said. "I'll go see." Again the harsh caress stroked his hair, and the Templar rose, and went away.

The King sank down on the sand. Another horse came stumbling and snorting up out of the river past him; he heard someone call out in a shaky voice. He ground his fists into his eyes, trying to clear his vision a little, feeling much safer with the river between him and the Saracens. Quickly he cast around him for the rest of his army.

Save for the dozen Templars now gathered on the bank just behind him, he saw no one. If any of the other Christian knights had gotten across the river alive, they had not waited for anybody else, they had run as soon as they reached dry ground. He sank down again, exhausted, and put his head down on his knees.

⬦ "German," Stephen said. "Where's German?"

"German is gone," said Rannulf. Naked and drenched, he was shivering uncontrollably. "He lost his saddle, and his mail pulled him under."

Richard le Mesne said, "God rest his soul," and crossed himself. Just beyond him, Stephen turned his face away.

The Templars gathered on the dark bank of the river. "We need a master," Richard Bear said. "Who has been here longest? Saint?"

"Thirteen years by Whitsun," Rannulf said, and gave the others a moment to say something, but nobody else spoke. He said, "Very well, then. Listen. We have two orders: the one is to protect the King, and the other is to get back to Jerusalem. We'll head due west to the high road." He looked around the circle, from face to face. Most of them were men of the Jerusalem Temple. They all looked tired, and some were hurt. "Get your horses and gear together. Build a fire. We'll rest up a little while and ride."

He straightened, his back stiff and creaking. Richard le Mesne walked up to him. "What condition is your horse in?"

"I don't have a horse," Rannulf said. He was thinking of German, which he knew he should not; he was thinking of German in his mail coat, sliding under the water. He crossed himself.

Bear never thought about anything but the immediate. "My horse is pretty much finished. There are some stray nags down at the far end of this meadow, here; let me go catch a few."

Rannulf nodded. "Take some help. Where's the King?"

Bear gave a jerk of his head down the river. "Going nowhere." He turned toward the other knights. On the blank sand above the river, near a snarl of drifted wood, the King lay curled like a puppy. Rannulf went by close enough to see that the boy was only asleep, and then circled around behind the brush, pissed, and went on a little way and knelt on the soft wet ground, close by the rushing of the river.

German, he thought. German, damn you, German, go and die on me. His hand moved up and down, back and forth. He had not thought before how much he liked German.

For a moment he felt the defeat like the iron cold of the river, dragging him down.

He said his prayers several times, asking God to tell him what he should do. No answer came to him, but he began to feel easier, and he decided he was already doing as God willed. He asked God to heal his throbbing arm. He said a Credo for German, and for the other men now rolling like boulders along the bottom of the river. He hoped that Gerard de Ridford was dead.

He shook off another wave of black hopelessness. He had to keep going: the King was in his charge, and Jerusalem lay over the mountains. The river would not hold the Saracens off for long. In the morning they would come after him. He got to his feet, going back toward the other men.

"Saint?" Richard le Mesne trudged across the sandy meadow toward him. The King was still asleep. Rannulf went to help Bear with the horses.

The other men had made a fire, on the bank of the river, and over it they cooked strips of meat cut from a drowned horse. Roasting this flesh on sticks, they sat almost in the leaping flames, and nobody said anything, except Stephen.

"German, and Hilaire, and Pedro—I saw them all die. God, I can't believe it!"

"Oh, shut up, Stephen," someone said wearily.

"I'm not going to shut up. My friends are dead, my brothers, my—my—German is dead, and I can't do anything, I can't save them, I can't avenge them; damn it, I can't even go find their bodies and give them a decent Christian burial."

Rannulf went away from him, out along the river bank. Through the dark, Bear led up some horses to him. He said, "You'll want the big bay, but I want him, too. I'll cast sticks with you for him."

"No, take him," Rannulf said. "The black horse there is good enough for me."

Several of the horses had reached this bank of the river without their riders, and Bear had caught four of them. The biggest and strongest was the bay he wanted, but the black had a quick, alert way about him. He also had no saddle. Rannulf went to one of the other horses, which did have a saddle, and began to strip its harness off.

Richard said, "We can use these other horses to rig up a sling for the whelp."

Behind them, at the fire, Stephen's voice rose in a tired whine. "Why did God do this to us? Why did God turn his back on us, if He loves us so much?"

There was a rumble of argument, or maybe agreement. Under the saddle, Rannulf found a heavy blanket, doubled up; it was soaked through, but when he shook it out it was large enough to cover him. Gratefully he wrapped the rough wool around himself and strapped it fast with his sword belt.

By the fire, Stephen kept on. "We're supposed to be God's knights.

Why did God destroy us, then? It's a lie, it's all a lie, and German is dead, and I don't care anymore!"

Richard was bridling the bay horse. Across its poll, he stared at Rannulf. "You're the Master, you should stop him from talking like that."

"He's just afraid," Rannulf said. "Everybody's afraid."

The other men had been listening in silence, but now another voice picked up Stephen's song. "There's no sense in going back to Jerusalem. They'll just hate us there anyway for losing."

Somebody else said, "God has abandoned us."

"If you want to leave, then go!"

This voice rang out so sharp and clear that Rannulf turned around to see. The young King walked out of the shadows into the flickering yellow fireglow. He still wore his fancy embroidered surcoat, filthy from the river, but no crown, no helmet, no cap, nothing masked his face, and the dance of the firelight made his broken features seem worse even than in good light. His voice crackled with life. "Go! Nobody will know, nobody will remember you, nobody will care. I am going back to Jerusalem. Those who come with me, I shall love, and God forever loves—the rest of you, go, into the dark and the wilderness, go!"

Rannulf turned back to his horse. "I don't think he'll need the sling." Bear grunted, amused.

The King called out, "Sir Rannulf! When do we ride out?"

"At your order, Sire."

"I give the order now!" The King strode toward him. "Where is my horse?" Behind him, around the fire, the other men were getting to their feet, their eyes downcast, their shoulders slumped, but following him nonetheless.

Bear brought up the King's horse. The other men scattered to their mounts. One last Templar remained defiantly by the fire, his feet among the glowing coals, his hands peeling off the last scraps of the roast meat from a stick and popping them into his mouth. Rannulf went over to him.

"Mouse," he said, "get up."

"I'm not going." The young man's voice had a steely whine to it. "I'm not doing this anymore."

"Get up," Rannulf said, "or I'll beat the shit out of you and take you along anyway."

The boy was still. For a moment Rannulf thought he would have to hit him; he unbuckled his belt, disencumbering himself from the blanket, and then Stephen got up and walked away toward the horses. Rannulf gave a long involuntary shudder. He was glad that Stephen hadn't needed hitting. He wasn't sure if he could have given much of a blow. He stooped down for the blanket, to cover his nakedness, and his knees griped and his back twinged. He felt stupid and old, an old man wrapped in a blanket in the dark. Now it was starting to rain again. He went to his horse and mounted.

✦ Stephen knotted his saddle girth and brought the stirrup down. Already on their horses, Rannulf and Richard le Mesne were holding a quick council with the King; Rannulf was saying, "If we follow the high road, we should reach the spring at Cresson by dawn. Save the horses." Turning, he raised his voice in a command to the rest of them. "Couple up. Form two columns. Bear, pair with the King and lead off." In the general stir that followed this, he reined his horse around by Stephen. "You ride with me."

"What, you don't trust me?" Stephen asked. He was cold; his mail was already clammy, his toes numb, his fingertips like ice. Rannulf made no answer to him, but swung around knee to knee with him, as the double column formed and rode away. Together they took up the tail of it.

Stephen hunched his shoulders, expecting a sermon, now that they were riding out, but to his amazement the older knight only folded his arms around himself, slumped down in his saddle, and went to sleep. Stephen gritted his teeth together. Indistinct in the dark, the two files of horsemen ahead of him clattered across the shoulder of the hill. The moon was ahead of them now, sliding down the far side of the sky, leading them home.

He thought of German with an ache that sometimes forced a groan out of him. He should have accepted German's love. Gone forever now. He felt robbed of something vital, broken off at the shared boundary. He wanted to talk but beside him there was only Rannulf, bundled in the stinking blanket and sleeping like a lump; as his horse climbed up and down the uneven trail Rannulf swayed and lurched along like baggage. Stephen wondered how anybody could sleep like that on the back of a horse. How anybody could sleep like that after the day they had just done.

The rain stopped. They rode east, where there had been no rain. Quickly Stephen went from being too wet to being too dry; none of them had anything left to drink. When the dawn was breaking, the column halted on the slope just below the crest of a ridge, and Rannulf woke up.

The other men were speaking in murmurs, looking around them.

"Where are we? Where should we go now?" This barren hillside seemed like every other: sand and sand-colored rock sprinkled with tough, ugly grass. The dew on the grass caught Stephen's eyes; his throat was dry with thirst. Rannulf lifted his reins and trotted his horse around the column to the front, and Stephen followed him.

Richard le Mesne and the young King were waiting at the head of the column, but Rannulf only waved his hand to them, beckoned to Stephen to follow him, and rode on ahead, up to the summit of the ridge. Stephen nudged his horse into a quick lope to catch up with him.

The dawn was brightening steadily. The clouds had drifted off into the western sky. A dent through the grass, the road cut diagonally across the steep angle of the slope. Rannulf took his horse along it at a short canter, Stephen a step behind him. At the crest of the ridge, they stopped.

The slope behind them lay in darkness; the slope before them was washed with the dawn light, so that every stalk and every tiny stone threw a shadow. The road cut deep into the dry ground, knifing back and forth along the slope toward the sink below. There in the crease of the land a long line of thorny brush grew, noisy with chattering birds.

Stephen's heart jumped. Where brush grew there was water, down there, somewhere. His horse pushed its nose forward against the bridle, and gave a wicker. Water, certainly. Rannulf rode on several paces down the road, and then reined in again. Stephen went after him, stopped when he stopped, and followed when he rode on, eager, almost whining, but again Rannulf drew up after only a few strides. Stephen's horse lunged forward, and he snatched it down hard; but he wanted to scream at Rannulf to go on, to the water, to the water.

Shapeless in the filthy blanket, Rannulf stood in his stirrups, sniffed at the air like a wolf. Stephen's mouth ached. *Go,* his mind screamed. *Go!* The other knight's horse tossed its head impatiently, and tiptoed around the road, circling against the hard hand on its reins.

The racket of the birds raged hotter as the sun rose, and the flock began to leave the trees. From the black stitchwork of the branches, they scattered into the air, and flew up, circling, spreading out over the barren hillside.

Abruptly the whole flock wheeled around and fluttered off toward the west, and Rannulf spun his horse and galloped back up the road. Stephen gaped at him a moment, startled, and out of a gulley in the side of the hill there rushed a stream of screaming Saracens.

Camel-kickers. The dun beasts lumbered across the slope, seeming too ungainly to move fast. On either hip they carried an archer. In the moment while he wrenched his horse around to follow Rannulf,

Stephen saw the wild ripple of their robes, the bend of their arms, the flex of their bows, and then their arrows ribboned the air. His horse seemed stuck in place, its hoofs clattering frantically at the road. An arrow whispered by him. He shot forward through the grass across the summit of the ridge.

Rannulf was waiting for him; the other Templars and the King were already rushing away across the slope, giving up the road, making for the height of the next hill. Stephen flattened down in his saddle, pushing his tired horse on. Rannulf galloped beside him. Hooting and howling, the Saracens streamed across the ridge after them.

The slope steepened. Stephen's horse scrabbled for footing on the loose rocky ground. Rannulf got in front of him, and swerved along the edge of a ravine that opened like a wound in the hillside, and Stephen's horse veered after. There was no trail, and quickly no flat ground, between the hill rising sheer to the sky and the ravine plunging away into a depth still full of night shadows. Rannulf with no signal turned his horse and plowed straight down.

Stephen's horse balked at that, skidded back to a stop. The shrieks of the Saracens needling his ears, Stephen lifted the horse off the cliff with hands and spurs and hurtled down the bank after Rannulf. They went down in a tumble of rock and sand, the horse sitting on its tail, its forelegs out straight in front of it, and when they reached the foot the horse bounced so high Stephen nearly fell off.

The Saracens had pulled up, on the ledge above, and were screaming insults and shooting occasional arrows after them. Stephen's horse pushed wearily up the far slope, easier and shorter than the pitch downward, and reaching the wide meadow beyond followed Rannulf in among the other Templars.

They were lined up along the height, facing the Saracens across the ravine; for a moment, while their horses blew, they shouted at each other and shook their fists and made faces. Rannulf pushed past the other men to Bear.

"We're in trouble. They're ahead of us; they must have circled around past Lake Tiberias."

Stephen's horse carried him into the center of this discussion, practically into the lap of the King. He muttered an apology, which young Baudouin ignored, all his attention fastened on the other two Templars. Bear braced his hands on the pommel of his saddle.

"Can we get around them?"

Rannulf scratched at his beard. "We have to find water, first of all." He jabbed with his chin toward the east. "There's a well, down the far side of that peak. It's out of the way, but it's safe."

The King said, "Is it on the road back to Jerusalem?"

Bear said, without looking at him, "Unless we get some water and rest these horses Jerusalem might as well lie beyond the sea."

Stubbornly, the King said, "I can't bear to take a step in the wrong direction. I want to keep on."

Rannulf reached out and clapped him on the arm. "We're doing that. Pay heed." He jerked his head, nodding back over his shoulder at the camel archers still watching and calling insults at them across the ravine. "They'll be looking for us now, watching the road for us. We have to do something else. Follow me." But he did not move; he stayed with one hand on the King's arm, staring at him. "Follow me," he said, again.

The King said, "Lead us."

"Good." Rannulf backed his horse out of the tight press of horses and started away.

He took them across the barren dry hill, toward the west; they fell back into the double column, with Stephen riding on Rannulf's right hand. As the day sharpened his dry throat hurt, and his belly flattened painfully against his backbone. He felt himself shrivelling up like a leaf. Rannulf turned to him, after a little while, and said, "Sleep."

"I can't," Stephen said.

The Norman laughed at him. "Sleep, Mouse," he said, again, and said no more, but led them on down the crease between two hills. Stephen stared ahead. He knew he could not sleep, not in such danger, in such strange country.

Then, moments later, it seemed, he was waking up again. His horse was blowing and snorting frantically, shouldering in among other horses, and he realized that they had found some water.

He let his reins slide through his fingers. This was no well, no village; all around were small bushy trees, their branches like crooked arms, their thin dark leaves like spread fingers. Beyond rose the broken face of a cliff of sandy stone. The pool was so small he could not see it for the horses pressed in to drink from it. He could feel his mount's belly pumping in long draughts of the water. The other men had all dismounted, except the young King, slumped wearily in his saddle, his gnawed face grey.

Now Bear pushed through the horses; he had a leather cup in his hand. At the shoulder of the King's horse he stopped and held out the cup, and Stephen saw it was full of murky water.

Bear said, "Sire, the horses are drinking this pool dry. Take this, while there is still some left."

The other men were gathering around, collecting their reins, their eyes sharp. Many staring at the cup. Stephen's mount lifted its head, satisfied. The young King took the water from Bear and looked from one to the next of the other men.

"I cannot drink when so many are thirsty." He held the cup out to Stephen, who was closest to him.

For a moment, craven, Stephen saw only the diseased hand offering him this water. He raised his eyes to the King's ruined face, and saw through to the glory of the King's soul. He remembered what German had said, and he knew himself blessed at this gesture.

"Thank you, Sire." He took the cup from the King's hands.

The water was in his hands, and his thirst was strong, but the King's grace was stronger still. He thought, In a few hours I may be dead anyway. He said, "I will not drink before my brothers," and offered the cup to Rannulf, standing beside him.

The other knight gave him a strange look, and passed the cup on to the next man, and so it went, from hand to hand, none drinking, until the cup came back to the King. The leper took it again, and said, in a voice that shook, "You are the most perfect knights any king has ever had."

He drank; they all drank, and there was exactly one cup for each of them.

They rode on through the hills. At day's end they came down into a gentle valley, opening away from them into the west, so that the sun seemed to roll away along it toward the edge of the world. The road lay down the middle of it, between the tended melon fields and orchards of an oasis. In their double column the knights trotted down into a stand of palm trees, where there was a well, and some mud-walled huts.

Stephen stiffened up, his hair prickling. There were people here, and they were sandpigs.

They were coming forward, to watch the knights ride up, half a dozen lean brown men in dusty robes, several naked children. By the well, as the knights approached, two women rose hastily, lifted baskets onto their heads, and walked away, straight as columns under their bulky burdens. Among the slender branchless stalks of the trees Stephen saw camels grazing. His hand went to the hilt of his sword. He wondered what Rannulf thought he was doing.

Rannulf ignored the people. He led the knights straight to the well, which stood inside a low brick wall. Putting one hand up, he brought the column to a halt. He had shucked off the filthy blanket earlier, and tied it behind his saddle; he had his sword belt looped over his shoulder. Now, half-naked, he slid down from his horse, tossed his reins and his sword to Stephen, and went to the well and began to lower the bucket into it.

Stephen dismounted, as the other knights were doing. The local people were gathering around to peer at them, but they left a good distance between them and the Templars. There were a lot of women and children, not many men. Stephen began to feel easier. He hung Rannulf's sword on his saddle and turned to his own horse to loosen the girths. "Who are these people?"

"Bedouin," Rannulf said. He brought up the dripping bucket and emptied it into the trough at the foot of the well. "They won't make trouble, there's too many of us. Anyway, they're probably Christian." The horses crowded up in a ring, greedy, and he dropped the bucket into the well again. One of the other knights stepped forward and took the pull rope from him.

"I'll do this, Saint."

Rannulf stooped over the trough, dipped up a handful of the water, and drank some of it. The horses and the other men crowded up toward the trough, the horses setting up a frantic thirsty rumble of nickers. Rannulf slid back out of the way, and turned, looking at the Bedouin.

"Where are you going?" Stephen asked him.

"I'm hungry," Rannulf said. He went toward the Bedouin, his hand out, and began to jabber in Arabic.

Stephen stood staring after him, astonished. He knew none of the words but the outstretched hand and the stoop of Rannulf's head were unmistakable: Rannulf was begging. Stephen's pride blazed up. He tore his eyes away, ashamed. His stomach growled. He shoved his way through the crowd to the water.

A few moments later Rannulf came back, and sat down on the wall around the well. He was chewing. Stephen tried to hold back, but his hunger drove him; he went up to the other knight, and saw he had a round of flatbread in his hand.

Stephen said, "You beg, like a cripple or a blind man." He sat down on the wall next to Rannulf, his gaze nailed to the bread he was too proud to ask for.

"I'm a monk," Rannulf said. "God feeds me. What, do you want me to take it by force of arms?" The other men were coming up to him, and he tore bits off the bread and gave them out.

"That would be better," Stephen said. "At least then we would all eat." This poor little bit of bread wasn't nearly enough; most of them got nothing. The King gave his piece to someone else. He was hiding himself in the midst of the knights, shy of the strangers standing around them, closer now, all curious black eyes. The children crouched in the dust; the women held the corners of their shawls across their faces. Stephen's hand went to his sword hilt again. It would be easy to take whatever they needed from these people.

Out of this crowd came an old woman, a basket in her arms. Her face, all sags and dewlaps, was dabbled with blue marks. "Templar," she said, in broken French. "Templar. God keep the holy knights." She pulled the napkin off the basket, and it was full of loaves. Setting the basket down, she backed away, and offered it to them with a grand sweep of her arm.

"You see," Rannulf said, to Stephen. "Eat." The knight let go of his sword hilt, amazed, and reached out and took a warm round slab of the bread.

Rannulf's arm hurt, a hot throbbing ache deep inside the arrow wound. He held it down in a bucket of water full of salt and hyssop while his other hand stuffed bread into his mouth. Beside him Stephen Mouse held out the cup, and Rannulf drank until it was empty, and then turned and filled it again from the trough.

The Templars sat around the well, the King in their midst. The women had brought three baskets of bread, now mostly gone, but as Rannulf reached for the last piece, a girl came up with another full basket. The rest of the villagers milled around the well, staring and muttering. The bolder children were patting the Templars' horses, tethered in a neat line by the well. Night was falling.

The King said, "By now Saladin could have taken Jerusalem."

Rannulf shook his head. "First he will chase down all he can of our army, all broken up as it is—he won't leave any remnant behind him. Not after Ramleh." He was still half-naked, and the night was cold. He said, "I need a shirt."

He said this in Arabic, without looking at anyone; among the clustered Bedouin there was a sudden brisk turmoil.

The King said, "But surely he will strike at Jerusalem next."

"We will reach Jerusalem before he does," Rannulf said. "I promise you."

Bear said, "Saint, they have a church here. We could hold a service."

The old woman came back, who was the leader of this clan, in her arms a load of cloth; she laid this down in the dust before Rannulf. She did not draw immediately away. The bones of her face propped up the skin like a tent; blue tattoos marked her forehead and her cheeks.

She said to him, "You are hurt. Let me see your arm."

He shook his head. "I am bound to God; no woman can touch me."

"God have mercy on you," she said. "I have a potion that will speed the work."

"God's mercy is enough," he said. "We need your church."

"I will send you the priest," she said.

"No. No priest. And tell these other people, when we go inside, they are to stay away until we come out again."

She said, "It is done. Holy one, say prayers for us, who have nourished you." She backed away, and he picked up the mass of cloth; it was a long loose robe with a hood. He put it on and sat down again among the other men.

Bear said, "Saint, this was Mouse's first battle. We have to make him dead."

Stephen's head snapped up. "What?"

Rannulf glanced at him, and nodded to Bear. "Yes, you're right. Very well. What about him?" He jabbed with his chin at the King.

The King said, "I will hear Mass with you."

"This is a Templar ceremony," Rannulf said.

The other men murmured, and pushed closer, intent. Among them Felix van Janke said, "He's as good as one of us."

"Oh, better," Rannulf said. "But he is not a Templar."

The King said, loudly, "I will hear Mass. I care not who says it."

Stephen said, "What are you going to do to me?"

Rannulf said to the King, "You will not betray us?"

Baudouin blinked at him. "Betray you. How? No, I shall never betray you."

"Very well," Rannulf said. "You can come into the church with us, but you must not leave before we all leave. And you must say the service with us. If you cannot, then shut your eyes, so that later you can say you saw nothing."

"I will," the King said. Stephen's eyes were wide with worry. Rannulf clapped him on the shoulder and went off to find a handful of dust and a handful of ashes.

The night lay deep above the village, a well of clear cool darkness below the fine spray of the stars. King Baudouin followed the other men to the little church, which was just another hut, with a bigger door than the others, and a porch like a lip. Rannulf and Richard le Mesne were standing on the porch; Rannulf had his belted sword in his hand, and he stooped and leaned the scabbard against the wall beside the door. In the long burnoose he looked like a Saracen.

The King crossed himself. "God keep us all." He went between Rannulf and the other knight, into the little church, and the other men followed him in, and shut the door.

The hut was so small the twelve of them filled it. There was a low stone altar, covered with a cloth, where they had already lit two small lamps. As the King went in, one of the knights was taking the Cross down from the wall.

The King's breath stopped. He felt Rannulf's eyes on him. Other men's eyes. Watching to see how he took this, if he truly were one of them. The knight at the altar, alone of them all, had brought his sword into the church, and with a thong he fixed the iron blade, point down, in the place where the Cross had hung.

That made a Cross. Slowly the King drew breath again. This was not so strange. He went in among the knights waiting before the altar.

Some of them were kneeling, saying prayers, and he sank down also onto his knees, and gave thanks to God who had preserved him. He begged God to let him reach Jerusalem before Saladin, to give him the chance to defend his city. He prayed to God that he might die in battle, suddenly and cleanly, and not just rot away.

Then all the knights stood, and gathered close around the altar. In their midst was the young redheaded knight Stephen, whom they called Mouse. He looked frightened; he knew not what they would do to him. The knights said nothing to him, but Bear and the German knight named Felx went to him and took his clothes off, all but his drawers. Then, putting their hands on his shoulders, they pushed him down to kneel on the packed earth before the altar.

Rannulf came up before him, his two hands fisted, and knelt down facing Stephen. Bear stood behind him, and with one hand bowed Stephen's head.

Rannulf said, "Stretch out your hands, Mouse."

The knight held out his hands before him, palms up. The knights were gathered very close around him, body to body, like a wall. Rannulf raised one of his fists over Stephen's left hand, stretched out open before him, and poured dust into Stephen's palm. "This dust is your dust," he said. He held up the other fist over Stephen's right hand, and poured ashes into Stephen's palm. "This ash is your ash."

"Amen," said all the other knights, in their ring around them.

Rannulf took hold of Stephen's wrists. "Stephen, do you give your life to God?"

"I do," Stephen said, in an unsteady voice.

Rannulf turned Stephen's hands over, so that the ash and the dust spilled out onto the ground.

"Now you are already dead. Therefore be unafraid of dying, and when God calls you, go gladly, because a soul freely given is surely saved. Henceforth, turn away from the community of living men, but keep only to us, your brothers, who are dead also." He put his hands on Stephen's shoulders and bowed his head down. "Oremus."

The other knights knelt down close around them, and laid their hands on Stephen, and in one voice, they lifted up the words of the Credo.

"I believe in God, the Father Almighty, Creator of Heaven and Earth, and in His only Son . . ."

The King had watched all this silently, but as they prayed the words came to his lips, and he said them with the knights. His chest was tight. This surely was heresy, blasphemy, damnable sin. Yet he understood it; his heart spoke these same words to him. He was one of them.

The knights stepped back, falling into three rows, in which he stood in the last, and Stephen came up beside him, still all but naked. There was a smear of ash on his cheek. He was weeping; his hands shook. He said his prayers in a voice thick with feeling.

They began to say the Mass, all together. The King joined them, full-hearted, eager. The Mass was straight enough. Some of the knights stumbled through the Latin, obviously knowing it only by rote, and Rannulf, in front of them, said no sermon, but they all recited the miserere, the Kyrie, the Credo, the paternoster. Rannulf said the words of the miracle that brought Christ into their midst. They passed a loaf of bread from hand to hand, and a cup of water from the well.

The King broke off a bite of the bread, and drank a sip of the water; he thought he tasted flesh and blood.

After the cup came Rannulf. He stood before each man in turn, and said, "God gives you this." Leaning forward he kissed the knight on the mouth. "God gives you this." He struck the knight a blow across the head. The knight at once knelt, his head bowed, deep in prayer.

The King held fast, his mind churning, wondering if this would come to him. This was certainly heresy. He should turn aside. Shut his eyes, as Rannulf had said. Yet he could not draw back. He belonged with them. Rannulf was coming along the row toward him. Now all the Templars were kneeling down, all but him and Rannulf.

The Templar stopped before him. "God gives you this." Baudouin felt the jar of the mouth on his, surprisingly hard. "God gives you this." And the blow knocked him dizzy to the floor.

✦ They slept that night in the church. In the morning, before dawn broke, they went out and found their horses, which the villagers had kept, fed and watered, and they wound their way south over the hills. The rains had brought the new grass up, rising green through the straw, and in the hollows and furrows of the land there was still some water standing, like gifts from heaven. In the evening, they came back at last to the highway to Jerusalem, where it climbed up through a groove between rocky upthrusting hills. At the foot of the long shallow slope leading up into the pass, some great boulders erupted out of the hillside, like roc's eggs half-buried in the sand, and here the Templars stopped and sheltered, and Rannulf sent two of the knights off to scout the heights.

"You're so cautious," the King said, bitterly. "We will never get back to Jerusalem." He was stiff all over, and his vision kept fading away; he could not see even to unbridle his horse. Rannulf pushed him to one side and undid the latches of the bridle for him. The two scouts were coming back, excited.

One was Richard Bear. He said, half-breathless, "There are forty Turkish bowmen up in the pass."

The King leaned heavily on his horse. One more obstacle in his way. But at least he was seeing better now.

Rannulf said, "Only bowmen? Horses or camels?"

"I looked over the whole camp. Just archers, light armor, small horses, no pack animals. They've been there less than a day, by the looks of their fires. They have no servants and no supplies."

The King said, "Can we go around them?"

"Probably," Rannulf said.

Bear turned toward Baudouin and nodded. "Back up, circle around to the east, catch the road at Qonatria. Another day's ride."

Rannulf said, "I say let's take them."

"What?" Bear blurted out an oath, and crossed himself, as if that canceled it.

"We need to give some wounds. We've been run all over hell with our tails between our legs, we can use a little revenge."

"How do you propose we get it—the twelve of us charge straight uphill into their arrows? That's a long way with no cover, and our horses are worn out."

"No no no." Rannulf's voice was a feline murmur. "Remember those sheep we passed, in the afternoon? Go bring me back a flock of sheep."

⊕ Rannulf had said, "Think about German. Don't you want to pay them off for German?"

Now Stephen was creeping along on his hands and knees among a flock of smelly sheep, climbing an interminable hill. The sheep, ewes and little newborn lambs, kept bunching together and shying away from him, and from the other men hidden in their midst, and the shepherds kept up a constant frantic whistling and whooping to drive them on. The ground was stony. Stephen's back hurt from going along bent over.

He poked his head up above the tide of wooly backs. They were still well below the height, where the cliff rose in a spire of rock, stripped of grass, gaunt against the blue sky. Up near the front of the flock, Rannulf walked, a staff in his hand, the hood of his burnoose pulled over his close-cropped hair. Stephen sank down beneath the waves of the sheep again.

This did not seem like the work of knights. His knees were cut from the hard ground, his fingertips were skinned. He had slung his sword over his back, to keep it out of the way, and the belt was strangling him. He could see none of the other men, was glad of that—he felt like a fool.

Up ahead, a sharp, commanding call rang out. Stephen sank down to the dirt, his breath stuck in his nostrils. The sheep baaed and pattered around him. He reached out and clutched a handful of wool. Still clean and white, a lamb climbed over him, bleating, to get to its mother; a foul clotted string hung off its underline.

The commanding bellow sounded again, and another voice answered, familiar: Rannulf.

This was the hard part. Stephen's eyes itched suddenly, his lungs built up a cough, his legs ached. He let go of the sheep he was clutching, slipped around beneath her neck and past the ewe and lamb beyond her, and so made his way toward the edge of the flock, until he could see out past the dirty wool of legs and bellies.

They were in the saddle of the pass. Forty yards up the slope, at the foot of the spire of rock, the Saracen bowmen were scattered around their campfires, most of them sitting and lying on the ground. Only three of them had come down to deal with the flock of sheep. Directly in front of Rannulf stood a big, bushy-bearded man in a leather breastplate, his hands on his hips. His bow, unstrung, was hanging on his back. He gestured toward the sheep, and Rannulf gave a shrug, spread his hands, chattered in Arabic.

The big man stamped past him, toward the sheep, looking them over with a definite appetitive interest. Perhaps he wanted to buy one for camp meat. Or intended just to take it. Rannulf came after him, talking plaintively, but the bowman cut him off with a sweep of his hand, and began to point to the sheep, and then, abruptly, he caught sight of Stephen among the ewes.

His mouth opened, his eyes popped, and he swung around, his arms flailing. As he wheeled, Rannulf closed with him, drawing a long knife from his sleeve. Stephen bolted up out of the flock, his sword already in his hand. On the steep slope ahead of him, Rannulf grappled with the burly Turk, and Stephen rushed to help, but before he could reach them Rannulf drove his knife to the hilt in the Turk's armpit.

"Take them!" Rannulf's voice rose in a hoarse bellow. He let the burly Turk drop. "Out! Out!"

Stephen charged past him toward the rest of the Saracens. The two men waiting on the stony hillside had seen their commander die; one was scrambling away back toward their camp, screeching, and the other had jerked a knife from his belt and set himself. Now as the other Templars charged up out of the sheep, he lost heart, and wheeled to run. In three jumps Stephen caught him and clubbed him down with his sword.

For German, he thought. For German.

Up there in the shadow of the spire of the rock, the other Turks were scrambling toward their bows. The slope seemed impossibly steep. He would never reach them before they shot him down. In a row they were flexing their bows to string them, some already kneeling to put their arrows to the nock. But all around him were the other Templars. He felt their strength drive him up, he felt their power in his arms; a fever seized him, and he flung himself onward.

Rannulf howled, off to his left, and the other Templars roared an answer. Stephen clambered the last few yards into the Turkish camp. Before him was the massed enemy, a thicket of arrows. Behind the taut bowstrings, the flexed curves of the bows, he saw the gleam of their eyes, heard the shriek of their voices. The tip of an arrow swung toward him, and Stephen's sword struck through the bow and the string and the arrow and the arm, and like German the Turk died.

Stephen plunged on past the first campfire. He could hear Bear roaring behind him. The Turks were trying to run. Near the foot of the rock spire, two of them stood fast, and he attacked them. Before he struck a blow three more Templars were leaping in beside him, and the Turks went down before them like corn before the reapers.

A horse galloped down on him, zig-zagging, and he jumped to catch it and the horse dodged nimbly past him and fled away. He saw a wounded Turk limping and struggling toward the rocks, trying to escape, and sprang on him and killed him.

Behind him, someone was screaming, and screaming, and then the screaming abruptly stopped.

He straightened, panting, his sword clutched in both hands. In a daze he looked around him. He was almost to the foot of the rock spire, where a campfire burned. Down the way he had come, the sheep were clattering and blathering away back toward their pastures, their shepherds hasty at their heels. The ground below the rock was spotted with dead Turks.

The other Templars were roaming around picking at the bodies; they clustered around the two campfires, eating whatever they could find. The fighting was over. Stephen crossed himself, his hand shaking.

For German. But German was still gone. A storm of fear swept over him, his mind teemed with broken images, wounded men, and dying men, men like him, dead; he felt sick to his stomach. He managed to get his sword belt around his waist again, and ran the blade into its scabbard.

Rannulf came up to him, carrying a dripping chunk of roast meat. "Here, it's rabbit." He held out the joint, with the bare bone sticking out of the end of it; for a moment Stephen saw it as a tiny arm reaching toward him.

"No," he said. "No." And sat down hard.

Rannulf said nothing, only stood there by him, eating the roasted meat. They had left the young King and another man at the foot of the slope, with their horses; they were coming up now at a gallop, raising dust. The scent of the cooked meat reached Stephen's nose, and suddenly he was hungry. He took in a deep breath, feeling better. He remembered striking blows, and knew he had slain men—he had won, he had lived, they had won. His head whirled. A sudden triumph heated him like a flame.

Rannulf was looking down at him.

"Well?"

"I'm hungry," Stephen said, and the other knight laughed, and held out the joint of meat to him. By the time the horses had reached them, he had gnawed the bone to the bare white. His blood sang. German, he thought. German, I avenged you. With his brothers he bounded into his saddle, and bolted for Jerusalem.

Stephen had not changed, but the world had. The world had shrunk down close around him, become no bigger than this moment, this warmth of sunshine on his back, this breath.

Before, in idle times like this, he had daydreamed of distant things: his home, his sisters, and the future, which seemed distant, also, a comfortable space before him, stretching away toward salvation, decked with great deeds.

Now his mind shrank from thinking like that, it made him angry to catch himself at it, as if it were a trick he was too old to fall for. He thought about food, and getting his hauberk down to the armory to be mended, and how he would teach his new horse not to pull on the bit.

Behind him, the city was so quiet he could hear a single persistent vendor calling, streets away. Some carpenters were working inside the gate tower, shuffling and banging wood and rapping with hammers. Stephen leaned against the wall, the stone warm under his hands, the wind soft. The gate was shut and barred on both sides, with the heavy grille of the portcullis lowered, because at any moment Saladin was going to appear before Jerusalem. And none could open that gate, nor go through it in either direction, without the word of Stephen de l'Aigle, from which he was deriving an outsized satisfaction.

He had just let Rannulf and three sergeants out; in fact, he could still see them riding along the road to the east. Looking for Saladin. Rannulf knew everything first, he remembered, and remembered who had told him that, and turned his head, closing that memory off. The two sergeants assigned to Stephen's command were pacing in opposite directions along the rampart. Outside on the road a man with a donkey was plodding toward the city, and some fifteen feet behind him, a woman with a basket; because the gate was so hard to open, he would not let them in until more of a crowd had gathered, or someone important appeared. Then, probably, they would have to wait again to pay the toll.

And once being here, they might regret it. Looking east, he scanned the horizon with a keen eye, wondering where Saladin was.

Since the King and the eleven Templars had reached Jerusalem they had heard nothing else of the army that had broken up at the Litani River. There were a few knights and sergeants left in the garrisons of the Holy City, old men, cripples, and sick; they manned the walls, and the King ordered all the gates and posterns closed, and no one to go in or out save by David's Gate. The churches were filled, and the market-places were empty. The vendor crying in the next street was going from barred and shuttered door to barred and shuttered door.

And yet the day was sweet, the wind merry; Stephen leaned against the wall and watched the hills and knew no more care than a baby.

One of his sergeants called out, and he turned and saw the King riding along the street inside the wall.

Stephen went nimbly down the stairs. The King rode a tall bay horse; after him came half a dozen other riders, all in bright clothes, and Baudouin himself wore a long coat of scarlet silk. He reined his horse in.

"Ho, Mouse, how goes it?"

"All's well, Sire."

"I'll come up and look. Hold." Throwing his reins to a page, he swung one leg across his horse's withers and slid to the ground. "Bili, come with me," he said, and went up the wide stone steps toward the rampart.

There, the carpenters had seen him coming, and all boiled out of the tower, still carrying their tools, and stood there bowing and cheering. The King's face contorted in a gruesome smile, and he waved a Cross over them. Stephen, coming up the steps behind him, had to move down a little to find room on the crowded rampart; another person had come after him, and he heard the rustle of silk and smelled roses and realized, suddenly, that he was standing in front of the Princess of Jerusalem. He stepped to one side with a murmured apology. The King was thanking the carpenters in terms that had the workmen's faces red as apples, and they bobbed up and down before him a while longer, swearing eternal fealty, thousands of prayers, all their children named for him, until their foreman hustled them back to work.

The King turned to look out over the wall to the east. "Nothing yet," he said.

His sister glided up beside him. Her slim white hand was delicately shaped, the knuckles smooth as pearls. Stephen wondered what she was doing here; all the rest of the court had left for the safety of the coast. She looked out toward Judea. "Would they have to come from that direction?"

The King's shoulders lifted the glossy silk of his coat. "It doesn't matter, really, once they're here." He leaned over the wall, looking down at the road. "Are those people waiting to get in?"

"Yes, Sire," Stephen said.

"Let them in, then," the King said, and turned and went back down the stairs. Stephen called to the porters, who set to work to unbar the inner gate and the outer gate, and raise the portcullis; by the time the gate was open and the serfs with their donkey and basket were shuffling through the archway, the King and his sister and their party had gone on out of sight along the wall.

Stephen leaned down from the rampart to call to the people coming in through the gate. "You can thank the King you aren't still outside waiting."

The man with the donkey turned a fierce face on him. "God bless our good King Baudouin!" The old woman gave a breathy cackle of agreement.

The porters were already closing the gate again, and swinging the bar across it. Stephen looked out over the wall, and saw dust on the road, and called out, "Hurry! Get those teeth down!" He jumped up onto the top of the wall, to see the better.

The dust plume spread like a stain across the sky. Under it, coming out between the hills into clear sight, a band of horsemen was trudging up the road. Stephen shaded his eyes. "Stand down," he said. His voice was gusty with relief. "These are Christian men, at least." He climbed down onto the rampart again and sent one of his sergeants on to bring the King back.

✦ There on the road before the gate, at the head of fifty knights, was a stocky red-headed man in a surcoat barred red and black. He looked much taken aback to see King Baudouin. Stiffly he said, "Sire. Good it is to see you here. The report was something otherwise."

King Baudouin smiled down at him. "Good day, my lord of Kerak. I'd like to hear that report."

Beside him, suddenly, Stephen Mouse said, "Sire—another army."

"Templars," someone else murmured, and all along the wall, the folk come to witness pressed closer to the edge, leaning out; Baudouin heard his sister's voice, on the far side of the gate. The King was still looking intently down at Renaud de Chatillon, the Wolf of Kerak, who had briefly been Prince of Antioch and still quartered the great Bohemund's arms on his badge.

"What had you heard, my lord? And from whom?"

Then the oncoming band of men galloped up, drawing all attention to them, and their leader rushed in between Kerak and the gate. His black horse reared, and the magnificent rider tossed his cloak aside, and seized the hilt of his sword.

"Get away, my lord—you have no power in Jerusalem, this is my city!"

Kerak sat motionless, his hands demurely folded on the pommel of his saddle. "There's a superior claim," he said, and nodded up toward the gate.

Twisting in his saddle, Gerard de Ridford turned his face toward the top of the wall. When he saw the King his eyes bulged. "Sire," he said. "Sire. You are alive."

"God be thanked for it," King Baudouin said. "And you also, sir, are alive, for which God be thanked again." He looked over the little army following the Templar Marshall. "Is this the whole number of you?"

The Templar made no answer. He and Kerak were back to staring at each other like two dogs at a bear-baiting. The King turned to Stephen and said, low, "Where is Rannulf?"

Stephen was watching the men below them. "I don't know, Sire."

Kerak lifted his head. "Sire, I am here to help you defend Jerusalem. Give me leave to bring my men inside the walls."

De Ridford wheeled around; being so far below the King's level he had the squat aspect of a toad. "Let them stay out here!" He waved his arm at the gate. "Open for me; I demand it."

The King wiped his hand over his face. "Ah, if only Cousin Tripoli were here, to make a complete set. Yes. My lord Marshall, of course you may bring in your men, who are doubtless weary and perhaps hurt. Go at once to the Temple, and then report to me at my citadel."

As he spoke, Stephen was moving toward the gate, murmuring orders to the porters, and the crowd swung around and scrambled down from the wall to cheer the Templars' entry into the city. The King leaned on his elbow, looking down at Renaud de Chatillon's blocky red head.

"Have you considered, my lord, where you would quarter so many men?"

"Sire, my wife's family has a palace here." He was married to one of the de Millys.

"And you swear to keep the peace?"

The Wolf of Kerak lifted his hand to witness. "As God saves me."

"Then, to help defend the city, I will let you enter, but you must keep good order. Attend me soon at my citadel."

"I am at the King's service." The red head dipped in a courtesy. The gates were opening, the Templars forming a double file to go through. Kerak rode away down the road a few paces, and gathered his men around him, and spoke to them. The King watched them. Lifting his head, he swept his gaze around the horizon; for a moment, perversely, he was hoping to see Saladin's army.

✠ "I would rather have twice as many Templars," the King said, "and half as many of Kerak's men."

They were riding through the great marketplace, which was so empty the sound of their horses' hoofs echoed off the high surrounding walls. There had been no market here for days. On the wide flat pavement the wind spun the loose sand into ripples. With her heel Sibylla gigged her mare to catch up with her brother's horse.

"If these came back, perhaps more will, also—perhaps they are only now making their way back again, Uncle Joscelin and the others." Baudouin d'Ibelin had not come back. She remembered the solid warmth of his chest under her hands. Somewhere he might lie now dead and cold. She swallowed. "Maybe they will all come home again."

The King said, "I can't expect that. I've got to stand up with what I actually have."

He saw it differently than she did, she realized, with a start: not as the loss of individual men, uncles and lovers, but as a collective weakness. Her mood lowered. Around her suddenly the world seemed like a great mill grinding up the people in it.

She said, "When will there be a market again? It would be good to see the streets with living people in them."

"The Templars will arrange that," he said. "We have to keep order, and watch the gates, and they will do that, too. We must bring in all that we can from the countryside, to sustain us in a siege, and to keep it from being there to sustain Saladin. And we must wait. That's the worst."

They had come to the far side of the marketplace. A yell faintly reached her ears. "What's that?" she said, looking around her, and the King spurred his horse into a gallop.

"Bati!" He raced into the next street, and she followed. Up ahead some people were fighting. Her brother galloped straight down on them. Sibylla called out to him—he was alone, they were many—and saw he would not stop and raced her horse after him.

He charged into the midst of the crowd, scattering them; coming on his heels, she saw there had been no fight, really, only a pack of men beating three ragged beggars. She reined in. The men who surrounded them wore Kerak's red-and-black. One of them leapt forward, grabbing for her brother's rein.

"Who the hell are you, to hinder us?"

The King reached up, and threw back the hood of his cloak. At the sight of his face, a gasp went up from all the men around them, and many stepped back, and someone swore.

"Sire." The knight before him let go of the King's rein. He was tall, well set up, with a shock of yellow-white hair. Sibylla realized she knew him: Guile of Kerak, the Wolf's bastard, and chief captain. Even as she recognized him she hardened with dislike.

Kerak's son said, "Sire, we did not know it was you; you should not go about so unattended."

Sibylla rode up beside her brother. "Well, hello, Guile. Hardly into the city, and already making trouble."

Her brother laughed. "You see I am perfectly well attended, Guile."

Before them, the white-haired knight drew back a pace, frowning up at them. "Making trouble! We only seek to help keep the city—on my lord's order." He waved his hand toward the beggars, who were crouched at the feet of the King's horse, clutching their rags around them. "My lord of Kerak says to get all these people off the streets."

The King said, "Then obey him, and get yourselves off the streets."

Guile put his cap back on. "Well, my lord of Kerak ordered me—"

"Now," the King said.

He was leaning forward, his gaze steady on the white-haired knight. Guile stood for a moment, his jaw set. His gaze slid toward Sibylla. Finally he said, "Yes, Sire," and saluted the King. Baudouin watched him collect his knights and ride away.

Sibylla was looking down at the beggars, huddled in the street. "Would a monastery not take them in?"

The King leaned down from his saddle. "Go," he said to the beggars. "Stay out of sight. In the morning, come to the kitchen gate of the citadel, you shall have food there. Go."

The beggars skittered off; one stopped long enough to seize hold of the King's stirrup, and kiss his shoe. Like winddrift they fluttered and flapped down the street. The King turned, and with his sister beside him they rode back toward the citadel.

Sibylla said nothing. She had always thought the war was like a great tournament, all banners and glory. They came to the gate into the citadel; Alys met them there, wringing her hands, her face screwed up like a child's. With her was the King's page, who was the son of Balian d'Ibelin. He was crying. His father was also missing. A hard lump formed in Sibylla's throat. She went with Baudouin into the courtyard, and got down from her horse, and went with Alys to the kitchen, to see that the beggars would be fed.

✦ Late in the night, Stephen woke with a start, and sat up, looking around the Crypt. In the next row, Rannulf was sitting down on his cot, taking his boots off.

"Oh. It's you," Stephen said. "De Ridford is here."

"I saw," Rannulf said. He fell backward onto the bed, his feet still on the floor; after a moment, slowly, he dragged his legs up and stretched out.

"And Kerak, too. His men are swaggering all around the streets looking for trouble."

"We may need them," Rannulf said. "Saladin's taken the castle at Jacob's Ford, with no one to hinder him, and hung the heads of the garrison on the walls."

"Chastelet," Stephen said.

His mind showed him the great castle, the shining oiled wood of the walls, the splendid arras, the new stone, still raw-edged. He remembered dreaming he might one day rule there. Another thing sealed over in his memory. He said, "Then Saladin will come here next?" But Rannulf was already asleep.

✦ In the morning, the Templars went to Mass, and then they gathered in the refectory. There, under the lamps, they took up their places in the ranks.

They stood still a moment, in silence, looking around at the great gaps in their lines; there were more spaces than there were men. Of the officers, only de Ridford and Gilbert Erail, the Seneschal, remained. Of the brother knights, one in four.

There was a long silence. Then, at no spoken word, the brother knights all moved up, until they stood solid again, shoulder to shoulder, facing the officers.

Rannulf took one step forward, his gaze on de Ridford and Gilbert Erail, and he said, "We should elect a new master."

De Ridford's flushed face jerked in a grimace. "Odo de Saint-Amand always championed you, even when you went far beyond bounds. Now as soon as he is down you want to displace him."

At that a growl of comment went through the assembled knights. Rannulf did not look around. In the rows of men behind him were many who hated him. Many also who did not. He kept his gaze fixed on de Ridford, standing before him under the lamp.

"Odo is dead, or a prisoner," Rannulf said. "Most of the Temple with him. Saladin will go through us like water unless we have a master who can lead us."

De Ridford's voice was harsh. "We need a Grand Chapter meeting to elect a master. That could take a year."

"Exactly," Rannulf said. "Too long. But we could hold our own election. We do it in the field, all the time, we did it after the battle on the Litani. We have to have a master."

"And you think it should be you," de Ridford said.

"I can do it better than anybody else."

Now the rumbling voices behind him erupted into a roar. "Yes! Yes!"

"Lead us, Rannulf!"

"Wait for Odo—he may still appear."

"Rannulf Fitznobody! Get back, get out of here, you pig; I won't follow you!"

De Ridford was glaring at Rannulf, his lips pulled back from his teeth. Low-voiced, he said, like an echo, "You pig."

Gilbert Erail folded his arms over his chest, his eyes shifting from de Ridford to Rannulf. "We need more men. That's the important thing. We can strip the garrisons in Cyprus and in Europe—by Whitsunday we could fill this hall again."

Rannulf said, "We can't wait until Whitsunday. Saladin may be here tomorrow."

The assembled knights were still loudly arguing. De Ridford cast a look at them, and swung back to Rannulf, and said, "No. Get back in your rank."

Rannulf clenched his jaw against the surge of his temper; he stood rooted where he was, and the Marshall's face went hot.

"Obey me!" he said, and Rannulf stepped back into the front rank of the men.

But another came forward at once, saying, clear-voiced, "I agree with Rannulf. We should elect new officers."

The other men shouted so that the vaulted ceiling rang; someone began to stamp his feet, and others picked that up, and a dozen voices began to chant: "Yes! Yes! Yes!"

"No," others bellowed out, and the chanting dissolved into a beestorm of boos and hisses.

In front of them all, facing the two officers, Stephen de l'Aigle lifted his voice again.

"We have to have a master. It isn't just Saladin; we've got other problems. You saw how many men that red lord brought into the city."

From the ranks, Felx van Janke called, "And who are making trouble already in the streets and in the Under City."

De Ridford said, "Odo de Saint-Amand is Master of this Order! I will tolerate no effort to displace him." He strode toward Stephen, his face warped into a heavy scowl. "Stand back and keep quiet around your betters, sapling."

Stephen did not move. "I claim the right to speak. And I think me no sapling anymore, my lord. That battle thinned the forest and I seem to be one of the standards around here now."

De Ridford said, "No election!"

Rannulf said, "Not until they bring in more bodies, anyway, is that it?" A ripple of laughter went through the ranks behind him. He threw a quick look over his shoulder. He was realizing that he had a good chance here. For once there were a lot of men here who supported him, and there was Stephen Mouse, talking like a prince and keeping the door open.

Gilbert Erail stepped forward, narrow-eyed, always watching for advantage. "Whatever we do, we can't fight among ourselves. This slick-tongued Frenchman here is right: Kerak is in the city and his army is as strong as we are, and then there's Saladin, and God may send us a few other tests, God being all-wise."

Again the knights began to stamp and chant, some calling for an election, and some against. Rannulf shouted out, "Vote on the election, then!" He flung his words after de Ridford, who was pacing away across the hall. "Bring it to the pitch, Marshall. Count us!"

De Ridford wheeled around. "Very well. But Odo shall know of it—how you repaid his championship of you. Let all men know you are treacherous." He shot a look at the Seneschal.

Gilbert stood forward a few steps. "Let those who will elect a new master now, go to the right, and those who will not, go to the left."

Rannulf went to the right, in past the columns that held up the roof, and turned to look into the center of the room again. He closed both hands on his sword hilt. His heart was a hammer in his chest. Half the massed knights had come with him, and half to the other side, but when they were counted, there was one more on the left side than the right.

De Ridford's voice seemed suddenly free and high. "Then we shall wait. God be thanked."

Gilbert said, "Close ranks, we have other work."

They all tramped out into the middle of the hall. Rannulf stood staring down at the floor. He had fallen short by a single man. He wondered if he would ever have such an opening again; the sour sinking feeling in his belly told him he would not. God wills it, he thought. He felt suddenly like a worthless speck of dust floating in the air, Rannulf Fitznobody, a skin full of nothing.

De Ridford said, "Rannulf, since you want command, we will make you commander of Jerusalem. Keep this place in order, if you're so good at this."

Rannulf lifted his head. "Yes, my lord." He could not meet the Marshall's eyes, afraid to see his look of triumph. With the others he went shuffling out of the refectory.

It had been a near-run thing, de Ridford thought, a very near-run thing: he had come within one man's vote of losing the Mastery of the Temple to a renegade churl with no family and no honor.

He was still brooding on Rannulf Fitzwilliam's crimes and failings when he went up to the King's citadel, to talk over the defense of the city. To his surprise, the Princess was there, looking pale and pensive; she sat beside her brother's throne on a little stool, her women behind her in the shadows. She was so out of place that de Ridford himself almost said something, but Kerak jumped into it first.

"Sire, the woman ought to be gone from here. There is no place for her here." The Wolf tramped across the room from the window, where he had been standing, staring out at the walls.

De Ridford at once saw his opening; he gave a quick smile to the Princess, and rose to her support. "My lord, she is Princess of Jerusalem, what other place does she have?"

Kerak wheeled toward him, as if he had not seen the Templar before. "Ah, you speak folly."

The King said, "Leave off, leave off; you will not spit at each other in front of me, and Saladin almost at the gates. Do you wish, Sibylla, we could arrange for you to be taken off somewhere safer."

She perched on the stool, her hands one over the other on her knee. She said, "I am staying here."

"Nobly said." De Ridford exchanged a long harsh look with Kerak. The older man snorted, his meaty lips twisting.

"Words, words. Put her in mail and give her a sword, and see how noble she looks."

The King's voice snapped with anger. "My lord, I said, leave off! I will not endure this biting one another. We have Jerusalem to defend; let's talk about that."

"Good, let's do that." The Wolf stuck his face forward, his jaw leading like a prow. "I came here to help you against the Mahounders. But we're shut up idle, out of the way, and given no part in the defense of the city. Give me command! I'll show you how to hold Jerusalem."

De Ridford set his fist on his hip. "We already know how to hold Jerusalem, my lord, against whoever comes against us. God gave us the Holy City, and we need no help from you!"

The King said, "Yes. The officer in charge of the city is the commander, as I recall—"

"He fell at the Litani," de Ridford said, clipped. This was crossing another of his vexations. "We have elected someone else to the post, an ordinary knight, for what of better." He shot an oblique look at Kerak, whose random hatred could perhaps be focussed to some valuable end.

"Who?" the King asked.

"Rannulf Fitzwilliam," said de Ridford, and then remembered, suddenly, that the King already knew him.

The King straightened. His shapeless monster face was framed against the figured silks and shaved velvets of his clothes and cushions; there were sores all along his lips. His voice rang with certainty.

"There is no better man in my whole kingdom. He will keep this city, by his sword and by his faith, and I shall support him utterly at it."

Kerak's eyes glinted. He turned, and walked away across the room, his back impudently to the King. Baudouin hurled words after him. "My lord Kerak, it is the business of the Templars to keep order, leave them to it. You need but hold your men in readiness. When Saladin marches, we shall plan against him according to his course. In the meantime, let Rannulf Fitzwilliam do his work, he is very able at it."

De Ridford stepped back a pace. For a moment he could not endure this, the heaping of praise on another man, on a man he despised, but he forced himself to stay cool, to take the long view. He had already found out that Rannulf was one of the knights who accompanied the King back from the Litani River; obviously the Norman had ingratiated himself with Baudouin, more evidence of his perfidy and ambition.

But also, perhaps, something that could be used. For some while de Ridford had been seeking a way inside the King's trust.

Kerak said, "Is that your word on it, then, Sire? I am to sit idle?"

"You are to wait," the King said. "You have my leave, my lord."

Kerak wheeled, and bowed, and stamped out of the room, with no more grace about it than a stablehand. The Marshall de Ridford said, "Sire, beware, he is a man without prudence."

The King said, "I know him well, my lord. But we can deal with him. As to the office of commander of Jerusalem, Rannulf is an excellent choice; bring him with you, when you come next."

De Ridford's smile hurt his cheeks. He said, "As you wish, Sire."

"I hope to have reports from you as necessary."

"Yes, Sire," de Ridford said.

"You may go."

"Yes, Sire." The Marshall bowed, and left.

The King waved to his page to bring him a cup of wine; beside him, Sibylla gave a shake of her head.

"They are all at odds. And yet we are in dire peril!"

"They are fighting men," Baudouin said. He drank deep of the heady, sustaining wine. "When there is no enemy in front of them they fight each other."

"Yes," she said, "they are as much a danger to Jerusalem as the Saracens."

He laughed, as if she made some kind of joke. She gave him a sharp look. The page brought her a cup of the wine also, and she sent him for the aquamanile and watered the wine. The chamberlain was at the door, waiting to be summoned, and she gave him a hard look to keep him away and turned to her brother. "Are you tired? Perhaps you should rest."

"Bili," he said, irritated, "stop mothering me. You can leave, if you wish."

"No," she said. "I want to be here, and see what you do."

"Very well," he said, and nodded to the chamberlain.

A delegation from the merchants of the High City came in, to discuss opening their markets. She watched how her brother handled this, how he spoke evenly and courteously to each man, looking full at him, although he gave up nothing; the merchants left resigned to his commands, if not satisfied. He was a good King. The more she saw of him the more she admired his craft. Yet God was steadily destroying him, while men like Kerak flourished like a blowfly on carrion.

She suppressed a start of anger at God, who dealt so cruelly with her brother. But God was good, and there had to be some purpose in it; and she was beginning to divine that the purpose lay in her, somehow, Sibylla, Queen of Jerusalem.

A steady trickle of men came through the court, asking favors of the King, bringing him reports and complaints and offers. She watched how he dealt with them all, drinking the while of the strong red wine. This was truly King's work, to direct all men's fortunes. Yet she saw nothing in it beyond a woman's grasp.

What was it they did, anyway, she thought, that men believed was so past women? They fought, but she could find men to fight in her name.

And in fact their readiness to fight made more trouble than it solved, and because of it, they solved very little, in the end. She could escape them, and eliminate the need for them, by simply not fighting any wars.

As for the rest of it, she could be the equal of any of them. Certainly she could be as reckless as Kerak, and as treacherous as Tripoli, as ambitious as de Ridford, as clever as the King himself.

She turned her face away from the room, to guard her thoughts, and that brought her gaze to the window, and out the window, to the wall of the city, the high upper story of David's Gate, the limitless sky beyond.

"Bili," he said, after a while, "everybody's gone, and we won't ride the wall until after Sext; shall we play chess?"

She swung around toward him, back into the game. "Oh, yes," she said. "Bring the board, I want to play."

✦ "While Saladin threatens us all it seems short-sighted to quarrel amongst ourselves," de Ridford said. He had caught up with Kerak in the street.

Kerak's mouth curled into a sneer. "Since I have come into this country my chiefest struggle has been with craven Christians."

"In any case, if you have difficulties in Jerusalem, your quarrel's not with me, but with Rannulf Fitzwilliam." He glanced behind Kerak, looking over his knights. "You have more men than this, surely?" Kerak's white-haired bastard was not among the half-dozen following him now.

Kerak said smoothly, "I am well attended."

De Ridford said nothing for a moment. They were riding along the great street of the city, which led from David's Gate back to the Temple; the shops along the way were all closed up, the gates all locked. He liked the city this way, still and empty; he hated the usual bustle of it, its stew of sights and sounds, the flocks of little faceless people who thought they were important when they mattered nothing.

Kerak was different. Kerak was going to serve him, although of course the Wolf would never know that.

The Marshall of the Temple said, "When Saladin comes we must stand together, and fight together, in God's name, and our own."

"Well it is you are a monk, giving me all these sermons." Kerak's voice grated. They were coming to the crossroads, where he would ride down to his palace near Bethesda Fountain. Kerak drew rein. His head swiveled on the thick creased column of his neck, his eyes narrow.

"My men are knights, not common foot-draggers to be shivvied around and locked up like women. I can't promise they will abide by some other man's commands than mine."

De Ridford smiled at him. "As I said, your quarrel is with Rannulf Fitzwilliam." His horse carried him tiptoe past the Lord of Kerak, up toward the Temple haram looming against the sky. He said, "Do what you must, my lord. Till seeing." He gigged his horse into a lope along the steep road that led to the Stables of Solomon, under the Temple pavement.

⟐ Stephen said, "What am I supposed to do with this?" He took the stick that Felx van Janke was handing to him.

"You've never fought with staves?" Felx shot a quick look at him. "The drawbacks of being rich." He held out another stick to Bear, who took it and laid it down beside him. They were sitting on the steps above the practice yard, waiting for the bells to ring for Sext. Felx dropped down next to them, his long legs thrust out.

"Why are we getting sticks?" Stephen asked.

Bear said, "We're going out to do dirty work in the streets. Rannulf doesn't want anybody sliced up; it goes against the vow, you see. So we get the staves. You've never used one? Stay on your horse and use it like a lance."

Felx said, "I had four brothers. One sword among us." He rolled the stave over his wrist, caught it with the other hand, and spun it back again. "A good stick's more tidy, anyway." His head rose; he looked past Stephen, back up the steps, and called, "Well? When do we go out? Are we going to get some supper this time?"

"Probably not," Rannulf said. He came down among them, stopped on the steps, looking up at the sky. "I want everybody in the saddle by Nones. I wish it would rain; that would make this easier. Mouse, I need your help."

"What do you want me to do?" Stephen said.

"Hold," Bear said. "Here comes the Marshall." The three men on the steps all stood, putting down their staves. De Ridford sauntered up to them. His full sandy beard was combed and even, and his hair hung down almost to his shoulders. His clothes were fine as a lord's. His gaze swept them, putting each of them aside, until he came to Rannulf, and then he smiled.

"Well, commander. I understand Kerak rules the streets now. Are you going to let that continue?"

Rannulf said, "No, my lord." His hands slid behind his back. He had a way of standing like a kicked dog when officers talked to him.

"Good. I attended on the King, today. We spoke of you." De Ridford's voice was sleek. "The King thinks very well of you. I think I may have misjudged you. Give good service henceforth, and you shall find me your friend."

Rannulf said, "Thank you, my lord." Stephen looked sharply at him.

"Do not disappoint me in the matter of the Lord of Kerak. I shall hear your report at Compline."

"Yes, my lord."

The bells began to ring. De Ridford said, "Continue," and went away up the steps.

Stephen watched him go, amazed. Felx and Bear went swiftly down to the practice yard; Rannulf grabbed Stephen by the arm and held him. "Stay."

De Ridford went up over the top of the steps and disappeared from sight. Staring after him, Stephen said, "God's blood. What was that about?"

"Never mind," Rannulf said, and gave him a shake. "I need you to do something; now, pay attention."

When the pages brought in their dinner, Alys looked at the tray and burst into tears.

"Oh, God, oh, God," she cried, "why did we not go with the Greeks to Acre? Why didn't we go with your mother to Ascalon? Now we're going to die here, and there isn't even anything to eat."

"Shut up," Sibylla said. She stared down at the tray, where there was only a loaf of bread and a little cheese—although very handsomely presented—on an enamel dish, with a silver knife. She broke the bread, and cut a piece of the cheese, while Alys snuffled and dripped.

"I said, be quiet." Sibylla glanced around her; over by the door, two pages waited, hollow-eyed, their lips tight. Alys gave a great sloppy sob, and Sibylla flung the bread at her.

"You are worthless, Alysette. Go back to bed and cry into the covers." The Princess jerked her head toward the pages again; the look of weary terror in their faces stoked her temper, and she snapped, "Stop standing around! Bring my cloak." She turned a furious gaze back on poor Alys, her anger a torch against this fear creeping like a grey fungus over everything around her. "I will attend my brother. There at least among the men I shall not hear puling and lamenting." She got up, took the cloak, and went alone down the stairs.

Her hands were cold. The sky was bundled with dank heavy clouds.

She stood on the steps of the tower looking across the courtyard.

It was the endless waiting that wore her down. Every day, they waited for some news, sifted through every change of the wind, every wisp of dust for some portent of what was to come, but there was no news, only boredom, unanswered questions, doubts and frets. She beat her fists together, willing something to happen.

The door to the opposite tower opened, and her brother came out.

He saw her at once, and waved to her. She went forward a few steps. The grooms were bringing their horses up out of the stable, so that they could ride around the corner to David's Gate and wait there for the messenger. One little busy boil of expectation in the middle of the dull day. Still it was something to do. She called to her brother, mounted her horse, and went side by side with him out to the street.

As they rode, the bells rang for Sext. The messenger was supposed to arrive exactly at Sext. Already, as they approached the gate, there was a crowd of people in the street; they raised a cheer for the King, and one too for Sibylla. She lifted her hand, smiling. It did well to look happy for these folk, to seem confident, and their cheers buoyed her. But already her back was tightening, her nerves on edge; she lifted her gaze, and scanned the walls, all lined with Templars.

The gateway was open, the portcullis raised. She and her brother rode out to the top of the road, and drew rein. The road was empty.

Baudouin said, "Well, now, where is he?" He stared away down the road. She knew he saw imperfectly; he masked it, but she knew him better than anyone else. She moved closer to him, and saw for him.

"There's no sign of anyone. No smoke, no dust." She knew from days of this what to look for. "The sky is clear, to the east, but there are clouds coming in from the sea; there could be more rain."

He said, "Good. Rain keeps people off the streets."

"Who is in the streets?"

His shoulders moved, twitching off some irritation. "Kerak is not restraining his men; they are going around at night, and there's certainly going to be trouble."

She turned, looking up at the wall again; the Templar guards slouched against the rampart. Then one flung out his arm, pointing outward, and she turned, and gave a cry.

"There's the messenger."

The King grunted. The messenger labored up the road, a small man, unarmored, on a small fleet horse. The people on the wall began to scream and shout at him long before he reached them, and as he reached them, he was already saying his news.

Which was no news. "Nothing yet," he said.

The King nodded. "Very good. Go in and rest."

The crowd on the walls cheered, and rapidly left. The messenger rode in through the gate, and the King and Sibylla followed him. She fought against her lowering mood. Every day for a week they had come here, to wait for the messenger, to hear, "Nothing yet." Every day, they cranked themselves up for something to happen, and every day, the same: "Nothing yet."

He would never say anything else. He himself was the message, the words just a frill. What they waited for was the day he did not come, which would mean that Saladin was on the march, had intercepted the messenger, and killed him.

She went after her brother, back to the citadel, to another day of useless tedious waiting. "What are you going to do about Kerak?" she asked. Like a man, she seized on the nearest available enemy.

Her brother let go of his reins; the grooms came up to help him out of his saddle. "Nothing. Let the Templars handle it." He played one against the other, she saw, like a chess game. Coldly she wondered what part in this game he had for her.

To be Queen, as he was King. That was what he wanted for her. She girded herself for that. She would be Queen, and then everything would change. She would save the Kingdom. She watched her brother half-fall down out of his saddle into the arms of the groom; for an instant, she caught herself wishing he would die, and let her in. She shut her eyes, and swept the thought away.

"Sibylla!"

She looked up; Alys stood in the door of the tower, waving her arms. "Sibylla! Come eat. The cheese is actually very good." She looked much happier. As always, food had given her heart. Sibylla climbed down from her saddle and went off toward another day's boredom.

✦ Rannulf was a great knight, Stephen thought, but he was a very bad officer; he took the whole business too seriously. He had laid a heavy hand on the city, allowing all the shops and suks to open only from Sext until Nones, and no one to be on the streets after Vespers; he had packed the gates with men and sent patrols around in fours rather than twos.

Now all he had to do was make people obey him, which of course was something different.

In particular he had to make Kerak's men obey him. Sitting his horse at the edge of the Under City's suk, Stephen looked out across the crowd and saw dozens of red-and-black jerkins, none showing any signs of heading on up to the High City and their quarters.

But then the Nones bells had not rung yet. The suk still boiled with a surging noisy crowd, many of them folk in from the countryside seeking shelter from the Saracens, many others down from the High City to buy extra food, and to break the tension with some momentary pleasure. They crowded around the wineshops and the dice games, and the people of the suk worked them in a hundred practiced ways, as they worked all the world as it passed in its endless stream through Jerusalem. Stephen looked around the crowd again, marking Kerak's men.

Halfway down the irregular wedge-shaped marketplace, a head white as a dandelion caught his eye. He let out his breath in a hiss. He had been hoping Guile of Kerak would go somewhere else to get himself in trouble. Stephen reached for his reins, and backed his horse up; Rannulf appeared by his stirrup, on foot.

"You see him?"

"I don't want to do this," Stephen said.

"Who cares what you want?" Rannulf said. "Get going." He backed off, hiding in the crowd, and Stephen rode out across the suk, toward Guile, sitting slouched on a tall bay horse, with two other knights beside him.

They saw him coming; their faces set, wary, and Guile said, "Well, if it isn't one of Jesus' little soldiers."

Stephen rode up beside him. In the crowd just around them he made out a score of Kerak's men, all armed. He faced Guile, and said, "Look, I have my orders. I'm supposed to clear this place out, come Nones, and that means you, too."

Guile watched him cooly. "I don't take orders from psalm-singing Cross-kissing poor little soldiers for Christ." The man beside him laughed. Everybody was watching Stephen.

He shrugged. "Look, I'm just doing what I'm told to do. If it were me, I wouldn't care, and in fact I don't care much now. I'm sick of this. I haven't been out of the saddle since Matins." He could not meet Guile's eyes; he stared away over the crowd. "Do you have anything to drink?"

"Sure," Guile said. "What's your name?" He gestured to the man on his left, and a leather wineskin came across to Stephen. He told them his name, and drank a little; they talked about the war, mostly about how they would carve Saladin into pieces, and then drifted off across the suk to a dice game, down near the fountain. The Syrian throwing the dice gave one glancing look at Stephen and stopped cheating. Guile got down off his horse and played several passes, winning some money. He was half-drunk, and winning made him boisterous; he laughed with his two friends, and reached for the wineskin again. Up in the High City, the first bells began to ring.

Stephen said, "That's Nones. The suk will shut down now."

Guile laughed. "You don't think anybody will actually pay any attention to that, do you?"

"I just follow orders. You know you're supposed to be back inside walls by Vespers." One of the knights handed him the wineskin and he drank.

Guile said, "How do you propose to get me there?" His voice grated.

Stephen lifted one hand, palm out, placating him. "Not me. I was just mentioning it. I told you, I'm sick of all of this." He tossed the wineskin to the man behind Guile. "At Vespers, I get to go back to the Temple and sleep. Unless of course my officer decides otherwise."

Guile said, "He's an ass. Nobody's going to listen to him. Maybe there is a war, but life has to go on."

"Yes, I tend to agree with you." Stephen turned his head, looking around the suk. Up on the hill, all the bells of Jerusalem were clanging, and around the suk, the merchants were reeling in their awnings, and shuttering their stalls.

Even the Syrian who ran the dice game was closing; he knelt, rolling up the gamecloth, and when Guile let out a yip of protest, he only shook his head.

"If I mean to be here tomorrow, my lord, I must not be here today." He tucked the roll of cloth under his arm and hurried off.

Guile muttered under his breath, looking around him. With the shops closed, the crowd was scattering, people with homes going back to them, and people without hunting for some other shelter. Kerak's men were bunching together around Guile, most of them on horseback, and he drew them back around the fountain, in the shadow of the hill-side.

"Well, I guess we have to make our own fun."

Stephen reined his horse back a little, out of the thick of these other men. He looked furtively around him, seeing no sign of any other Templar; the suk was all but empty, only a few of the beggars lingering, their eyes on Guile and his men. Guile sent some of his knights to drive them off, and the beggars crept away into the narrow lanes and alleys of the Under City. Kerak's men were going nowhere. Most of them sat and lounged around by the fountain; one tried to climb the steep side of the cistern that fed it. Somebody produced a handful of dice and another game started up.

Guile came over to Stephen. "Why are you hanging around here?"

Stephen lifted one shoulder. "I'm supposed to patrol the suk. Until Vespers. Then I'm going to bed."

"Pray first, though, hunh." Guile smirked at him.

"Oh, yes," Stephen said. "Lots of prayer."

"You dogsbodies live a pretty sorry life, I guess. No fun at all."

"Oh," Stephen said, "I wouldn't say that."

"Really." Guile's tongue ran over his lower lip. "You mean, you do have some excitement, now and then?"

"A vow," Stephen said, "is made to break. And a little hocus-pocus, some crisscross, and it's whole again. Right?"

Guile's smile widened. "I understand." He cast a look around them at the empty suk. "I guess you'd know where to find what you wanted."

"Pretty much."

"On the other hand, you're still a monk."

Stephen shifted in his saddle, his hand on his hip. "You mean, do I know where to get women."

Guile laughed, his eyes glinting under his white brows. "Now you're warm."

Stephen shook his head, turning his gaze away. "I can't help you."

"I guess not. Being a monk. I'll bet you haven't dipped it in years, have you?"

Stephen stared steadily away; he fought down the urge to pound his fist into Guile's face. He said, "I know a woman who'll oblige, but just you—not these others." He took the skin and upended it over his mouth, taking a good long draught; he lowered the skin and plugged it, in no hurry to say more.

Guile was staring at him. Apparently Guile had not dipped it himself in some while. "Some Syrian whore?"

"No, she's Frankish, clean, and sweet. But she only does noblemen."

That was the right thing to say. Guile sat back, smiling, expansive. "How much?"

Stephen looked away again. He had no idea what a whore might cost; the whole idea of whores made him sick. "That's between you and her."

"All right. Good. Take me to her."

Stephen said, "Don't let the rest of these pigs know where we're going."

Guile turned, and called vaguely to the other men to wait where they were. He and Stephen drifted away from the fountain, across the empty suk. Stephen said, "Out there in the desert, do you get a lot of work?"

"No, we live like kings. When my lord Kerak leads us, we always win, and we take home such booty our horses stagger in the carrying of it, and when we are at home, we game, or hear music, and eat the finest meats, and drink the best wines in Outremer."

"Good," Stephen said. "Maybe I'll come out there and join you."

"It's not a monkish life."

"I'm sick of the monkish life." Stephen guided him into a narrow lane between two high blank walls. "I'm ready for a little fun now and then."

"I'll wager on it." Guile turned and laughed at him. "Whatever makes a man to take up such a life voluntarily?" They went up the hill and around a curve, with houses close all around, and out of the corners Rannulf and Felx and Bear pounced on Guile and hauled him off his horse.

Stephen wiped his hand over his face, watching. Bear got Guile's arms behind him, and Felx had him by the hair; Kerak's man flung himself uselessly against their grip, and they muscled him quickly down. When he opened his mouth to scream, Felx's hand clamped down over his face. Panting, Guile subsided.

Rannulf went up in front of him. "Now, baby, I don't want any trouble from you. In a moment we're going down to the suk and you're going to tell your men to get back up to the High City where they belong, and then you're going to stay there."

Guile's eyes blazed. Felx lowered his hand. Guile shot one furious glance past Rannulf's shoulder at Stephen and faced the commander of Jerusalem.

"Let me go! Fight me hand to hand and see what comes of it!"

"Oh, no," Rannulf said. "I don't fight other Christians. You're going to do as I say, or I'll make sure you don't even walk for a week." He nodded to Bear. "Snug him up."

Bear had his arms twined intricately through Guile's; he brought his fists up, and Guile snapped stiffly erect and exhaled a whine of pain. Rannulf watched him, remote. Guile bit his teeth together, not saying anything, and Rannulf nodded once more to Bear. "Do it again."

"No," Guile gasped, before Bear could hurt him. "I'll give the order."

"Good," Rannulf said, and stepped back. "Let him go."

Bear uncoiled his arms from Guile's and released him. Kerak's man stood glowering around at the four Templars. "I'll get you for this."

"Will you," Rannulf said. "Mouse, bring his horse."

Stephen led over Guile's horse. The white-haired knight reached for his reins. "You treacherous bastard," he said, under his breath.

"No," Stephen said. "Maybe I'm treacherous, but you're the bastard." He reined around to keep Guile in front of him; Felx was leading the other Templars' horses out of the lane. They rode down to see that Kerak's men did as they were told.

CHAPTER XV

The King leaned heavily on the pommel of his saddle, his hands lumpy under his gloves. "There is the chapel on the Mount of Olives, that Father began. I would like to finish it, someday." He was not looking toward the Mount of Olives, but down the road, where the messenger would first appear. If he came.

"Let's go up there, later." Sibylla turned, half-standing in her stirrups, to look up at the hillside to the east of them. The city's hucksters sold rosaries made of olive wood and olive pits they claimed were taken from the mount but which they actually gathered on the slopes south of the city; there were no olive trees on the hill, only ragged spires of cypress, and clumpy weedy underbrush. She saw no sign of the chapel. "What has to be done?" She avoided looking off down the road.

The King said, "It needs ornament. Statues, and furniture. It's a pretty place, and it would be good, I think, to build something, instead of always fighting."

His voice was flat. The messenger was late. Above them, on the rampart of the wall, several other people waited, and no one spoke, and no one watched the road, save the King, who looked nowhere else.

Sibylla was still staring at the Mount of Olives. "There are some excellent craftsmen in Acre, who could do the statues. Let me help you. We could do it together."

"Good. I was hoping you would like the idea." Her brother's voice strained, trying to stretch this out, to cover the vast uncertainty of waiting, and then, above them, someone shouted.

"He comes!"

Sibylla's whole body went soft with relief; she brought a sigh up out of her lungs, and her brother faced her, and their eyes met. Up on the rampart, the dozen people watching were cheering and clapping.

"More than one! Look, there, who rides with him?"

"A knight—three knights!"

"Who is it?" her brother murmured, and she turned her gaze down the road.

Far down there, the messenger in his brown leather jack was driving his exhausted horse on toward the city; three men followed him, sitting tall on big horses. Knights. One caught her eye. She recognized his slouched shoulders, the way he held his head, and a cry escaped her.

"It's Uncle Joscelin!"

The King said, "Joscelin. What's he doing here? Something's happened." He tilted forward, his eyes peering down the road.

All along the wall, cheers rose; more people were pushing up along the rampart, passing the news back to the street below. Sibylla turned back toward the oncoming riders. She raised one hand above her head, and waved, and among the weary men climbing the road toward her, an arm rose in answer.

Something in that gesture lifted her heart. She knew, suddenly, as if an angel told her, that the war was over, at least for now. She drew a breath, and it seemed her first free breath in days and days. The messenger booted his horse toward them. As soon as he was within earshot, he was shouting.

"They've turned back! Saladin has turned back!"

Now from the wall such a roar of a cheer went up that Sibylla's horse shied, and the King reached out and grabbed hold of her rein. She laughed at him. As if she could not master her own horse. "We're saved, Bati," she said, giddy. "We're saved."

Then, through all the wild cheering and excitement, she saw his face slack with disappointment. He let go of her reins. "I am doomed to die in bed," he said, heavily, and swung his horse around, and rode to meet the messenger.

The day was cold; the pages were piling wood onto the hearth. The King stood just behind them. He felt nothing of the heat of the fire, but the flames satisfied his eyes, a visual music. Behind him, by the throne, his uncle Joscelin was talking to Sibylla; Kerak had just swaggered into the room, and was glaring all around, grunting and coughing. The chamberlain rapped his staff on the floor and announced the Marshall of the Temple of Jerusalem, and Gerard de Ridford strode in the door. Rannulf Fitzwilliam slouched along behind him. The King went across the room to his throne and sat down.

"Draw around me," he said, and the men moved up in a semi-circle around the throne, the three lords in front, and their underlings on their heels. The Princess came quietly to stand behind the throne. The King signed to the chamberlain to shut the door, and spoke to this council.

"I am grateful to you for coming here. I need advice on some matters. First let me hear what you think of this latest turn. Why did Saladin retreat?"

Kerak spoke first, at once, careless that he had seen nothing of the campaign. "He is a Turk. He has no gift of reason; everything he does is unfathomable." His head jerked up, throwing a nod at Sibylla, just behind Baudouin's shoulder. "Sire, she ought not to be here."

The King said, "She is my heiress, she will rule, she stays." He turned at once to Joscelin, shutting Kerak out. "Uncle, why did Saladin give up, when he had Jerusalem all but in his grasp?"

Joscelin said, "God saved us. When they made me prisoner, by the Litani River, they were saying they would be in Jerusalem by Ramadan. They took hundreds of prisoners—the Ibelins, the Master of the Temple—all of us who could raise good ransoms, they sent off to Damascus, where it looked as if we would sit for weeks; but then a few days ago the Sultan suddenly showed up, and let us all go on our paroles."

Kerak said, "It's a trick of some kind."

The King said, "You saw the Sultan Saladin, Uncle?"

"Not at the Litani River," Joscelin said. "But in Damascus, only a few days ago, I was face to face with him for more than an hour, talking over the ransoms. He is in command, and in no hurry." He gave a shake of his head, looking gloomy. "God will not allow Jerusalem to fall into the hands of the faithless. But this time it was damned close."

The King said, "I have a plan to forestall the next time, which I will tell you in a moment. But it requires a truce, and I am glad he wants to talk. Whom shall we send to Damascus?"

"Send nobody," Kerak said. "It's a trick, and no good will come of it for us—I say, fight him! He must be weak, to give up as he did. If we attack now, we might break him."

The King said, "If words were men, my lord Kerak, you would lead an army numberless as the sands. But now we have about one hundred fifty knights among us, and if he wants a truce, I'm very minded to give it to him."

"Bah," Kerak said. "You are all city soldiers. Greeks. Jews." He turned and walked off across the room, pushing through his followers.

The King said, "To negotiate this truce, I believe I should send Tripoli."

De Ridford lunged forward. "Sire. You cannot mean this."

"I do mean it."

"Sire, at the Litani River, he abandoned us to the enemy. He is Saladin's friend, he was a hostage for years at their court—"

"All the more reason for sending him," the King said. "He understands them, he gets along well with them."

"He betrayed us at the Litani River! He will betray us again."

"A truce is in his best interest," the King said. "I always trust men to pursue their own ends as faithfully as they say they're going to pursue mine."

Joscelin said, "Well, I'm not going to go back to Damascus, I have to go home to Nablus and put things in order there, and so does everybody else. Tripoli is the only one to go; the King is right."

Baudouin thanked him with a glance; slow and mild and white-hearted, his uncle was worth six Keraks. De Ridford set one fist on his hip, his face hard as a wedge.

"The Temple insists then that you send some of us, as well. We shall know the value of this truce." He nodded his head behind him. "Rannulf Fitzwilliam here could go. He speaks the language; he is used to dealing with the Saracens."

In among the row of lesser men, Rannulf lifted his head. Kerak turned, by the window, and gave him a dagger of a look. The King said, "I agree. We shall send Rannulf also. And some priest, perhaps Saint-George, since it is after all Damascus."

His throat was dry; he put out his hand, and a page gave him a cup of wine. He gathered himself for the next leap. Thus far it had gone well enough. The men before him were muttering in agreement; Kerak was still staring at Rannulf. The King drank of the strong dark wine. It surprised him that de Ridford had put forth Rannulf's name, but it fit too well with Baudouin's own purposes to quibble.

He said, "When we have this truce, I mean to send out an appeal to Christendom, to send us another Crusade."

That startled them; all their voices rose at once. He drank again, the wine cushioning the jags and jolts of this work; he was tired, he felt the power running out of him like a draining wound, and yet the hardest was to come. Kerak stepped forward.

"The Crusade is a false dream, Sire. None will answer, and we will wait in vain, and do nothing in the meantime. Trust in God, and take our swords in our hands, and attack the enemy. That is the way of the true Soldier of the Cross!"

His own men called out in agreement, some clapping their hands. De Ridford was scowling, and Joscelin gave a shake of his head.

"Sire, my lord Kerak has some point. The people in the West don't care about us anymore, except to make sermons about how we're suffering for our sins, and deserve to lose."

The King had come to the moment he dreaded; he felt his sister's presence behind him, and could not put this off anymore. He said, "I mean to seek out some great prince to lead the new Crusade. And to win his support I will offer him the dearest prizes in my gift: Holy Sepulcher, the city of Jerusalem, my crown, and for his wife and queen, my sister." Into the sudden electric silence, he went on, "The King of the Romans is unmarried. And there is the English prince, Richard Lionheart, who is known to support the Crusade, and who is reputed to be a second Roland."

Kerak said, "I say it is a false hope, Sire."

Although he sat facing forward, toward the men, the King's attention was on his sister, who stood behind him, and who neither moved nor spoke. He only nodded at Kerak. "Say what you will, my lord. I am determined to preserve this Kingdom."

Joscelin said, "Whatever you choose to do, Sire, I shall follow. God gave this burden to you, and not to me. But now let me take leave, unless there is more you require of me."

"Go, my lord. Thank you very much. God be with you."

"And with your spirit," Joscelin said, and went around the throne and spoke briefly to Sibylla, and kissed her, and went out. The King sat watching the room before him. De Ridford had beckoned for a page, and now took a cup of the wine from him. Rannulf was staring at the floor. Sibylla's presence here confounded him, as, somehow, it did Kerak, who seemed much subdued.

"My lord Kerak," the King said. "Now that the danger to Jerusalem is past, you too will wish to return to your own country, I am sure."

The Lord of Kerak turned, now, standing among his men, his white-haired son beside him. "Sire, some of my men desire to use this chance to worship at the holy shrines." The Wolf bowed his head in piety. A little late, his hand rose and made a quick crossing of his breast. His deepset eyes glittered.

"Keep the peace, my lord," Baudouin said. "And may God speed you home again."

"God keep you." Kerak backed up two steps, turned, and marched out, his men close on his heels.

De Ridford said, "My lord, by your leave," and bowed, but the King lifted his hand.

"No. Stay a moment." He hitched himself up higher on the throne. "I heard nothing from you, my lord Marshall, in favor of the Crusade or against."

De Ridford's wide shoulders rose and fell, his hands on his belt. "The

Temple fights the Crusade every day, Sire. Even now, men come to join us from all over Christendom, and they wait not for princes, nor do they require the earthly rewards of a crown and a beautiful queen." He bowed elegantly to Sibylla. Turning his head slightly, he gathered Rannulf Fitzwilliam in with a glance. "My brothers and I ask only to serve. We have put ourselves in God's hands, not those of some worldly prince."

The King said, "Well said, my lord." He looked past de Ridford, to Rannulf. "Saint. What think you of it?"

Rannulf said, "My lord the Marshall speaks for me."

"Why do you think Saladin retreated?"

The knight stirred, as if the question nettled him. His eyes met Baudouin's. "I wish I knew."

Then Sibylla spoke, her voice clear and bitter. "Perhaps he withdrew because he wearies of the war. Perhaps he stopped fighting because he wants peace. He has asked to talk of peace, and all you offer him is unrelenting war."

Rannulf dropped his gaze, and said nothing. Beside him, de Ridford said, "My lady, this Sultan has said he would purge the Holy Land of the very air we breathe."

"No," Sibylla said. She moved up to stand at her brother's right hand. Her voice was taut with reined-in anger. "I will hear it from the man my brother sends to talk peace to the Sultan. If he will talk peace at all."

Baudouin shifted in his place; he saw her fist clench at her side, and knew where her rage sprang from. Rannulf gave her nothing, kept his head turned away from her, and his gaze lowered. De Ridford wheeled around, sharp with words. "You villain! Answer this noblewoman. I order it."

Rannulf said, to the floor, "Yes, Princess."

She said, "Why do you think Saladin withdrew, if not because he knows God is with us, and will keep us always, and so all he does is futile? And so he may be minded to seek a peace with us?"

"Yes, Princess."

"That is no answer."

"Yes, Princess."

She struck out with her hand, swept the King's wine cup off the table; with a clatter and a clang, it hit the floor on the far side of the room. "You will not answer me, even under orders! What perverse pride is this, parading as humility? You wrap yourself in that vow, as if you were better than the rest of us, like the Pharisee in the parable."

"Yes, Princess."

"Well, remember me in your prayers, holy warrior. Although as you turn humility into pride, and obedience into mockery, so you would likely turn prayers into curses."

"Yes, Princess," Rannulf said. "Non militia, sed malitia."

Baudouin broke into a smile, and Sibylla gave a startled burst of laughter. The joke disarmed her; her hand opened, the long slim fingers flexing. For a moment no one spoke. Baudouin sagged down into the throne, too tired to keep upright anymore, his muscles feeble. He thought he had done what he intended, and he said, "My lords Templar, you have my leave to go."

They went. Sibylla said, "God's teeth, Rannulf Fitzwilliam makes me angry, he makes me want to hit him. What do you like so much in him?"

"He is honest," the King said. "A virtue priced beyond pearls, and a lot rarer."

"A virtue you are not applying to me. What is this of a new marriage for me?"

"The Crusade needs a great leader. The King of the Romans, or Prince Richard of England."

"You did not speak to me of this, before."

The King had not, because he had expected her to object; so he had proclaimed his intentions before the world, to bind her fast before she could escape. "Each of us has a duty, Bili. This is yours."

"I am a widow. By law I can choose my own husband."

"You would choose someone you know, which would be a calamity. And someone you could master, which would be a worse calamity."

"My lord," she said, "you have betrayed me. The while you have taught me to be Queen, and now you want to make me just a pawn again."

"I am trying to give you a king to rule with you, to save Jerusalem. You will do as I command you, because you are Princess, because you are my sister." He knew if he kept on he would break her to this, the only way to save Jerusalem.

"Am I to have no word in this at all? I will not do it, Bati."

"Sibylla. You're no virgin; don't act like one. You married William merrily enough."

"I was a little girl! All I thought of was the wedding, the clothes, the jewels, and the excitement, and how much he would love me. Nobody told me about the—you don't know, Bati. I am not a virgin, but you are. You don't know."

"I know that there must come some great lord from the West, with the army only such a man can muster, or this Kingdom will fall. And the way to bring such a man here is to offer him what he cannot have in the West. And I will hear no more—"

"To save Jerusalem you would give it away."

"I will hear no more!"

"What do you know of this English prince, save that he has broad rich lands of his own, and is a mighty warrior, and so will save us, surely, from the Saracens. But so doing, he will be greater than us, he will owe us nothing, and we will owe him everything."

He said, "I will hear no more from you concerning this, my sister, save that you will submit to it."

A little silence. She said, in a different voice, "I will not, my lord." She gathered herself. In the back of the room her women stirred, making ready to follow her. "By your leave, Sire, I shall go."

"Come back when you are ready to agree to it," her brother said. She left.

◈ In the street, de Ridford said, "That is a dangerous woman."

Rannulf said, "All women are dangerous."

He was staring straight ahead down the narrow street. It was the middle of the afternoon, and the word of the Sultan's retreat had gotten all over. The people were crowding forth out of their houses into the street; the city boomed alive after the long anxious waiting behind walls. By the fountain, the old men had gotten out their chess game, and the women waited in lines with their jars and pitchers. The wineseller on the corner was in the street rolling up the shutters of his shop. There would be drunken men all over the city tonight. The pieman came by, singing of his wares in a high cracked voice.

Rannulf noticed all of this, but only with his eyes. The Princess had laid hold of his mind. He could not shake off the memory of the exchange with her, how she had challenged him; he ran the words over and over through his memory, devout as prayer.

He realized that de Ridford had spoken to him. He said, "I have my vow." Which she had crashed through like a spiderweb.

De Ridford said, "Nonetheless, you must deal with her, as it is expedient. She is the heiress of the Kingdom. When the King dies, the crown will fall into her lap. But you, you have the address of a plowboy. I kept expecting you to pull your forelock. I've never seen anybody else who can be both obsequious and arrogant at the same time."

Rannulf gave him a sideways look. He saw no reason to trade insults with de Ridford. Nothing in the Marshall's new show of tolerance convinced him the feud between them was over. De Ridford turned toward him again.

"Yet something can be made of you, I think. You know why I have placed you in this embassy."

"Not really, no."

"Well, I'm sure it will eventually occur to you. I want to know everything Tripoli does in Damascus. Mark especially the Sultan's countenance toward him."

"This is not my line of work."

"I have never understood quite what your line of work is, other than to bedevil me, but you will obey orders, won't you."

"Yes, my lord," Rannulf said.

"And I have another order. Kerak has been treading the edge, all through this, and now that there is no more immediate danger from Saladin, he will push as far as he can. This wanting to pray at the shrines is a sham. He will try something, and when he does, I want you to make sure he never wants to see Jerusalem again. Is that in your line of work?"

"Yes, my lord."

"Then do it," de Ridford said.

That night Rannulf dreamed of the Princess Sibylla.

He was in a dark wood, and he saw her on the path. Now she did not do battle with him, as she had in her brother's court; she ran away from him. He chased her, and he caught her under the trees, and he dragged her down on the ground and raped her.

He never saw her face. He woke immediately. He was lying on his cot in the Crypt, in the flickering light of the lamp; all around him the other men slept in a low chorus of snores and breathings. The dream had been so real, so real.

He crossed himself. His penis was painfully hard inside his drawers. He forced his way through a paternoster, trying to wring himself limp, but it did no good. He wanted to conquer her. He remembered, in the dream, her hips shivering against him, her hair wrapped around his wrists. Impossible she did not know what he had done to her, that across the city in her silken bed she did not dream this too. Her fault. She had tempted him. Come to him in the dream and seduced him. His hand slid down to his crotch. Before he sinned any more he rolled onto his stomach and buried his head in his arms.

He could never possess her, even if somehow he were freed of the vow; she would go to some prince, a fair-haired magnificence who walked on carpets all day long and used men like Rannulf to hold his horse. Even in the dream, he had had to steal her.

Even in his dreams he did evil. And if she did not know, God certainly knew. He made himself say prayers, over and over again, until the Matins bells began to ring. Later that morning, he heard that the Princess had left Jerusalem.

✦ Kerak's men did not leave. In bands, they roamed Jerusalem, taking whatever they wanted from the shops and stalls, and abusing the local people. On de Ridford's order, Rannulf got out all the knights of the Temple, armed with staves, and they fought Kerak's men back and forth through the streets and down into the Under City.

By sundown a steady drizzle was falling. The cold and the rain defeated Kerak's men as much as the Templars with their staves; half of them gave up, and went into the penitential cell in the Temple, and the rest fled the city.

The winter night lay heavy on Jerusalem. The rain was falling harder, freezing into streaks of sleet. With every step Rannulf's horse skidded along the icy pavement. The city's horde of beggars had crept into the cracks and chinks of the walls, into the gateways and alleys, and the Templars went around with their staves, and roused them, and drove them all down toward the sheep market.

There someone had piled up dung and trash and broken barrels and set a torch to it. In the driving sleet the wretched poor gathered close around the heat and the light. Their very number made a sort of shelter. A few loaves appeared, and some wine. The Templars dismounted, and went in among them, and standing shoulder to shoulder with the beggars and the drunks, they stretched out their hands to the warmth of the flames.

On the embassy to Damascus, Rannulf took Stephen de l'Aigle, Felx van Janke, and Richard le Mesne, and two sergeants to run errands. They all rode to Lake Tiberias to meet the Count of Tripoli, the King's chief legate. The Count was married to the Lady of Tiberias, whose castle stood above the pretty waters of the lake, which was the Sea of Galilee, where Jesus had been a fisherman. The four Templars arrived at the castle in the afternoon, and were taken at once into a little hall, where the Count received them.

Raymond of Tripoli was a slight man, shorter than Rannulf by a full head, his chestnut hair balding up the front of his skull like a retreating wave. When the chamberlain said Rannulf's name, Tripoli's head jerked, and he gave the Templar an angry glare.

"Rannulf Fitzwilliam. I know who you are; I've heard all about you for years, none of it good. Why the Order should send you on this embassy, I cannot know, save it be to insult me." He walked toward Rannulf, his hands behind his back, and the words coming clipped and harsh. "I am insulted. I want to have as little to do with you as possible. We leave in the morning. You can ride rearguard. In Damascus, stay away from me, and keep your mouth shut. Do you hear me?"

"I'm listening," Rannulf said.

The Count's eyes widened; his lips barely moved. "Get out."

Rannulf turned on his heel and walked out of the room; the other three men followed him. The chamberlain sent a page to take them to their quarters. Nobody said anything, until they were in a bare little back room near the stable, and the door shut.

Stephen exploded. "How dare he speak of insult! What's the matter with you? You should have knocked him across the hall!"

"He hates the Order," Rannulf said. The room was dank, even in midsummer, with moss growing along the foot of the wall; the only furniture was a table, two chairs, and a cot without a tick. He said, "I'm not staying here," and opened up the door and went out and around the corner of the wall, to the stable.

The sergeants had taken the Templars' horses into an unused corner of the stable near the hay ricks, and set their packs and saddles against the wall. The sun was going down and the stable was already dark. Rannulf climbed up on the side of the hay rick and flopped open the wooden cover on the window, which let in a little bit of late light. Felx and Richard broke open their packs and took their rolled blankets from their saddles; Stephen prowled restlessly around, still simmering at Tripoli's reception of them.

"I thought he just hated de Ridford."

"Well," Rannulf said. "He's broad-minded." Standing on the side of the rick, he dumped several armsful of hay on the floor, jumped down, and kicked it into a sort of bed.

"Is he going to feed us?" Bear asked. The sergeants had brought in a pail of water, and he squatted down to wash his face.

"Probably not," Rannulf said. "He's tight as a nun's butt, Tripoli." He pointed at one of the sergeants. "Go find the cellarer and get some wine for us."

Stephen said, "What's between him and de Ridford?"

Rannulf sat down on his new bed and reached for his pack. "When de Ridford came to Outremer he was not a Templar. He gave his service to Tripoli, in exchange for which Tripoli promised him the first heiress in the Count's gift. And before long there was an heiress, a de Botrun girl, but a merchant of Genoa offered Tripoli her weight in gold for her, and the Count forgot about de Ridford, and put the lady on the scales." Out of the pack he took a loaf of bread, broke it, and passed around the pieces.

Stephen laughed. Slowly he began settling himself down, finding his saddle and his pack. "Why did he join the Temple? And why did the Temple take him?"

"His uncle was the Seneschal," said Felx. "And Odo likes him, for some reason."

"He kisses Odo's boots," Bear said, out of the gathering darkness. He was lying down, his head on his saddle, his hands folded like an effigy's over his breast.

Rannulf took another loaf from his pack. "Odo used him to handle the King's mother and the rest of the court. Odo had his uses for everybody." The sergeant came back with a small keg of wine and a single wooden cup, and they passed it around them; with the sergeants they made a close circle. "De Ridford loves double dealing."

"Yes," Stephen said. "Like this with you. Why do you trust him?"

"Does it look as if I trust him?" Rannulf leaned back against the wall.

His bad shoulder ached. "I've never been to Damascus. And they have Odo there; I'd like to see him."

"Maybe you can talk the Sultan into taking ransom for him," Stephen said.

Felx gave a grunt of a laugh. "The Sultan would have ransomed him with the others. I promise you, the problem isn't the Sultan. I'm glad we're going—I hear Damascus is beautiful, and rich as Constantinople."

Rannulf snorted. "Nothing is as rich as Constantinople."

"Have you been there?" Stephen asked.

"I came through Constantinople on my way out here, in the year of the earthquakes," Rannulf said. "I was lost in the city for three days. And for two of them, I didn't even care."

"Is it beautiful?" Stephen asked.

"It's dirty, and it's noisy. And beautiful, yes, but mostly it's big, the buildings are huge, the streets are jammed with people, even at the dead of night there is something going on, everywhere. In a single hour you see more than in a whole lifetime anywhere else. It's all lit with lamps, everywhere, so that it's never dark, and the Greeks are like mosquitoes, they're always on you, trying to get another drop of your blood." He shook his head, bringing himself back to this stable, the horses champing and stirring up the straw, and Bear, already asleep, snoring gently in the shadows. Thinking of Constantinople still gave him a quick burst of longing, as if he had seen a vision of a higher life he could not attain. "I almost stayed there, I almost gave up the vow and just stayed." He crossed himself.

Stephen said, "I almost give up the vow every day."

"Every Matins," Felx said. "When the bell rings. Between the first and second stroke."

Rannulf said, "Well, since we're speaking of bells, Compline is going to ring soon, and I have some orders for you. Stay away from Tripoli's men. From now on, no talking on the march. Ride in columns."

"There's four of us," Stephen said. "Six, counting the sergeants."

"Do as I tell you. I'm sending the sergeants back." The wine cup came around again. "I brought enough corn for the horses, but I only have bread for four men. Tripoli will not keep us, and between here and Damascus I think there may be very little for anybody to eat."

The two sergeants murmured, protesting; one said, "We can forage."

"Don't argue with me," Rannulf said. "You're going back. In fact you ought to go back tonight, and save me your breakfast."

One sergeant groaned. The other said, "We need the sleep, Saint, soften up."

"Is that all?" Felx said. "No psalms or sermons?"

"Say your prayers," Rannulf said. Outside the bell was ringing. He locked his hands together and bent his head, and while the others mumbled through their paternosters he pretended he was praying too. He was not praying. He had not prayed in weeks, not since he had fallen in love with the Princess Sibylla.

✦ The Damascus road crossed the high grassy bluffs called the Goulan, the path a deep dusty dent through barren pasture turning into flat desert scrub. From the heights, Rannulf twisted in his saddle and looked back, and at the far edge of the land saw the glitter of the Mediterranean: all the Holy Land lay beneath his eyes, taken in a single look.

Just before noon the next day, they came to a well, a green patch in the dull brown land, where there was a village with a little church. At Tripoli's passage a few minutes earlier the people had come in from their fields and out of their houses to watch, but now they were going back to work. The Templars took over the church, turned the priest out, shut the windows up, locked the doors, hung the sword over the altar, and gathered there to arrange the Mass.

Rannulf said, "I don't want to serve it."

They stood before the altar. Stephen had brought some wine from Tiberias, and was pouring it into one of the church vessels. Bear glowered at Rannulf, "What's the matter with you? Why are you such an old woman lately?"

Stephen said quickly, "I will serve it."

Bear swung toward him. "You know it? All of it?"

"I know it," Stephen said. He laid a loaf of bread on the altar. "Get ready."

Rannulf, Felx, and Bear lined up before the altar, and Stephen began to lead the service, in a clear voice and good churchly Latin. Rannulf kept still, his head down, his hands folded before him. He was at the low end of the row of men, and when the bread came around, and the cup of wine, he put them down. Stephen came along, giving the kiss and the blow, and Rannulf turned away.

The other men prayed on a while; Rannulf went out as soon as he could. Stephen came after him in the churchyard, in a hot temper. "Why am I unworthy?"

Rannulf picked up his sword, which he had left outside the church door. "Nobody's worthy. What do you mean?" He looped the belt over his shoulder and walked across the village common to his horse.

"You would not take the sacrament from me."

"It has nothing to do with you," Rannulf said, surprised. He had left his horse by the well. A crowd of little boys surrounded it; he brushed in through their midst and led the horse away a few steps.

"What is it then?" Stephen asked.

Rannulf mounted his horse. "No concern of yours." They had to catch up with Tripoli, who fortunately did not travel very fast. Felx and Bear were coming out of the church. Stephen mounted and rode up stirrup to stirrup with Rannulf.

"Bear's right, you've been in a fit, lately."

"Then why do you follow me?" Rannulf said, angry.

"God loves madmen. We're hoping a little of it rubs off."

Rannulf growled at him. "You're light as a girl, Mouse." He reined around, headed toward the road, and the other two men got on their horses and followed him. They fell into columns, Stephen on Rannulf's right, and went at a quick trot down the road after Tripoli.

◈ Just after sundown, they caught up with Tripoli at a caravanserai on the desert where there was neither bread nor wine nor fodder for the horses; Tripoli's men were fighting and arguing over a few stems of hay when the Templars rode to the far end of the horse pen, tied their horses to the fence, and fed them of the corn brought in their packs. There was only water to drink, but Rannulf had bread enough to fill the four knights' stomachs. Tripoli's men took note of this, from a distance.

After they had eaten, they said the Compline office, and went to sleep, and before dawn the pounding of drums and the braying of horns brought them leaping up out of their blankets. The sky was still dark but all along the edge of the world the light ran pink and orange and blue, and surrounding the caravanserai were Saracen horsemen, packed together stirrup to stirrup, a wall of gleaming breastplates and fluttering yellow cloaks.

The rapid rhythmic drumming never stopped, a relentless pounding in the ears. Rannulf said, "They've sent an escort. We'll say Matins on the march." He went to saddle his horse.

The Saracen soldiers were Kurdish lancers from the Halka, Saladin's elite troops, armored and greaved, their helmets tufted with yellow plumes, their surcoats of yellow silk. Their magnificent horses wore yellow saddlecloths and yellow tassels on their bridles. They carried lances with six-inch double-edged steel points. The drums beat constantly. The Christians formed their columns, Tripoli and his forty men first, and the Templars at the end, and rode out the gate between two ranks of the lancers, as if between two rows of knives.

When they had gone on a way, a servant came back and demanded that Rannulf attend the Count of Tripoli. With Felx van Janke, he rode up along the side of the column, until he came to the Count, who rode beside a wiry Saracen in the splendid clothes of a prince.

"My lord Emir." Tripoli spoke as if the words tasted bad to him. "This is the Templars' commander, Rannulf Fitzwilliam by name, an ordinary knight, I believe." His gaze skimmed past Rannulf. "I present you to the lord Turanshah Mohammed ibn Ayyub, master of shields and cupbearer to the Sultan."

Rannulf knew this name: it was the Sultan's brother, who was said to be closer to Saladin than any other. Tripoli had spoken French and so he spoke French. "I am honored, my lord."

The slim man on Tripoli's far side watched him steadily, his head at a proud angle. He said, in Arabic, "Only four Templars. Are we slighted?" Lifting his hand, he summoned other men out of the pack behind him. Now he spoke French, accented, and a little kinked. "The Sultan has sent some servants of his, to attend to you while you are his guests." Three men in long robes and turbans circled their horses around the front of the column and fell in beside Rannulf and Felx.

Rannulf said, without enthusiasm, "The Sultan is generous." He saw they would be watched and followed and fenced in the whole of this trip.

"If you are in need of anything, we shall supply it," said the Sultan's brother.

Rannulf said, "The Sultan is generous. We need nothing."

Tripoli coughed. The Saracen princeling said, "By an oversight this inn was not stocked sufficiently with food and fodder—we shall supply you and your horses."

Rannulf said, again, "We need nothing." He was watching Tripoli through the corner of his eye, to see how he took this; the Count's face, sloping down from his high round forehead to his small and pointed chin, showed nothing but his harsh dislike of Rannulf. Rannulf bowed his head slightly. "By your leave, my lord, I shall go back to my position."

"Go," Tripoli said, and Rannulf swung out and with Felx beside him cantered back along the column toward his own men. Half the yellow lancers now rode in a disorderly mass behind the Templars; there would be no falling back on this day's march. The three Saracen servants who were trailing along after him were not soldiers, maybe courtiers, in silk gowns and boots of red leather, riding slim-legged mares with braided manes. Under their sharp, curious eyes the Templars rode along in their marching order, facing forward, saying nothing.

The high road climbed through hills like grey-brown slabs of rock tilting up from the sand. From the pass at the crest of the range, they could see all across the broad flat desert to the blue mountains. In the north one peak wore a snowy cap, like a captive cloud. The river lay like a darker ribbon through the low ground; where the city stood, the stream broke into many separate streams, and the gold of the desert burst into a jewel-like green. They rode on toward it all afternoon. As they drew near, the scent of oranges sweetened the air; the white walls of the city rose from the dense green groves and garden of the oasis. The last sunlight shone on domes and spires, on the tiled gate where they entered in.

Inside the city, a mob waited for them, shouting and restless. The Kurdish drummers set up their steady thrumming but the uproar of the crowd drowned them out. The lancers made a great show of galloping up on either side of the Christians, shielding them from this threat: the arms of the mob waved sticks and stones in the air, and their voices were ugly.

They crossed a square, also packed with angry people; beyond the thickets of their bodies Rannulf could see a vast sprawling building, faced with blue tiles, decorated in swirling designs like writing. The mob began to throw rocks at them, and the Kurds shouted and shook their lances and made short dashes into the mass of the people, to drive them away.

They rode along a covered street, straight as Roman work, which was lined with shops and stalls overflowing with goods: heaps of oranges, stacks of flatbread, and piles of cloth, and other things, the metalwork tools and toys for which the city's craftsmen were famous. Under the tangy scent of the oranges, and the sharp smoky smell of all cities, there was another trace in the air, like rotting flowers.

Across a wide pavement as big as the pavement of the Temple itself, they came to a high white wall, set in it a second gate, a grille of iron fixed with plaques of gold, and here they stopped, and the Sultan him-self met them.

The lancers fell back to form a curved wall of horsemen stretching all across the pavement. In the open archway of the gate, the Sultan sat on a white camel, comparisoned in cloth of gold and scarlet silk. A ser-vant held a parasol over him, although the sun was almost gone. An-other servant, a black man, stood at the shoulder of the camel, and whenever anybody talked, he talked: Rannulf guessed he was changing the French into Arabic. There were two rows of archers on either side of the gate, carrying double-curved horn bows, and at the top of the wall, other soldiers stood half-hidden behind a battlement. Rannulf could not see how they were armed.

Tripoli ranged his company in two ranks before the Sultan; the Bishop of Saint-George with his attendants took the right end of the front line, and Rannulf took his men to the left. From here he got his first good look at al-Nasr al-Malik Salah ad-Din Yusuf ibn Ayyub, Sultan of Cairo and Damascus.

He was slight, like his brother, with large dark eyes, and a quick, forceful way of looking around him, as if he saw everything immediately. He wore a white turban, but Rannulf knew he was bald beneath it, bald as a peeled egg. Remembering how he knew, he smiled.

Tripoli was introducing his company, but the Sultan had seen Rannulf's smile. Stiffly perched on the camel, his hands folded before him, he directed an unblinking look into the ranks of the Templars.

When Tripoli had finished the catalogue of his own men, the Sultan said, "Make these piebald knights known to me."

Tripoli turned, and began the introduction of them, but when he said Rannulf's name, the Sultan waved him silent. Bolt upright as if he might by sheer will make up for his lack of size, the Sultan riveted the knight with his stare.

"Who is this man? He smiles, as if he knows me. I do not recall that I have met him."

He spoke in Arabic, and the servant beside his camel raised his voice to translate, but Rannulf answered him at once. "It was at Ramleh, lord. We did not meet, exactly."

With the eyes of all the Saracens on him, he knew how coarse and harsh he looked, his jerkin frayed along the hems, his beard tangled and untrimmed. He saw how the men around the Sultan were staring at him, hiding smiles behind their hands. But the Sultan seemed to have lost interest in him. Maybe he had forgotten what had happened at Ramleh. With a nod, he let Tripoli go on with his introductions, and after a while the Christians were led into the palace, and there taken to the rooms where they would stay.

◈ "This is beautiful," Stephen said, walking slowly through the sun-washed room. Under his feet lay a cream-colored carpet, trimmed with a border of green and gold. He put one hand out and drew his fingertips across the inlaid wood of a table, polished to a golden glow. "Simply beautiful."

Inside the palace wall, there were gardens and parks; the Saracens had led them to a grove of lemon trees, where the fruit hung ripening. Here, set off from the rest of the palace, was a house of white brick, with three big rooms, and a balcony looking out on the lemon grove.

The three rooms made even the King's hall in his citadel of Jerusalem look like a kennel. Open and airy, they were full of light, and yet shady and cool; carved white screens of stone stood before the windows, so that the sun cast patterns of shadow onto the walls. When the wind blew through the branches of the lemon trees outside the house, the shadows danced and shivered. Plants like tall green fountains stood in the corners of the room. On the table a scatter of agates and carbuncles caught the random sunlight. Stephen's gaze sought out the servant Ali, standing by the door with Rannulf. "Beautiful," he said, again.

He shut his eyes a moment. He was not supposed to think that way. Bear and Felx were wandering around the chambers, handling everything, like bumpkins. Now Bear with a cry pounced on the pretty jewels on the table. Stephen went over to where Rannulf stood with the handsome servant.

Rannulf was saying, "Where are our horses?"

Ali said, "We shall care for your horses. You have no need for them here." He turned, lifting his hand, and in through the door came a parade of other servants, each carrying a basket or a ewer. Stephen's mouth suddenly sprang with water; he smelled roasted meat, and onions, and fresh warm bread.

Beside him, Rannulf said, "I would like to go out to see Damascus. Such as I saw of it coming here seemed beautiful, and interesting."

Ali bowed, more with his eyes than his head; like all the Saracens he clearly thought the Templars were little better than peasants. "I shall ask. But I doubt it very much. You saw, coming here, how the crowd would have torn you to pieces. For your own safety, you must remain inside the palace wall."

He was tall, bonelessly supple, his face quick and lively, with high cheekbones and a full, sensuous mouth. Ever since he joined them on the road here, Stephen had been admiring that mouth, in some imaginative detail. The servant sensed his gaze, and gave him a flash of a smile.

"Well, then," Rannulf said. "Are we allowed to go where we please in the palace?"

Ali inclined his head an inch. "Probably it would be best for you simply to stay here. We shall provide for you. Tomorrow the Sultan will honor you as his guests at a formal banquet, which I believe you will find a feast for all your senses." He gave a faint, wicked sniff, nosing Rannulf, who stank. "We shall provide you with suitable clothing."

Felx came out of the next room. "Saint, there are no bells here."

"I know," Rannulf said. He jerked his thumb at Stephen. "Go in the other room and run those slaves out; we ought to say Vespers." Turning to Ali, he said, "Get out. We're busy now. I'll call you when I need you."

On his way into the next room, where the servants were unpacking the food, Stephen glanced back, and saw how Ali bridled up at the knight's curt orders; at once he thought, Not a servant, that one. He went on and ordered out the other slaves, and in the front room with the other Templars he knelt down and said his prayers.

Turanshah said, "They need a truce, so much is clear. We should get easily what we want from them. Tripoli will be a help; he always is. We must be sure to give him every favor, and watch him every moment. The priest is of no consequence, it seems to me. He is exhausted from the mere journey here, he'll sleep through it all."

The Sultan nodded. After the meeting with the Franks, he had withdrawn to his private chambers, where he could rest a little. He had spent most of the day listening to people from Mosul, where there was an uprising against his authority, and from Baghdad, where the caliph was balking at his suggestions for dealing with Mosul; the matter of the Franks was only one of the several problems that beset him.

Of all his troubles, the Franks pricked deepest. He was fifty years old, and for most of his life he had worked to free Islam from the oppression of the Kingdom of Jerusalem. He imagined himself a surgeon, who would draw the poisoned barb from the body of the faith.

Twice he had attacked them. The first time, learning that all the Franks were busy in the north, he had rushed up out of Egypt with every man he could muster. Sweeping through the country, he had been utterly certain of the victory, until, as he crossed the wadi near Ramleh, he looked up to see a little band of Christians tearing through his whole vast army as if it were a cloud of gnats. The second time, when his advance guard broke the Frankish army on the bank of the Litani River, Jerusalem had been his to seize, and yet he had not been able to close his hands upon it. This baffled him: it was as if he faced some magic spell, strongest where it seemed weak.

"What of the Templars?" his brother Turanshah said. "Who was that you spoke to? How could you have met him at Ramleh?"

"Not the city. He meant the battle we fought, near there, where we might very well have met, he and I, had I not been running so fast."

He remembered that very well, that moment at the wadi near Ramleh, and the black-and-white horseman battering through his guards. He remembered the nightmare struggle to get away, how he had fallen out of the litter, and entangled himself in the drapery, losing his turban. He had looked and felt like a fool, and he had been glad of his life, grateful to Allah for sparing his life, foolish or not.

Now here he was again, that black devil of a knight.

In through a side door, his nephew Ali came into the room, and bowed deeply to him, with a murmur of greeting. The Sultan sat down on a couch, watching his nephew with expectation. "Well, what have you to tell me?"

Ali shrugged his shoulders. "The Templars are stalled and slopped, my lord."

From the other men, even the servants bringing in the meal, a general laugh arose; they liked this condescension. They wanted the Franks to be mere brutes. The Sultan laced his fingers together. "Give me your impression of them."

Ali stood gracefully in the center of the room. He was the Sultan's favorite nephew, for his quick, subtle mind as much as for his personal beauty. He said, "They are as crude and rough as most of their kind. The commander is no better than the rest: he has the manner of a boor, he puts my teeth on edge. One of the other men called him Saint, which must be some kind of joke."

He spoke the name in Frankish. The Sultan translated it into Arabic. "Al-Wali. He does seem an unlikely friend of God."

"Saint," said Turanshah sharply. "I wish I'd known that earlier. This is the Templar who has all the merchants bribed to bring him news."

"Is he?" The Sultan lifted his eyebrows, interested. "What is his office?"

"I don't know. He has no title that I've heard. But he's a spy, that I am sure of."

Ali said, "Tripoli said he was an ordinary knight."

"Yes," Turanshah said. "But Tripoli dislikes him very much, which seems odd—you would think an ordinary knight beneath Tripoli's interest."

The Sultan laughed. "I fear my dear Count dislikes most of his fellow Christians." He fingered his beard. After this, he had still more work: a meeting with the cadi of Damascus, letters to write to Mosul and Baghdad. He nodded to Ali. "Watch them all closely. Especially al-Wali. Don't let him outside the palace compound. We've gone to a great deal of trouble to convince them this is a healthy, bustling city they're visiting, so let's not jeopardize that. I'll see Tripoli alone tomorrow, just for a few minutes, to remind him what great friends we are. As for this Templar, let's see if we can buy him, or failing that, break him a little."

Turanshah grunted at him. "Why—because he made you run at Ramleh?"

"Friends of God should prove their callings," the Sultan said.

"He'll certainly try to leave the palace," Ali said. "He's already asked."

"Good," the Sultan said. "If he does, make him suffer for it." The Sultan touched his beard with his fingers. "Before he leaves Damascus, I want him made a fool of, whether he knows it or not."

✦ In the morning the Saracens brought them fresh robes. Stephen had just gotten up and said his morning office; he was sitting in the big front room in the sun. Bear and Felx were in the next room and Rannulf had disappeared somewhere. The Saracens, Ali at their head, brought in white cotton robes, neatly folded, with sashes of black and yellow, and slippers, like women's shoes. Under Ali's direction the slaves laid all these things out on the table.

Stephen's interest keened. Through the tail of his eye he watched Ali as the tall Saracen ordered the other servants around. The underlings went away into the next room, where the food was kept, and the other goods. Ali lingered. He said, "Perhaps you would care to put on cooler clothing. The day will be extremely hot."

Stephen lifted his head, and met the other man's eyes. At once his loins tightened; he saw the same quickening interest in Ali, the same reckless flicker of excitement. He made himself calm. He was not supposed to feel like this.

He said, "We wear only what the Order gives us." He smiled at Ali. "If you were in Jerusalem, would you wear a Templar robe?"

Ali lowered his eyes, as if to hide his thoughts. His long brown hands were ringed in gold. "In Jerusalem we all go as pilgrims, do we not? But we are not in Jerusalem. This is Damascus, where it will be very hot today." He waved his hand at the table. "Where you would be more comfortable dressed as we dress."

Stephen stood up, his blood on fire; he caught the outstretched hand. "I want to be comfortable," he said, and leaned forward and kissed Ali's full-lipped, passionate mouth.

Ali pulled violently away from him. His black eyes remained fixed on Stephen's. In a low voice, he said, "This cannot be. We are enemies, you and I."

Stephen said, "I don't want that. I don't believe it." He reached out again, and caught Ali by the hand, and again kissed him, and this time the other man returned the kiss, and his arm went around Stephen's waist.

Stephen murmured, triumphant. He slid his free hand down between them, but the Damascene drew back.

"Not here," he said. "Can you get away?"

"Yes. Maybe." Stephen still held his hand, and wanted to kiss him again, but then someone called out, in the next room. He realized how close the others were.

Ali said, "Later." He turned, pulling his hand out of Stephen's, and went swiftly away.

Stephen stood where he was, still savoring the kiss. He had an erection. He turned around, looking out through the screens into the windblown green murmuring of the lemon grove, remembering where he was. He wanted Ali, but he was seeing other things, all around this, like shadows in the white glare of his lust.

He went out through the next room to the balcony, and leaned against the rail; below him the lemon grove covered the gentle downward slope. He thought of his vow, and wondered where Rannulf was.

He shut his eyes. The scent of the lemon grove tingled in his nostrils. It wasn't as if he were in Jerusalem. This wasn't really anyplace; he felt as if it were noplace, a hole in the world. As if what he did here wasn't really happening.

Even as he thought this, he felt it all slipping away from him, all the surfaces of things, all the meanings, sliding and slipping away.

He looked down into the lemon grove again. Now he saw Rannulf, walking through the trees. The black-haired Norman went off toward the outer wall. A few moments later, a Saracen stole furtively along the path after him.

Here, not even Rannulf knew what was going on. Stephen wiped his hand over his face. His body sang with a half-controlled excitement. His body was real. Ali's body was real. He turned and went back into the pleasure house.

✦ The palace was built in concentric rings, each circle higher and more elegant, each girdled by a wall; in the midafternoon the knights went up through a gate, and across the gardens there and through another gate, to the great hall, where they were to be the guests of the Sultan at a feast.

This hall was as big as the refectory of the Temple, with columns of veined brown marble holding up the vaulted ceiling. The walls were painted in amazing designs of flowers and birds, and the floor was glossy polished stone. They sat at a horseshoe of tables so wide the people at the other end were out of earshot. When the four Templars went in, on the open floor in the middle of the tables, a dozen girls were dancing, dressed only in sheer silk, and not much of that.

Bear, walking behind Rannulf, gave a yelp of outraged chastity, and Felx muttered something that was not a prayer. Rannulf got a momentary eyeful of a bouncing, pink-nippled breast and tore his gaze away. His temper jerked up short. With the other Templars he sat down behind the table, in one arm of the horseshoe, and he turned and looked up at the Sultan's dais.

There on the dais, among his officers, the Sultan was staring back at him.

Neither of them looked away. Rannulf felt the hair rising on the back of his neck. A red flush colored the Sultan's cheeks. Beside him, one of the other Saracens, the brother, had seen this crossed stare, and was looking from one to the other. On Rannulf's left Stephen moved, suddenly, with a creak of the furniture. He had noticed it too. Rannulf swiveled his head forward again, toward the dancing girls, and aimed his gaze down at the table.

Stephen said, "I didn't know they jiggled like that."

"Shut up," Rannulf said. The music played with his ears. He wanted to get up and leave, he wanted to move, to shake off the assaults of temptation, drill his body back into obedience, but he had to sit here and be attacked. The servants were constantly bringing more dishes, and taking away others, so that the table was a shifting pattern, different colors, different shapes of platters. The slaves moved around him, brushing up against him, leaning past him with bowls of sugared nuts, sweets smelling of cinnamon and clove, skewered meats dripping their warm juices. He ate only the bread. Even when they brought figs and dates, which he loved, he ate only the bread.

The other men were yielding. In low voices, they exclaimed at the flavors of the food, and they were peering at the women, and bobbing back and forth with the music. Richard Bear said, "Why are they watching us so hard?"

Felx rumbled a laugh. "Maybe they've never seen Templars so close. Saint, is it true the water here is poisonous?"

Rannulf said, "I have never been to an oasis where the people weren't half-sick all the time. Drink the wine." He reached for his cup. The Saracens were not supposed to drink wine, but they were providing it for the Franks in endless measure. Up on the Sultan's dais, where Tripoli sat, a burst of unrestrained laughter rose. Midway along the horseshoe of the table, the Bishop of Saint-George had fallen asleep.

Stephen said, "What's next, hashish and poppy-juice? I have to piss."

"Go," Rannulf said.

Stephen left. No longer hungry, Rannulf brushed his hands together; a servant brought him a napkin. The soft cloth smelled like flowers. He dropped it instantly to the table, so alive to these temptations that merely smelling flowers seemed to him to be a sin. The music ended, and the girls went off through the curtained arch at the foot of the hall.

"My lord Count." The black man had come out to translate for the Sultan. He had the sleek, full face and feathery voice of a eunuch. "May you enjoy your visit to Damascus, the most beautiful and ancient of all cities, from whose clay God shaped Adam. While you are here let us set before you all joys and delights, and if there should be anything you desire that we can provide, you need only speak to have it."

Tripoli stood up. In his own high, reedy voice, and his own Arabic, he said his answer, just as ritual. "May Allah preserve the most excellent Sultan of Damascus and Cairo!" He went on like that for a while. The black man sat close to the Sultan, unnecessary. Rannulf wondered where the eunuch had learned French.

Felx said, "What's wrong with him, anyway?"

Bear turned and smirked at him, obviously pleased to know something Felx didn't. "He's been gelded."

The big Deutschlander's wooly yellow eyebrows arched up; his lips pursed. "And that turns them black?" he said, innocently.

Rannulf glanced over at him and laughed, and Bear, suddenly ruddy, laughed also; Felx licked his lips. He was drinking hard, and eating uninhibitedly of all the fine food. Sitting in place, he bounced. Tripoli had done with his speech, and now the black man stood up, and spoke French; around the sleeping Bishop, his servants hastily jostled him and whispered him awake.

"To the Bishop of Saint-George, welcome to Damascus, where Saint George is buried, where Saint Paul first came face to face with his destiny, may your visit here magnify your faith and ours."

The Bishop groaned and struggled to his feet. He had no Arabic and had to speak French, and the black eunuch sat close by the Sultan and changed the words for him.

When the Bishop was done, the black man turned toward the Templars.

"To the warriors of the Temple of Jerusalem, also, let us offer the hand of greeting. Welcome to the oldest and greatest of all cities, mother of Constantinople and Cairo, Bokhara and Baghdad, where all men mingle in peace, and do the works of God."

Rannulf had no use for this. "Thank you," he said. "I'm very glad to be here."

Caught short, the rest of the table only stared at him a moment in silence, and then among the Sultan's company a few smiles appeared. They thought him simple. Probably they were right. The Sultan leaned forward slightly.

"You speak the language of the Koran quite well."

"Not really," Rannulf said. He stood, as he always did when a lord spoke to him; he clasped his hands behind his back. "Marketplace Arabic."

"Do you know the Koran?"

"Not at all. Some phrases, nothing else."

"How well do you know your own Bible?"

"Little enough. I am not a man for books."

"These are more than mere books, certainly—the roots of faith. Do you love your faith?"

The Templar's head rose. "Sultan, this talk leads nowhere. All that matters to me is the war. To you, also, I think, nothing matters except the war, and you are on one side, and I on the other—I have what you want: what's the use of talking about anything else?"

In a rising babble of other people's voices, the Sultan said, smoothly, "What's the use of talking about that?" In the thicket of his beard his teeth showed. "You came here for some reason; what is the Temple's end in this?"

"You hold one of my brothers prisoner, Odo de Saint-Amand, I want to see him."

The Sultan looked down and then up again, nodding with his eyes. "Certainly."

"We will support a truce, if one can be made between you and the King."

"I suppose I should be pleased at the reassurance, given your well-known treachery in such matters."

"We obey God," Rannulf said. "Not pieces of paper."

The Count of Tripoli spoke in a loud clear voice. "This is not the place to discuss policy, my lord Sultan, my lord Templar."

"I beg my lord the Count's pardon," Rannulf said, and sat down again.

"What was that about?" Bear asked, his eyes wide. He spoke no Arabic.

Rannulf shrugged. "He will let me see Odo."

"It didn't seem that affable," Bear said.

Just beyond him, Felx was leaning forward to look at Rannulf. "No. What's going on here, Saint?"

"Just talking," Rannulf said. The black spokesman was up again, performing, in French, another long speech about the wonders of Damascus, where Abel and Nimrod were buried, and John the Baptist's head, which perhaps explained the dancers.

Rannulf cast a wide look around the hall again. The servants were pattering around with their burdens of food and drink, more than anyone could eat, as if they had so much of everything they never thought of saving it. Yet he remembered, coming here, how the hostelry had not had meat, or corn for the horses.

He wanted to get out into the city. That seemed impossible; guards walked the outside wall, and they were following him wherever he went. He was a prisoner here. In the open space between the tables two jugglers were tossing up a whirl of oranges. By the door another man waited, his face painted like a puppet, his hands full of sticks. Stephen had not come back. Rannulf lowered his eyes and sat there with his hands on his knees, bored, waiting for the dinner to end, so that he could go do something more interesting.

✦ Stephen went out of the hall through a side arcade, into the darkness of a garden. The night was warm, the air still and heavy; the peppery scent of blown flowers reached his nose. He made water, and stood a moment, in the dark, not knowing what to do, and then Ali came up beside him.

They said nothing. Silently they went off side by side, down through the overgrown garden, and into a stand of trees. Stephen's heart hammered, feeling too large for his chest; his mouth was dry, and his palms sweating. He followed Ali through the little wood, where they came to a pond of water, hidden away inside the hedge of the trees.

They stopped at the edge of the water, and still neither of them spoke; Ali began to take off his clothes. His face burning, his hands trembling, Stephen kept his gaze on the water, and got out of his jerkin, his boots, his shirt, and his leggings; he took off his close-fitting lambskin drawers, part of his Templar vow, that he was never supposed to remove. Still without looking at Ali, still without speaking, he waded out into the water.

Ali followed him. Thigh-deep in the water, Stephen reached his arms out before him into the dark and dove.

The water enveloped him. Warm and soft, it rippled over his skin like a thousand playful fingers; he swam down into its embrace until his outstretched hands touched the rock bottom of the pond, and then he shot upward toward the surface, turning over as he swam, the water streaming over his chest and between his thighs and through his hair.

A wild exhilaration filled him. He wanted to shout, to scream. His skin tingled; his blood pulsed like a hot wind in his veins. He broke through the surface of the pond, his mouth open, gulping air. Ali was beside him. They plunged under the surface again, side by side, their bodies coiling together like snakes, slick and taut. Stephen caught Ali around the waist and held him; they struggled together in a delicious combat, their arms wound around one another. With a low laugh Ali twisted away, and Stephen pursued him, caught him at the edge of the pool, and took him there, half in and half out of the water. Afterward, he held Ali pinned under him for a while, his chest against Ali's back, and his face buried in the other man's hair. His whole body sang.

Ali murmured to him, and Stephen moved back, letting him go; as their bodies separated the air rushed in between them, suddenly cool on his skin. He wheeled back into the pond, diving into the deep caress of the water; he tumbled and twisted in the water, delighting in himself, in his body, in being only a body, soulless, guiltless, careless, alive. At the far side of the pond Ali caught up with him, and put one arm around him, and in his ear whispered, "Now it's my turn."

Stephen pulled away, still caught in the giddy glory of release, but Ali held him, stronger than he had realized, and forced him down under him. Stephen flung his arms out, and got two handfuls of the tall grass growing at the edge of the water, and yielded, and the yielding was as sweet as the conquest.

⬥ They lay side by side on the grass. Stephen was loathe to speak; he wanted to keep the purity of this moment, so edged with problems. Ali touched him.

"Do you do this in Jerusalem?"

Stephen laughed. He felt himself shrinking back inside himself. Rolling onto his side, he reached out and stroked the Saracen's face. "No. My vow forbids it. If I were caught I'd be in a lot of trouble."

"Then—" Ali caught hold of his hand. "I am the first?"

Stephen laughed at that, at the hopeful note in the other man's voice; a rush of tenderness flooded him. He felt as if he had known this other man all his life. Had waited for him, all his life. He said, "No. Not the first." He pulled Ali's hand toward him and kissed it. "I should go back. I don't want them wondering where I am."

He could hear Ali smiling, in the way his voice sounded. "My dear, they are busy until very late, and if all goes as it should, they will be in no way able to wonder about you." He leaned over Stephen and kissed him. Stephen shut his eyes. In a few days, he would go back to the Temple, this would be over. He pushed that off the edge of the world. Bending his head, he kissed Ali's shoulder.

⊕ In the late evening when Rannulf and the other Templars finally staggered back to the house in the lemon grove, Stephen was already there, alone, and wearing one of the long Saracen robes. Just inside the threshold, Rannulf dumped Felx on the floor and left him where he landed. Bear had stopped singing, at least, but now he was crying, and he wobbled mournfully away into the next room, a flask of wine in each hand. Rannulf stared at Stephen.

"Enjoying yourself?"

"I felt sick, so I left the palace, and came back here," Stephen said. "I was tired. There were all those women."

"Yes, women being a real weakness of yours."

"What exactly are you getting at?"

Rannulf said, "Come out on the balcony, it's hot in here." He went across the next room, dark and empty, to the little overhang above the lemon grove. Stephen followed him.

"What happened, after I left?"

Rannulf leaned on the railing of the balcony; even in the dark he could see the men down under the trees, watching them. "Nothing much. They are trying to feed us to death, and with Felx and Bear, it may work."

Stephen said, "Well, maybe we should just relax and be raped, you know, Rannulf. They do say Eden was in Damascus."

Rannulf said nothing; his hands closed into fists. Whatever Stephen had done, it hadn't been rape. He forced his hands open; keep your temper, he thought. Don't think, just watch.

"Who were you with?" he said.

Beside him, Stephen shifted his weight, his foot rasping on the balcony floor. "What do you mean? I just—"

"Don't lie to me. You were with one of the Saracens." He swung around toward the redheaded knight, pieces clicking together in his mind. "Ali."

Stephen jerked, as if a dart had hit him. Rannulf nodded at him. "Yes: Ali. I knew he was too smooth to be a servant. He's a spy. You know that? Everything you tell him will go straight to the Sultan."

In the dark he could not see Stephen's face, only his shape, indistinct in the flowing Saracen clothes. Stephen's voice came harsh out of this shadow.

"You see everything cramped and narrow and full of hate, Rannulf. Everybody is your enemy, or somebody to be used."

"Will you spy on him for me?"

"No!" Stephen took a step away from him; he lifted one hand, fisted. "This isn't that way, Rannulf. This has nothing to do with you, or Jerusalem, or the Temple, or the war. Stay out. Understand me?" He banged the fist lightly on Rannulf's chest. "Stay out." He turned and walked back into the hot, perfumed air of the pleasure house.

Rannulf watched him go, morose. The Saracens seemed one step ahead of him, and they were peeling away his men like husks; in front of him he saw nothing but traps. Standing in front of the railing, he thought of saying the Compline office, but the will to do it would not come to him. God would give him no help; God watched to see how he did. God perhaps had given him up. He was tired, but loathe to go inside the pleasure house, and instead he lay down on the balcony, pillowed his head on his arm, and went to sleep in the open air.

Turanshah said, "The King of Jerusalem is sick, perhaps close to death. Sometimes blind. Yet he still commands these men, he still has power over them. He must be an amazing fellow."

The Sultan came back into the middle of the room, shedding his long coat and turban. A servant came up quickly with a cup of sherbet for him, and he sat down near the lamp and refreshed his mouth and tongue with the cool drink. "The King of Jerusalem is a great adversary, a sickly boy with the soul of a lion. May Allah rot his bones. What about the Templar?"

"Aren't you giving too much importance to this knight?"

"Importance. The Templars are the firebrands of the Franks. I have seen, and you also, how a dozen of them will charge without any hesitation at thousands of our men, and how sometimes that charge puts thousands of our men to rout—as if they cast some spell over us! As if they were a black wind rising from hell. Yet I have met Templars, now and then, and they seem ordinary men, just ordinary men. This one is different. This one, perhaps, is the key, and I want to find out what that key opens."

Turanshah said flatly, "He was certainly unpleasant enough at the reception. He needs a whipping."

"Good. Let's give him one. Ali?"

Ali was standing on the far side of the room, half-turned away, as if he had no interest. He did not answer; the Sultan had to say his name a second time before he turned.

"Yes, Uncle."

"You weren't at the reception."

"I hate crowds," Ali said. He came into the middle of the room, his chin up, and his hands together.

"How are the Templars behaving themselves? Are they accepting our generous hospitality in the proper spirit of not bothering to look deeper?"

Ali gave a brisk shake of his head. His voice was crisp. "Not at all. Their captain is snooping all around. Clearly he means to get into the city somehow. I suggest you watch the wall."

"I told you he's a spy," Turanshah said, with satisfaction. "I hope he does go over the wall. We're ready for him; we'll give him a lesson."

The Sultan was still watching Ali, suspicious; in his nephew's manner he saw that Ali was concealing something. Then another idea overtook him. He gave his attention to Turanshah.

"Why wait for him to step into the trap? Surely we can lure him in."

"Oh, certainly." His brother smiled at him.

"Good," the Sultan said. He remembered Ramleh, again, and the knight battering at him. "Let's do that. Let him see we are not to be toyed with. Give him some room. Let him go over the wall. And then break him for it."

annulf," Odo said. "What are you doing here? I never expected to see you again." He rolled over; when he moved, he dragged after him the heavy links of his chain. Yet he smiled as easily as ever, a gleam in his pale eyes. "Do the Saracens know they've let the snake into the fishpond?"

Behind Rannulf the door shut. At the sound of the latch closing on him, his stomach clenched. He crossed the rush-strewn dungeon, stooping under the sloping ceiling, and squatted on his heels beside his officer.

"They are suspicious. They're watching me every step."

"Don't cross them," Odo said. "I don't want company."

The Master of the Temple of Jerusalem lay on a tick of straw, a blanket covering him. His hair straggled around his face and down over his shoulders, and his skin was pale as fishmeat; the bottom half of his body seemed not to move much.

"Are you all right?" Rannulf asked.

Odo lifted one shoulder. "I live."

Rannulf twitched the blanket back. Odo wore only a long shirt. On his wrists there were iron bracelets, and ropes of chain led from them, under the blanket, to a ring in the wall. His right ankle was chained, also, but his left leg Rannulf did not see at first.

"What's this metal?" He knew the other Frankish prisoners had been kept like guests, not criminals.

"Oh. I annoyed the Sultan. Something about a nephew." Odo pulled the blanket over himself again, but not before Rannulf saw that his left leg, half-hidden under the shirt tail, was withered and twisted like a dry stick, no bigger than the bones.

"I broke it, in the battle," Odo said. "It's never healed. God's will. You were right, Saint. We should not have charged them. I'm glad you got away, and I hope de Ridford died."

"No," Rannulf said. "He's back in Jerusalem."

Odo gave a shake of his head. He looked much older, the mass of his chest and shoulders sinking below his bones, his skin sagging from his neck; he lay there in the wreckage of himself. His face was clear and calm. "When we are all cold as stones he will be quick and making trouble."

Rannulf shrugged away de Ridford. He could not take his eyes from Odo's face. "There's some talk of getting you ransomed."

"No," Odo said. "That's why I am here. They wanted to trade me for some sprig of the Sultan's, held hostage at Margat, and I refused. I am a Knight Templar and not a unit of exchange. I miscalculated. Now I am suffering for it. That seems fair enough to me."

"To me also," Rannulf said.

"And with this leg, I could not fight again, anyway."

"Probably not," Rannulf said.

"Say prayers for me. And before you go, Saint, shrive me."

Rannulf gave a slight start. He knew at once he could not refuse. He turned his head to one side, and put his hand up between them. "Confess, then, brother."

The Master spoke in a low voice. "Forgive me, Jesus, for I have sinned." He gave a catalog of his slips and crashes, all as ordinary as any other man's.

"Are you contrite?" Rannulf asked.

"I am heartily sorry for having offended God, who made me and deserves all my love."

"Then I absolve you." Rannulf made the sign of the Cross over him. His mouth was dry. He felt like a thief, stealing into God's place, hearing with God's ears. Odo seemed to him already in a state of grace.

He said, "Father, give me a blessing."

The Master of the Jerusalem Temple gave a growl of a laugh, and sank back down on the straw. "This is your blessing. Fight this bastard to your last breath. And tell my brothers how I have fared." He turned his face away and shut his eyes. The chains clicked and ticked together. Rannulf got up and went to the door, and the turnkey, waiting on the other side, opened it for him at once.

✤ The dungeon was in a tower on the far side of the palace compound; three guards escorted him back to the pleasure house, walking him briskly along in their midst, letting him see nothing. The path crossed the brow of a slope, and from the top of it, for a moment, he could see down over the distant wall into the white clutter of the city; out of the sprawl of roofs and treetops rose the needle towers of the mosques. He stretched his neck, trying to see more, and the guard behind him put a hand on his back and pushed him on.

"Keep going!"

"A beautiful city," he said. "I wish I could see it."

"Oh, certainly, certainly." The guard on his left laughed. "You wish you could see Damascus. And it is beautiful, but not for you, faithless one."

They went on down through the lemon grove to the pleasure house. Rannulf's steps slowed; those white rooms were a prison to him. Music drifted out of the window, pipes, tambourines, a little drum. He heard Bear call out in a laughing voice.

Two of the guards went off. The third, the one who had spoken to him, lingered by him. Rannulf stopped on the terrace outside the pleasure house, loathe to go in.

The guard said, quietly, "You want to see Damascus?"

Rannulf's head swiveled toward him. "Yes."

"Do you have any money?"

He had no money; but this was promising. "Yes."

"I will help you get over the wall," the guard said. "For dinars."

Rannulf looked around them, to see if anyone was watching. He said, "How many dinars?"

The guard said, "Bring me all you can. In a little while, go down to the wall, and wait there. I will find you." He moved off at once, to join the other guards, sitting down on a bench by the door. Rannulf went into the pleasure house, excited.

At once he knew there were women here. His senses quickened, every nerve stirring. He went into the big sunlit front room; the musicians were all women, wearing almost nothing, and two other girls were going around the place, putting out baskets of fruit and sweets. Felx van Janke stood by the door, smiling. When Rannulf appeared, he pulled the smile in, but the lascivious glint remained in his eyes.

He said, "Did you see Odo?" But his mind was not on Odo. Through the corner of his eye he was looking across the room.

Rannulf said, "I saw him." He could hear Bear's voice, in the side chamber, and in there with him a light laugh sounded.

"Well, that's good," Felx said, not listening much.

Rannulf said, "Who brought these women in here?"

Felx shrugged. "I don't know. What are you going to do about it?"

"Me? Nothing." Rannulf crossed himself. "I'm hot. I think I'll change my clothes." He went on across the sunny room to the far doorway.

This led into the room where the servants kept food and drink and things to serve it all in, and where they had put the cotton djellabahs they had brought for the Templars to wear. At the far end of the long dim room three or four Saracen girls were gathered, talking among themselves, and giggling. When Rannulf came in, they hushed, and stared at him.

He ignored them, or tried to; they were soft, round-limbed, young and tender, they made his palms itch. He went to the cupboard, took off his Templar clothes, all but his drawers, and put on one of the soft clean white robes. He pulled his boots off, but he would not wear the slippers. He told himself he would walk his feet to blisters before he put them into shoes like that. Barefoot, he went out again to the front room.

Felx was sitting on the cushioned couch, and a slender girl with long black hair was holding out a cup to him. The tall Saracen called Ali stood in the doorway. Rannulf went up to him.

"We are sworn to avoid women."

The Saracen smiled at him, his eyes glittering. "They are merely servants. You must have servants to attend you."

"Then I am going out into the garden," Rannulf said. "Am I permitted that?"

Ali nodded with his eyes, looking down, then up; Rannulf had seen the Sultan do this; he saw much of the Sultan in Ali. The Saracen said, "The garden and the lemon grove are permitted you."

"Thank you," Rannulf said, and went out.

✠ In among the lemon trees, he stopped, and looked back toward the pleasure house. No one was following him. Two of the guards remained in front of the door but the one who had spoken to him was gone. He rubbed his hands down the front of the djellabah and the soft touch of the cotton startled him: the cloth caressed his skin; it seemed sinful just to be wearing it.

He stood under the lemon trees a while, patient, watching the pleasure house. They wanted him to go down to the wall, but he saw no purpose in doing what they wanted. They had given him some freedom, which he meant to use. He settled down on his heels beside the lemon tree, waiting for his chance.

✠ Inside the pleasure house, a girl gave a long voluptuous scream. Ali's nose wrinkled in disgust, and he moved off to the far edge of the terrace. He glanced around, toward the lemon grove, wondering where the Templar captain had gone; by now he should be under the wall, taking the bait.

From the pleasure house came a crash, like glass breaking, and the music suddenly picked up again. Somebody whooped. The Kurdish guards were peering in the door; one went to the next window, and looked in over the sill.

Stephen came out the door, moving fast, as if he were escaping. He wore the long white djellabah, sashed in red silk; he walked with a long-legged, leonine saunter. It was this in him that had first drawn Ali to him, this animal grace, and now Ali grew keen at the sight of him, excited. Stephen crossed the terrace, coming toward him, and as he walked, he lifted his head, and their eyes met, and Stephen smiled. Ali moved toward him, his hands out.

"Let's get away from here," Stephen said.

"Certainly. Would you like to see the rest of the palace?"

"You shouldn't trust me," Stephen said. "What if I'm a spy?"

Ali laughed. They started off together, climbing the path of white stones toward the gate in the next wall. Ali held Stephen by the hand. "You are too noble, my dear. I know you're not a spy. But don't you want to know who I am?"

"No," Stephen said, and looked away.

Ali laughed again, not understanding. "Well, then, I won't tell you. But I insist on the pleasure of showing you one of the most beautiful places on earth."

He thought, when Stephen had seen the palace, he would come to know without having to be told who Ali was.

They strode away across the grassy slope, studded with gardens of half-blown roses. Stephen looked avidly all around him, his eyes wide. Ali held his hand, as if tethering him down. He wanted to talk, but he could see that Stephen shied from talking. As if that gave Ali too much.

When Stephen had seen all the palace, when he knew who Ali was, he would be halfway won.

They were coming to the wall, rising through a tangle of vines; a row of cypress screened part of it, where a path lay beaten through the high seeding grass. Ali led Stephen in through the grass, behind the cypress trees. There was a little door in the wall, unguarded. While Ali opened it, Stephen turned, looking out through the green fence of the cypress.

"What is it?" Ali asked.

"I thought I saw somebody following us," Stephen said.

Ali grunted, amused. "What are you afraid of? This is my place. Here I go wherever I please, and you too, if you are with me." He pushed the door open, and let Stephen go through ahead of him.

They came out at the bottom of another long upslope; at the top of it was a large building, the upper-story windows shaped in pointed arches, the ground story rimmed by an arcade, its roof of red tile, its open side of pointed arches. The slope between was terraced into gardens.

Ali said, "This is the kitchen garden, when of course it is planted, and up there are the factories and kitchens and storerooms." He looked at Stephen, expecting to see him impressed, but Stephen was looking back through the half-open doorway again.

"Where is Rannulf?" he said.

His temper nudged, Ali frowned at him. "I assure you, your captain is being very adequately dealt with." By now the surly Templar would be over the wall, would be in the hands of Turanshah's men, suffering as he deserved. "Come along, Stephen, let's enjoy this together. Forget about your companions for a while." He reached out and took hold of Stephen's hand, and Stephen came willingly after him.

✦ Rannulf slipped through the half-open door and stood at the foot of a climbing slope, neatly layered into broad ledges, on which grew rows of vegetables, now all gone to weeds. Stars of mullein covered the ground between the stalky-bolted cabbages; the flowering carrots stood waist-high to him. He went up from ledge to ledge, wondering where all the food for this great palace was coming from, because it certainly was not coming from this garden.

He had waited a long while before he came through the hidden door, to let Ali and Stephen get well ahead of him. Now this whole slope seemed deserted. Coming on a path he found an old hoe, and picked it up and carried it along, as if he were a workman. A little way on, he acquired a lantern also, and a rake. He saw no one, not until he had climbed up through the garden, and come to a terrace, bordered in thick green hedges. On the far side of the terrace rose a two-story building, its windows cut gracefully in loops, like hands meeting at the fingertips. In the shade of the porches, two Kurdish guards stood with their lances cocked out to the side.

Between them and Rannulf at the terrace's edge was a throng of people, wiry sun-blackened men in loincloths, and women swathed to the eyes, balancing great heaps of white laundry on their heads. Along the front of the terrace, big cauldrons boiled, and the women were washing linens and drawing them out again, and then spreading them to dry on the hedges. The men were clustered in the shade, doing nothing but talking.

Rannulf wanted talk. Carrying his tools, his servile head bowed, he went in among them, and sat down at the side of the terrace, where there was a stone wall. The men were eating lentils and onions out of a common bowl; one of them was bragging about bringing in a load of fruit all the way from the Jezireh.

"I knew I would get a very fine price, and I have, but it has put some fear into me. In Allah's name, I have not seen this city so empty, not in all my life."

"You should have been here when they brought the Franks in. We all had to go out and yell and wave our arms, so that it looked as if there were people in the streets. We got a penny apiece, and sore throats."

"Is there plague along the Tigris?" someone asked.

"None in my village, let praises rise to Allah. Where has everybody gone from here? They cannot all be dead."

Several voices rose at once, lamenting. Rannulf crept in among these men, following the aroma of the lentils. No one heeded him. They were used to strangers coming in from the country to make their fortunes feeding the palace, and here his black hair and eyes were a help to him. He kept a careful watch on the Kurdish guards in the arcade.

"Ay, ay," said the man directly in front of him. "The Sultan himself will flee Damascus, when he has dealt with the Franks. Spit on them! The plague is our punishment for not driving them into the sea."

Rannulf had come within reach of the bowl. He murmured under his breath, not the Arabic blessing, but close, and dipped his fingers into the brown mess of the lentils, and began to eat. He sat on his heels, as they did. He ate as they did, with the first two fingers of his right hand only. Their voices fed his ears.

"Have you seen the Franks?"

"Have we seen them. Have we seen them. They are ugly as ogres, with their long teeth and blue skin, and their watery eyes. I believe those who say they are hatched from eggs laid in dunghills."

"The Sultan will get the best of them."

"Ay, ay, would I had such faith."

"I have heard some among them are Templars."

"Templars!" Across the bowl a hand rose in the sign against evil.

"Yes! And that one is no less than Ithiel himself."

The talk hushed, a little. One man gave a loud laugh. "Faugh. There is no Ithiel."

"My cousin who carries a lance for Taqi ad-Din has seen him with his own eyes. The tip of his spear sends forth lightning, and wherever his black horse treads the land is sown with corpses."

"There is no Ithiel." One loud voice, another laugh. For a while no one spoke. Rannulf licked his fingers, his belly full, and his ears full.

"Soft, now, here comes dear Ahmed."

Rannulf looked up, and swiftly lowered his eyes again. His muscles tightened. A lancer in a tasseled helmet was strutting across the terrace toward them.

The men around him sent up a chorus of greetings. "Ahmed!" "Allah's blessings on you, valiant soldier!" Their heads bobbed in brisk little bows. The Kurd stopped in front of them.

"I see you're all keeping busy, as usual. What a pack of sluggards!"

"No, no, Ahmed, it's just so hot, that's all."

"Blessings on you, Ahmed!"

"Valiant soldier!"

Rannulf bowed his head up and down like a fool, with the rest of them; if they caught him spying, they would chain him to a wall, like Odo, and he did not think he could bear that as well as Odo did. He wondered if he had long teeth, and watery eyes.

The Kurd moved on. Behind his back, the talk changed. "Look at him strut!"

"Yes, if only he fought so well against the Franks."

"The lazy sack of shit."

Rannulf drew back toward the wall again, keeping his eyes down, and his ears open.

"What would he do, if he came face to face with Ithiel?"

◈ Ali said, "What do you think?" He beckoned to the servants, who came and moved away the remains of their dinner.

"It's magnificent," Stephen said.

He looked around this room again, still absorbing the details of its beauty. They had walked all over the palace, seeing everything, before they came here, to Ali's own apartment. This was the best place of all, a warm quiet room, so simply furnished it seemed almost severe, the long straight lines of the low wooden tables, the fluid shapes of the lamps, the geometric red clay tiles of the floor; in one corner there stood a leafy little tree in a pot, confronting all this order with its welcome, anarchistic profusion. Stephen admired this room with all his heart.

"Rannulf says Damascus isn't as fine as Constantinople, but I don't believe it."

"Is it much like Paris?"

"Paris is a dump," Stephen said, and Ali burst out laughing.

"You're wonderful, Stephen. I'm having a wonderful time with you."

Stephen lay back on his side on the couch. "Yes, I'm very happy."

They spoke French; Stephen had attempted a little Arabic, once or twice, but Ali had laughed at him. He did not want Ali to laugh at him. They had been together almost the whole day, and he had seen splendid halls and fountains, gardens, a library, a blue-tiled bathhouse, the Sultan's own little mosque like a jewel made of white stone. They had made love on the grass. The food had been delicious, apricots and lamb, little onions stuffed with pine nuts, fruit poached in spiced syrup, and even the wine was fair enough. In a few moments, he intended to make love again.

"How long have you been a Templar?" Ali asked.

"I came out here last year."

"Did you fight at Ramleh?"

Stephen shook his head. He wanted to stay off this line of talk; he had to keep this separate from that other life. But Ali was intent, his eyes sharp, his body tilted forward under the elegant drapery of his robe.

"What about the battle last autumn? We call it the Gift of the River, you probably have some other name for it."

"The Litani River," Stephen said. He reached for the wine cup; he was slightly drunk. "God punished us for our sins, whatever they happened to be at the time." He looked into the cup, swirling the wine around the inside. "You know, I had an old aunt who said she could tell the future from the patterns the wine makes on the inside of the cup."

"Did she. How curious." Ali with his fingertip circled the bone of Stephen's ankle. He was much less interested in the future than in the past. "Fortunate that you escaped that battle, where we made a harvest of your kind."

Stephen watched the wine slick the surface of the cup. "God willed it." He moved his bare foot away from Ali.

The Saracen reached out and gripped his ankle. "Very true. God wills that we—whose cause is righteous—shall triumph over you."

Stephen said, "I don't want to talk about this, Ali."

"Why not? Because you will have to admit to yourself that I'm right?" Ali's eyes burned. He let go of Stephen's ankle and stretched out his hand, palm up. "Please, Stephen. I like you very much. I don't want to see you destroyed, as surely we will destroy you and all your sort in the end."

"You're no better than Rannulf," Stephen said, angry.

Ali's face settled. "I assure you. I am in another category utterly from your oafish brigand of a commander." He drew back, his head high, putting on a cast of arrogance and power. "I can save you, Stephen, if you'll let me."

Stephen reached for the wine cup and drained it. "Thank you," he said. "I'm getting out of here." He stood up, swaying, his stomach doing a hurtle up into his throat.

"Where are you going?" Ali said. There was a knock on the door; he glanced around, and a servant came quickly through the room to answer.

Stephen said, "I'm a Templar, Ali. Maybe I don't keep my vow very well, but I'm still a Templar, and you made the mistake of reminding me." He started toward the door, and then the servant stepped back, and two guards came in.

Ali reached out, and gripped Stephen's arm, and held him. "What's going on?" He had switched to Arabic, which Stephen understood far better than he spoke.

"My lord, we can't find him," the first guard said.

"What?"

"The Jerusalem knight. Al-Wali. We can't find him. Dawud waited for him by the wall but he never came. We've searched all the streets around the palace wall—"

Stephen gave a shout of laughter. Ali flung him a nasty glare and turned back to the guards. "Go find him. Get everybody in the palace out there, go through every house, but find him."

The first guard said, "Yes, my lord." He saluted, and they both hurried out the door. Ali wheeled toward Stephen.

"Where is he?" His voice snapped.

Stephen beamed at him. "I have no idea. I certainly wouldn't tell you if I did."

Ali growled. "You are inexplicable to me. Come." He pushed Stephen ahead of him, out the door.

The Sultan said, "My dear Count, it is not my own cause I champion here. It is Islam itself that has been wounded, sorely
wounded, by the deeds of you faithless barbarians. Now they
say you are sending for more Christians from Frankland, to come here
and kill my people and drive them from their homes. And to help you
do this I am to provide you with a period of truce. This hardly seems
good policy to me."

He put the silver cup down on the table between him and Tripoli.
These apartments, where Tripoli was staying, were on the south side of
the palace, facing away from the city; tall windows opened in three of
the four walls and the untainted breezes blew in from the garden and
from the clean and holy desert beyond. The Sultan was glad he had come
down here. He needed to get away from his court; the court was too
merry, too loud, feverishly loud and merry, a dance among the graves.
But he had to entertain them, to keep them here, to make this gambit
work.

Now he and Tripoli talked their way along the little winding paths
of diplomacy, sure-footed among deceits; they knew each other so well
they could even smile as they lied. Tripoli was smiling now. He lounged
on a cushioned chair, his small round-fingered hands raised.

"My lord Sultan, you distress me more than I can tell you. For years
we have been friends, we have spoken together on many things, I have
been your guest, you have been mine, and now suddenly you seem to
have discovered we are enemies." He smiled. "You sadden me very
much, my friend."

"You and I are friends," said Salah ad-Din Yusuf. "Your faith and
mine are deadly enemies." He nodded to a servant, who came with an
iced pitcher, and filled his cup again. "I need money, Count. You need
time. I will sell you time for money, but it will not come cheaply for you."

"Yes," Tripoli said. "What did you have in mind, my lord?"

"I want five hundred thousand michaels for each year of the truce."
The Sultan leaned forward, tapping the table between them with his

forefinger. "And my nephew Tariq is to be released from Margat, and the other hostages of my people are to be released, and you shall release my people who now pay you tribute from their tribute."

Tripoli blinked at him. "My dear Sultan. Perhaps a few of the stars as well."

"If it can be arranged."

The Count laughed. He wasted no time in anger. He was all but an Arab, Tripoli, who understood every undertone, every quiver of a syllable, every second and third meaning, and would spend days braiding them together and taking them apart again. Instinctively he would compromise, and at this point Salah ad-Din would accept any compromise as a victory.

Tripoli said, "The King has no money to pay such a huge price, my lord Sultan. You cannot ask a stone to bleed."

"The Templars have money," the Sultan said.

A ripple of annoyance crossed Tripoli's face. "They certainly do. Money which is not within my reach, or the King's reach, either, unfortunately." He leaned forward for an almond cake from the dish on the table. Salah ad-Din had noticed that Tripoli always ate everything set in front of him, and yet he never fattened. He broke the cake in half in his two hands. "Let us talk sensibly here, my friend. You worry too much about the Crusade. There will be no help forthcoming from the Franks beyond the sea; they care nothing for the kingdom of the Cross. But the King will soon die. When he does, help me become King, and then between you and me we can make a good and lasting peace."

The Sultan did not say that he would have no peace until he held Jerusalem. He said, "Who are the heirs of Baudouin the Leper?"

Tripoli put down one half of the cake and broke the other half into pieces. His nails were bitten down to the quick. "The King's sister Sibylla is his heir, a mere girl, careless as a butterfly. She has a baby son. And there is a much younger half-sister, Isobel. A council of the barons could be induced to overturn their rights. If I had enough money, I could buy the crown."

The Sultan said, "With enough money, a fool buys a gold coffin." He was thinking of his enemy, the boy King of Jerusalem, who fought him with such a heart, and such a will. He admired Baudouin the Leper much more than he wanted to. He thought Tripoli would have been an easier opponent. "I wish I could come face to face one day with your King."

"No, you don't," said Tripoli. "It's like looking at an unburied corpse." In some ways he was still, profoundly, a mere barbarian. "He should die and have done with it. What is it?"

A servant had come into the room, and stood bowing and waving his hands, trying to attract attention. The Sultan's eyes sharpened. Behind him, he saw his nephew Ali, waiting in the doorway, and he said, "With your permission, my lord Count, I think this is my concern. Yes."

Ali came in, hastily. His face was flushed. Behind him was a man with cropped red hair and a full red beard, whom the Sultan did not know, but whom Tripoli knew: the Count stood up suddenly, saying, "What are you doing here?"

Ali said, "Uncle, my lord, call your guards, you must protect yourself."

Behind him, the redheaded man said to Tripoli, in French, "They've lost Rannulf."

"Oh," said Tripoli. His gaze flicked toward the Sultan. "Well, that's a mistake."

Salah ad-Din sat where he was, his hands on his knees. "Ali, what is going on?"

His nephew said, "My lord, the Templar al-Wali is missing. He could be anywhere, even inside the palace somewhere. You yourself could be in mortal danger."

"Truly," the Sultan said. He jerked his attention toward Tripoli, and the redheaded man, who he realized now was a Templar; why he was with Ali the Sultan put aside for later consideration. "Is he of evil intent? What sort of man did you bring into my court?"

Tripoli said, "Not one I would want roaming freely through my palace. I thought you were keeping them under control."

The Sultan nodded to Ali. "Call my guards. I will go back to my own apartments until he is found. When he is found, bring him to me." He stood, coming face to face with the redheaded knight. "Your comrade is foolish to attempt this. He is only assuring himself of trouble. If you tell us where he is, it will go easier with you in the end."

"I'm sure it would," the knight said, composed, "but I'm not telling you anything."

"Ali, take him and chain him until his friend is found."

Tripoli said, "These men are your guests, my lord Sultan, you may not misuse them."

"They are misusing me," the Sultan said, making ready to leave, and then the door opened again, and he lifted his head, and past the shoulders of the other men he looked straight into the black eyes of the Templar called Saint.

Salah ad-Din gave a violent start. Around him the room fell suddenly quiet, and the Templar walked in among them. "Looking for me?" He went through their midst to the couch and dropped down onto it, as if he were master here. He was barefoot. The djellabah he wore was already stained and filthy. His gaze was fixed on the Sultan. "I bow before the magnificence of the Sultan of Cairo and Damascus, beloved of Allah, Master of Realms and Dominions." He did not bow.

Ali said, "Guards," and the Sultan raised his hand to stop him.

"No. Don't be a fool. More of a fool. You may go. My lord Count will stay, and this other knight, and—" He gestured toward the couch. "The rest of you will leave us."

Quickly they filed out of the room. The Sultan sat down again on his chair. He could not bring himself to look at the man on the couch. "What is it, monk?"

"I want to get out of here," the Templar said. "I did not come to the Holy Land to die of pox, and this city is rotten with it. Make this truce, now, so I can take my men and leave."

The Sultan folded his arms together. All his grand designs were dwindling down fast to a small practicality. He said, "I have set my conditions for a truce. Match them, and it is done."

Tripoli said, "Is there plague in the city?"

"There is sickness in every city."

The Templar's voice was relentless. "There was plague in your army, too, wasn't there, at Jacob's Ford—that was why you did not attack Jerusalem: all your men were dying of the pox. You can't get an army together without everybody falling sick. You're no threat to anybody, right now. Mouse, bring me something to drink."

The redheaded knight obeyed him, crossing the room to the table where the wine ewer stood, and then moving to stand beside the couch. If he had joined Ali in an indiscretion clearly he had come out again on the same side he had gone in. The Sultan made one last attempt to master this. He lifted his gaze to Tripoli. "Are you lord here, or is this clod?"

Tripoli said, "I want a three-year truce, my lord. No payment, no exchanges of prisoners." His eyes were steady; behind the fringe of his moustache his lips hardly seemed to move.

The Sultan was quiet. He still did not look at the man sprawling on the couch as if he owned this palace, as if he ruled this world. The Templar said, "If you do not give us the truce, Sultan, I will go back to Jerusalem for three hundred of my brothers, and we will come and take this city, and there is nobody here to prevent us from doing it."

"You're bluffing," Salah ad-Din said, curt. Now he did turn and stare at the Templar. "I crushed your brotherhood at the Litani River. There aren't three hundred of you left."

The knight sneered at him. "We are like dragon's teeth, Sultan. We grow back."

Salah ad-Din studied him a moment, the hard black eyes unblinking, the mouth in the dense beard heavy with a sensuality that should not have been so resistent to seduction. The Sultan saw little chance now of gaining anything out of this negotiation, save some necessary room to maneuver. It would be a relief to be able to leave Damascus, to go up to the mountains for the rest of the summer's heat, to escape from the plague. He needed the truce. He needed money but he would find it elsewhere. He wanted his nephew out of Margat but that would have to wait. He nodded to Tripoli.

"Very well, I can accept that. A truce of three years."

"Excellent," Tripoli said. "I'll send for a scribe." He glanced at the Templar. "Does that satisfy you?"

The Templar stood. He took the cup from the redheaded man, and drank it empty. "I will hold to it," he said, and put the cup down, and walked out the door, the other knight on his heels.

Tripoli sat back in the cushions of his chair, tenting his fingers together, his eyes brimming with amusement. "You know, my lord, we have a saying, something about supping with the devil, to whom that particular Templar bears a close familial resemblance. You should have been honest with us from the beginning." There was a little of the priest in him; he brandished a forefinger. "You see there is some danger in being too elaborate."

"Bah," the Sultan said. "You Franks, you're all damned. Get some servants in here, close the windows."

Bear moaned, his eyes bleary. "God's blood, I've been poisoned." His horse shifted sideways and he swayed in his saddle as if he were about to fall off.

Stephen gathered his reins and mounted. They had all heard about the plague in Damascus; now half the palace was gathered in this open court, making ready to escape from the diseased city. The Templars had moved off toward the wall, to get by themselves, and the palace folk were avoiding them anyway. Felx came up through the gate from the stable, leading his horse and a packhorse. Rannulf rode on his heels, with another packhorse.

Over in the middle of the courtyard horns blared. Tripoli and the Sultan were exchanging more ceremonial remarks. A pattering of applause went up. Felx slung his stirrup leather over his saddle and checked his girths.

"Truce, false," he said. "It's a long way to come for a few words."

Stephen said, "Oh, I didn't mind it."

Ali was over there, in the crowd around the Sultan. Stephen turned his eyes away. He would be glad to be gone from here, out of the way of sin. On the other hand, he felt like a god. Rannulf mounted his horse and swung around to yell at them.

"Form up! Move, Felx, or you'll walk back to Jerusalem."

"I'll walk on your black heart," Felx muttered.

If he heard that, Rannulf ignored it. The Norman knight trotted his horse up and down in front of the other Templars. His voice was sharp, pitched just loud enough to reach their ears. "Now, listen to me. Since you all had such a wonderful time, you must know you're going to do penance, and here it is. I begged some corn for the horses, but I could get no food for us; we'll be fasting all the way back to Tiberias."

Bear hissed between his teeth. "I can't eat anyway." He put one hand to his forehead.

Felx said, "Do we have an escort again?"

"They're letting us ride vanguard this time," Rannulf said. "If there's a Saracen who can keep pace with us, I want to see him do it."

In the crowd around the Sultan and the Count of Tripoli, a cheer rose; the Sultan was giving Tripoli a splendid chestnut horse, dressed in gaudy cloths and harness. From the ranks of the Sultan's guard a rider jogged across the pavement toward the Templars. Recognizing him, Stephen straightened, wondering what he should say, but it was Rannulf that Ali approached.

"Al-Wali!" His voice was harsh. "My uncle the most excellent Sultan, in the name of Allah, bids me tell you he will not offend you by offering you gifts."

Rannulf sidestepped his horse around to face him. "The Sultan has given me fitting gifts."

Ali's voice rose, loud enough to reach all ears. "He would show you some honor, for the sake of his honor and that of Allah, and so he will give you, not treasure or beauty, but a promise. You have met twice now, he says. Twice now you have been the victor, but the time will come when he will put your head on a stake." Without looking at Stephen, he wheeled his mare and loped away.

Bear said, "I'd sooner the treasure and beauty."

Rannulf hacked out one of his unpleasant laughs. "Let's go."

◈ By midday they had outdistanced the last of the Saracen escort. They climbed through the pass in the hills and spent the night on the desert west of there, eating nothing, drinking water, one man always sitting up to keep watch. Stephen woke before dawn, his belly raging with hunger, his ears full of the Matins bells. As he wakened wide, the tolling of the bell became the moan of the desert wind.

He lifted his head. The other men slept around him on the ground. Rannulf was sitting watch, cross-legged, his head bowed. Silently Stephen got up, and went off a little to relieve himself and say his prayers. Felx and Bear slept on. Stephen sat down next to Rannulf.

"I have to confess."

"Do it," Rannulf said.

Stephen went quickly through the formula, one hand up, fingers splayed, between his face and Rannulf's, and got through his sins at a gallop, burying Ali among luxury and gluttony and a few other abstractions. His stomach hurt. It seemed important to have his sins removed before they reached Jerusalem. Afterward he sat staring into the darkness, struggling with the memory. Beside him Rannulf suddenly crossed himself.

"Mouse. I want you to shrive me."

Stephen lifted his head, pulled out of his own thoughts. He had said his confession to others of the Temple but he had never heard one before; quickly he got his mind into the other half of the ritual. He said, "Tell it."

Rannulf lifted one hand between them, his gaze aimed steadily somewhere else. Stephen looked down at the ground.

"Forgive me, Jesus, for I have sinned," Rannulf said. He fell still for a while. Stephen waited, puzzled; Rannulf said nothing for so long a time he wondered if the other knight had fallen asleep.

Then at last Rannulf said, "There's a woman."

"In Damascus?" Stephen blurted, and almost looked at him.

"No. In Jerusalem. I've never touched her. But I want her. I dream of her. I think of her all the time." He said, intensely, "I love her."

Stephen watched his own hands in the dark. He said his part of the ritual. "Are you contrite?"

"No," Rannulf said.

"Can I absolve you, then?" He remembered how Rannulf had refused to serve the Mass or receive the Sacrament, on the way here, and guessed the answer.

"No," Rannulf said.

Stephen reached out and took hold of Rannulf's hand. The other knight closed his fingers on him. Neither of them spoke. Stephen wondered who the woman was, and gave up at once. They sat like that until the sun rose and the other men woke up.

The city of Ascalon, Sibylla thought, was like the sheep in the fable, that fattened between two packs of wolves. She laid her hand on the railing of the terrace and looked out over the city. To the west the sea ran dark and blue out as far as her sight reached, out to where the sky began; as the waves rushed on toward Ascalon, they paled, turned green as Chinese stone, and then broke into tumbling white that flooded along the beaches in a restless, ceaseless surge, gnawing and clawing at the shore like wolves.

The shore itself rose in white waves, the sand waves of the desert that prowled up out of the south with the furnace wind of Arabia. When the wind rose, its shrivelling blast howled like wolves.

Between the dunes and the surf Ascalon raised its towers. For centuries the city had given way as it had to, so that to south and west her earlier boundaries were marked with broken walls, great tilted blocks of plastered stone like the upshrugging shoulders of some giant under the coastal plain, walls half-buried in drifted sand, tumbled into the sea, eroded down to their granite ribs. Yet the advance of the desert made the beaches on which the city grew, and the sea made tolerable the desert's burning heat; and cradled in this enmity Ascalon prospered.

The city clustered around its many wells. Beneath the clattering fronds of the palm trees, in the shrill marketplaces, in the crowded streets, the people lived and worked as they had since the days of Abraham and Isaac. Their houses incorporated stone from Roman days; their great public baths displayed mosaics showing scenes of Alexander. They spoke a language that traded in foreign words as the merchants traded in foreign goods, and in the bazaar all races met: a jet-black Abyssinian dickered with a red-headed Circassian merchant, or a yellow man in a silk cap.

It was, Sibylla thought, a city that could balance on opposites, and wring profit from contention. She had always loved it best of all the cities of Outremer. Now it seemed to her a sermon on her destiny.

This day her destiny seemed ambiguous. She drew her gaze from the city and faced the man beside her on the terrace.

"What did my brother say to you?"

The Patriarch of Jerusalem was a client of her mother's. His name was Heraclius but behind his back the court called him Montargent, because everything he did turned on money. He was flawlessly composed, clean and fragrant, his lavish vestment immaculate, his beard combed and trimmed. He always smiled. He said, "Alas, my child, the King will not allow even the mention of your name."

She could see he enjoyed telling her that. She stared back at him, steady-eyed. "I can assume you gave the task some effort?"

"My dear, I was persistent."

She said, "Thank you, Father." She turned away from him, but he would not be dismissed; he pushed more bad news at her. "The King is adamant. I heard it from others there as well, how he silences anyone who dares speak for you. I fear, Princess, you have no place anymore in his favor."

She said, "Is he well?"

"Well?" Montargent gave a laugh cracked with disbelief. "He is all but blind, and holds audience only from Prime to Tierce, before he must get back into his bed. The more wonder his ferocious spirit toward you, who might comfort him in his final days. Ah, this vale of tears."

These words stung. The contempt in the priest's voice hurt worse than the news he brought. She said, "He still rules. He does his will. He has made this truce. Thank you. I shall repay you." She turned and walked off down the terrace. Behind her the patriarch strolled away in a cloud of his hangers-on.

Sibylla wrung her hands together. She missed Baudouin sorely. She had come to Ascalon soon after the quarrel with him. Half the court was here for the summer: her mother, and her little son, with all their household, and some of every great family in Outremer, Ibelins and Millys and Plancys and Courtenays. Every day another great reception, another feast on the beach; always the same people, different clothes, different settings. After a while she had sent a message to Jerusalem, offering to forgive him, but he had sent it back, the seal unbroken.

She had asked other people to go between them; no one could get him to listen. When the Patriarch had offered, she had been desperate enough to accept, all the while knowing the thing foredoomed. Until she bent to his will her brother would have nothing to do with her. Until she did her duty.

She knew he was sick. She was afraid he would die, that she would never see him again.

The terrace was a broad flagged skirt along three sides of the palace; a stone railing guarded the edge. Beyond the railing the land swept away in a stretch of gardens, with statues of birds and animals among the dense tended shrubbery, and cypress trees in rows. From the terrace a stone stair led down into a fountain shaped like a great stone shell, set in a little pocket of a lawn. Alys joined her, carrying some flowers out of the garden boxes around the courtyard. She gave Sibylla a quick, searching look.

"You look angry."

"It came to nothing. And he is a wicked man, even for a priest."

Alys said, "You should never deal with these people. He has the most awful reputation." She held up some of the posies she had picked. "Smell this, isn't it beautiful? We should make some perfume while we're here."

Sibylla buried her nose in a handful of soft pink petals. The scent cloyed in her nostrils. They went to the corner; the great many-leveled palace courtyard was covered with people, talking in little groups, their voices a general buzz, their clothes a bright mosaic against the grey marble. She stopped. Below her, on the next level, she saw Montargent, smiling, talking, and knew he would tell everybody her brother hated her.

For a moment she shrank away from them. They would all stare at her. Smile to her face and talk behind her back. Alys went on a few steps, and turned and looked back, puzzled. Sibylla shook her skirts out. She reminded herself of Ascalon, steady between tumults. Head high, she went down into the court.

✦ The great sprawling palace of Ascalon was called the Salome Palace, after the niece of King Herod, who had lived here, according to the stories. Certainly it was very old, like a little city in itself, with living quarters and kitchens, baths and workshops, stables and vineyards, and a graveyard. From its long southern front two opposing staircases descended, through three levels of landings and gardens, to a wide circular courtyard before the entrance gate. Agnes de Courtenay liked to have her gatherings on this many-leveled terrace. She sat on the topmost landing, where the fresh breeze reached, and she could see everything. Her grandson leaned on her knee, and she fed him grapes.

"There is your daughter again," Amalric de Lusignan said.

He had just returned from France, where he had gone the year before. Agnes was surprised to find that she had missed him; quickly she had restored him as her favorite, excusing the Plancy cadet who had taken his place. She glanced down onto the second level, where Sibylla had appeared around the side of the palace. Reaching down, she lifted Sibylla's son up onto her lap and kissed him.

"Now, sit still, sonny, I shall teach you statecraft. See how they swarm around her." Wherever Sibylla walked, the people turned, bowing and pushing closer, all in waves like windblown wheat.

Amalric said, "She's prettier now than when I left. Is she still favoring Baudouin d'Ibelin?"

Agnes gave a cackle of amusement. "Not much." Captured after the Battle on the Litani River, Baudouin d'Ibelin had come back from Damascus encumbered by a crushing ransom. While in the Saracens' hands he had bragged openly that he would soon be King of Jerusalem, and the Sultan had assessed him in that light. Sibylla was furious with him and would not receive him, nor even speak to him, save as she had to. "He went off to Constantinople. The Emperor's hinted at helping him pay his ransom. There is de Ridford. Send down for him; I must sound him out about this truce."

"De Ridford," Amalric said. He turned and nodded, and one of the pages went off down the stairs. "Still as he was when I left—a wax candle monk. Does he have women?"

"Not that I can discover. His lust is power; he could second as a bung-puller, he is that crooked."

Her gaze went to Sibylla again. Her daughter was climbing up the stairs toward her, stopping every few steps to talk to someone else. The little boy on Agnes' lap was trying to get down, and she let him go. "She should marry again, she is too fixed on men's affairs of late. Her brother seduced her into it, and now that they have quarreled he won't even talk to her. She needs a man who will make her be a woman."

"She could have her pick," Amalric said. "That one, there, for instance—see how he stares at her."

Agnes followed his eyes, and the discreet tilt of his smooth-shaven chin. On the landing just below Sibylla a tall man stood alone, in the corner of the rail, watching the girl above him. He wore a long-tailed cap over his yellow-white hair. His coat was red and black. She said, "Guile of Kerak."

"Is that who that is." Amalric came forward a few paces, to look closer.

"The Wolf's bastard," Agnes said. "Got on his wife's tiring maid when he was Prince of Antioch. Risen now to be the Wolf's right arm.

Everything is the same but the hair." The way he looked at Sibylla ran-
kled, rousing a motherly ire. "He is baseborn. He should not even walk
among my court, much less ogle my daughter."

Amalric laughed. "If you would exclude everybody with a question
in his quarterings, lady, there would be nobody here, not even you."

"Ah, you cur! What a tongue."

"Now you complain."

Agnes hissed at him. Her grandson was climbing onto the railing, and
she snapped her fingers and pointed, and a page hurried after him.
Sibylla came up the steps. Balancing on the rail, the little boy went by
her, and she by him, and neither of them remarked the other. Agnes saw
this, with a wrench at her heart; she saw her daughter straying off into
a wasteland of men's doings, missing what was best in a woman's life.
She lifted her face, smiling, and held out her hands.

"Dear girl. Come and give me a kiss. You look beautiful. Umm-
mmm."

Sibylla bent, and pecked at her mother's cheek, her eyes elsewhere.
"You look very well, my lady." Her cousin Alys, round as a dumpling,
puffed and panted up the steps after her, carrying masses of pink quar-
trefoil; Sibylla turned at once, and commanded the other girl here and
there, putting the flowers around. A servant brought her a stool but
Sibylla did not sit down, only gave orders.

"They smell wonderful," Agnes said. "Do sit, my girl—you make me
restless, standing above me like that."

Sibylla plopped down gracelessly on the stool. "There. Does that
please you?"

"Quite." Agnes patted her on the arm. "That dress is very becoming,
the color fits you perfectly." She turned her head slightly toward Amalric, who needed no more hint than that, but drifted off across the flagstone terrace, toward the stone railing, which Alys was decking with
masses of pink flowers, a very pretty effect.

Sibylla said, "What, are you going to lecture me again about marry-
ing?"

Her mother said, "It's better to have a man than not, my dear." Her
gaze shifted, down a flight of steps, to the next landing, where the
lutenist sat; several people stood around listening. One who did not listen was Guile of Kerak, leaning up against the railing, staring at her
daughter. "For one thing, they protect you."

That angered Sibylla, who swiveled to face her, chin high and eyes
flashing. "I protect myself, Mother. I am no fearful, clinging wife."

Agnes lifted her eyebrows at her. "You are innocent, Sibylla. I understand you have taken to going off alone, without even sweet Alys here, which is very dangerous; what do you think you are up to?"

"I like to go around the city, and Alys will not ride." Sibylla smoothed her skirt down, flattening the embroidery under her fingers. She was never still; her foot tapped, her eyes searched around the many-layered terraces. At the top of the stairs, the Templar Marshall Gerard de Ridford stood, smiling, waiting to be noticed, and Agnes nodded to him.

"My lord Marshall. I am very glad to see you. You must tell me about this truce the King my son has concluded with Damascus."

The Templar Marshall bowed over her hand. "My lady, I have only heard of it what you have heard. Until I go back to Jerusalem I have no opinion." He turned to Sibylla. "My lady Princess, I am very pleased to see you."

"My lord Templar."

Agnes said, "In three years' truce we can rebuild the kingdom. It seems suspicious that Tripoli should have gotten us so much in return for nothing. Saladin must have fallen asleep."

"Oh," de Ridford said, "Tripoli has sold us out again, certainly. I placed some of my men with him, on the mission to Damascus. When I return to Jerusalem, I shall know more."

Sibylla said, "You all hate Tripoli, you can see nothing good in what he does. Yet the truce seems to me of more value than the Crusade."

Agnes blinked, startled at that; de Ridford chuckled. "The Crusade, certainly, is worth no more than the truce. My lady, my dear Princess." He was taking himself away; Agnes waved him off, and he went across the flagstones, toward Amalric and his French news.

Sibylla said, "If Saladin will make truce with us for three years, when he has such an advantage, then he might make peace forever."

"Dear girl," Agnes said. "There is no such place as forever. My advice to you is to speak more carefully around the men. If they think you're loose-tongued, they'll say less in your company."

"Mother," Sibylla said, "you are all connivance. Could one of us make some private contact with Saladin?"

Agnes sat bolt upright, shocked. "One of us? You mean, you or me? God's love, girl, what are you thinking of?" She cast a quick look around her, to see who might be listening; no one was listening. Amalric and de Ridford were the closest people to them, save for the dreamy, inattentive page behind her, and the two men were off in a corner talking. She reached out and clutched her daughter's arm.

"Listen to me, girl. I know not what foolishness your brother has stuffed into your head, but it is wicked folly, if it leads you into this—

keep your hands out of this. Do not go behind their backs to Saladin. Do you understand me?"

Sibylla jerked her arm out of her mother's grasp. Her eyes were dark with temper. "Do not handle me, mother."

"Do you understand?"

"I know," Sibylla said, "that if we go on as we are, the Kingdom is lost." She stared away, her fists in her lap, her foot tapping on the floor again. Her cheeks were ruddy. Agnes chewed her lip, frowning. She knew Sibylla too well to think she would abandon this idea simply because her mother told her to do so.

Ideas were slippery, unmanageable, especially the treacherous idea of peace. Agnes had learned early to confine her dealings to people, who were easy, and solid, and real. Now here was her daughter, entangled in that net of dreams. She gave a little shake of her head, alarmed.

The trouble with coming out here by herself, Sibylla thought, was that she had no one to talk to. She had brought a groom and a page, of course, but she missed Alys, whose company so amplified her pleasure, who provided a reliably appreciative audience for Sibylla's clever observations and remarks, and who often had observations and remarks of her own, although seldom as clever as Sibylla's. With Alys to be cautious, Sibylla could be bolder; with Alys to sound her constant alarums, Sibylla could more easily laugh alarming things off.

Like this Egyptian show. She had ridden down the little slope from the Salome Palace, out to the broad beach that was one of Ascalon's chief thoroughfares, and found a crowd gathered to watch a story show. This was something common enough; Ascalon stood at the convergence of several trade routes, and there was a regular trade in entertainment.

The show was already going on, and the local people watching were yelling and laughing in huge enjoyment of it. The stage was only a square cut out in an upright board, with a drapery around it; the figures were made of cloth, with faces sewn on, and huge hands. Held aloft on sticks they waggled and sailed around in the space framed in the board, more like birds than people, swooping at each other, while from under the drapery came the shrieky voices of the players.

One of the figures had a big red cross on the front of it. When Sibylla had been there a moment, a man in a flat cap who had been watching from the side of the stage turned and went around behind it, and the figure with the cross was yanked down out of sight. Almost at once another figure took its place, this one wearing a Turkish turban.

Sibylla frowned. She wondered if she should be offended at this.

Now the figure in the turban was taking a merciless drubbing from the other figure, which, she realized now, was dressed to be an Arab. This was probably an insult; she saw how the crowd watched her, over their shoulders, through the corners of their eyes. They would expect her to do something. On the stage the Arab was now chasing the Turk around and around, as, had she not been here, it would have chased the Crusader.

She wondered what Baudouin would do.

That gave her an idea. She reached into her purse, got out a couple of coins, and gave them to her page. "Take these to the players. Tell them the next time, they may leave the Crusader in view, as in Ascalon we are wide-minded." She said this loudly, so that everybody nearby could hear her.

The page ran off through the crowd, which parted to let him through. On the stage the figures stopped in midair; the page slowed, approaching, and a man in a cap came out from behind the stage and took the money and heard the boy speak. Turning, he scanned the crowd, saw Sibylla, and swept her a huge bow.

The crowd cheered. The players came out from behind the stage, the figures on their hands, and bowed to her as well, and made the figures bow. With a cool wave, Sibylla called the page to her, and rode away down the street.

Her heart was pounding. She had done well, she had done as Baudouin would.

The beach stretched away before her, swarming with people hawking goods and people buying them, with beggars and loiterers enjoying the sun. The wind being light, two tubby Genose merchantmen had stood in to anchor in the open roads of the sea, and a steady stream of little boats rocked up and down the waves between them and the shore. Sibylla rode along behind a woman balancing a basket neatly on her head; in the basket lay a dozen long silver fish. Three brown men rushed along beside Sibylla's horse, their hands uplifted, streaming strings of coral beads.

"Lady! Lady!"

At a sign from her, the groom rode up and chased them off. She veered up toward the inland side of the beach, where in the clustered little shops was a merchant who had promised her black pearls.

The merchant, who was from Basra, sat under a palm tree and showed her jewels in little bags of brocaded silk. She haggled with him a little, not much wanting what he had, but thinking he might carry messages for her to Saladin; then something her mother had said once came back to her. The Templars ruled the roads, and all that travelled on them. She went out again, having bought nothing and given nothing away.

Her groom held her bay mare by the reins, down at the edge of the street; as she came away from the merchant, a woman with sores on her face came up, her palm cupped, and Sibylla gave her money, which brought on a tide of beggars. As she was giving a coin into each filthy pleading hand a shout sounded, in the street.

She turned her head; her groom had been dozing, and jerked his head up. The page came dashing in from the street.

"They're beating up the puppet show!" The child's face was red with indignation. "Princess! Stop them! Look!"

"Help me." Sibylla grabbed her reins in one hand, and the cantle of her saddle with the other, and the groom gave her a practiced boost. From the vantage of her saddle she could see over the heads of the crowd now milling and pushing around the end of the street, where the stage for the show still stood, surrounded by its flapping drapery. Around it three men on horseback were fighting with some men on foot.

Sibylla cried out, angry; she saw the show's drapery caught on a sword blade, and ripped away, she saw the stage go down. The players were trying to defend what was left of their work, their bare arms raised against the swords and horses of the three men harrying them. Sibylla was halfway to this rout when she saw among the mounted men the white head of Guile of Kerak.

Her hands tightened on her reins. Guile frightened her. But she could not draw back now. She thought of Baudouin again, and spurred her horse into a short lope across the shelving beach and in among the crouching players, who were trying to gather up their show and flee.

She plunged into their midst, and they shrank from her as from another enemy. She wheeled to face Guile of Kerak.

"What are you doing here? What right do you have to take arms against these people?"

Startled, Guile's horse backed up two steps from her, its nose poking the air. The white-haired knight had a whip in his hand, with which he had been worrying the players, and he swung it around toward her, as if he meant to strike her.

She flinched back, and he laughed. On his long shark-jaw the new beard glittered like sprinkled sand. He said, "Princess, you should not go around without an escort." The two men with him stopped what they were doing, and waited behind him, their gazes on her.

Everybody's gaze was on her. She felt the stabs of a thousand looks:

the crowd pressing in now on all sides, the three knights before her, the players huddled behind her; she knew some other mounted men had come up on the edge of the crowd, but she was too intent on Guile to see who they were.

She fixed her gaze on Guile; she made her voice strong and clear.

"I need no escort here in Ascalon. These people love me."

The crowd let out its breath in a yell of agreement, and she took courage from that. Guile's thin lips kinked into a smile. His gaze moved from her face, travelled down leisurely over her body, in a way that made her feel naked. When he looked into her eyes again his smile widened.

"You should not be out here, Princess. I'll take you back where you belong." He reached for the reins of her horse.

She shouted, furious, and yanked on her reins, backing her mare out of his reach. Guile lunged after her, one long arm grabbing, grabbing, and she raised her whip and slashed him across the wrist. He jerked his arm back, and in a fury, a breathless, heedless rage, she spurred her mare forward and swung her whip at his face.

He recoiled, his arm cocked in front of him, and when the lash struck his hand he caught hold of it and yanked it from her. The crowd around them gave her no room to escape. The knight swung toward her, his face clenched and his teeth bared. He flung down her whip, and he reached for her with both hands.

Before he could touch her, someone else drove through the crowd and wedged his horse between them, a second rider flying on his heels. "Hands off her, Whitehair!"

Guile roared. He gripped the hilt of his sword; Sibylla, now tucked in behind the two newcomers' horses, saw these two men reach for their weapons, and cried, "No! Stop!" She reached out and caught hold of the arm of the nearest rider.

Guile was backing away, his face flushed red as raw meat. "She was here alone, in the street, alone," he shouted. "I was doing a knight's duty!"

The man who had rushed in between them said calmly, "Your duty's done, then. Leave off." He turned to face her, and she saw he was Amalric de Lusignan, her mother's favorite.

Her throat and cheeks prickled up. She had not wanted to be rescued, especially not by him. She said, "Thank you, Sir Amalric." Guile, she saw, through the corner of her eye, was leaving.

Her mother's lover said, "Princess, you are too brave." His keen attention was following Guile. She glanced at the other man, beside her, the man whose arm she had caught; he had much the same look as

Amalric, with long blonde hair and a quick smile, which he gave her now, but he was poor in dress, almost shabby.

She said, "Guile is a filthy swine. Shameful it is that here, surrounded by strangers and infidels, the threat comes from one I know, and another Christian, too." Turning, she cast around for the Egyptian players, but they had vanished; even the stage was gone. "Shameful what they did to these poor people."

Amalric crossed his hands on his saddlebows. A garnet hung in his left earlobe. His coat was of yellow satin, embroidered with green and set with gold studs. She saw why her mother liked him, with his shaggy good looks set off by splendid dress.

He said, "God helps those who do right. May we ride along with you?" His nod took in the other rider. "This is my younger brother Guy, who followed me out from France."

She glanced around at his brother, who had dismounted, and picked her riding whip up off the ground. "Welcome, my lord."

He brought her the whip, and stood looking up at her. "Thank you, my lady. I am come, surely, but how *well,* I cannot say."

"Bah," Amalric said. "What courtesy is this for a princess, you dog? Princess, where are you going? I am showing my brother here the sights, would you help me?"

Guy went back to his horse and mounted. Sibylla swung her mare around to ride between the two men, and they went off along the beach. Her servants fell in unobtrusively behind them. She looked again at the brother. "Then you came here against your will, sir?"

"Ah, lady," he said, "I came with the best will, I came all this way to fight and die for Jesus Christ, and I but step foot on the wharf, and there is a three years' truce announced. God laughs at me."

"Oh," she said, "if that's the whole of it, that you shall not die soon, I think you will not be disconsolate very long."

He laughed. If he were truly disconsolate then he wore it excellently well; he had an air about him of merriment and expectation of good things, although his coat was out at the elbows and frayed at the cuffs.

She wanted to like him; she guarded herself against that. Turned to Amalric, on her left hand.

"I thought you were gone home to France forever. Did you come back for the Cross, or for my mother's sake?"

Amalric reared his head back, his eyes widening. He had bristly eyebrows as fair as his hair. "Princess. What a set of traps that is. Better shall I say that I came back to set eyes once again on the prettiest Princess in Christendom."

She snorted at him. "You are a flirt, my lord."

"I! Not at all, a flirt's victim merely. My brother is the flirt. Guy?"

She turned around, ready for another compliment, but the brother was staring around him, open-mouthed, paying no heed to her or to anybody else, but only to Ascalon. Amalric gave a laugh. "Guy! Come back, come back!"

His brother jerked around toward them. "Oh. Your pardon, my lady. But this is the fairest city I have ever seen. Now, look there, what tower is that?"

"That is the Tower of the Virgin," Sibylla said, pointing. They had come to the city wall, which reached down along the beach and out into the sea; beyond it, past a cluster of green palms, rose a watertower. "My father the King of Jerusalem built it."

They turned and went along the street that followed the wall inland, through a grove of palm trees. By the well there, some women were drawing water, and singing in a strange language. The street was lined with stone walls buttressed every few yards with old marble statues, windworn, the noses broken off the pocky faces, like ghosts in the plaster. Sibylla told the brothers how the city had resisted the Crusaders for years and years, until the Saracens named her the Virgin of Syria; how at last her father King Amalric took the place by siege. They passed through the domed shadow of the basilica. Guy gaped and exclaimed at everything; he lapped up everything she said. But not for her sake. It was Ascalon that beguiled him. His brother paid her extravagant compliments, which she valued little; had Guy paid her compliments, she would have hardly noticed them, but because he did not, she wanted him to, very dearly, and by the time they returned to Salome she was determined to have his admiration, whatever the means.

◈ Later, she found Agnes at the big table in the hall with her chamberlain, talking about money matters. Sibylla sat there a moment, her hands in her lap, listening to them discuss the cost of wax candles.

Her mother sent the chamberlain off and frowned at her. "Well, I hear you made a sensation in the market today. Whatever do you think of, when you do these things?"

"Oh. Since you already know the gist, I'll go straight to the end. I want you to send Guile away."

"I shall certainly do so." Her mother rolled up the papers before her, which held the accounts of her household. "I forbid you to go around by yourself in the city. Amalric said there was a single groom with you, and a little boy."

This led into Sibylla's second reason for coming here. She reached out and took a quill from the table and drew it through her fingers. "Please thank Amalric for me—he saved me from grievous sin. I would have plucked Guile's eyes out, if they hadn't stopped me."

Her mother hooted. She tied the rolls with ribbon and put them into the little chest before her on the table. "Amalric tells it differently."

"I'm sure he does. He's funny; I like him." Casually, lightly: "Who is this brother he has brought back with him?"

Agnes tossed her head up, angry, and sniffed. "Bah. That fellow! I wish he'd never come from France." She swung down the lid of the chest, and fastened the latch. "I shall require you tomorrow, when Maria d'Ibelin comes." A page came forward and took the chest.

"I'll be with you." Sibylla brushed the feather over her cheek. She wondered what Guy de Lusignan had done to annoy her mother; her imagination leapt, and she liked him even better.

"We have to find another lutenist. Or have the rest of them play without Marco. She will surely remark on how bad he is; I cannot bear to hear it."

"Isabelle de Plancy has a good lutenist," Sibylla said idly. "I'll send Alys over in the morning, to beg him from her." She wasted only the edge of her mind on her mother's small busy doings. She had larger dreams.

And larger problems. Now that her brother had concluded his truce with Saladin, he would advance his scheme for a new Crusade. She would face more expectations that she marry some prince, to save Jerusalem.

She could forestall that. She could marry as she willed, if she was quick enough.

She saw no harm in it, and some advantage. She needed a knight, to deal with men like Guile. Jerusalem needed a king. Her brother was the perfect knight, but he was lost to her. And soon, perhaps, he would be lost to all Jerusalem, and then the power would fall on her to make a new king.

A king who would be, first, her knight. Who would work her will. Who would have no loyalty save to her. Agnes was talking fretfully about the cook, who was French and loved garlic beyond all measure. Sibylla stroked the feather over her cheek again, soft as a caress.

Her mind went back to Guy de Lusignan, new come from France, sweet-natured and innocent. He seemed the solution to her problem. He had no one here, no connections, save his brother. If she raised him up, he would owe everything to her—he would have to do whatever she required of him. And she liked him. He was kind, and handsome; he reminded her somehow of her brother. Her brother, as he might have been.

God meant her to be Queen of Jerusalem. God would confer His grace on whomever she chose. Whatever she did, God willed. She reached out and laid the feather down on the polished surface of the table, lifted her head, and smiled.

The younger people had formed a circle, on the green grass beyond the lower terrace, and were dancing a round dance; in the center, a girl with a cushion waited for the music to stop. Agnes de Courtenay paused on the stair, her eyes on the swaying circle. De Ridford came up beside her.

"Oh, the joys of youth," Agnes said.

The Marshall of the Temple said, "I cannot believe I was ever so frivolous."

"No, no, not you." She smiled at him. "Whose every step shakes the world. Will there be an election for Master of the Temple?"

"Yes, soon. Odo de Saint-Amand is not coming back from Damascus."

"What would be required for you to win it?" She tried not to sound too eager, too greedy, but the chance to have the Master of the Temple in her debt tested her self-restraint.

He shook his head at her. "I don't want to win this one. Nobody wants to win this one. The King will send the Master of the Temple back to Europe, to preach the new Crusade. He'll do no fighting, lead no army; he'll just trudge from court to court for years, eating down the table, and smiling until his cheeks crack."

"Ah," she said. She watched the circle of the dancers turn, a slow, intricate rhythm, two steps to the right, three to the left, and then spin; as the girls spun, their skirts belled out a moment, green and gold.

The music abruptly broke off, and the girl in the center of the circle—it was Alys of Beersheba—dropped her cushion down before one of the men, and knelt on it, and he knelt on it also, and they exchanged a demure little peck of a kiss.

De Ridford said, "The Princess does not dance."

Sibylla and a man with shoulder-length blonde hair were coming in from the garden. Agnes said, "She seems to have a new friend."

"So I see. Who is he?"

"Guy de Lusignan," Agnes said. "Amalric's younger brother, fresh arrived from France."

"Oh," said de Ridford. "A shrewd move, my lady."

"You praise my daughter's choice of men, sir?" Agnes arched her brows at him.

He was very handsome when he laughed, his eyes shining, his teeth fine and even. He said, "No, lady. Your choice. As always." And laughed again.

CHAPTER XXI

You are just returned from Damascus, where you served on the embassy to the Sultan," Gilbert Erail said.

"Yes, my lord," the four Templars said, in unison. They stood in front of the whole chapter; the great refectory was quiet around them. Gilbert's voice rang flat and loud through the stone hall.

"Let Richard le Mesne answer."

Bear stepped forward. "Yes, my lord."

"I understand there was a truce arranged, between the King and the Sultan—is this true of your knowledge?"

"I heard the treaty read, my lord."

"Was anything base or unworthy given to the Sultan for it?"

"No, my lord. It was simple enough, just three years of truce, and no more."

De Ridford stood beside the Seneschal. He said, "Why then did the Sultan agree to it?" The ranks of the knights rumbled with low voices.

The Seneschal ignored them, but went on questioning Bear. "Did any of your brothers act in any way base or unworthy of the Order?"

"No, my lord," Bear said.

Rannulf looked down at his feet, smiling. They had been in a fever of contrition all the way back from Damascus. The Seneschal said, "Felx van Janke, answer."

Dutcher stepped forward. Because of his bald head he was allowed to keep a hat on during chapter meetings. Gilbert laced his crippled hand through his beard, his hooded eyes half-closed.

"Did any of your brothers act in any way base or unworthy of the Order?"

"No, my lord," Felx said.

"What did you see of the Count of Tripoli?"

"Very little, my lord. He kept to his part, and we to ours."

De Ridford said, "Then he may have made some secret treaty with the Sultan, without your knowledge. In fact you might as well have been in Jerusalem as Damascus, for all you had to do with the treaty, or so it sounds."

Felx said, "If we hadn't been there—"

Sharply, Gilbert broke in. "No, answer me alone. My lord Marshall, keep still."

"You ask the wrong questions," de Ridford growled.

"Perhaps I do, but it is my duty to ask them." Gilbert nodded to Felx. "You saw little of Tripoli, then? How did he act toward you?"

Felx hawed a moment, and Gilbert went in at this hint. "Answer me at once. How did Tripoli act toward you?"

"My lord, he dismissed us."

The chapter burst into loud talk. Gilbert raised his hands and patted down the noise. "He dismissed you!"

"He spoke very scornfully to us, and said he was insulted we had come."

"And how did you answer this scorn and insult?"

"My lord, we kept aside, and avoided him."

De Ridford grunted. "And this you call maintaining the honor of the Order!"

"My lord Marshall, as you would uphold the honor of the Order," Gilbert said, harsh-voiced, "then obey the Rule. Felx, in Damascus, saw you the Sultan?"

"Several times, my lord."

"And how did he act toward you?"

"My lord," Felx said, "he knows who his enemies are."

That made the whole chapter laugh. Gilbert Erail said, "Then I think it likely you upheld the honor of the Order. Stephen de l'Aigle, answer me."

An arm's length to Rannulf's left, Mouse stepped forward. "My lord Seneschal."

"Did any of your brothers act in any way base or unworthy of the Order?"

"No, my lord."

"What think you of Tripoli?"

"My lord, he hates us. He would not keep us at his table, or ride with us. He is like one with the Sultan, who treats him very well, and gives him presents, but to us the Sultan gave a promise of a battle to the death."

"God wills it," said Gilbert Erail. "What do you know of the making of the truce?"

"My lord, I was there when they agreed to it—" Mouse turned his head, and stared hard at de Ridford— "and it was as it reads: three years' truce, nothing given or taken."

"Rannulf Fitzwilliam, answer me."

Rannulf stepped forward, his hands clasped behind his back. "Yes, my lord."

"You saw Odo de Saint-Amand?"

"Yes, my lord."

"Is he well, and well-kept?"

"My lord, he is sick, and in a dungeon, and he says he will stay there until he dies, rather than let the Sultan turn him into money."

A roar of voices resounded through the refectory. Gilbert stared at him. "What of this truce?"

"It's a good truce, my lord."

"There was no hidden deal struck?"

"No, my lord."

"Will the Sultan keep it?"

"My lord, he has no choice. His country is full of plague, he cannot bring an army together, there are risings and rebels all over."

"Then this is why he made the truce."

"Yes, my lord."

"Why did you get on so ill with Tripoli?"

"My lord, I had no difficulty with Tripoli. He and the Sultan love each other, but when I needed him to stand fast with me, he did."

"Very good," Gilbert Erail said. "You have done good service; God will reward you. Go back."

The four men moved back into their places in the ranks. Rannulf stood at the left-hand end of the front row now. He turned, and looked around him at the other knights. While he was away in Damascus, two shiploads of men had come to join the chapter. Every day, more arrived, new recruits from France and Flanders and Germany, older men from the garrisons on Cyprus and the coast. Under the high ceiling of the refectory, hung with banners and ropes and cobwebs, the hall that had been nearly empty a few months before was now half-full again. His chest swelled. What he had promised Saladin was coming to pass. He felt the Temple all around him, a greater self, immortal. Gilbert was calling them to the holy office; Rannulf bowed his head with the rest of them and set his palms together, and this time, for once, he could pray.

✦ The Crypt was infested with black rats that crept through chinks in the stonework and ran along the beams of the ceiling. One day soon after they came back from Damascus, when there was nothing else to do, Rannulf took six of the knights into the room, and while they pulled the beds away from the walls and stuffed smoking rags into the cracks between the stones, he sat on a stool in the middle of the room, and shot the fleeing rats with a crossbow.

Stephen said, "This is the kind of work I would have given to sergeants." He had taken off his shirt; even in the summer the Crypt was usually cold, but the hard work had warmed him. Rannulf said, "What would you rather do, soap saddles?" He had the bolts laid out on his knee, and he slapped another into the bone slot on the box of the crossbow and set the trigger. Stephen went to help Felx van Janke and Ponce le Brun drag a bed away from the wall.

From the space behind it a dozen lank black bodies dashed, gibbering and squeaking, darting in all directions. Stephen dodged toward the middle of the room, which was prudent anyway because Rannulf shot at every rat he saw, careless of who was in between. The bow fired with a flat snap. The bolt nipped one furry black body up out of the swarm and smacked it against the stone wall. Rannulf reloaded and fired again, three times, four; the squeaking died away. Most of the rats had found cover. The four that had not lay on the floor, twitching and bleeding.

"Help me," said Ponce.

Stephen put his shoulder to an oaken chest and heaved it away from the wall. Outside the window, somebody was walking by, going toward the door. Stephen saw who it was, but he thought Rannulf did not, until Rannulf wheeled around and fired.

The door opened, just as the six-inch crossbow bolt buried itself to the vanes in the wooden jamb. Gerard de Ridford stood on the threshold. Coolly he looked at the bolt quivering heart-high in the doorframe beside him; he raised his eyes to Rannulf.

Rannulf said, "I beg your pardon, my lord Marshall."

De Ridford said, "Your aim is faulty. Give that work to someone better at it; I am going to see the King, and I want you to accompany me."

"Mouse," Rannulf said. He took the bolt out of the crossbow and got down from the stool. "Shoot the rats." He went across the room to take his jerkin and followed de Ridford out of the room.

De Ridford said, in a tone of mild injury, "Here I thought we were brothers."

"I missed, didn't I?" Rannulf said.

The Marshall laughed. "You know, sometimes I think you have more wit than I first supposed." They went down to the stables, under the corner of the great haram pavement, and rode out across Jerusalem to the citadel.

In the street, on the way, de Ridford started in again. "Did you enjoy yourself, in Damascus? I saw how you smiled, when le Mesne denied it."

"Everybody to his own vices," Rannulf said.

"But yours are more peculiar than other men's. Le Mesne, and van Janke, I understand. Even de l'Aigle makes sense to me." They had come to the citadel, and de Ridford went first through the gate. A train of camels crowded the yard between the two towers; the porters were unloading them of sacks and baskets, goods for the King's kitchens. De Ridford went into the tower and led the way up the stairs, past the rows of people at their endless waiting. The chamberlain announced them at once.

The King sat crumpled up among the cushions and bolsters of his throne. His eyes were glassy. The swollen, discolored skin of his face looked half-cooked. The two Templars went up before him and bowed.

De Ridford said, "God keep you, Sire. I am at your service, and Rannulf Fitzwilliam here, with me."

"Yes, thank you for answering me." The King hitched himself a little higher in the cushioned throne. His head seemed too heavy for him. His eyes stared at nothing. He was blind, Rannulf realized; he had been half-blind, when Rannulf last saw him, but now he saw nothing at all. His lips were split and bleeding and his voice wheezed up like something squeezed out of him. "Have you tested this truce, my lord Marshall?"

"I have investigated it, Sire, and know it to be fairly struck."

"Good. Then I have you with me. I am summoning the whole council of the Kingdom here for Christmas, and then we shall send out the call for the Crusade." The King swung his head to one side, turning away. "God cannot mean the fate of Jerusalem to turn on a woman's virtue."

Rannulf looked at him; he had heard that the Princess Sibylla still defied him, refused to marry to serve his policy, lived openly with some unknown knight. The King held one hand out, and a page came from behind the throne and put a cup of wine into his grasp, and closed his fingers around it.

The King said, "Rannulf. Tell me of the Sultan."

Rannulf said, "When we got there, Damascus was full of plague, and half-deserted. But he wanted us to think that it throve, and so he put on a show of a thriving city, with such crowds, and such shops and goods, I believed it, until I learned otherwise. That was what most impressed me, that he could do such a thing."

"You talked to him?"

"Somewhat. That was double-tongued, too."

De Ridford laughed. The King drank of the wine, spilling some of it on his chin; the page came back, and took the cup, and gave him a napkin, and the King swabbed at his face with it. He said, "What did you think of him?"

"That he has more of everything than we do. More people, more money, more land. More power."

"He does not have the one true and living God," said de Ridford. "Which is all that matters."

The King said, "And the plague has him stopped now."

"For now," Rannulf said. "There's something going on in the east, too, some rebellion. The plague is bad there, too, between the rivers. He needs the truce, and he certainly cannot fight."

"God save us from this pox," the King said.

Rannulf said, quietly, "God save us from this Sultan."

"Amen," de Ridford said.

"God may," the King said. "I will send for a new Crusade. My lord Marshall, have you considered the other thing I asked you?"

"I have, Sire," de Ridford said, smoothly. He nodded to Rannulf. "The King has asked me to provide him with a guard of our brethren, to stand watch over him day and night. I think you best suited for this duty."

Rannulf started. He said, "I have no wish to leave the Temple."

The King said, "I promise you, it will be only for a little while."

De Ridford said, "You are ordered to this duty, which you will take up."

"Take it," the King said. "I have no strength to argue with you."

"I will serve you, Sire," Rannulf said.

"Good," the King said. "Make arrangements. You have my leave."

The Templars went out again; in the street, de Ridford turned, and said, "I have just made you virtually King of Jerusalem, and you are too stupid to see the advantage in it. Which of course makes you perfect for my purposes. Keep him safe, and out of reach, is all I ask. I have already sown his mind with Tripoli's evils; can his foolish sister but bridle her headlong spirit, all shall be as I will it."

Rannulf said, "I will do this to serve the King, and not you. I will not be your spy."

"No, no. But I will know everyone who sees him, or tries to, and you will tell me especially should Tripoli seek the King's ear, in anything. And you will do this for the sake of the Order, hmm?"

Rannulf had already told him he would not; he saw no use in re-
peating it. He said, "I need men. I cannot do it alone."

"Take those you trust. I know already who they are; you will arrive
at it eventually." De Ridford smiled at him. "I ask nothing of you beyond your ability. You should thank me for seeing to your advancement."

"Thank you," Rannulf said.

The Temple held an election for Master, and elected Arnold da
Toroga, a Spanish knight. At Christmastide the King sent out the call
for a new Crusade, and his sister Sibylla married Guy de Lusignan, a
Poitevin knight nobody had ever heard of, who had been in the Holy
Land only a few months.

The King gave his sister's new husband the cities of Jaffa and Ascalon, and the title of Count of Jaffa, so that she would not be married to a landless man. But Baudouin would not receive the new-married pair; although he longed for his sister's company again, his pride controlled him.

Then the war came back.

Kerak had always disdained the truce, and he did not wait for the Crusade. In the year after Tripoli's return from Damascus, the Wolf built boats in his castle of Montreal and carried them on camels across the southern desert to Aqaba, and launched them on the Sea of Egypt. Packed with the Bedouin who supported him, this fleet raided all along the Arabian coast, threatening even Mecca. Kerak went back to the Ultrajordain, his pirates were all caught and hanged, and Saladin called his army out of the Syrian desert and led them on Jerusalem again.

The King was too sick to ride, too blind to see faces. He summoned all the knights in Outremer, and at the head of this army, borne in a litter, he went out to fight Saladin. They met on the Plain of Esdraelon, in the north of the kingdom.

The King had the Templars with him, to see for him, and carry his orders around, and make sure that he was obeyed. He arranged his army on the western edge of the swampy plain, where to attack him Saladin would have to cross the marshes and then expose himself on all sides to the charges of the knights. Saladin remained on the eastern edge of the plain. The King's scouts and spies reported that his great army was rapidly eating up the surrounding country.

The King sent to the knights of his army that they should parade and cavort in front of the Saracens, and draw them out to fight. So every day between the two armies there were single combats and flashy little melees. But Saladin would not launch a mass attack; Baudouin grew tired of waiting.

His sister's husband joined the army, leading some twenty men and a hundred footsoldiers. The King lay on his cot and heard the news of this, how the Count of Jaffa rode through the camp to the blowing of brass horns, a dozen banners flying, with a crowd of servants and a string of pack animals, and set up a little court of his own in the middle of Baudouin's army.

"Everything so new you can still smell the dyestuffs," Mouse told him. "Even their horseshoes shine."

The King laughed, but his heart ached. He missed his sister. He thought he saw a way back to her. He said, "Summon him to the council tonight, we shall look him over from close up."

But when the council met that night, in the King's tent, Jaffa had not come. Instead he sent a message, that he had joined the army to fight for the Cross, but that he would not greet King Baudouin as a brother until the King apologize for mistreating Guy's wife.

The King heard this and stiffened; the words jangled in his ears. For a moment he thought of dismissing Guy from the army and sending the Templars to do the job. His anger disoriented him. The noises of the other men shuffling into the tent blurred into a general roar, and he had to work to remember what was actually around him. For a moment his mind was blank; the black void engulfed him.

He fought down a surge of terror. He knew he sat in the back of the tent, with the Templars standing on either side of him, and beginning with them, he forced himself to remember, to rebuild it all in his mind; the arch of the silk above his head and the space around him, full of people; he made himself give the people faces, and then came to realize that Jaffa's messenger still stood in front of him, waiting for an answer.

He said, "Hell freezes, first. Tell your master that. Go."

From the inchoate darkness before him came a murmur of leave-taking. He put his hand out, and someone—one of the Templars—put a cup into it. He drank deep.

"Come up around me," he said, in a loud voice, to the darkness. "I shall hear your counsel."

They gathered around him; they talked over the stand-off, and how to lure Saladin into the trap set for him. Tripoli and de Ridford got into an argument, and the King, in a rage, shouted them to silence. With so little life left to him it infuriated him that they would waste his time on their stupid quarrel. The hot bolt of his anger sustained him; he called forth each man in his turn, got from him what he knew, and gave him orders, and when he was done, sent them all away and then sank down, exhausted.

The black nothing surrounded him. There was silence.

He said, "Who is there?"

"Mouse," said the knight, beside him. "And Felx. Do you wish anything, Sire?"

"I'm tired," the King said and put his hand out, and they lifted him. Then he heard Tripoli's voice, somewhere at a distance.

"No. He must hear us. Let me by!"

"Hold," the King said. "Sit me down again." Lifting his voice, he called, "My lord of Tripoli, come here."

They set him down on the chair again. His mouth was dry; he put out his hand, and they gave him wine to drink. His weary mind struggled to remember what Tripoli looked like, a face that he had known since babyhood. The voice helped.

"Sire, we have come to speak to you as your loyal men, and as the barons of this kingdom."

He grunted. He could see already that this was going somewhere unpleasant. "Which loyal men are these?"

"Sire, I am here, and Balian d'Ibelin, Reginald of Sidon, a few other men."

The King's temper simmered again, that uplifting fire. He said, "I see. Speak, then."

His voice warned them. Tripoli said nothing; the others coughed and cleared their throats. At last Balian said, "Sire, for the sake of the kingdom, you ought to yield the throne."

"Really," the King said. His rage felt like an iron man inside his skin. "To whom?"

Tripoli said, "Sire, you have served beyond all our hopes—"

"And will serve yet," the King said. "God gave me this task, to defend Jerusalem, and this body to do it with, and I will go on doing it until God himself removes me. Now, leave me."

Tripoli said, "Sire, you must—"

"Leave me," the King said, his throat raw, his brain beating in his skull, "leave me before I have them throw you out." He raised his hand, and in a rush the men before him were moving. He felt the Templars brush by him on either side, and heard them all hurrying noisily away, toward the front of the tent. He sank down in the chair.

He said, aloud, "I should, he is right, I should let him be King."

"No," Rannulf said, beside him. "You are the King, you should have seen them quake when you railed at them."

His voice startled Baudouin, who had not known he was there. He put his arms out, and the Templar lifted him. One of the others came and helped him bear the King away to his cot, and take off his crown and his robe and shoes, and lay him down. Dust and ashes, he thought. Ashes and dust. What was it he clung to with such a fervor? He could feel nothing, see nothing; his ears were full of sounds, but most of them were illusions. Yet through this ran some edge of understanding, a little ripple of a connection with the world. If he lost that seam he would disappear. The world would disappear. His mind reeled.

He said, "Rannulf, why does the Sultan not attack?"

The knight said, "He's gotten too clever. He sees the trap. But he'll have to move soon, he's running out of forage."

"When the battle starts—" The King swallowed. A longing rose in him so strong and sweet it made him groan. "I want to lead the first charge. Swear this to me, that you will obey me in this. If you have to tie me to the horse. If Saladin but gives me the opening, I will die like a man."

"Sire," Mouse said.

"Swear it," the King said.

"We swear," they all said, together.

He laid his head down on the pillow. He was exhausted but if he let go, if he gave up to the darkness, how would he ever find his way back again? So needing to sleep he battled against it, until at last sleep crushed him like a cross.

In the end Saladin backed off. With his whole huge army he faded away into the desert. The Franks took King Baudouin back to Jerusalem. He was dying, and all knew it. The summer heat oppressed him, and he sent to his sister's husband, Guy, Count of Jaffa, and asked him to give him Jaffa in trade for Jerusalem, because he longed for the cool and the sweet air of the seacoast. And he wanted also to see his sister again, to reconcile himself with her.

But Sibylla was in childbed. Her husband the Count took no counsel with her, only sent immediately back to the King that for the sake of pride and honor, and the mortal insult that Baudouin had dealt him and his wife, Jaffa would give him nothing.

Then the King called up all the great men of the Kingdom, the patriarch and the Masters of the Hospitallers and the Templars, and the Count of Tripoli who was in the city by chance, Philip de Milly and Balian d'Ibelin and young Humphrey de Toron, the King's uncle Joscelin de Courtenay, and even the lord of Kerak. Before this council he disinherited his sister and her husband, and he changed the succession from her to her son by her first marriage, who was six years old. If the child died before he was of major age, then Tripoli was to get the crown. If he died older, but without issue, the Pope and the Emperor should name the new King.

De Ridford argued against it, as much as he dared, but the King would hear no persuasions.

He set up a council of all the barons to rule as Regent. He excluded Sibylla and her husband from any part in the governance of the Kingdom. He wanted to name Tripoli as the guardian of the child King, but the Count refused, saying if the boy died, he would surely be accused of murdering him. So Joscelin de Courtenay was his great-nephew's guardian. As the child's bodyguard King Baudouin chose Rannulf Fitzwilliam.

Baudouin was so weak now he could not lift his head by himself, but to the last he was the lord of Jerusalem, and the greatest men of his kingdom submitted to his will. They swore to his testament in the Church of the Holy Sepulcher, each man with his hand on the empty marble box that was the emblem of their faith, the proof that death could not hold them. But death was waiting there among them as they signed and sealed the charter.

The King went into his citadel and lay down in his bed. His mother came down from Nablus, and he said good-by to her, and sent her away. He took the viaticum, and called the Templars around him.

"My life is over; I know I shall not get up again. I am not afraid of dying. In all my life I regret only one thing, which is that I lost my sister, through my own fault, commanding her to do what I should not even have asked of her. For the rest, I am content. God gave me charge of Jerusalem, and I have kept faith with that. As for my dying I shall do that away from the eyes of the crowd, and without a constant looking in to see if I am gone yet. Send everybody else away. Henceforth, only you four shall be around me, and tend to me. And tell no one how I fare, no one, until I am dead. And then I don't care whom you tell."

But the King did not die at once. Ordinary things went on. He lay in his bed and listened to the four men around him. Among themselves they spoke a crossbreed of Latin and French, with odd bits of Arabic mixed in. Rannulf bullied them all like an older brother.

"Getting enough to eat?"

"He left his whole meal, all that food would go to waste."

"Well, I can see you aren't going to let that happen."

The King said, "Let him eat it. What are you, a bishop? Let me tell you, Saint, I have little patience with all this holy deprivation. I have never touched a woman, my beard stopped growing long ago, I have no pleasures left; everything you do for God's sake, God makes me do, and I know it is worthless. In me, sickness, in you, vanity. So let him eat."

"You're dying," Rannulf told him, close by. "You're safe from sin. He wallows in it." Hands tugged and pulled at Baudouin's covers, rough, as if Rannulf knew that through the numbness of his flesh Baudouin could feel only roughness, pulling, and tugs. His vision was a field of sparkles and blobs of light; his ears popped and crackled so that sometimes he could hardly hear anything else.

Sometimes his mind stuck, clogged on one word, one thought. Then dreams swam up from the depths of him, memories, old fears and yearnings, and he wondered how long he could go on keeping track of what was real.

The ordinary voices of the men, saying their prayers.

He was tired, and near the end, now.

"Someone bring me drink." He could still make noise.

Felx came; he knew even before the voice sounded, he knew them all by touch. The Netherlander's slow and careful hands sat him up and fed him watered wine. Felx always watered the wine.

"What are you doing now?" In among the aimless tweaks in his hearing there was a real sound, somewhere between grinding and bells, a chiming of metal.

"Mouse is cutting Saint's hair," Felx said.

A scissors. His imagination assembled it for him, all out of that one noise: Rannulf on a stool, his head bent, submissive for once, the redheaded knight behind him with the twinned knives in his hand. The bits of black hair falling.

"Will you cut my hair?"

They washed his hair, using some potion against lice that Bear had gotten in the Under City, and combed it and cut it. He slept; when he woke they dressed him, sat him up in crowds of pillows, brought him food he did not eat. Eating seemed extraneous now, when he was so close to dying.

He knew how close he was, he could feel his mind giving way. It could be worse, he thought; he could be so dazed and useless, and not die. He forgot things, important things, which bothered him.

"Did my sister have her baby?"

"Back at Candlemas, Sire."

"Oh. Convenient." He struggled with a fog in the middle of his mind. "Why does she not come to see me?"

No answer. He knew the answer, anyway. He lay still, feigning sleep. He was asleep more and more now.

Often the chamberlain came to the door, trying to gain audience for this one, and that one; Rannulf told him to send them all away.

This time he brought a message, a piece of paper.

"What's that?"

"Abu Hamid's mark. I have to answer this. Mouse, you come with me."

"Where are you going?" Baudouin asked, but no one heard him. Or perhaps he had only said it in his mind.

Maybe it all happened only in his mind. Maybe he was already dead, and this was hell.

The summer heat beat down on the suk, and the air rippled above the buildings. On the flat roofs the grass that had grown green there during the spring rains was withered to white straw. Rannulf left his horse with Stephen, and went down between two shops to the back door into the house of Abu Hamid, who had summoned him.

This door opened into a shadowy room with white plastered walls, cooler than the outdoors. Rannulf went in, expecting to find the merchant or one of his friends, and stopped short, his jaw dropping open. At the far end of the room, the Princess Sibylla turned and faced him.

For a moment he could not take his eyes from her. He had not seen her since before she married. She stared calmly back at him through the shadows of the room until he mastered himself and lowered his eyes.

"Thank you for coming," she said.

"I would not have, had I known it was you," he said, staring at the floor.

"I am aware of that." She was moving up the room toward him. "But I have come to plead with you, Rannulf, to beg you to take me to my brother."

The softness of her footstep was a thunder on his nerves. He shook his head. "There is nothing you can do. He has bound the succession in iron bands, with safeguards all around, you cannot break it."

"Ah," she said. "What you think of me! I don't care about the succession, Saint. He's dying. I have to see him before he dies. Please. I shall go to my knees before you." He heard the susurrus of her skirts; he shut his eyes, unwilling to see her humble herself. She said, "I beg you. Take me to him."

He crossed himself; what decided him was not her desire, but that he knew the King's. He said, "I will take you."

"Thank you," she said. "Let me fetch my cloak."

✦ The room was dark, and stank of steeped herbs and human slops. Sibylla said, on the threshold, "Bati?" She was already weeping. She had promised herself she would be serene, she would show no frailty, but the tears flooded down her cheeks. "Bati?" She crossed the room to the raised bed; she forgot about the Templars behind her, she saw only the carcass of her brother lying on the bed.

He was dead. She was too late. She laid her head down on his chest and sobbed.

The Templars left them alone. Under her head his chest heaved. From his wrecked flesh his voice rose as if from the bottom of a well. "Bili?" His head turned, his arms twitched, trying to reach for her. "Bili," he whispered. "You came. You did come after all." She gathered him into her arms, laughing with relief, and sprinkled him with her tears.

Toward evening, two of the Templars came back into the room: Rannulf, and the handsome redheaded knight inexplicably called Mouse. Her brother was asleep. Sibylla drew back, turning her gaze on the two men.

"I want to stay until the end," she said. "But no one else must know that I am here."

Rannulf went to the King's bedside. The knight Mouse said, "You have no women with you, Princess, it's not seemly."

"I don't care," she said. "I want to stay."

"She can stay," Rannulf said. He lit the lamp on the King's bedstead. "Mouse, go fetch her something to eat. Call Felx and Bear and put them on guard at the door."

The redheaded knight went out again. Sibylla crossed the room to the window; she could hear doves calling, in the stonework just outside. The sun was going down, the sky like bloody rags. Below, in the courtyard, a sentry called out and another answered, passing the word. The sill of the window was still warm under her hand.

Coming here had cost her something. Her husband considered his feud with the King to be the measure of his own greatness. If he found out she was not in Beersheba, with Alys and the baby, where she had made as if to go, there would be trouble. She had lied to him to get around the trouble.

He would never find out. She was good at lying.

The cost was worth it. She went to her brother again.

He lay in the rucked covers, his breathing loud and harsh. His hair was cut short, like a Templar's. His face was unrecognizable beneath the crusty, swollen sores. The bedclothes stank of sweat. She said, "Does he always sound like that?" Gathering the embroidered coverlets in her hands she tried to straighten them. "Help me," she said. "Lift him."

The knight came obediently up beside her, and cradled the King in his arms and held him while she smoothed the bed. He said, "He sounds worse and worse."

She said, "Once, he was the most beautiful boy. They all said I should have been the boy, and he the girl, he was so much more beautiful than I. His hair was down to his shoulders, long yellow curls, and he had eyes like my father's. My father could look at you like pins going through you."

"I remember him," the knight said.

She laid the pillows down. "Here, put him to rest." Standing back, she watched her brother stretched on the bed. Leaning forward, she reached out to draw the cover up. The knight had begun to do that, and their hands touched.

At the touch he recoiled; he jerked his hand back as if she burned him. She wheeled around, angry. "Am I so hateful to you?"

"No, Princess," he said. He was staring at the floor again, as he always did.

"Ah," she said. "I cannot understand you."

She turned back to her brother, tucking the cover around him. Behind her the knight was silent. Yet his silence and his downcast look no longer shut her out. Somehow, in touching him, she had pierced the magic armor of his vow.

Mouse returned, with servants bringing bread and cheese and wine; he had brought two women, too, but Rannulf sent them away immediately. The knights who had been outside standing guard came in, a big bald man with a blonde beard, and a bigger dark-haired man, and they all ate together, Sibylla among them, like peasants, sitting on the floor. Mouse, who had a pretty, courtly way about him, broke her bread for her and filled her cup. After, the four men knelt down and said their prayers.

Sibylla went to the bed and stood looking down at her brother. She thought of times in their youth, of hunting with their father in the wilderness and going to Mass on Christmas. He slept, his mouth open and the breath sawing in and out of his throat. She stroked her hand over his cropped hair, but he did not awaken. She wondered if he had received the Sacrament. Tears began to slip down her face. She had always loved him; as children they had been allies against their mother, their nurses, the regent Tripoli, the countless meaching sycophantic schemers and bribers around them. She thought bitterly she would give up her prospects for the crown, give up her husband, give up everything, to have her brother back again.

She thought of her new daughter, in Beersheba, providing her excuse. She would not give up her daughter.

Rannulf and Mouse went out. The other two knights lay down on their cots, on the far side of the room, and slept. They had brought in a cot for her also and put it at the foot of the bed, but she did not lie down on it. She felt alone now, and easier. It felt good to be by herself, and not to have to worry about how everything she did would seem to Guy. She went about the room picking up some of the mess. The night had at last subdued the baking summer heat. Through the window the air rushed in a cool torrent. She leaned on the sill, pushing her face into the breath of the night, and looked out over Jerusalem. After living a while in breezy, orange-scented Jaffa she found this city strange and harsh.

Something in it summoned her, some call to be greater.

"Bili."

She wheeled. Her brother had wakened, his head turned on the pillows, and she went to his side. "Here I am." She put her hand on his hand.

His fingers moved feebly against hers. "I thought I dreamed it." The words crept from him, slurred, run together. "Where is your baby?"

"She's with Alys, she's safe and well. She's so pretty, Bati, she is as pretty as a new rose. I wish you could see her. We've named her Alice, for his mother, but we all call her Jolie."

"You love her, then," he said.

"Yes. More than anything."

"Good." He was running out of strength. "I'm . . ." His mouth moved but nothing came out. His head rolled on the pillow.

"Bati. What do you want?"

His lips moved. She went across the room to the door and opened it. "Please, help me," she said into the dark outside, and the door pushed wide and Rannulf came in.

He went straight to the bed and leaned over the King; she stood by the foot of the bed, watching. There was a cup on the table, and the Templar lifted the King up in the circle of his arm and gave him to drink. She saw that he did not drink.

She said, "Has he received the Sacrament?"

The knight nodded. Laying her brother down again, he said, low, "God gives you this." He went back to the door and pulled in the latch, then returned to the bed and stood at the head of it, his hands on the hilt of his sword. Sibylla sat down by the bed to wait.

✠ Rannulf fell asleep on his feet; deep in the night, the bell for vigils woke him. The room was quiet. Three candles burned steadily on the chest by the bed. The King lay on his back, his breathing ragged. His sister slept also; sitting on the stool, she had laid her head down on the bed by the King's feet, and fallen asleep that way.

Rannulf opened the door onto the stairway, and looked out. Stephen and Felx were there, under the torch on the landing, saying the vigils office. He left the door slightly open, and went back to the bed.

He stood looking down at the Princess; it seemed less of a sin to look at her as she slept. She had taken off her headdress, and her hair lay in heavy coils around her. Her cheek was ruddy, her mouth half open. Twice he reached out to touch her, to waken her; each time he drew his hand back. Finally he stooped and lifted her up in his arms, her legs draped in her long skirts, and her head against his shoulder.

For a moment he held her, looking into her face, her eyelid delicate as a shell and her mouth reckless. If he could have held her like that forever he would never have moved again. She stirred, her head turning, and he laid her down on the cot.

He went to the head of the King's bed, crossed himself, and said the vigils office. The door opened, and Stephen came in. Rannulf went to the empty cot under the window and lay down on it, but for a long while he could not sleep, and his arms where he had touched her seemed scalded to the bone.

✠ Late in the afternoon, the King died. They summoned the priests, and servants, and various lords; it did not matter now, they let anyone into the room who cared to enter. The four Templars themselves left, even before the body did.

Sibylla said, "I have to go back to Jaffa, and I want no one to know I was ever in Jerusalem."

Rannulf said, "How did you get here? Through Abu Hamid?"

She nodded. "He can arrange my return."

"Mouse and I will take you down to the Under City."

So, in the evening, wrapped and hooded in a cloak, and with a Templar riding on either stirrup, she took the road down into the Under City.

She was exhausted. She could not think of her brother; that he was dead had no meaning for her yet, nothing seemed to have changed.

She had to think about what would happen next. About how she would save the Kingdom.

From the first she had seen the futility in her brother's elaborate schemes to keep her from the throne. The new King would be her son, who was only six, and frail. The Regency was given to a council, and she knew this kingdom: no such council as her brother had contrived would ever rule here. In their quarrels and rivalries she could maneuver to get what she wanted. Many on the Council were her enemies, but she had her friends there also: her uncle Joscelin and de Ridford, who would see to her interests.

Bracketed between the Templars, she was coming down into the suk. The goatpens were empty, the produce market closed. The merchants were taking in their stalls, unhooking awnings from poles, and gathering up the goods unsold during the day. By the fountain the women of the Under City had gathered with their jugs. Abu Hamid's servants were rolling up the carpets that had covered the ground in front of his house, showing off some jugs of brass which now tumbled carelessly into a basket.

She glanced at the knight on her left hand, considering how to draw him tighter to her.

She said, "Saint, when you were in Damascus, how could the Sultan have been persuaded to give us a true peace?"

Rannulf said, "There can be no peace between him and me. I have what he wants."

This was of no use to her, and its clarity was dangerous. Her hand tightened on the reins. Her voice harshened. "You make it seem so simple."

"It is simple," he said. "Not easy."

"God's grace," she said, angry. "What a saint. And the blood all over you."

"Even Jesus had to die," he said. He made the sign of the Cross over the cross on his chest. The Templars drew rein at the front gate of the merchant's house. Sibylla spoke to the knight beside her.

"You blaspheme, Saint. Jesus died to save us; not to glorify death, but to defeat it. We cannot go on fighting with the Saracens, we must find some way to live with them."

Rannulf turned toward her; he looked full at her, his eyes black as hellfire and no shame in them, no humility, only a hateful, saintly arrogance. "This may be your Kingdom, Princess," he said. "But it's my war. Mouse, take her."

Now he averted his gaze, cutting her off. She said quietly, so that only he could hear her, "You devil. Damn you, you are the angel of death." The red knight dismounted and came around to lift her down from her horse. Still simmering with her balked temper, she went on ahead of him through the gate, and he spoke to the porter, who ran off for his master. She turned to Mouse.

"Thank you," she said. "I shall not forget how well you have helped me."

"Princess," he said. "I loved the King."

Startled at the feeling in his voice, she put out her hands to him, and then remembered and drew back. "I know, Mouse."

"He needed you, and you came," he said. "If you ever need me, Princess, call me." He bowed his head to her, and he went out the gate again.

She stood looking after him, her mind brought unprepared back to her brother, and for the first time, a pang of unbearable grief pierced her heart. Outside, beyond the walls, a wail of voices went up.

"The King! The King!" The news had reached the suk.

She stiffened, helpless, laid open utterly to this. Abu Hamid hastened toward her, his face contorted. "My lady! My lady, is it true?"

"Yes," she said, her voice shaking. "The King is dead. Our good King Baudouin is dead." Up in the Holy City, the bells began to toll. She buried her face in her hands, and cried.

✠ Rannulf did not go to the palace, but went back to the Temple, to the church of the Rock, and knelt down before the altar and tried to pray.

The church was empty. The Rock rolled out before him like a petrified sea, its crumpled and dented surface pooled with shadows. Overhead, beyond the lamps, the dome seemed distant as a dream. He thought of German, who in this place had called him a renegade.

Deep in his left forearm, the old wound throbbed, what he thought of as German's wound.

He could not pray. He hated God. His mind churned with a filthy and sinful rage against God. He sat back on his heels and looked out across the Rock, the way to Heaven.

The King was dead, whom Rannulf had loved, taken not honorably and nobly but piece by rotten piece. As if God were evil, and despised good, and destroyed it everywhere he found it. It was not as the priests said. It was not the world that was wicked; the world was sweet and good and full of beauties, but God blighted it all, save what was false, and that God magnified.

God had slain the King, while worthless men like Kerak throve, and that was all the proof Rannulf needed; he judged God guilty.

In his forearm the wound pulsed like flowing blood.

He remembered how she had cursed him, at the end. His chest ached. He loved her. For a whole day he had lived in the same room with her, he had spoken to her; she had touched him, he had held her. Although he had tried to keep his gaze from her, her image was graven on his mind: her clear, wide eyes, the blade of her cheekbone, her stubborn, sensuous mouth. And she was selfless as an angel. She had come to her brother in his extremity and loved him, as pure and good as the waters of Eden, and not even that had softened God's heart, not even that had saved Baudouin.

He gripped the front of his jerkin in both fists, as if he would pull the Cross off his chest.

I defy you, he thought, too craven to say it out loud. I am your knight no more. Strike me where I stand, or wither me up like an uprooted weed, but I will pray to you and fight for you no more. He lurched onto his feet like a drunken man and staggered out of the church.

CHAPTER XXIII

Everybody called the new King Baudouinet. He was small for his age, and not strong. They brought him from his grand-mother's house in Nablus, and crowned him in the Church of the Holy Sepulcher, in robes too big for him, with a crown too heavy for his head.

He sat straight and solemn on the throne, and the men around him told him what to say, and he said it. He was apt enough. He listened carefully to his great-uncle Joscelin, who explained everything to him, and he quickly learned the little speeches required of him and said them very well.

Saladin sent an embassy to him, to attend the coronation, and presented the Sultan's compliments. The little King received them in the hall of the citadel, with two of his Templar guards flanking him, Stephen to the left of the throne, Rannulf to the right.

The Sultan's chief legate was the black eunuch, gorgeous in a gold-trimmed robe, his head shaven clean as a shelled egg. He spoke the Sultan's greetings in excellent French, and offered the little King some presents. Behind him, in among his attendants, Stephen saw a face familiar to him.

His heart jumped. He had not seen Ali in more than two years, but the sight of him woke everything up again. The tall Saracen was watching him, as well; their eyes met, and between them a spark leapt like a bolt of lightning.

The eunuch had laid a tray of little gifts at the King's feet. Baudouinet was bending forward to peer at them, excited. "Show me these things." He pointed.

The eunuch murmured something, and glanced behind him; smoothly he stepped aside, and Ali came forward and went down on one knee in front of the silver tray. "Your Highness must permit me the honor." Picking up a little silver cone, he spun it between his fingers and dropped it onto the tray, where it whirled and hummed; the King crowed. He had scooted forward to the very edge of the throne, and perched on it like a little bird, his knees up.

"What's that?"

Ali took another of the toys and twisted a key in its belly. "This is Greek work, your Highness." The toy clanked and flapped and made grotesque noises. Stephen realized it was supposed to be some kind of animal. Baudouinet laughed and clapped his hands.

"Is it permitted to address your Highness' guards?" Ali asked smoothly. He picked up another of the objects on the tray.

Baudouinet looked sharply into the Saracen's face. "Why do you want to do that?"

Stephen almost laughed out loud at Ali's look; all his subtlety brought to nothing, the Kurdish prince fumbled a while, hunting a good answer, and said, finally, "I knew them both in Damascus, Sire."

"Then speak to them," the little King said. "But show me that first." He pointed to the toy in Ali's hand.

This was an enamel frog, which hopped. Ali lifted his head. He glanced briefly at Stephen, and turned to Rannulf, and spoke Arabic.

"My uncle bade me tell you that the meeting on the Plain of Esdraelon was a draw."

Rannulf shifted on his feet, his hands on the hilt of his sword. "He backed off. He can call it what he wants."

Ali stood up, leaving the child on the throne to play by himself. "He also bade me give you his sincere sympathies on the death of your King. He had a profound respect for Baudouin the Leper."

"That I will accept," Rannulf said.

"While I am in Jerusalem, I would like to visit the holy places of Islam."

"You may go wherever you wish," Rannulf said. "I have nothing to hide from you."

"I would like very much to go into the Haram al-Sharif," Ali said.

"Do you want a guide?" Rannulf said. "Mouse will take you." He turned his head and looked at Stephen. "Go with him. Make sure he sees everything he wants to."

Stephen met Ali's gaze again, eager. "Yes, my lord."

✦ The air inside was cold. Ali went forward, across the curved ambulatory, into one of the archways, and stood looking at the Rock.

For a moment he was beyond himself, gazing on the massive outcrop where Mohammed had begun his rise to Heaven; in him something rose up also, trying to follow. He bowed his head, and said some prayers of thanks and praise.

After a while he remembered Stephen, behind him, and straightened. He laid his hand on the iron railing in front of him. "What is this?"

"People were chipping away pieces of the Rock to take home with them," Stephen said. "We put the railing up to keep them off."

Ali said, "Barbarians."

"A fair number of these people were Saracens."

Ali laughed. "Barbarians," he said, again. He was looking out over the Rock; the cold silence of the place impressed him. The air seemed blue from the blue interior wall of the dome. On the Rock was a stone altar, with a cup on it, and a book.

He said, "You hold your services here."

"Twice a day," Stephen said.

Ali shook his head. "It cannot be as holy to you as it is to me." It angered him to see the altar on the Rock.

"This is the center of the world. Directly over us is Heaven, directly under us is hell. This is what we are fighting over, isn't it?" Stephen came up to stand next to Ali, like a challenge. "I love this place. I come in here whenever I can. This is the closest place on earth to God. Don't tell me I don't hold it holy."

Ali faced him, his temper rising, and caught himself. "We are defiling it, then, by arguing here."

Stephen's set hard look relaxed. "Yes," he said. "Thank you." He crossed himself. Ali stood watching him, pulled unwillingly to some understanding. He turned and looked at the Rock, its dark surface tossed like a frozen ocean.

He said, "What happens when we are in the right place to fight, Stephen? Will you kill me? Will I kill you?"

"If God wills it," Stephen said.

"You say that when you can't think of anything else to say."

Stephen said nothing, looking down. Ali struggled with himself. Someone came into the church, going through another arch to the railing, knelt there a moment, and went out again. The busy scraping of his steps died away. The silence seemed more pure for it. Ali felt the cold of the air on his skin like a burning. Directly above him was God. He felt pulled upward in every strand.

For the first time he did not surrender. For the first time, he rebelled, he clung to himself.

Stephen said, "Where I lived, before I came here, the old people said that God keeps a great hall in Heaven, and there he gathers the men who die fighting for him, the truest warriors, and the best, and they keep company in that hall until the battle at the end of the world. Maybe at that table some are Christian men, and some are Saracen."

Ali said, harshly, "You believe in fables."

"I have to believe in something."

"Is this a common failing of the Order? What does al-Wali believe?"

Stephen said, "Poverty, chastity, and obeying orders."

"Soon your Order will elect a new master. Will they choose him?"

Stephen shook his head. "Nobody will vote for Rannulf. He has more enemies than a beggar has lice. If you want to talk about politics, let's get out of here." He bent his knee and crossed himself and led Ali away out of the mosque.

Ali followed him. On the wide pavement, he stood a moment, looking toward the hulking building at the edge of the haram, which was the mosque al-Aqsa, now defiled under a weight of Christian idolatry. They were a race of idiots, he thought, his heart sore. He looked at the red knight beside him, with his loose easy stride, his high-headed bearing, a beautiful young beast. The enemy. They walked together across the open, sunlit pavement, toward al-Aqsa.

"Not like Damascus," Stephen said. "This is our refectory. That long wing is the dormitory, and the armory is around the back."

Ali swept a look around him. A steady stream of men went in and out of the long low building Stephen had called the dormitory; by their white jerkins they were the knights. Many others, not knights, hurried and toiled around the pavement. Off to his left, where a string of slender white columns formed an arcade, there were knots of people working; by a forge waited a string of the rangy, coarse-headed horses the knights rode, and he could hear the ringing of hammers and smell the hot iron; as he watched, two men carrying a handtruck, stacked with long loaves of bread and rounds of cheese, wove their way through the shifting tide of people around al-Aqsa and went inside. At another angle, a groom led several horses away across the pavement at a jog.

Ali lifted his eyes from the bustle and purpose of the Temple Mount and scanned what he could see of the walls of Jerusalem, set with high square towers, running off to the north and west. Crouched like a lioness on this spur of rock, with steep defiles on three sides, the city was impregnable, if she were well garrisoned and supplied.

He said, "You don't live here now."

"No," Stephen said. "I live in the citadel, with the King. I wish I were here, guarding the King is boring." He led Ali around to the side of the great old mosque, to a yard where there were posts set in the ground;

before each post stood a man in armor with a sword. "We all work here every day, with our weapons. These are novices, which is why they can't hit."

Ali watched the rows of young men sweating and groaning with their swords. "They seem to be hitting well enough to me."

"Oh," Stephen said, "we'll teach them to fight like Templars."

Ali turned, and looked down the great complex. From here he could see nearly all of it, and much of the city beyond, of which it took up such a huge part. Against his will he was impressed. He knew why they were letting him see this. In the rows of workshops by the arcade, in the practice yards, around the refectory, crowds of men worked and slacked and talked, dozens of men, hundreds. The Temple had recovered.

Stephen said, "Where are you staying?" They walked off along the edge of the pavement.

"In a palace in the city. Across the gate from where we met today." On their left rose the top of the wall, massive dressed stones, the color of honey, set almost seamlessly together. Beyond them the hillside plunged away into a barren valley.

"La Plaisance," Stephen said. He was smiling, in the tangled red mat of his beard. "That's a pretty enough place, isn't it?"

"It's a very agreeable surprise, actually. There's even a bath, and the gardens are fine."

"I've been there," Stephen said. "The King's grandmother stays there when she is in Jerusalem. I could meet you in the garden." Their hands brushed together, swinging between them as they walked.

Ali's mouth was dry. There were people everywhere here; the burden of secrecy shackled him. He said, "I'm sure this is very dangerous for you."

"I'll take the chance," Stephen said. "Tonight. In the garden?"

Ali said, "I'll be there. After dark." Their hands touched again, as if by accident. Their little fingers hooked together and instantly slipped apart. Ahead of them were more crowds of men. Ali ran his tongue over his lips. His uncle was not going to be happy with this. Yet his body felt electric, and he could not keep from smiling.

✦ Rannulf was in the Under City, in the suk, eating dates, and talking to the camel-drivers. Stephen went up beside him, and waited until the other knight chose to see him there.

"Well?" Rannulf said, finally.

"They've left. I made sure he saw everything you wanted, the towers, the gates. If he didn't know before how strong this city is, he does now."

"Good," Rannulf said.

"He said something odd. He said we are going to have another election soon. Is that true?"

Rannulf's head turned sharply toward him, his black eyes wide. "Did he."

"Yes. Do you know anything about this?"

"I heard a rumor, from Cyprus, that's all. Arnold da Toroga died in Paris, preaching the Crusade; we need a new master." Rannulf spat out a date stone. "The bastard has better spies than I do. He knows more than I do."

"He knows the gross, not the fine," Stephen said. "He asked if you would be elected."

Rannulf laughed. He looked at Stephen through the corner of his eye. "What did you tell him?"

"I said you had no chance," Stephen said.

Rannulf turned away. Stephen followed him off across the suk, toward the fountain.

"Should I have lied?"

"No," Rannulf said. "You did well, Mouse. You did everything right."

✧ What Stephen had said gnawed on Rannulf. Although he knew he could never win the election, he wanted to be Master. He thought if he could not serve God anymore, he could at least be Master of the Temple.

With Stephen, he went to the Temple, to the practice butts, and took his sword and began to work at the butt with it. It had been a long while since he had done any sword work. He stood square to the post, and hacked at it with the blade, alternating forehands and backhands, as he always did; his arms began to ache almost at once.

Behind him, Stephen gave a low whistle, and he lowered the sword and turned around.

De Ridford was standing on the step nearby, watching him. Rannulf wore only his shirt, which was soaked through with sweat; he wiped his forearm over his face.

De Ridford said, smiling, "You are supposed to practice in full mail."

"Bring it up in a chapter meeting," Rannulf said. He took the sword up again.

De Ridford waited, patient. When Rannulf stopped, his arms throbbing, the Marshall said, "I wonder how you manage to get through all these fights, Rannulf, your form is so bad."

"Is that what you came over here to tell me?"

"Actually, no." The Marshall came a step closer. "You know the castle Montgisor?"

"I have been there."

"There is to be a council. I will go, and you will accompany me. We shall leave in the morning."

"A council," Rannulf said sharply. "In whose interest?"

"Some great men of the Kingdom. You have a little power now, you ought to learn to use it."

Rannulf laid his forearm on the butt, and leaned on it, studying de Ridford's face; the Marshall's eyes closed like a cat's, sleek, assured. Rannulf said, "My orders are to guard the King."

"Your men are capable." De Ridford glanced past him, toward Stephen, and nodded to Rannulf. "This is an order. Kerak will be there, Courtenay, Jaffa, perhaps the Princess herself. The fate of this Kingdom will turn on what is said there."

Rannulf said, "Well, I doubt that." He stared straight at de Ridford, letting a little silence grow up to cover his sudden eagerness. He said, "I'll go."

"Yes." The grease of de Ridford's smile slid across his face again. "You should change your stroke; you look like a butcher." Leisurely, he went away, back up the short stone stair that led to the dormitory.

Rannulf stood staring after him. Stephen came up beside him.

"This stinks. You're going alone, with him at your back?"

"I have to obey orders," Rannulf said.

She might be there. He might see her again.

"Rannulf, this is a trap."

"What am I supposed to do?" He stripped off his shirt and dried his face and chest on the cloth. "I have to obey orders. Are you going to hit?"

Stephen glared at him a moment longer, turned to the butts, and drew his sword. Rannulf sat on the foot of the staircase and watched his brother hack away at the post. The grey mood that had grown over him ever since the King died had abruptly lifted a little. In Montgisor, if de Ridford gave him the opening, he would prove to the Marshall what a real butcher he was. De Ridford was the clear favorite to win the election; if Rannulf got rid of him, then he might have more of a chance. And he might see Sibylla again. He clubbed his fists together and set his chin on them, willing himself patient.

ell, you can stay here if you want," Agnes said, "but I am
going back to Nablus." She turned, looking Sibylla over with
a single, eviscerating glance. "Where have you been now,
dressed like that?"

"Out hunting with Guy." Sibylla wore a long plain skirt, and boots,
with a white coif over her head. She followed her mother through the
door, and into the bright sun of the courtyard.

"You are a beautiful woman, dear, when you dress properly." Agnes
stopped at the edge of the courtyard and looked around. "When you
dress like that, you might as well be a potter's daughter. Naturally, nobody else is ready yet."

Sibylla looked out across the dusty courtyard. The castle Montgisor
was set on a hilltop above the plain, a squat bailey and two towers inside a curtain wall, with some wooden outbuildings. They had chosen
to meet here because it was Sibylla's, part of her morgengab from her
first marriage.

But since his arrival the night before, the Lord of Kerak had taken
it over, and his men walked along the ramparts; his men stood at the
gates. Guy seemed not to notice this, but Sibylla felt it like a gall.

Her mother said, "You'll be the only woman here. I hope it makes
you happy."

Up from the stable, in the cellar under the opposite tower, a groom
led several horses by their bridles. Behind them four more men struggled along with the huge box litter her mother traveled in, bulky as a
ship with its curtains and chair.

"You're really going," Sibylla said. "I wish you would stay. What
about the baby?"

"The baby is darling, and you can bring her to me at Nablus so that
I can fuss over her all I want." Agnes pulled on her gloves. On each
cheekbone she wore a powdery badge of rouge. "This place is comfort-
less as a cave, and nothing will happen here, save the men poke and prod
each other. But learn your lesson, my girl."

Sibylla folded her arms over her breast. Her mother had her points. Montgisor was cold, and smelled, and it was already crowded, with half the men who were to gather here yet to arrive. Someone was at the gate now, trying to get in. On the rampart Kerak's guards stirred; among them she saw the white head of the Wolf's bastard son, Guile.

She could not leave. She had summoned all her party here to talk over how to deal with the new Regency, and she had to stay here, or have no say, and have no power in it.

She said, "Uncle Joscelin will be here soon."

Her mother settled her hat on her head and tied the scarf. "Yes. Pay attention to him. He may be a fat old man but he has a feel for the way things are going." Out in the courtyard, the grooms were hitching up the litter to the mules that carried it. A cart rolled up from the stable to carry her chests and her maids. Agnes nodded toward the gate. "There's de Ridford. Watch out for him. And stay away from Kerak." She was going, laying down a trail of admonitions as she left.

Sibylla looked over at the gate tower, a massive stone lump above the wall; in its shadow she saw de Ridford, big and booming, his fine head thrown back. He rode out into the sunlight of the courtyard.

Behind him, in the crowd following him, was another Templar she knew: Rannulf Fitzwilliam. She said, unthinking, "What is he doing here?"

"Who?" Her mother turned, sharp-eyed, looking where she was looking.

"No," Sibylla said. "I was wrong; it is no one."

Agnes caught the lie in her voice, and stared at the Templar like a stork watching frogs, but she did not know him. Sibylla drew back, out of her mother's way. Suddenly she was glad Agnes was going. Her mother always knew her mind too well. It was easier to fool men. She stepped into the cool of the doorway, out of the dust, to wait for her husband.

✥ "Are you going to stand for this?" Rannulf asked.

De Ridford led him up the steps toward the castle's hall, where the Princess and the Count of Jaffa would receive them. "I shall know the meaning of it. Keep still. I will brook no insolence from you before these great ones." The sight of Kerak's men everywhere had the Marshall on edge; but he saw possibilities in it. The guard who let them in to the hall wore Jaffa's livery, at least. They strode into a dank, low-ceilinged room, where by the hearth the Princess of Jerusalem sat, her husband beside her.

"Welcome, my lord Marshall. My lord commander."

De Ridford trotted out a parade of rote greetings. She seemed older, the Princess, some of her fire banked. Jaffa stood beside her, his hand on the back of her chair, as if he would spring on anyone who came near her. De Ridford had not met him before.

"My lord Jaffa, my good wishes to you."

"My lord Marshall." Jaffa's voice was too loud. He looked beyond de Ridford. "You brought none of your men with you?"

"Only this knight, here," de Ridford said. "I assume I am among friends. Obviously my lord of Kerak is of another opinion."

In the chair, the Princess stirred suddenly, her chin rising, and would have spoken; but her husband's hand dropped to her shoulder. Guy said, "My lord Kerak will keep order, at my command. I see no such difficulty in this as other people see." He shrugged off even the burden of thinking about it, and smiled, as if that made everything better. "The hunting is said to be excellent here. I invite you to join me riding after antelope, one morning soon."

De Ridford said, "As you wish, my lord."

Behind him, there was a growl. "What the hell is that?" Rannulf said.

De Ridford smiled, looking straight ahead. "Hold your tongue." To Jaffa, he said, "Heed him not: he is a wolf's head; he has no courtesy." The Princess was watching all this intently.

"Courtesy," Rannulf said. "I will take no orders from Kerak, my lord."

De Ridford wheeled around to face him. "You are dismissed. Go out and see to our establishment."

Rannulf stared at him a moment, not moving, and de Ridford braced himself, but then the other knight turned on his heel and walked away.

Jaffa said, with broad amusement, "One of your trusted officers?"

De Ridford said, "He is not a courtier. I ask your pardon for him." He had brought Rannulf here for one reason only, to get rid of him; the opportunities for doing that seemed to be multiplying. He bowed again to Jaffa. "Yes, my lord, I would indeed like to run antelope, whenever you wish."

In the sunlit courtyard, Rannulf stood looking around him, letting the heat go down from the crossed words with de Ridford. He did not mind being sent out of the hall. He hated seeing her with Jaffa's hand on her.

Kerak's men were all over the place; as he stood looking a half-dozen men in red coats came out of the gatehouse, with Guile of Kerak himself leading them. They went off across the courtyard, toward the stables, which lay on lower ground. Rannulf walked back the way they had come, to the gatehouse, and climbed the staircase to the upper story.

He leaned on the stone sill of the window, looking down on the courtyard, seeing everything. The courtyard bustled with people, servants carrying things, and Kerak's soldiers, and other men-at-arms. While he watched, some of Kerak's men harried a servant girl until she dropped her basket and ran for the shelter of the kitchen. Those men not Kerak's kept carefully out of the way, looking elsewhere.

The messy uproar bothered him, used as he was to the rigor of the Temple. If he had command here, he would make all these men keep step and say please. The urge to power kindled him; he saw himself a lord greater than Jaffa, worthy of Jaffa's wife.

Through this vision, as if through a rippling flame, he saw himself as he was, lowborn and ordinary, and alone. Down below, de Ridford came out of the hall; from here he looked smaller, as if Rannulf could stretch down his arm and pluck him up between thumb and forefinger and dash his brains out on the stone of the walls.

As he thought this, his mind leapt on, saw de Ridford dead, and Rannulf himself made Master of the Order. He led the defense of the Kingdom, beat back Saladin, and she loved him, not in the open, but in secret; they met in secret, and she loved him back, and the sons she bore to Guy de Lusignan were Rannulf's sons.

That burnt. He shut his eyes, and put his hands over his face. He could not see what to do. Every course he imagined led only into darker twistings and turnings. His heart cankered, blood-sick, and he realized suddenly how much he missed his vow.

Guy de Lusignan wasn't quite sure what he was doing, but whatever it was, it had taken a landless, penniless, patronless younger son halfway across the world, made him Count of Jaffa, given him a beautiful Princess for his wife, and brought him to the foot of the throne of Jerusalem. He meant to keep on doing it, whatever it was he was doing, for as long and as far as it went.

But it all depended on Sibylla, and now Sibylla was angry at him.

"I don't understand you," he said. "Why won't you go hunting with me tomorrow?"

"Because there is too much to do here," she said. She sat on the big bed of their chamber, holding the little girl, Jolie, in her arms. "I need you—they must see you are ready to lead them."

Guy laughed. "I don't see anybody here willing to be led. Like that Templar, facing against his lord; could I lead him? And they are all like that, all cross-grained."

"Those two Templars have a long-standing feud," she said. She looked baffled, as if he should know all these things. He did not want to know these things, the thousand little jealousies and hatreds of this kingdom, close as a family. He wanted to go out and run antelope, the fastest, finest sport he had ever done, far better than sitting around talking about policy. He went over to his wife, and sat next to her, looking down at the baby in her arms.

"Ours," he said, and kissed his wife.

"At least Uncle Joscelin will be here soon," she said, as if he had done nothing. "He always travels with a lot of men. He will balance Kerak."

Guy muttered under his breath. "Kerak. He's an old man, living on his name. He has you all bemused. I'm going down to see about some horses for coursing antelope. Will you come?"

"No—I have to nurse the baby," she said. "Go on, look at the horses; maybe I will go with you, later, if there is a horse for me."

"Good," he said, pleased. She wasn't angry anymore. He swept his hand up under her hair; suddenly he wanted to make love to her, to prove again that she belonged to him. But she was bent over the baby, and he knew better than to come between her and the baby. "I love you," he said, and kissed the top of her head, and went out.

◈ She had made a mistake, Sibylla thought; she had married the wrong man.

When Guy had gone she sat on the floor of the chamber and played with the baby, who was just learning to sit up well by herself. Sibylla had taught her to play a little game, hiding behind her hands, while her mother pretended to search for her.

"Where is Jolie? Oh, where is she?"

Behind her upraised hands, the baby gave a liquid gurgle of delight. Sibylla searched for her under the cushion.

Guy had given her this little girl; for that alone she would always love him. Sometimes she thought Jolie was worth more than the whole Kingdom of Jerusalem, and she would forego being Queen after all, just to be Jolie's mother.

For Jolie's sake, she would be Queen, and she would bring peace to Jerusalem. If Guy disappointed her, she had other means. God would not let her fail; God would cover her mistakes.

Alys came in, shaking her head. "I think we shall have to starve, that's all."

Sibylla had just found Jolie, in behind her hands, and the two of them were sharing the immense delight of reunion, the child cooing and laughing, and climbing into her mother's arms. Sibylla kissed her silky head. Slowly she realized that Alys was still fussing.

"What's the matter?"

"I can't go out to see to dinner. As soon as I step into the open, the men there come at me." Alys plumped down on her stool, her face red. "One of them, I stuck my scissors in him, Sibylla, I did."

"Good for you," Sibylla said.

Alys struck her fist on her knee. "No! I don't want to do such things!" Suddenly tears stood brimming in her eyes. "I won't go out, Sibylla. Not until it's safe."

"Very well," Sibylla said, surprised. "We'll send the pages." She curled Jolie in her arms, in the cradle of her love.

◈ Night came; the council began that they had come here to hold. Guy de Lusignan leaned on the back of the double chair he would share later with his wife, and watched the men filling up this little hall. Half the power of Outremer was here, all turning like the·planets around him. Whatever he said, they listened to. He sat in the place of honor, and all sat below him, older men, noble lords, soldiers who had fought here for years. Servants jumped at his least nod. He lifted his finger, and everybody bowed.

This continually surprised him. He loved Sibylla, who was clever, and pretty, who had given him a baby daughter of whom he was surprisingly fond, but now she wasn't even heiress of Jerusalem anymore. Her brother's death had thrown more barriers in her way than it removed. And yet these people went on fawning on him as if he would be King tomorrow.

Beside him, the Templar Marshall, de Ridford, said, "The Princess will soon grace us with her company?"

Guy said, "She will sup with us." His wife's uncle, Joscelin de Courtenay, Count of Edessa, was coming in. He had arrived at Montgisor that afternoon, with a horde of his men, too many to quarter in the castle; they had taken over the village, driving the peasants out to sleep in the fields. Joscelin de Courtenay was another one like Kerak, a big noise in a satin coat, and Guy could not understand why everybody gave him so much deference.

Hugely fat, grunting and huffing and quaking, Joscelin reached his place at the table, and stood behind his chair looking around; Guy went around the carved arm of the double chair and sat down, and all the other lords sat also. The lower end of the hall was crowded with men who had no place at the tables, the knights and hangers-on of the lords, and here again, now, suddenly, another fight was breaking out. Guy gave a little shake of his head. Kerak could not even keep order in a place like this: why was everybody so shy of him? He sat back in the chair, watching Guile of Kerak and his men kick the fighting apart.

His wife came into the hall.

She sent no one on before her to announce her. She merely came into the doorway, and stood there, until suddenly the knowledge she was there swept across the room, and all men turned. They fell still at once. Even the lords rose up in their places; among the lesser men many went down on one knee to her.

She stood there a moment longer. She wore a long gown of blue silk, with a skirt of many filmy layers, and a short velvet jacket, a little darker blue, intricately embroidered in silver thread. Her hair was coiled under a coif of silver lace. The sight of her always moved him to joy, and she quieted the riotous hall; she brought it instantly to a peace and calm Kerak's men could never have achieved with all the swords in Christendom. She was the sweetest girl in the whole world, and Guy knew himself a king already, just in having her. Proudly he went forward, to bring her to the place of honor at the table.

✦ De Ridford dropped the gnawed bone back onto the platter, and wiped his greasy fingers on a napkin; small and mean as the castle was, yet it served good food, and the wine was excellent. He glanced at Guy de Lusignan, on his left, to congratulate him on this, but the Count of Jaffa as usual was nose to nose with his wife, making poor company.

The Templar Marshall turned instead to the Princess' uncle, Joscelin de Courtenay, who was sitting on his right. "The food is excellent," he said.

Joscelin had finished eating. He sat plumped back in his chair, his belly heaped up in front of him like a miser's treasure. "Damned excellent. Thank Agnes. She staffed the place."

"A pity she had to leave." De Ridford always learned a lot from Agnes de Courtenay, who knew the intimate pulse of Outremer.

Joscelin shrugged. "Maybe. I wish Sibylla would leave, and let us get on with the man talk."

De Ridford laughed. His gaze swung around toward the high seat again, and he lifted his voice, to reach Kerak, sitting beyond it. "My lord Kerak, are you going to keep this latest truce?"

Kerak leaned his elbows on the table. "I can't fight two wars at once. The question is, what are we going to do about Tripoli?"

Joscelin belched. "Not in front of Sibylla. Don't bore the ladies." He waved his hand, and one of his pages hurried up to bring him a cup of wine.

"Not at all," Sibylla said, and twisted to face Kerak. "Why, my lord, what do you want to do about Tripoli?"

Kerak's face suffused with color. He craned himself out across the table to stare past her at de Ridford and Joscelin. "I say we get all our men together and attack him, right now, before he attacks us."

Joscelin muttered something under his breath; de Ridford gave a quick look around him to see who was overhearing this. Finally Joscelin said, "Well, he's in a pretty strong position."

The Princess' voice rose, sharp. "You mean, you would actually consider such a thing?"

Kerak's thick lips curled into a sneer. "No, you have no belly for it, do you—this is why women cannot rule."

Guy said, "Now, Sibylla, listen to me."

She ignored him; she sat rigid in her place, her gaze aimed like a sword at Kerak. "I would give more consideration to your opinions on the matter, my lord, did you yourself not blunder from disaster to disaster."

De Ridford blinked, startled at this brazen boldness from a tender girl. The truth in it impressed him also. Guy had hold of his wife's arm. De Ridford canted forward to see the Wolf's face; the whole hall had quieted to listen to this argument. Kerak sneered. He said, "If you were a man, I would slap you down, for speaking so."

De Ridford lifted his voice. "You would have to go through me to do it, my lord, I promise you." Several other men barked out their support for this.

Sibylla said, "I will not allow talk of an attack on my kinsman Tripoli, no matter how evilly he has treated me. Such talk only weakens us all."

Joscelin said, "Where is Tripoli now?"

"In the north," de Ridford said. "And as Edessa says, he is very strong. The question should be more what he may do to us, than what we may do to him."

Sibylla said, "What, he might attack us?"

Joscelin laced his fingers together across the mound of his belly. "Never. It would cost too much." He erupted softly in another bubbling gaseous belch.

De Ridford laughed. Guy de Lusignan slumped back in the high seat, looking bored. His wife sat upright, her long hands in her lap, and was about to speak, then a servant came into the hall and hurried down the table to her.

"My lady Princess, the baby cries, and she will not be soothed."

The Princess sat as she had been, bolt upright, staring forward, but now a little frown appeared between her brows. She hesitated only a moment. Turning to Jaffa, she said, "I have to go. I shall see you later. My lords, good evening." Rising, she brought them all up onto their feet, and until she had reached the door and gone, she held the gaze of every man there.

Guy sat down again. "The baby's cutting teeth," he said, to no one in particular.

Joscelin said, "Ah, she's a sharp tongue in her head, Sibylla. Like Agnes."

"She has some peculiar notions," Guy said. "The women here, you know, it's not like France."

Kerak said, "If you want my advice, Jaffa, lock her up in a tower!"

Guy bridled up, angry; de Ridford reached out, and gripped his arm. "Well, maybe, but at least wait until she makes you King," he said.

"I shall never be King," Guy said. He settled back into his chair. "Tripoli is nearer to being King than I; all he has to do is poison the brat ahead of him."

De Ridford shook him. "You know nothing of the ways of Outremer. I promise you, you will be King, and Tripoli, never."

Guy blinked at him, his blue eyes clear with sudden hope. "You think so."

"Believe me," De Ridford said.

Guy sat back, struggling to fit this large and lofty idea into a mind no bigger than a baby's tooth. Down at the low end of the hall the ordinary men were fighting for the bits left over from their masters' meal. Joscelin was falling asleep, his hands tucked over his belly. Kerak had gotten into a bawling argument with someone half the room away.

De Ridford cast a glance down the table. At the very end, Rannulf Fitzwilliam sat, his elbows planted on the table, a cup before him; as de Ridford watched, he drained the cup, and reached across the table for the ewer to fill it up again.

Good, de Ridford thought. Drink hard, you fool, drink yourself witless, what little wit you have.

Watching the hall, the ceaseless small fighting among these men, he knew exactly how to deal with Rannulf; the Norman's own nasty temper would be the end of him. In fact, the whole council was going along very well. He sat back on the bench, away from the table, replete.

CHAPTER XXV

Rannulf woke up in the back of the stable under a hay rick. He had no notion how he had gotten there; he had drunk himself blind the night before, and now his head was pounding and his belly hurt. He went into the stable yard and soaked his head in the trough, drank the cold water until his stomach swelled, vomited, and drank again.

After that, he still felt bad. Around him the stablehands and grooms were leading the horses out to the trough, and he went away toward the wall, and tried to sort his mind out. He had to find some way back to God. He went around behind the bailey to the chapel.

The chapel was small, and empty, its bare floor swept, only a little rug in the middle. The candles were unlit. The book lay open in the center of the altar. He knelt down and tried to pray. The words would not pass his lips. Nothing out there answered him, and he knew God had given up on him.

"Saint."

Startled, he was on his feet before he saw her. She had come in through the side door of the chapel, the same one he had come through, and she stood by the pulpit. He said, "Princess, what are you doing here?" He glanced around them; they were alone.

The heat rose in him, the old lust, and the vow was gone, now.

She said, "I wanted to talk to you. I need your help." Innocent, she came forward, her gaze direct. "I want to make a secret connection with Saladin."

"God's eyes," he said. "You don't know what you're asking."

"I do know. I want peace. I want my children to live in Jerusalem at peace with all the world. The only way to do that is to come to terms with the Saracens."

"Saladin will not stop fighting us until every one of us is dead, Princess. Or until he is dead. And then there will be another Saladin."

"He made two truces; he can make another, to last forever." She came on, pressing her argument. She was within his reach. Through the thin silk of her sleeves he could see her arms, round and soft. Her skin like silk.

He said, "He uses the truce to get ready to make war. So do we. The longer the truce, the harder the war after it."

"No," she said, her voice rising, sharper; she was losing her temper with him. "All you care to do is kill people. Your war, your holy war, that's all you know, and all you want. That's why you're a Templar, isn't it? So you can kill without sin."

He said, "I'll show you why I am a Templar." He grabbed her, one hand on her arm, the other on her throat, and pulled her hard against him.

Her eyes widened, white-rimmed. With a whine she twisted vainly in his grip, and he bent over her, his mouth open to kiss her.

Overhead, a bell spoke, tolling Nones.

The great voice sent a shudder through him. He let go of her. Turning, he went off a few steps into the dark of the chapel, his head down, ashamed. "I'm sorry," he said.

He thought she would run, or scream, or call for help. She said, her voice rasping, "Don't tell me you're sorry. Tell me you will do as I ask."

He lifted his eyes and looked at her again. "No. I won't."

She had her fingers to her throat; at his answer her face twisted in fury. "Ah, you—" She turned and went out of the chapel.

He stood still a moment, his mind scattered. He had been about to force her. She had come to him for help, and he had jumped her like a wolf on a doe. The strokes of the bell shivered the air around him. He felt torn into a thousand pieces. He could not pray and he had no right being in this place. He walked out of the chapel.

✦ Guy said, "Are you all right? You look pretty twitchy."

Sibylla sank down on the high seat beside him. "I'm perfectly well."

Under the table his hand came creeping up her knee. "How is my little comfit?" He meant the baby, Jolie.

"Oh, she's fine." She looked out across the room, wishing he would be quiet.

The nobles were moving around the hall, sitting down, having waited until she and her husband took their places. On her right hand Kerak sagged in his chair, already bawling for drink; Guile stood behind him, to serve him. Her uncle Joscelin sat on Guy's left, and beyond him, de Ridford, wiping his mouth on a napkin.

Her gaze slid past him, on down to the low end of the table, where Rannulf Fitzwilliam sat on the bench. He was drinking. He would not look at her; as always he kept his gaze down, full of false monkish pride. She hated him, for refusing her, for attacking her. Her throat still hurt; she had wrapped her coif around under her chin, to hide the bruise, but Guy would surely see it later; she would have to lie.

If she told him, he would see that the Templar suffered for what he had done.

Her skin roughened. She felt like a fool for thinking she could enlist his help.

Guy's hand squeezed her knee. "What's wrong?"

She shook her head. "Nothing."

"I think you ought to stay away from these gatherings, anyway." He waved his hand at the hall. "It's like a barracks."

She mumbled something. Abruptly she did wish for the quiet and comfort of her room, for Alys to serve her and talk to her, for Jolie's un-limited love. Around them the men spoke and laughed, a general roar that filled the room. The servants brought dishes to them. She and Guy shared a plate, and he put the tenderest meats before her, broke the bread into pieces for her, gave her the cup first, before he drank.

She leaned on him, grateful for his affection. "You're good to me, dar-ling. You never say no to me."

"You've never made it necessary." He kissed her brow.

Kerak and Joscelin were shouting back and forth along the table. Leaning forward to aim his words past Guy and Sibylla, the Wolf called, "Those Saracen blades bend like whips, and they hold an edge better than ours."

Joscelin said, "Not the sword wins the battle, but the arm that wields it." He sprawled on the bench, taking his winecup from a page. He had gotten so fat he could not sit up straight anymore.

Kerak planted his elbows on the table. "Nonetheless, a good sword helps. I would not like to face any enemy with only a stick or a stone in my hand."

"I have seen men fight as well with sticks as with swords," said de Ridford, suddenly. "I agree with my lord Count, it is the man who wins, not the weapon."

"Oh, so," Kerak said, with a laugh. "Put a man with a stick against a man with a sword, and see who is left standing at the end."

De Ridford said, "My men use staves, keeping order in the streets of Jerusalem, and they are masters at it. I would set any of them against any of your swordsmen, my lord, with utmost confidence."

Guy looked around. Up and down the table the other talk quieted; they sensed a contest, and they all loved a fight. Kerak and de Ridford were staring at each other, and the Marshall began to smile, smooth as cream. He said, "In fact, I will pit Rannulf, here, against your Guile, there, any time, my lord."

A jubilant yell went up from the listeners. Down at the end of the table, Rannulf at last lifted his gaze from the floor.

He said, "We aren't supposed to fight for sport." His voice was less than steady; Sibylla realized he was drunk.

De Ridford gave him only half a glance. "I'm ordering you."

Kerak bawled, "He's wiggling out, Marshall, see? He knows he can't do it." He twisted, looking back over his shoulder at Guile behind him.

"He'll do it," de Ridford said. "Bring him a stave."

Guile said, "Let's put it to the trial." He strode forward to the table just down from his father, and stepped up onto it, among the platters and cups, and jumped across to the open floor beyond. The servants shrank back out of his way. He drew his sword, and swaggering he went down the length of the hall, swishing the blade back and forth, while the men at the tables yelled and clapped their hands in rhythm. Sibylla glanced down at Rannulf again.

He sat still, his face sour, watching Guile; then he turned, and gave such a look to de Ridford that Sibylla murmured under her breath. Guy put his arm around her. Up from the door came a man with a stick, six feet long, and as thick as her wrist, and Rannulf stood, and walked around the end of the table and out into the middle of the hall.

Guile backed away from him a few steps, the sword cocked in his right hand, his left arm spread away from his body. The onlookers hushed so that Sibylla could hear the crackling of the fire in the huge hearth. Rannulf took the stave from the servant; he held it at the middle, one-handed, and banged it once or twice on the straw-covered floor. His gaze never left Guile.

Joscelin said, "A hundred michaels on the sword. This Templar's going down the hill."

De Ridford said, quietly, "He's a little long in the tooth, Rannulf, but I have seen him fight with this weapon; he is brilliant at it." Sibylla looked at him sharply. She knew he hated Rannulf.

Guy said, "I'll take the stave, my lord Count."

Kerak slapped his hand on the table. "Shall we have the lady begin this?"

"No," she said, sharply, without thinking, and the men around her laughed.

"Squeamish, darling," Guy said. "Do you want to leave?"

Her gaze followed the two men in the middle of the hall; they were circling each other, step by step. Her hair stood on end. She said, "No."

Kerak banged his hand on the table again. "All right, then. Begin!"

Guile bounded forward at once, slashing with the sword; the blade sang through the air. Rannulf moved out of his way. Now he held the stave in both hands, slantwise across his body. Guile leapt at him again, and again Rannulf avoided his rush, sidling around to his left, the sword slicing uselessly through the space between them. Guile lost his smile.

"He will not fight!"

"Damn you," Kerak shouted. "Take it to him!"

Guile lunged, the sword pointfirst. Rannulf stepped in past the blade and thrust the stave between Guile's knees and tripped him. The watching crowd bellowed. Guile landed on his backside, and bounced up again at once, his face red.

Sibylla sat back, smiling behind her hand. She loved to see Guile humbled. Down the table from her, Kerak gave a howl of rage. "Get him! Cut him!"

Two-handed, Guile hacked a flurry of blows at Rannulf's head; again and again the upraised stave turned the blade aside. The parries were glancing, twisting, so that the sword never bit, and the stave never broke. Then Guile missed a stroke and the stave shot in past his guard, poked him in the stomach, and doubled him over. As he wobbled there, helpless, Rannulf went by him, back into the center of the room, and swung the stave around level and spanked him flat across the backside.

Sibylla sat back, clapping her hands together. All along the table, men were laughing now. With a startled bray of pain, Guile tottered off balance. Like a baited bull, he swung around toward his tormentor, and got the stave smack in the chest. His arm dropped. Staggering back, he came up hard against the edge of the table.

Rannulf lowered the stave. He started back toward his place, and amid a general roar of applause from the onlookers Guy turned to Joscelin, his face bright with amusement, and said, "My hundred michaels, please?"

Joscelin turned toward him, jovial, his mouth open to speak, and then Guile shot forward, raising his sword again, and leapt on Rannulf when his back was turned.

Sibylla cried out, furious, and rose halfway out of her chair. A yell went up from the watching room. Rannulf flinched, warned, and the sword missed him by an inch, carried down past his elbow, and hit the table so hard the blade stuck fast. Rannulf spun around. The stave whirled in his hands; he whacked the sword flying out of Guile's grip, and then flailed at him, milling blows to Guile's head and ribs, the stave a blur in the air, and under this drubbing Guile went down hard on the floor and curled up, his arms clasped over his skull.

Kerak was standing in his place, screaming to his son to get up, to fight back. Around the table the other men were merely screaming. Sibylla's hand hurt. She looked down in surprise and saw her fist clenched, as if she fought. Her head throbbed with a sudden, violent ache; her heart raced.

Guy said, "Now, that's a piece of work."

De Ridford's voice was fat with gloating. "He is a Templar."

Rannulf was going back to his place at the table. As he passed, the men watching shouted, and leaned out to clap his shoulder, touch his arm; he ignored them all. He reached his place, and sat down again, and turned his gaze down to the floor. Guile crept away, and went unobtrusively back to the wall behind his father.

Guy turned, beckoning to a page. "Take the Templar the best wine we have, with my regards."

Kerak wheeled, glaring at Guile. "You're rotten. You can't even beat an old man with a stick."

Sibylla pried her clenched fist open. She sat staring into the middle of the hall; the sword lay there on the straw, forgotten.

It was in her, too, the lust to fight. She had felt it, as much as anyone, watching this combat, the gross beauty of it, and the power. She saw, suddenly, how hard it would be to make peace. Her chest tightened; she remembered railing at him in righteous indignation, as if she knew better.

She wondered what she did know. She turned to Guy.

"I want to go up to Jolie."

Guy's arm tightened around her. "I'll take you." He turned, and waved to a page. He had learned the manner of a king; every move he made was royal now. She thought she had liked him better as he had been when she first met him, in his worn old coat, without the pearl in his ear. She was learning too many things tonight, too much at once. When she rose, all the men stood, and she went out of their midst toward the shelter of her room and her child.

❧ Rannulf went into the stable, to tend his horse, and Guile and several of his men set on him. They gave him no warning, but they chose a bad place for it, narrow, and dark, where they got in each other's way, and he stayed in the fight long enough to stick his knife to the haft in Guile's chest.

The other men pulled him off, and saw what he had done. Abruptly they stopped beating him. Two of them held him by the arms, and another went for Kerak.

The Wolf came, red-eyed. He saw his son, and knelt down and felt the wound, and saw that his son was dead. Then he got up, and came up face-to-face with Rannulf.

Rannulf's arms were twisted behind his back. He looked into Kerak's face and said, "It took six of them, Wolf. Remember that."

Kerak drew his knife. "Where is de Ridford? Tell him I'm going to kill his man, here!"

Another knight said, "De Ridford went out somewhere. That's why we knew he'd be alone."

"Go on, Kerak," Rannulf said. "Kill me. De Ridford wants me dead. He set me up for this; you're doing what he wants."

Kerak drew his arm back. The blade a long steel sliver in the dark. Rannulf's gut clenched. Kerak turned his head. "Can I do it?"

"Ah, you coward," Rannulf said, disgusted.

"He's an officer of the Temple," somebody said. "He has two hundred brothers to avenge him. You have to get de Ridford to agree to it, or we'll be fighting them for years."

Kerak turned, and punched Rannulf in the face with the fist that held the dagger. "Go find de Ridford." He cocked his arm back and hit Rannulf again.

◈ Rannulf blinked his eyes open, fighting for consciousness; he was lying on his face on the floor, his bound arms twisted behind him, numb to the shoulder. His head hurt. He wondered how long he had been out, and how much longer before he died.

Under him was a plank floor. All around him were the boots and legs of his captors, shuffling around; they were doing something behind him that he could not see. Past the legs and boots he saw the close walls of a little room, all hung with weapons: the armory.

He shut his eyes. His head throbbed, and his arms ached; every time he breathed a hard pain stabbed him in the chest. Something broken. He wanted them to kill him now, before they decided to make a game out of breaking him.

He wanted them to kill him, but he was afraid of dying.

Above his head, somebody said, "He's awake," and a blow thudded into his hip.

"Good. The old man wants to see him cry a little."

"You know, I never really liked Guile much until now."

There was a laugh at that, and somebody hit him again. He lay still, his teeth clenched against the whimper in his throat. They would kill him, eventually, and he would go to hell. He was back in the time before God, when he had been one of these men, doing evil for the fun of it, and now he would go on dying forever. A cold terror flooded him; he bit his tongue; he tasted blood in his mouth.

Hands on his arms dragged him up, halfway onto his feet, and they swung him around. Now he saw what they had been doing. They had pried up the grate out of a hole in the floor, opening the way into a pit under the armory. They were going to throw him down into that pit. His wits flew. He gave a yell, and began to fight, a useless desperate struggle. They rained blows on him. Laughed, and kicked and cursed him, and dragged him headfirst to the pit and hurled him in.

◈ Sibylla slept late into the morning; when she woke, the baby curled in her arm, Guy was gone, out hunting again. Alys was directing the servants around with their breakfast of peaches and clabbered milk and bread.

"This is a terrible place," Alys said. "Now they're talking about hanging somebody."

"Hanging someone. Who?" Sibylla sat up. The baby smelled ripe, and she laid her down on the covers, and sent one of the maids for fresh clothes for her.

"Some Templar," Alys said. She sat down and broke one of the rolls open. "They're only waiting for the other one to come back and allow it. I hate these people. I hate Kerak."

"I'm not too fond of Kerak either," Sibylla said, slowly. With the maid standing there to hand her the clean clothes and take away the dirty ones, she began to unwrap her daughter's swaddlings. "Send somebody out to find out for me where the Templar is now."

◈ Joscelin said, "I don't want to do this. Kerak's like a badger when he thinks you've crossed him."

Sibylla hooked her arm through his. Two of Joscelin's knights were coming along after them. On ahead of them, through the gateway, his captain galloped off down the road, to rouse the rest of Joscelin's army and bring them up to Montgisor.

She hoped they would be unnecessary. The palms of her hands were clammy and she could not stop clearing her throat. "Montgisor is my castle, Uncle. He does not rule here." This was going to be hard, maybe impossible. "What will it do to us, if we let him do as he pleases? Who can rule then?"

Joscelin's head swayed toward her; his eyes blinked. "Yes," he said. "I know." Turning, he beckoned to the men behind him, and sent them to try the door of the gatehouse. He and Sibylla stood side by side in the yard watching.

The door was locked from the inside. Joscelin said, "Knock," and one of his men lifted his fist and rapped on the door. At once the door cracked slightly ajar.

"Open for my lord the Count of Edessa," said Joscelin's man.

From the crack in the doorway: "My lord Kerak bade me let no one in."

"This is my lord the Count of Edessa," Joscelin's man said, again.

Sibylla lifted her voice. "I rule here, not Kerak; let us in."

The doorway said nothing more, but did not close, and after only an instant of the silence, Joscelin strode heavily forward.

"Let me in! Now!"

The door opened. Joscelin marched into the room beyond, and Sibylla trailed him; the other men stayed outside.

With the guard, they filled the little armory chamber, whose floor was made much smaller by the gaping hole in the center, its iron cover tipped back to one side.

Kerak's knight stood with his back to the wall, his eyes white. He said, "My lord, I have to follow orders."

Joscelin nodded at the hole in the floor. "He's down there?"

"My lord—"

"Bring him up."

The guard stood still a moment, swallowing. Joscelin's head came around. All his life, men had obeyed him; he looked outraged now that this one did not, and his voice swelled. "Bring him up!"

Sibylla could hear footsteps running toward them, outside in the yard. Her throat was dry. She moved over to one side of the room, her back to a rack of painted shields, and folded her arms over her breast. In through the door burst a knight in Kerak's color.

He saw, first, only that the guard was on his knees by the hole in the floor, getting ready to go down into it. "What are you doing, you idiot?" Then he saw Joscelin, and he froze, his head up, his fists at his sides. Then Kerak strode into the room.

This packed it, and the knight behind Kerak turned and left. The Wolf glared at Joscelin. "What are you doing?" The man climbing down into the hole in the floor had stopped to wait for orders.

Joscelin said, "You overreach." He turned to the man on the floor. "Go down, and bring him up."

Kerak said, "He killed my son."

Sibylla's throat was so dry she thought she might not get the words out. "This is my castle. You cannot do justice here. I alone can judge."

Kerak's head swiveled around toward her. His green eyes were feral. "Don't make an enemy of me, woman." He spoke to Joscelin in a hiss like a snake's. "I won't forget, Edessa. Don't take me lightly."

Joscelin said, "Let her judge the case. Now. Here." He looked down at the floor, where the guard had reappeared, and turned and gave Sibylla a deep look. "Sibylla?"

Sibylla nodded to him. Her arms were clasped around her, like a shield. The close presence of the men seemed to make it hard to breathe. The hole in the floor gave up a smell of rot and old water and dung. The guard knelt beside it, and reached down, and dragged the Templar up onto the floor; there he lay, half-conscious, his hands still wrapped around with the cut ends of the rope. Blood matted his short black hair.

Joscelin said, "What happened?"

"He killed my son," Kerak said. "Ask him. He will admit it."

Joscelin reached out one foot and pushed the Templar's body. "Can you hear us?"

The man groaned. His hands moved, pulling apart the bonds. Kerak thrust his head forward, his teeth bared. "It was his dagger. He admitted it."

"Who was there?" Sibylla asked. "Who saw?"

"No one," Kerak said. He gave her a crafty, gloating look. "Only the murderer, and my son and the men with him."

"Yes. Certainly, after last night, Guile knew he needed help with him." Sibylla shifted her weight to the other foot. "So they set on him, outnumbering him. I think him innocent."

Kerak bellowed, his arms flung up. "Women have no reason!" He fixed her with a pig's tiny glittering stare. "Do you think you've won anything? Do you think you've won anything?" White spume flew from his lips. He wheeled toward the door of the gatehouse. "Where are my men?" He strode out, shouting.

Joscelin was looking morosely at Sibylla. "Well, that looked fine enough," he said. "But what are you going to do now, Sibylla? They've half-killed him already; they'll finish the job as soon as we're gone."

On the floor, Rannulf moved. He rolled over, and Sibylla moved back hastily away from him. She looked out the door into the gate.

Several mounted men were riding up from the road. Joscelin's knights. More came after them, many more, clogging the gate yard. Her heart jumped. This was going to work. She looked down at Rannulf, who had gotten to his hands and knees.

"Saint. Can you ride?"

He staggered to his feet. The rags of his jerkin hung around his waist and his shirt was soaked with blood. He put out one hand to steady himself against the wall, and hung there a moment, breathing hard.

Joscelin said, "I'll get him a horse," and went to the door.

Sibylla turned toward the Templar, swaying on his feet, and said, under her breath, "You see, I pay my debts."

"I didn't know you owed me anything." He set off around the little room, hunting through the racks of weapons. With a murmur he took an old battered scabbard down from the wall. She knew he had found his own sword.

Joscelin tramped into the room again. "Quickly, now. There's a horse here. My men will block the gate for you, so that Kerak cannot follow, but we cannot do it long."

The Templar said, "Thank you, my lord." He went toward the door; on the way, as he came close by Sibylla, he said, "Thank you, Princess." He looked at her, their eyes meeting, just for a moment, and he went on and out the door.

Joscelin stood there staring at her. "What did that mean?"

She smiled at him, folding her arms across her breast again. "I don't understand you."

"What debts do you have with a Templar? With that Templar?" Joscelin's eyes narrowed. "You are Agnes' daughter, Sibylla."

Outside, there was a yell of outrage. Sibylla thought she could hear Kerak's raw bawling voice. She had defeated him; he would not rule in her castle. She had done justice here. She said, "Thank you, Uncle Joscelin." She went out to the gate yard, to help quell the angry uproar.

⬥ Rannulf knew they would be looking for him on the road to Jerusalem, and he swung away from it, striking out instead through the broken hills to the east, pierced with caves and watered with a hundred ancient wells. All the rest of the day and all night long he travelled, although he was exhausted, and sick, the pain in his chest working steadily deeper, down to his heart. He slept little, and dreamed much, of monsters, rising from the black flames of hell, gnawing and devouring him.

He was riding straight into the east. When the first light broke before him at the rim of the sky, he drew rein and dismounted from the horse, and turned around to face Jerusalem. His chest was a fiery bonecase, his head pulsed; he knew he was dying. He had to try to pray again, to beg God's forgiveness, to ask to be taken back again. Kneeling down he put his palms together, but the words would not leave his throat.

He sat slumped on the flat sandy ground, facing west, toward Jerusalem. Behind him the sun was rising in a wave of light. Suddenly he sensed around him a great voice roaring, so vast and perfect he could not hear it with his ears. His soul heard it, and a fearsome exaltation swelled him: for a moment he seemed to be lifting off the ground.

Then the call broke like glass breaking, into a million separate sounds, and all of these were audible: the shrill cries of birds, the scream of the wind, the thornbush rattling. The whole desert lightened toward the day. His shadow stretched over the ground before him like an arrow toward Jerusalem. The horizon streamed colors, blue into green brightening to gold, and then fading again into the colorless wash of the daylight.

Caught in this blast, exalted, he knew how stupid he had been. God had never given him up. God filled the world, God was everywhere, in the earth under him, in the wild skirling of the air, in the blaze of the rising sun; God pierced him through and through. He doubled over on the sand, surrendering himself to that measureless power, and the day flowed over him in a tide of light.

After that, almost at once, he began to get well.

CHAPTER XXVI

Felx said, "I went to the Temple this morning."

"See anything interesting?" Stephen said. He leaned against the doorjamb. He had just done a quick reconnaissance of the hall, before the little King came down for his daily audience. There was no one else in the hall save the pages and serving people, looking busy. On the stairs down to the lower door, there were already some petitioners waiting to see the King.

"Some interesting," Felx said. "They all think Rannulf isn't coming back from Montgisor."

Stephen frowned at him. "What does that mean?"

"De Ridford's taken him into a trap," Felx said. "Nobody's saying so. But as I said, they all think he's gone." He tugged on his ragged yellow beard. "Ponce le Brun even asked me who would command the King's guard now, with Rannulf out of the way."

"What!"

"He tried to pretend I had misunderstood him but I heard what he said."

Upstairs, the big door groaned open; the two knights turned and looked up, and the chamberlain came out of the great hall and took up his staff. He cleared his throat a few times, trying his voice. Stephen went to the doorway and stood beside it, and Felx stood on the far side. The chamberlain paced in, announcing the King in booming tones, and with two pages and a squire in front of him, and his nurse behind, the child entered the hall, walking very straight. Last of them all Richard le Mesne strolled by, yawning. Felx and Stephen closed on him from either side and steered him off into the corner where they could talk unheard.

"What is this?" Bear asked.

Stephen said, "Saint's in trouble."

"Unh." Bear lifted his head. "I knew this sounded like a bad idea."

Stephen said, "I say we go down there and get him."

"What about the King?" Bear said.

"One of us can stay by the King. Two of us go down and get Rannulf."

Bear said, "I'm going. If Saint's in trouble, I want to be there—he's saved my head so many times he owns it."

Felx said, "Anyway, we'll need a lot of help. You know who's at Montgisor. Besides that snake de Ridford there's Kerak, and Kerak's Guile—" In mid-sentence he stopped, staring across the room, his jaw hanging. Stephen swung around.

The crowd of little people waiting on the stairs was pushing through the hall, to present the morning's petitions to the King. Behind them, just inside the door, was Rannulf Fitzwilliam.

Bear said, under his breath, "Oh, well, and here I was hoping for a little excitement."

Stephen slapped the back of his hand across Felx's arm. "What, were you daydreaming?"

Felx growled at him. "Yes? Look at him."

Rannulf was angling across the room toward them. Felx was right: he had taken some hard hits. He was dragging himself along, and the whole left side of his face was bruised and swollen. Half his jerkin was gone. He came up into the midst of the Templars and looked around at them.

"Is this how you stand guard over the King?"

"What happened to you?" Stephen said. "Where's de Ridford?"

"As far as I know he's still at Montgisor," Rannulf said. He gave a wide look around the room and faced them again. "Bear, take the door. Felx, stand by the King. I'm going upstairs; I have to sleep." He turned around and walked over toward the door, weaving through the crowd of people standing around the boy King, who was delivering one of his rote speeches. In the doorway, Rannulf turned, and said, "Mouse," and Stephen went after him.

"We were just getting ready to come down there and get you," Stephen said, on the stairs.

"No, you weren't," Rannulf said. "You were staying here and doing what I ordered you to do when I left." He went slowly up the steps, and on the landing, he slumped against the wall. "Help me," he said.

Stephen stepped in beside him, took Rannulf's wrist in his hand, and looped Rannulf's arm over his shoulders. "What happened to you?" He walked, and Rannulf half-walked across the room to the cot by the window.

Rannulf's voice shook. "God healed me. God had mercy on me."

"What about de Ridford?" Stephen asked.

"I don't give a damn about de Ridford," Rannulf said. He sank down heavily on the cot. "Wake me up," he said, "if anything happens." He pulled at the blanket, lying down half on top of it, got a fold of it over his legs, and was immediately asleep.

✦ "If he dies before he's fourteen, Tripoli gets the crown. Isn't that the agreement?"

"One of the Leper's stratagems, buying the boy some protection. In truth if this child dies a child, the crown will belong to whoever can take and hold it."

"Which might as easily be Tripoli, as us."

"Or us, as easily as Tripoli."

"He is sickly, the boy."

"Yet he is only a boy. I cannot stomach . . ." Joscelin shook his head. "My niece is right. We cannot let the Crusade make murderers of us all. See what has befallen Kerak, now."

He nodded across the hall, toward the high table. No one sat there now, save Kerak; the Princess had come in and left, Guy de Lusignan beside her. The other men milled through the hall, talking and eating the last of the dinner meal, and getting ready to go out. Up behind the empty board, Kerak sat alone, his hands before him tilted up together, his gaze glassy.

De Ridford grunted in his chest. His plan had gone terribly wrong. He had heard the story over and over again, and it still unnerved him. He said, "God forgive me for bringing here the instrument of Guile's death." He crossed himself.

Joscelin said, "Guile is no great loss, it seems to me."

De Ridford murmured a leave, and drifted off across the hall, circling the table. Rannulf was out there somewhere, loose. De Ridford's back itched between his shoulder blades. He went up beside Kerak, and laid a hand on the older man's shoulder.

"You have my prayers, my lord, and for your son."

Kerak's steepled hands curled up into fists. "I want that son of a bitch who killed him. Will you give him to me?"

De Ridford sat down on the bench next to him. "You had him. You let him go."

Kerak thumped his fists down on the table. "He was the only son I had. My only child. Born on the wrong side of the blanket, and with his mother's rabbit-brain, but still—"

De Ridford said, "You have my sympathies. I shall pray for him." He was glad Guile was dead, Kerak's most loyal and most zealous commander. He was pleased with himself for getting Guile out of the way. "You should have settled matters with Rannulf when you had him in your hands."

"I'll kill him," Kerak said, mechanically.

"First kill the boy King. Rannulf is responsible for him. You will make him look the useless serf he is."

"That would profit Tripoli."

"Exactly. It will seem to profit Tripoli, and so Tripoli will be blamed." De Ridford liked this scheme, which had so many positive effects. "No one will object when we place the Princess on the throne. Perhaps we can find Rannulf guilty of helping to murder the King."

He had gone too far. Kerak shifted in his place, scowling at him. "God's eyes, you are full of knots as a net. Go. My son is dead. I can think of nothing other now; go." De Ridford left. Guy de Lusignan had come back into the hall, alone, and the Marshall of the Templars went to pile up a little more spiritual coin with him.

A few days later, the council done at Montgisor, he returned to Jerusalem. Before he had passed through David's Gate he had heard from the guards that Rannulf was back at the citadel. He decided to keep close, and let the other knight come to him with his threats and charges.

Rannulf did not come. After a few days, de Ridford began to worry a little, and he went on a pretext to the citadel, to come face-to-face with him, and force the issue.

But Baudouinet was sick, and no one was admitted into his presence, and his guards were shut up with him. The door to the hall stood closed, and the chamberlain let no one past the first landing of the stairway; on the steps, in the courtyard, a steadily growing crowd of people waited to see the King.

The Grand Chapter to elect the new Master was to be held in Jerusalem on Epiphany. De Ridford foresaw trouble; he had to know what Rannulf intended to do, before the chapter meeting. The Marshall had already counted all the votes. Agnes had given him money to buy those amenable to such persuasions. Others he had plied with whatever means seemed efficacious. He knew he would win on the first counting, if all went well.

Somehow Rannulf would overturn it. The fear grew in him like a fever. He went to Gilbert, and nagged the Seneschal into summoning Rannulf to a hearing before the two officers.

He had an excellent pretext. He said, "He murdered Guile of Kerak, a crime for which he must be punished."

Gilbert sent some sergeants across the city to the citadel, with the summons. He said, "What I've heard is that Guile went at him, with a lot of help, and Saint still got him."

"Don't call him that," de Ridford said. Gilbert smiled at him, his crippled hand stroking his beard. De Ridford went on, "Kerak has sworn vengeance. The whole Order will suffer if we are not seen to do justice."

A few moments later the sergeants came back without Rannulf. "He is on duty, he says, and will come when he can."

"On duty!" De Ridford wheeled around. "His duty is to the Order!" Now he was sure Rannulf plotted against him, and he shouted at Gilbert, "Drag him here by force! He has defied us, refused a command."

Gilbert said, "He says he will come when he can, my lord Marshall. Control yourself." And he was so obviously pleased with de Ridford's discomfiture that the Marshall stilled himself at once, and made no more issue of it.

The winter rains began. Christmas passed, and the officers of the other chapters came to the Temple, and the Grand Chapter met.

At first de Ridford thought, with relief, that Rannulf was ignoring this summons too. But when the refectory was full of the officers, the great shadowy space loud with the bustle of their talk and the stamping of their feet, like a stableful of horses, he saw the black-haired Norman standing at the left side of the front row, by himself.

De Ridford stared at him a moment, daring him to look back, but Rannulf only stared down at the floor.

They called the chapter meeting into being, said the prayers, and announced the election. Right away it was clear that only two men had any real support—de Ridford and Gilbert Erail. Through all the talk Rannulf stood with his eyes lowered, his hands folded on the hilt of his sword, saying nothing.

They called for the vote, and voted by rank, the greatest officers first. Man by man, de Ridford heard his name proclaimed, and knew himself becoming Master of the Temple. Although he had schemed for years for this, and done everything he could to guarantee it, yet as it became true he grew light-headed with surprise and pleasure, as if this had come on him all unlooked for.

Then it was Rannulf's turn, and he lifted his head, and now he did look at de Ridford, and his face was black with malice.

He said, "Obviously you are going to win this, de Ridford. But I will vote for Gilbert Erail, not because I like him much, nor because he is the best choice—he isn't—I am. But the choice is between him and you, and I would vote for a cur dog over you, de Ridford."

He lowered his eyes again, and said nothing more. De Ridford went hot as a furnace. He felt them all watching him; he felt as if he had been scourged in front of them. He could not strike back. To make a battle of this now would risk too much. He had to keep still and let the final few votes be called, and so in the moment of his triumph he was humiliated.

The chapter meeting ended, and the men filed out. By calculation De Ridford reached the doorway just as Rannulf did.

"I'll see you pay for that," he said.

Rannulf only laughed at him, and went out across the porch of the refectory. Stephen de l'Aigle was there waiting for him, with their horses. De Ridford stood watching them, his mouth dry. Rannulf's confidence frightened him. There had to be something in this he didn't know. He dared not move against Rannulf until he knew exactly what was going on. The two knights rode away across the pavement, down toward the gate to the city. De Ridford reminded himself he was their Master, he was Master of the Temple, the greatest army in the world; he bowed to no man save the Pope himself. Yet his knees shook. The next day he rode down to Nablus, where Joscelin de Courtenay held his court, and had the King's guardian transfer Baudouinet and his knights out of Jerusalem, to Acre in the north, for reasons of the boy's health.

CHAPTER XXVII

Agnes said, "Very nicely done, all of it. Your father would have been proud of you." Shading her eyes with her hand, she looked up at the front of the chapel, which stood among the dark cypresses of the Mount of Olives. "The statues are particularly fine."

"I remember coming here as a child," Sibylla said. "When only the walls were standing. I was afraid Baby Jesus would be rained on." At her elbow, Alys laughed.

Made of rosy stone in the new French style, the chapel seemed larger than it was. Her father had begun it, and her brother brought it along; now Sibylla was finishing it, taking a deep satisfaction from the task. This, she thought, was the real work of kings.

The porch of the chapel was set inside pointed arches; above them was a row of niches in the stone. In each of these niches an image would stand. The first was already in place, a sword-bearing archangel with a devil glowering at his feet. From the arch of his wings to the tip of his sword, the angel made a flawless curve of power, while the devil was squashed down like a toad, his face contorted, and his tongue sticking out.

Her mother said, "This is very handsome."

"The angel reminds me of de Ridford," Sibylla said.

Her mother laughed. "Oh, yes, and he would love to know it."

Sibylla thought, But the devil reminds me of Rannulf.

She lowered her eyes. Along the porch of the chapel, in a constant cloud of white dust, the workmen were raising a scaffolding, to lift the next statue to its niche. This one a pilgrim, praying, his head bent over his hands.

Behind her, a shriek went up. "Mama!"

She turned, gladdened; across the courtyard, cluttered with stone and piles of wood, her daughter toddled toward her. "Mama, see?"

Jolie's hair was a glinting tangle. Her face glowed through a mask of dirt. Her hands were full of pretty little stones; Sibylla bent over them, admiring each one. Lifting her head, she looked down across the courtyard and saw Guy walking toward her. He smiled; his face was the child's face, only older. She waved to him, and stood, lifting Jolie up into her arms.

"Gamma," Jolie said, and offered the sticky handfuls of rocks to her grandmother.

Agnes said, "You know they have shunted poor Baudouinet away to Acre."

Guy came up to them, his head raised, his gaze sweeping the chapel. "Not bad," he said. "The statues are very nice." He was being polite; such things did not interest him. He turned at once, and looked away, back toward Jerusalem, on its hill opposite. She had promised to go hunting with him, in the morning, to make up for spending today doing this.

Agnes said, "As I said, Baudouinet is off in Acre, and I am going there, to see him. I thought perhaps you would want to come."

"I," Sibylla said, startled.

Guy's head swiveled toward them. "Acre. Doesn't Tripoli control Acre? She can't go there."

Agnes said, "The King is sick. Perhaps very sick."

Sibylla turned, and summoned Alys with a look, and gave Jolie away to her. Guy said, "Well, she can't go to Acre. I won't allow it." His voice as he said this dropped into his chest.

Sibylla glanced at her mother; their gazes met, and across this bridge ran an instant's unspoken message. She said, "We should be going back, shouldn't we?"

Agnes smiled at her. "Yes, I suppose we should."

In Acre the King lived in the palace called Beauregard, at the north end of the city. Agnes went there with the Count of Tripoli, who was visiting the city, and a physician she knew, a Jew, far-famed, who was called Philip of Acre.

The palace was shut up tight, as if for a war; at every gate and door someone stopped them. Finally they came into the garden, at the back of the palace. Here another guard held them up, this one a Templar, tall, with a copper-colored beard, who would not let them pass, but sent word of their coming on down into the garden.

Her grandson came quickly, his face bright. "Grandmother!" He came up beside the redheaded knight, and took his hand. "Grandmother, this is my friend Mouse. He's a Knight Templar, he is very valiant and wonderful."

Agnes lifted her eyes to the knight. "Well met, Sir Mouse. That's quite a commendation."

The knight smiled at her. His eyes were blue; he carried himself with an arresting grace. He said, "Thank you, my lady. The King is pleased to glorify me." The King in fact hung on his hand, pulling on him, which the knight patiently endured.

Another Templar had followed the King up out of the garden, and the little boy glanced back at him.

"This is Saint. He is the chief of my bodyguard."

This knight had no such elegance of manner as the first. He stared at the ground, and mumbled something to Agnes. Tripoli pushed forward into the front of the conversation, talking to this Templar.

"I sent for you, a month ago, to present yourself to me. You never did."

The black knight said, "My orders are to defend the King. I said I would come when I could." He sounded irritated. His hair and beard were sooty black, and his clothes looked as if he slept in them. Agnes saw her grandson liked this one much less than the other; the child turned shy, when the black knight spoke, and kept close by red Mouse.

Tripoli said, "Then I will tell you now, Rannulf, while I am in Acre, I am Master of the city. Make no trouble for me."

The knight lifted his head slightly. His eyes were stony. "I have had three warnings from various places that someone means to kill the King. One was about Kerak. Two were about you."

Tripoli stiffened. "I assure you, I am not—"

"Considering that this is a little boy, I think it foul even for a damned Saracen, but for another Christian—"

"I am not plotting the King's life!"

"Good," the knight said. "Then there will be no problem."

"Are you done, now?" Agnes said. She turned to the other man she had brought with them, who had been standing silently all the while. "This is Philip of Acre, who is a physician. I have brought him here to view my grandson. If you will allow it."

The black knight ignored her. He went back to staring at the ground. The red knight said, "Yes, certainly. Here, little boy, let this hakim look you over."

The child had listened with a grave face to the talk of his proposed murder, but now he went forward bravely, with his big friend beside him. They took his coat and shirt off, and the physician studied him, smelled his breath, looked at the tips of his fingers, and laid one ear against his back, listening. After a moment he straightened, and with a gentle word sent the child away down the garden. The red knight followed him.

Agnes said, "What ails him, Philip?"

The physician watched the child go. The Jew was slight, dressed in a gown discreetly embroidered around the hem and the cuffs of the sleeves; he wore a cap like a silk tonsure. He turned to the black knight, and said, "How does he eat?"

The knight lifted his head. "We taste of all his food before he eats it. We handle everything he touches. Is he being poisoned?" He gave a sharp glance at Tripoli.

The physician smiled. "You are a Norman, aren't you. I've noticed men of your race have a predilection to the suspicion of poisoning. No, he isn't being poisoned. I believe my Christian colleagues in Salerno would say that he has too much of a cold humor. He's small and frail. His chest is full of cracklings and whistlings, the circles of his nails are blue, his color is bad." He turned to Agnes, and gave a little shake of his head. Not in his words, but in this gesture she knew her grandson's death decreed.

Her heart clenched. Her eyes sought after the child, sitting on the grass at the far side of the garden. Heavily, she said, "He's always been sickly. I thought he might grow better." She crossed herself.

The Templar was staring at the physician. He said, now, "You are Philip ben Ezra? I understand there is a physician by that name at the court in Damascus."

"My cousin," said Philip of Acre.

Tripoli had been watching the little boy, his face intent as a vulture's; now he swung around toward the black knight. "What interest is that of yours?"

"I'm interested in anybody connected with Damascus," the Templar said. "I have heard that Saladin is also sick."

Philip backed away, leaving the knight and Tripoli to stand face-to-face. The Count said stiffly, "Your duty, as you said, is to protect the King. Stay out of policy."

The knight said, "If he is sick, we should attack him. The Temple is at full strength again, it's November, the truce is over, and it's time to fight. The Sultan has a lot of problems. Now he's on his back. One little push might finish him."

Tripoli grunted at him. "He wants to extend the truce, which I am minded to do."

"Truces favor them, not us."

"I see no virtue in overthrowing Saladin; it would just cause chaos."

"Yes, he has a lot of sons and nephews. They might fight over the succession for years, which would be to our advantage."

"And whoever finally came to power might be much worse than Sal-adin, who is at least a reasonable and honorable man." Under pressure of argument Tripoli's voice sharpened to a sarcastic whine. "And what you obviously do not know, mewed up as you are in this little corner of the Kingdom, and narrow-minded anyway by virtue of your calling, is that the famine is everywhere. The price of corn even here in Acre is going up daily, and in the south there is no corn at all. We can't fight without food."

The knight said, "Attacking Saladin we could seize the Hauran, with its fields and orchards. We could hold all that territory at least through the harvest and feed the whole Kingdom on it."

"You have the mentality of a bandit. Which was probably your pro-fession before you took up cutting throats for Christ."

"No, before I took vows I cut throats for noblemen like you, who are too water-hearted to do it for themselves."

Agnes laughed. She said, "While you two are having at this, I think I shall desport myself with my grandson. Sir Templar, I have your per-mission?"

The knight stared down at the ground. He spoke to Tripoli, rather than directly to Agnes. "Tell her she may go down there. Ask her to send me Mouse."

Tripoli said, with a sneer, "Your own connection to Damascus."

"Yes," the knight said, "but his is through the back door."

Agnes was going off down the garden; she saw, puzzled, how Tripoli recoiled with distaste at that last remark. Tripoli and the black knight argued a while longer, and the Count left. Agnes spent the rest of the afternoon with her grandson, Templars hovering over her all the while.

When she saw Tripoli again, the following day, at his own palace, she said, "I wonder at you, my lord, letting that surly black-haired brute talk at you that way."

The Templar interested her. Under his icy skin he gave off a steady blast of heat. She was tempted to liberate him from his vow of chastity, but his discipline was formidable; she suspected he would refuse her. She consigned him to the luxury of her imagination.

"He's a swine," Tripoli said. "They are unfit companions for a young and tender prince."

Agnes said, "My grandson is dying, I doubt they can corrupt him overmuch. And they will protect him, you can see that. I pity the poor assassin who wanders into that den."

A servant brought her a cup of spiced wine. The rain was hammer-ing in off the sea, and even in this hall, where a fire blazed on the hearth,

Agnes could not warm herself. Her fingerbones ached.

Tripoli said, "All Templars are criminals. That one deserves a quick hanging."

"The two of you were quite amusing. He seems very well informed. What did you mean, he has his own connections in Damascus?"

"That other knight. The redheaded one. One of the Sultan's many nephews is his lover."

Agnes now understood the joke about the back door, and burst out laughing. Tripoli colored, his mouth sour. "You are merry, my lady," he said, stiffly. "Merry the devil at the news of sin." He stared away coldly into the drizzling rain.

The little boy grew steadily sicker. Agnes saw him every day; when he could not leave his bed, she sent again to her daughter, down in Jaffa, and this time Sibylla came, in secret, like a thief, so that Tripoli did not know she was there.

She had gotten past her husband by sending him off hunting, and told him some good lies, on top of it; but she would not go to see the little King. She said, "He has never been my child."

"Then what are you doing here?" Agnes said. Sibylla gave her no answer, but then Joscelin de Courtenay arrived, and Agnes saw them talking together and knew they were planning how to seize the advantage at the child's death. That was why she had come, then.

She went to her daughter again, and said, "Come see the boy. He may live only a few days more."

Sibylla was fretful, taut, her skin pale, her eyes sleek. She said, "Am I to have the chamberlain announce me? Hear, hear, my lord King, let me introduce you to your mother? What use is it?" In by the hearth, fat Joscelin de Courtenay sat with his feet to the fire, dozing.

That night, late, the Templars sent a servant to Agnes; and she went off across the city in the dark and the cold and the rain, and stood there by the bed and watched the little boy struggle for his last breath. When he was clay, she saw that the red knight was weeping, and the black knight beside him close to weeping.

Her heart was a knot in her chest. She went back to her palace, in the dawn cold, and woke her daughter in her bed.

Sibylla sat up, white as shell; before her mother could speak, she said, "I shall go today, I think. I shall go to see him today."

Agnes looked at her with eyes boiled dry. "He is dead."

Her daughter's lips parted. "Oh, no," she said.

"Yes," Agnes said. "And now he is out of your way, isn't he? And now you may do what you have plotted and planned for, all these years—that for which you have spent your honor and your child's life, and God knows what other, hidden prices—now, go be Queen of Jerusalem, my dear, and see what happiness it brings you." Then she rose, and went straight out of the palace, and went back to her own home of Nablus, and there, at last, alone, she untied her heart in a stream of tears.

✦ In the chapel of the palace Beauregard, the Templars stood watch over the little King's coffin, and Tripoli came, and Joscelin de Courtenay.

Tripoli said, "By the terms of the will of Baudouin the Leper, I am now King of Jerusalem."

Joscelin said, "That is so. But as we are kinsmen, and fellow Christians, I must warn you that Jerusalem is not safe for you."

Rannulf stood at the head of the coffin, his hands folded over the hilt of his sword, and looked straight ahead of him; the words of these men fell on his ears like evil music.

Tripoli said, "No, I fear not. De Ridford will seize any chance to interfere, and there is Kerak to consider also."

"You must make your claim as strong as you can," Joscelin said. "Go to Tiberias, and call a council there of all the great men of the Kingdom. Let that council proclaim you king." Joscelin laid his hand on the coffin. "The Templars will take this back to Jerusalem, and see to the burial. When everyone has accepted you as King, you can come into the city to be crowned."

Tripoli said, "What you are saying makes sense to me. I shall leave in the morning for Tiberias." He turned and went out of the chapel. Joscelin bent his knee, and said a prayer, and he too left.

Stephen said, "Joscelin said what Tripoli wanted to hear, and so he believed him."

The candles by the coffin were burning down, and Rannulf went forward and took new ones, and lit them, and set them into the melted stubs. Kneeling down, he crossed himself and said a paternoster. The candles made an island of light around the coffin; the rest of the chapel lay in darkness.

He felt all around him a great churning and stirring, all set in motion around this small death.

White-eyed, Stephen spoke into the silence; he said, "How can we trust anything, then? Tripoli is a clever man; if he is so easily gulled, what hope for somebody like me?"

"What else are you going to do?" Rannulf asked.

It was deep in the night, the vigils bell had long since sounded. Between them was a coffin, and the body of a child they had both loved. He felt as if Stephen talked to him across a widening chasm.

Stephen said, "I have to believe in something. I can't say my prayers to a void."

"Believe, then," Rannulf said.

"How can I, when I see how everybody else deludes himself? They are all as sure as I am. More! Because I doubt everything now."

Rannulf shifted his feet. In the darkness, he heard the sound of a door opening and shutting.

He said, "Just believe, Mouse. Either Jesus died for us, and so we can be saved, or he did not, and we are damned. So better to believe, either way."

"I can't," Mouse cried, and then, from the dark, she walked into the glow of the candles, up to the far side of the coffin.

Rannulf said, "I knew you were here. When Joscelin spoke, I heard your words in his voice."

Before the coffin, she stood slim and straight in a long white gown, her eyes huge. He was tired and he saw her in the middle of a well of streaming light. She spoke out of the light. "Tomorrow Tripoli leaves for Tiberias. And I for Jerusalem, and there I shall be crowned the Queen."

"Why are you coming here, now, and telling me this?"

"Because I want you to stay out of it. Of all the men in this kingdom, you alone I cannot foresee."

Rannulf shifted his feet. "How can I stay out of it? I am a knight of the Temple of Jerusalem."

"Then tell me you support me. I was born to this, to rule Jerusalem. Who else is there?"

"There is Tripoli. Who also talks about peace with Saladin."

"Tripoli is an usurper. God wills that I be Queen, Rannulf. I will bring God's purpose at last into being in this Kingdom. I will make peace, bring an end to the bloodshed—we turn the Holy Land into a slaughter ground, which should be the garden of the world!"

"God wills it," Rannulf said.

"No!" She flung a fiery look at him, like an angel's sword. "God does not will this endless war. God is not evil."

"God is not good. God is, is all."

"You blaspheme! You pull everything inside out, good is evil, murder is piety, life is hell, and Heaven is a battlefield. While people are suffering and dying you make sermons saying God wills it!"

Rannulf could not take his eyes from her. He leaned forward, and banged his knuckles on the coffin. "Sibylla, I stood guard over his deathbed. Where were you?"

Her eyes widened. Her mouth opened a moment, but she said nothing; she turned and walked away, back into the darkness.

Stephen said, "You called her by her name."

"Did I." He was exhausted. He wanted to sink into an oblivion of sleep.

"You've talked to her before," Stephen said.

"At Montgisor. When I killed Guile. They were going to hang me, and she saved me. She alone spoke for me, and saved my life. I love her. I would fight the whole world for her. I always end up fighting her instead."

"Now she will make herself Queen."

"God willing."

"And then what?"

"Then we obey orders. Which is all we ever do anyway. We never have all that much choice, do we? Why worry about it?"

"What about you and her?"

"What?"

"Have you slept with her?"

Rannulf's hand clenched. "Don't talk about her like that."

"You haven't, then."

"How could I? She's married, she is a princess, she'll be Queen of Jerusalem. I have no choice here either."

Stephen was staring keenly at him. "What if you did? What if you could have her, if you gave up God?"

"That will never happen," Rannulf said.

Stephen shook his head. "You're as bad as any of us, Rannulf. You have no faith either. You just give it away. Obeying orders. That's your faith, and that's nothing."

Rannulf made no answer. After a moment he crossed himself again. He knew Stephen was right. They stood there the rest of the night, and said nothing more to each other.

CHAPTER XXVIII

Guy de Lusignan reached Jerusalem just at sundown, as the gate was closing. The streets were full of Templars, standing guard on gates and on the walls, and riding in packs through the streets. Guy went straight to the citadel; in the courtyard, he met Gerard de Ridford.

The Master asked him, "Are you ready?"

Guy said, "I don't know. I don't understand what's going on. Where is my lady wife? She's supposed to be off in a convent in Sidon."

"She is here," the Master said. "She was in Acre, when the King died—she and Joscelin have handled things very well, so far. She's gotten Tripoli out of the way, and the Patriarch is of course amenable to anything. He has brought out the sacred oil and the crown and the cape; tomorrow he will anoint her Queen of Jerusalem."

Guy looked up at the tower, a square stone blade against the dark. A crack of yellow candlelight showed in the window. She had lied to him. All the while he had missed her, and wanted her back, and thought she was off doing pious works, but she had lied to him.

He wished he had not let de Ridford know this. Everybody would think him a fool, if they knew he could not control his own wife.

She was up there now, and he knew how tight she would be strung, so close to her goal; she would be burning. The fire in her drew him irresistibly. He started forward and the Master gripped his arm.

"No. Heed me. You remember, I told you once, you would be King of Jerusalem."

"You did," Guy said.

"Good. Now be guided by me. Tomorrow, when she takes the crown, she must give it to you. Promise her whatever you need to, but she has to give the crown to you, or all is lost—no man can follow a woman into war. And so Tripoli might still triumph."

Guy licked his lips. He had long before lost interest in de Ridford's endless fussing and plotting and tugging on strings. His gaze rose to the orange light in the window. "I have to see her," he said, and went for-

ward, across the courtyard to the staircase, and up. De Ridford followed, a few paces behind.

He hated this place, so close and dark. He had been here only once
before, to present himself to Baudouin the Leper, and he thought he
could still catch a taint of the stench of sickness and death, even on the
stairs. He went up through the crowded landing where people were jostled together in the dark, waiting, and into the hall beyond, with its three
narrow windows, its raised platform for the throne.

She did not sit on the throne, but stood in the middle of the hall, in
the light from all the lamps.

"No, why wonder?" she was saying, when he came in. "Tomorrow
night it shall all be done, and let him find out as he will." All around
her stood the men who supported her; the Master came in behind Guy.
She went on, "Until we see what he will do, no one is to move. Let him
misstep." Her voice was high and strong. As she spoke, she was turning to look from man to man, and now her gaze found Guy. Her face
opened in a blooming smile. "Ah, you are finally come." She stretched
out one arm to him.

He went up beside her, taking hold of her hand, and stood there next
to her. "Darling," he said, "you were supposed to be in a convent praying." He clutched her hand, holding her fast. His gaze searched her. He
wanted to get her away from all these people; a lusty urgency drove him,
he needed to possess her, to make certain of her. He glanced around him
at the packed room, at all these rivals.

He looked out over a field of bent backs. Just inside the door, the Master of the Temple lowered his head an inch. They were all bowing.
Amazed, he realized they were bowing to him. He clung to his wife's
hand, and looked down into her face, and saw her smile.

Guy felt a jolt of understanding, as if he had suddenly wakened up.
He was going to be the King. He struggled to get his mind around this
truth, that he was going to be King of Jerusalem. God was wonderful.
He almost laughed out loud. He still gripped his wife's hand; he lifted
it, and kissed it. His head swam. He could forgive her a few lies now.
He kissed her hand again, amazed.

✥ There was no pomp in this coronation. In haste they gathered under
the dome of Holy Sepulcher, the lords packed shoulder to shoulder in
rows before the altar, the Templars along the walls; here where only a
year before they had sworn to uphold the will of Baudouin the Leper,
they overturned his will, and saw Sibylla crowned the Queen.

She sat before the altar, facing them, the great cape around her like an ill-fitting carapace. When Heraclius set the iron crown on her head, she seemed to flinch, as if it weighed more than she had expected.

Then her husband knelt before her, the first of her vassals to do homage to her, and with her two hands she reached up, and from her sleek coiled hair she lifted the crown and set it on her husband's head. And then all the men before her gave a shout of triumph, as if they had seen something glorious.

✛ Half the lamps had gone out. In the dim light under the dome, the surface of the great Rock seemed to move and shift and seethe. At the edge of it Rannulf sat on his heels, his hands idle, and his mind idle, and de Ridford came up behind him.

Rannulf did not look around, and he said nothing. Finally de Ridford spoke. "You know Kerak has put a price on your head."

"If Kerak had any balls left he'd come after me himself."

The Master gave a grunt of a laugh. "I've always admired your sheer brass. It took me a while to realize it's all sham. What do you think Tripoli will do next?"

"He's in a very strong position. He holds the north in a solid block. Half of Outremer follows him and not this straw King you and the Princess have foisted on us. He has a truce with Saladin, that lets him turn his back on Damascus."

The Master walked up closer to the Rock, into the edge of Rannulf's field of vision. "Then you think he will attack us."

"No," Rannulf said. "He should. But he won't. He's too cautious. He'll wait and see, and then march and countermarch, and the longer Guy is King, the more King he is."

He had stood in Holy Sepulcher and watched her crowned. He had not seen her since then. But she would not leave his mind; even here, he thought of her, and not of God. And he hated her husband.

De Ridford hated Tripoli. "Then perhaps we should attack him."

"He's a Christian," Rannulf said.

"In name only! It's said he prays toward Mecca, in his own chapel— that he keeps an idol of Mohammed under the altar."

Rannulf laughed at that, for the first time looking around at de Ridford, who knew so little about his enemies. Of course de Ridford's chief enemy was Tripoli. The Master's face was intense as a fire, his eyes blazing.

"You laugh! And yet you yourself saw him with Saladin. I heard your men say how the Sultan loves him. Their testimony convicted him before the whole chapter—why does it not convince you?"

"He's a Christian, and my vow forbids me to strike against other Christians."

"Bah, you are his fool. He has you completely gulled. I suspect you and your guard failed your job, in Acre, and he poisoned the child King under your nose." The Master's eyes were narrow. "Or you are treacherous, and in league with him. No matter. I despise Tripoli, and I mean to destroy him, no matter what the cost. As for you, churl, whatever I order you to do, you will do, or I will cut you down. Hmmm? I'll have your own men cut you down. Do you understand?"

Rannulf considered that a moment; then he said, "Yes, my lord."

De Ridford smiled at him. "Someday, Rannulf, you will beg me for my favor." He went out of the church, his feet loud across the ambulatory.

Rannulf sat looking out at the Rock. Since he had come back to the Temple from Acre he had given himself up to the routine of its chores and hours, saying his offices when the bells rang, caring for his horses and his weapons, working at the practice butts, patrolling the city; he took a certain pleasure from having everything there before him, in knowing exactly what he would do next. Yet he was uneasy. He could feel something coming toward him that he had to be ready for. Sibylla played at being Queen, de Ridford blinded himself with his little feud with Tripoli, but there was something coming that could drown them all.

Mouse came up beside him. "What was that all about?"

"You heard him."

"What do you think he's going to do against Tripoli?"

"I don't know, and I don't much care, Mouse." Rannulf got up, his knees cracking, and bowed to the altar, and signed himself with the Cross. "Come down to the stable and help me with my new horse." He started away toward the door, Mouse walking beside him.

✠ In the spring, when the dyers were spreading their cloth to dry on the rooftops of Jerusalem, and the first caravans were moving along the Jaffa road, Saladin sent an embassy with his greetings to the new Queen and her King.

The Legate of the Name was Tabib the Ethiopian, the eunuch, who delivered the Sultan's speeches and gifts. Behind him, in among the other seconds, Ali stood with his hands folded, marking this new King.

Nobody knew anything of him, save that he had come from France, which seemed to spew forth a constant stream of these yellow-headed, loud-mouthed, energetic men. This one fit the mold. He was square-shouldered, jut-jawed, younger than Ali himself; he stood up before his throne, and his voice rang out through the crowded hall.

"I accept these presents and greetings from the Sultan of Damascus. But let him not think us weak, and easily bought off with pretty toys and words. My lord the Count of Tripoli made this truce between us and Damascus, but when the truce is over, let the Sultan beware: he will find us ready with our swords in our hands."

He spoke louder than he needed. Around him stood ranks of Templars, fencing him off. His pretty young queen sat behind him, on the double throne, and said nothing; but her eyes were always moving. Ali had already looked among the Templars, not finding the one he wanted to see.

Yet there were Templars everywhere, at all the gates, in the streets, on the walls. There would be no free roving around the city from shrine to shrine, this time; they had already made that obvious. Ali watched the tall, brown-bearded Master of the Temple walk up beside the King, and whisper in his ear, one hand on his elbow.

Tabib the Ethiopian made his leave-takings, and they went out of the citadel, down some narrow stairs to a courtyard full of horses. There more Templars escorted them off to the palace called La Plaisance. Ali saw he would make no contact this time with Stephen de l'Aigle.

He told himself that was a grace of God. Already in Damascus people had begun to talk about how eagerly he advanced this mission, which had been his idea, conceived even before the news came of the boy King's death. For months he had thought of nothing else. Now it had all come to dust. Inside La Plaisance, he left the other faithful to relax and joke and eat and clean up, and wandered away from room to room, his mood leaden.

Unlike the citadel, which was a fortress, this place was meant for comfort, as its name suggested. Its inside spaces were open sunlit galleries, some with mosaic floors, and some with painted walls, and there was even a bath, in the back wing, with fanciful fish on the tiles of the pool. Now La Plaisance stood all but empty, with only the embassy and their servants living there, and a few servants of the King to attend on them. He thought no one had lived here for a while, and found proof of this in a little gallery, where dried boughs left over from some festivity still hung along the walls, their dropped needles scattered in brown drifts across the floor.

He told himself this was a fitting figure for his pursuit of Stephen de l'Aigle, a withered bough, the dry husk of a memory, tucked off in an empty room in a palace in a hostile city. Crossing the black-and-white tile floor, he came to a door, and opened it.

A wave of colors rushed at him. He stepped out into bright sunlight, and the riot of a burgeoning springtime garden; a rush of little birds fluttered away at his approach, and scattered into the trees.

The air was warmer outside than inside. There was a sweet trace of fragrance in the giddy breeze. The garden had been untended for a while, like the palace, and had gone wild, daisies with hairy stalks lifting up among the clustered Turkish cups, and blown roses; a line of an old poem came into his mind, how the rose shed its petals like drops of blood across the wind of time. He went out into the middle of all this wild, secret beauty, delighting in it, and then there was suddenly someone behind him. He wheeled around, his hand flying to the dagger in his belt. Then, in a rush of relief and pleasure, he saw who it was.

"God—God—I thought never to see you again."

"Well, you were wrong," Stephen said, and came to him.

✠ "You spoke very harshly to the Sultan's man," Sibylla said. She sat down on the stool, and Alys came up behind her and began to take off her linen coif.

Guy said, "They are Saracens! They respect nothing except force, and the threat of force." Now that the morning's audience was done, he was making ready to go out hunting. He had no taste for the small steady work of being King.

Sibylla sat still, her head bent, while her cousin's hands worked down the back of her gown, undoing the laces. "If you start out talking fight with them you have nowhere to go. No room. It's like standing with your heels over the edge of a cliff."

"Don't tell me what to do," he said.

She was still a moment. Alys had undone the gown, and now lifted it up over her head and away. Guy went noisily around the room, looking for something. Since the coronation, he and Sibylla had not been easy with each other. Alys brought her a long loose coat to wear, and Sibylla put it on; she nodded to her cousin. "Go fetch Jolie to me."

"Yes, Highness." Alys went eagerly out. She liked the times they spent with the baby.

Sibylla sat down again on the stool, her gaze following her husband. "There are people in the embassy from Damascus who are not merely spokesmen and servants."

"What do you mean?"

"One of the men who stood behind the black man is a relative of Saladin's who has been here before."

His head swiveled toward her. "How do you know that?"

Pleased to have gotten his attention, she smiled at him. "The chamberlain recognized him."

He looked angry. That she knew something he did not seemed like an insult to him. He said, "Sibylla, stay out of this. You should go back to Jaffa, anyway."

"Well, I am not going back to Jaffa," she said. She knew he could do nothing to prevent her staying; he was King because of her, he needed her.

Alys came in, with the baby and her nurse. Seeing her mother, the little girl gave a scream of imperious pleasure. Sibylla went down on her knees and held out her arms, and Jolie ran headlong into them.

"That's my girl. That's my little Jolie."

Guy squatted down beside them. "My women," he said. He kissed Sibylla's cheek, and then the baby's. Sibylla put her arm around his neck, holding him there.

"Come with us. We shall go down to the suk in the Under City and watch the jugglers."

"God's love." He pulled violently away from her. "What are you taking her down there for?"

"There's always something to see in the Under City."

He stood up. "I don't want you going down there," he said. But he was already turning away. He had said what he wanted to say and now he would go off hunting, and she would take Jolie into the Under City. There was a delicate balance between them; they kept in place by constantly pulling in opposite directions. He called for his groom, who was waiting in the antechamber, and bent and kissed Sibylla again, and Jolie, gave them some good-byes, and went out.

Alys said, "He's angry."

"No, he's not," Sibylla said. Jolie trotted off across the room, toward the corner, where there was a lute; the child loved to pluck the strings, and even tried to sing. Sibylla followed her. "Send down for dinner, will you, Alysette?"

Alys waved a page off to this minor duty. "When will we go to the Under City?"

"Later. Nothing happens down there until after Nones, anyway." De Ridford would escort them. There was a caravan in from Egypt, with jugglers and shows. Also in the suk, a man she had to see.

That, too, Guy would mislike.

He could not stop her; he had given up trying. Had settled down into his proper role, which he had done very well, today, actually, in the audience. He was her sword. The Saracens would pay more heed to her overtures of peace if they thought Guy might attack them at any moment.

"Mama, see?" The little girl had pulled the lute into her lap.

"Show me."

Jolie banged on the strings with her hands, lifting her voice in a long quivering bray that was so like and yet so unlike a real song that Sibylla burst out laughing. Alys bustled by her, loudly scolding.

"No, no, little silly, not like that."

"No, leave her," Sibylla said. "Go tend to that, now." The servants were bringing in their dinner on trays; a clattering and babbling spread out through the room. Redirected, Alys bent her importance in a smooth arc back to the servants. Like Guy, she loved to give orders. Sibylla sat down, her back to the bustle, smiling at her daughter. "Play that again, Jolie."

✦ In the dark, in the warm silence, Ali said, "Come with me."

Stephen muttered something below words. He stretched, his body twisting on the bed, his arms wide. Ali laid his hands on the knight's chest, and pushed him down, and put his head down on him and listened to his heart beat.

"Come with me," he said, again.

Stephen fingered through his hair. "What do you mean?"

"Go back to Damascus with me, and live there. With me. How can I say this more clearly? What don't you understand?"

The hand stroked his hair until every nerve tingled. "How you could say it at all, that's what I don't understand."

"Ayyyahh." Ali pushed angrily away, and lay down on his back, alone. "What, it makes too much sense? My uncle is going to annihilate you, Stephen, your whole kingdom, your whole Order, all of you."

"Yes, well, as Saint says, he can try." Stephen moved again, rolling onto his side, his head propped on his hand. They had found this little room in a far corner of the palace; the high windows behind the bed opened on the white sky of the evening. Ali could not keep from touching him. He stretched out his arm and laid his hand on him.

"Are you in danger, coming here like this?"

"Maybe. Stop trying to rescue me. I am who I am, you are who you are, that's all. But in spite of everything, we're here, together. Can't you be glad of that? Isn't that good enough, for now? Because that's all there is, Ali."

Ali said, "No. You're being ingenuous, Stephen. It's more than just now for me, more than just sex. And I can't do it anymore like this. I can't be both your lover and your enemy."

Stephen said, "Come to Jerusalem. Be a Templar."

"Don't be ridiculous," Ali said.

"It was a joke."

"Obviously. But I'm being very serious. I will not go on like this. I love you, Stephen. I have thought of you constantly since we were together last. I have schemed and plotted like a wizard to get back to Jerusalem to see you. I want you with me. I want you in Damascus with me, forever."

Stephen listened, his face still; he said, "Or?"

"Or this is over between us."

For a moment Stephen said nothing, and did not move, but then he gathered himself. Slid off the bed, and stooped for his clothes. Ali said, "Where are you going?"

"Away," Stephen said.

"Damn you," Ali said, an edge in his voice. "Why are you doing this to me?"

"I'm not doing anything," Stephen said. He was putting on his leggings. "What I meant for a joke, you mean seriously. You're the one who's decided, Ali. Good-bye." He pulled his shirt on and went out.

"Stephen," Ali said.

There was no answer. The door swung half-open. Beyond lay part of the garden, and the trees behind it. He would go out over the wall at the back. Ali laid his head down on the bed and shut his eyes.

✠ After Vespers the tables in the refectory were set up for supper. At the ringing of a bell the knights filed into the hall and lined up along the walls, and listened with heads bowed to the words of the priest praising God. The bell rang again, and all together the knights went forward and sat down on the benches, and the food was brought in.

Rannulf sat at one end of the middle table, with Bear on his left, and Felx to Bear's left, but there was a little space between them.

Bear said, "Where is Mouse?" He reached across the table to take a loaf from the nearest basket. The clatter and rumble of the knights spread through the hall. It was their custom to amuse themselves during meals by getting the novices to recite psalms, and now one of the young men climbed onto the stool in the middle of the room and lifted his uncertain voice.

"By the rivers of Babylon we sat and wept, as we remembered Zion—"

"Oh, babble on," Felx muttered.

"Where is Mouse?"

Rannulf said, "He's not here."

On the stool the novice was stumbling through the verse; he forgot a word, and from all around the hall the other men whooped and whistled and threw chunks of bread at him. Bear said, "What are you going to do about that?"

"Do about what?" Rannulf said. The sergeants were bringing in big platters of meat. The sour stink of it reached his nose; for weeks they had been getting bad meat, because of the famine. He reached for another loaf of the bread. A sergeant came by and filled his cup.

"If I forget thee, O Jerusalem, let my right hand—unh—" The novice flung up his hands, warding off the bombardment. "Lose its cunning, may—may my tongue cleave to the roof of my mouth—"

Bear planted his elbows on the table. "I mean, what are you going to do about Mouse. And the damned sandpig he's busy plugging."

Felx slammed an elbow into him; Bear adjusted to it with a grunt. Rannulf said, "I'm not going to do anything."

Felx said, "I told you."

"O daughter of Babylon, doomed to destruction—unh—"

Rannulf said, "This is my favorite psalm, and he is butchering it." He broke the hard end off the loaf in his hands. "I won't hear anything against Mouse. Got that?" He cocked his arm back and threw. The novice was crouched on the stool, his arms over his head, bellowing through the hail.

"He who seizes your infants and dashes them against the rocks!" He bolted off the stool. The knights roared for another victim. In through the far door came Stephen.

He looked grim; he walked around the end of the table, and sat down between Rannulf and Bear. He put his hands up over his face. Above his bowed head Rannulf met Bear's eyes.

Another novice had taken his place on the stool; this one knew the virtue in a short psalm.

"How good and pleasant it is when brothers live together in unity!"

"I like this one," Felx said. "All that oil." Bear hung his arm over Mouse's shoulders. Rannulf ate another bite of bread.

CHAPTER XXIX

In the suk, when the beggar boy came up to him, Stephen thought at first he brought a message from Ali, and his hopes leapt. But it was not. The Queen wanted to see him, secretly, alone. Through his disappointment, there ran a cold trickle of warning: this was not a good idea. But he had said once, Call me.

He looked over his shoulder, off past the row of camels in front of Abu Hamid's, where Rannulf squatted on his heels talking to drovers. The other knight's back was to him. He did not see this. Stephen turned to the boy and nodded.

"Tell her I will come."

Stephen said, "I am doing this only for you. And only once."

"Thank you, Mouse," Sibylla said.

He stood aside, one hand out to the man waiting behind him. "My lady Queen, I present to you my lord Faruk ad-Din Ali ibn Aziz."

The Saracen prince stood where he was, staring at her, his eyes wide. He had the fine features and fair skin she had marked in other Kurds. He said, "To the Queen of Jerusalem, may God give peace." His French was excellent.

She said, "Thank you very much for consenting to this meeting, my lord. I have some messages for you to bear to your master, the lord Sultan, Salah ad-Din."

The Saracen watched her as if he had never seen a woman before. He said, "I shall convey them, Highness."

"One is a letter, which I have written." She turned, and Alys came forward with the letter in her hand. Alys' hand shook so the letter rattled. Sibylla said, "The other message is my personal assurance that if the Sultan will talk to me of a lasting peace, I will meet him anywhere he wishes."

The Saracen took the letter from her, with a little bow of his head. "I shall tell my uncle the Sultan what you have said to me, Highness."

"Thank you," she said, again.

That was all. He went out again, at once; Mouse followed him. Sibylla turned toward Alys. Lifting her hands, she adjusted her coif. "Well," she said. "It's begun now."

Alys said, "I hope my lord the King never finds out."

"I hope he does," Sibylla said. "Because then something will have come of it."

◈ Ali said, "She is beautiful. But so brazen. What sort of man is her husband, that he allows her to go about so freely?"

Stephen said, "She rules herself. She does as she pleases, and she always has."

"She must be miserably unhappy. Women need to be ruled."

Stephen laughed. "What do you know about women?" They had only a little way to go; they had met the Queen in a house by David's Gate, only a few blocks from La Plaisance. It was very late, well past vigils. They went down the great street a little, staying to the shadows of the houses on the right; to the left the high wall of the citadel reached its corner, and the dark expanses of the marketplace opened up away from them, stretching toward the hump of its vaulted roof.

Ali said, "Have you changed your mind?"

"No. My mind has never changed. I've been the same through all of this. I've loved you, honestly and well. You're the one who wants it to change." He stopped short, one hand out. "Hold."

"What?" Ali looked away down the street; ahead of them the buildings on either side loomed high above the narrow way, so that the street was utterly dark, and nothing moved there now, but a moment before, Stephen thought, something had moved.

Ali said, "I have to get back," and started to walk on down the street, and Stephen grabbed his arm.

"No, wait." He raised his voice a level. "Saint. Is that you?"

For a moment there was no answer, and then out of the dark of the street Rannulf walked. By his walk alone Stephen knew his temper; he collected himself. Rannulf came up to him and shoved him hard in the chest.

"What are you doing? You're giving de Ridford just what he wants."

Stephen yielded a step to him. "I'm not doing anything."

Rannulf shoved him again, pushing him back another step. "Go down and get my horse."

Stephen went around him, out into the street, and turned. Rannulf was facing Ali, his head thrust forward, his shoulders set, as if he were about to fight him. "Get out of my city."

"Your city," Ali said, his voice rough. He stood back, his head high. "You inflate yourself, dog-soldier. Do you think you're anything but chaff in the wind? I have seen enough of Jerusalem to know this is a city full of lies, and treacheries, and brewing hatreds."

"Then you won't mind leaving," Rannulf said. His head jerked toward Stephen. "Why aren't you bringing my horse?" Stephen went on, down the street, into the shadows, and found a horse there, tethered by the reins to a ring in the wall.

He mounted it, and rode back to Rannulf; Ali was gone.

Rannulf took hold of the high cantle of the saddle and vaulted up behind him.

"What did she say to him?"

"Nothing much." Stephen nudged the horse with its heels and started off down the dark street. He was tired. Seeing Ali again had opened up a well of feelings. "She gave him a letter."

Rannulf reached around him and got hold of his hand with the reins, and turned the horse around again, going back up the street. "Why did you do this? I refused to do this for her. Why did you?"

"I promised her once I would help her."

"Help her. Help de Ridford."

"De Ridford," Stephen said, contemptuous. Still doubled up on the horse, they were riding back across the end of the marketplace, and the horse swung off to the right, the way they rode on patrol, past the citadel. "De Ridford won't do anything to me."

The horse stopped. Rannulf said, "It isn't you I'm worried about." Stephen looked around, startled, because the horse had stopped of its own will, as if by habit, and looking up, he saw that from this place on the street he had a clear view past the gate of the citadel to the tower, where in the narrow third-floor window, a faint orange light shone.

The light went out. Rannulf moved, and the horse strode out again. Stephen said, "That's her room, isn't it. You come here every night, and stop, and watch. How does that fit with your vow, Saint?"

"Let's go home," Rannulf said. "I'm tired."

Tripoli stayed in the north, the heart of his power, and proclaimed himself King of Jerusalem. Most of the old families of Outremer supported him against Guy, the newcomer. Tripoli issued a decree that Sibylla and Guy were usurpers, and none should obey them. The Sultan sent an embassy to him, too, and Tripoli and the legate went before a council of nobles and reaffirmed the truce; Saladin even agreed to sell Tripoli shipments of the grain of the Hauran, to ease the famine there.

In the south, there was no food, and people starved.

Balian d'Ibelin, who supported Tripoli, came to Jerusalem, and talked long with Guy and Sibylla. De Ridford stood behind the throne, and whispered in the King's ear, and made sure he yielded nothing. Balian went back to Tripoli with a message of insult and defiance. The King and Queen issued a decree outlawing Tripoli, and declaring all his rights in the Kingdom forfeit, and all his vassals released from their obligations to him.

Tripoli sent out a call to all his knights. De Ridford promised Guy the support of the Templars, and for the first time, he suggested that they might eliminate Tripoli in some way other than war.

He was careful, putting forth this plan, because he had to keep it from the young Queen; he knew her mind, too feminine for statecraft; she would balk at the deception necessary to lure Tripoli into the trap. Guy had no such scruples. From the first he was eager for it, this scheme that would eliminate his rival without cost or danger to himself. Of course de Ridford only told the King a part of the scheme. He left vague how he and his knights would carry out the attack on Tripoli. An attack in which Rannulf Fitzwilliam would either break his vow, or die disgraced.

It would have worked. So sweet a plan, doing so many things so neatly, it would have worked like a Greek music box, except for Kerak, who in the late spring threw all their hopes and dreams into a tumult when he broke the truce again.

⊕ Jolie was crying steadily, her face screwed into a red knot, her fists pumping. "She's hot and tired," Sibylla said. "Alysette, take her down-stairs, will you? Put her in for her sleep." The child's ceaseless shrieks set her teeth on edge. She did not look at Guy, pacing up and down the room, up and down.

When Alys had gone, he wheeled around, and hurled words at Sibylla. "You'll torture even the child, for the sake of some old dusty pro-priety. It's stinking hot here, and only the beginning of the summer— I want to go back to Jaffa."

"We can't go back to Jaffa," she said. Her throat was raw from shout-ing at him. "As long as Saladin may come, we have to stay here, at the center of everything. Why can't you understand that?"

He tramped back across the room again. "This place is a hut, the food is awful, the hunting is awful—"

"There's going to be a war, Guy! What does it matter how the hunt-ing is?"

"I can fight a war from Jaffa. If we have to stay here, at least let's move over to that other palace, with the pretty rooms."

"La Plaisance," she said. He could not trouble to remember the name even of a place he liked. She sat down on the stool at the foot of the bed, her hands together, trying to get through this quarreling to somewhere calm again.

Guy said, "Well, then, let's move over there. There's a garden where the baby could play."

"We are King and Queen of Jerusalem," she said. "We must be here, in the citadel of Jerusalem, to rule. Especially in times of peril." In the door came a page, murmuring a name, and right on his heels the Master of the Temple appeared. Guy went forward to meet him. Sibylla watched him morosely from the stool. She did not want him here, but he walked in and out of her councils and her chambers as if he were the King. He bowed to her, to Guy, mouthed the right words, but there was no yielding to majesty in him, only the form of it.

Guy said, "What word from Kerak?"

Sibylla stood up, and went to stand beside him. Kerak had seized a caravan on the great highway, and thrown the people into his dungeons and the goods into his storerooms; they had sent him an order, to release everything, because this broke the truce they had with Saladin.

The Master shrugged. His shoulders looked broad as a wooden beam beneath the sweep of his voluminous Templar cloak. "I have heard nothing yet. But the news is not good. My spies have reported me that Saladin is gathering an army in the Hauran."

"Where's that?" Guy said, blankly.

Sibylla went a step past him, her hand on his arm to keep him still. She spoke to the Master of the Temple. "From the Hauran he can attack us as easily as Kerak. What is his intent?"

De Ridford swayed his head toward her. "We cannot say."

Guy said, "Kerak must return the booty. Breaking the truce, he is clearly in the wrong." He was taking on what she had come to think of as his Kingly Way, where he strutted and tossed his head back and spoke from the depths of his chest. "We must have the truce. Until we settle with Tripoli we cannot deal with the Saracens!"

De Ridford bowed again. "Sire, Kerak may yet bend."

Sibylla grunted at him. "No, he will not bend. Kerak has never turned to take a step back. We must punish him." She faced de Ridford, her mind full of a blossoming idea. "Or we could use him. Take Saladin, him, and Tripoli, and use them all at once."

Guy said, "Sibylla, sit down; it's too hot for this." De Ridford only lifted his eyebrows at her.

Angry, she walked away from both of them, into the center of the room, and wheeled to challenge them.

"What, is it too bold for you? Let me say it. We can ally with Saladin against Kerak."

Guy let out a half-strangled yelp. De Ridford's head rose, and his mouth fell slightly open. She smiled at them, taken so unawares, and plunged on.

"So doing, we can eliminate Kerak, once and for all. And bypass Tripoli—as part of the agreement with Saladin, we must force him to deal with us alone, and cut Tripoli out of it. So in one stroke we make ourselves true masters of the whole of the Kingdom."

"You're mad," Guy said. De Ridford said nothing, but was watching her thoughtfully.

She spoke to him, who seemed to be listening. "Kerak would not dare resist us both. There would be no fighting. We could just slap him down a little."

"He is a Christian knight," Guy said roughly, and came up beside her and took hold of her wrist. "We cannot attack another Christian."

She twisted her arm against his grip. "We have talked of attacking Tripoli, who is a fellow Christian."

"In name only," de Ridford said. "In truth he is as faithless as any Mahounder."

"Keep out of this, Sibylla," Guy said. "This is men's work." His hand tightened painfully on her wrist.

Between her teeth, she said, "If you think you can cow me that way, darling, you know me little. Let go of me."

She looked into his eyes; they stared at one another a moment, all the little blocks and levers of their life together falling into place; after a moment he let go of her arm.

He turned his back on her. Strutted off across the room again. "You don't know what you're talking about."

"I know better than you, I who have been beside the throne all my life."

"But I am King now!"

"Yet you must heed counsel. We are King and Queen together." She turned to de Ridford again, who had always supported her. "My lord, think of this, it seems to me the only way."

The knight spread a slow smile across his face, like a trap opening before her, and said, "You would have more chance of being heeded, my Queen, had you not already gone behind his Highness' back to Saladin." The breath ran out of her. She stared at him a moment, amazed, her mind blank, unready. Guy wheeled toward her, his face purpling.

"What? What is this? What is he saying?" He crossed the room in two long strides and caught her by the shoulders and shook her. "What have you done?"

She said, "Let me go!"

De Ridford said, "Sire, she is hysterical. For her own sake, put her away in seclusion, before she harms herself and others."

Sibylla let out a yell of rage and shame; she wrenched one arm out of her husband's grasp and slapped him across the face so hard her hand went numb. "Let go of me!" He staggered, and his hands opened; she backed up, away from him, free. But the two men blocked the way out. She could not escape. She faced them, the two of them, locked together in their muscular male stupidity.

Guy's jaw was set. "Is it true? You treated with Saladin behind my back?"

She saw no point in confessing; she turned a harsh glare toward de Ridford. "You have betrayed me, my lord. Well is it said that treachery is nature to a Templar."

He still smiled, but now he showed his teeth. "Well is it said that the vices of a man are more pleasing to God than the virtues of a woman. My Queen, you have betrayed us all."

Guy said, "She can stay here, since she likes it so much. I'll to the other place, across the city," and turned and walked out of the room. De Ridford stood a moment, watching her; she turned her back on him. A moment later she heard him leave, and the key turned in the lock.

✦ A little later, they sent Alys to her, and Jolie, and some maids. They kept the door onto the staircase locked. With so many people in it the tower room was breathlessly hot, and the child wept and wailed, and the maids fussed. Sibylla sat by the window and stared out across the roofs of Jerusalem.

The grass that grew every winter on the rooftops had withered down to a fringe of white straw. She remembered something from the Bible about that, the withering of hopes.

She knew that de Ridford had been planning this, somehow, from the very first, for years, since the first time he had stood in council with the men, and when she spoke, defended her. All the while, he had meant to sell her, one day, to his own advantage.

She had aided him. She had married Guy because he knew nothing of Outremer, because she could master him, and use him, and now Outremer had a king who knew nothing of the Kingdom, and whom any strong man could master and use.

She remembered once thinking that he reminded her of her brother. The thought brought tears to her eyes.

Alys murmured, "Will you have some dinner, dear?"

"No. Go away," she said.

Her brother had foreseen this. She remembered some words Baudouin had spoken to her that she had taken very ill. Now her heart ached like a fresh wound; she longed for him with new hurt, as if he had died yesterday.

She would not sit here, and give in.

She could send to her mother. Agnes was in Nablus. She would have lots of lectures and disapproving looks but she would help her, nonetheless. Others would help her. She had her friends, everywhere, even among the Templars. She had her party, like Guy's. Like Tripoli's. Like Kerak's. She saw the Kingdom broken into smaller and smaller pieces, with Saladin all around them.

She had done this. Looking back, she saw how everything she had done had led this way. Yet she had not meant it, she had intended something quite other.

The shell of her grand designs fell away, leaving her naked, and much smaller.

She would not stay in Jerusalem. She would do nothing more to divide her people and endanger the Kingdom, but she would not stay here tamely waiting on her husband.

Out beyond the gateway, in the street, she saw a brace of Templars riding by.

Then suddenly she thought of Rannulf Fitzwilliam, and a terrible longing filled her, something she had never felt before, a hunger, heart-deep. She got up, crossed the room, and picked up her daughter and held her, needing the shock of the warm, separate life, enfolded in her life, complete. But it was not complete. She paced back to the window, the child in her arms, and stared out across the city toward the Temple Mount.

✤ De Ridford went down the curved stone staircase that led from the Temple pavement to the stables, in the great cavern under the corner of the wall. In the yard there he came on Rannulf Fitzwilliam and Stephen de l'Aigle, taking the saddles off their horses.

The Master went into the shade of the cavern. "Well? What did you find out?"

Rannulf hung his saddle on the rack; a sergeant came up to take it away and clean it. "Saladin hasn't moved, and he won't, for a while, anyway. He's still gathering his army."

"Will he attack us, or Kerak?"

The knight took a rag and a brush and began to rub down the horse. "He has siege engines with him. But he has tried Kerak before and not made even a chip in its walls."

"Well, anyway," de Ridford said. "I have another task for you. The Queen has fled."

"What?" Rannulf straightened. Beyond him, Stephen appeared above the level of his horse's back, his gaze steady on de Ridford.

"Her husband—for her own sake—confined her, and she has run away, like the stupid slut she is. I want you to find her and bring her back here."

Rannulf turned his head, and looked back over his shoulder at Stephen; he faced de Ridford again. "My vow forbids me to deal with women."

"I don't care about your damned vow. I'm ordering you to do this. With your informants, you can find her, and I don't know anybody else who can." He sneered at Rannulf. "Take a column of men with you, they'll defend you against her."

"Yes, my lord," Rannulf said.

✦ "We should not leave them here," the boy said.

His father snarled at him. "Take the money," he said. Her skirts bunched up in one hand, Sibylla climbed out of the cart.

Alys still sat on the sacks of grain heaped up behind the drover's seat. Her cheeks were streaked with tears. She clutched Jolie in her arms, looking around her as if flames licked up the sides of the cart. Sibylla found her shoes, put them on, and took her purse from her belt.

She said, "Thank you. I shall never forget your kindness."

The drover harumphed at her. He showed her no respect. His wide dirty palm was thrust out toward her, demanding. She had told him that she was the Queen of Jerusalem, but she saw he did not believe her.

The boy believed her. He stood by the oxen, staring round-eyed at her. But then he had seen her as she had come to them, in her silks and satins; he had listened to her story, talked his father into bringing her here, found the rude Syrian clothes she wore now.

She paid silver into his father's palm. "Thank you," she said again. "You may go."

"I may go." The peasant mocked her, tilting his head from side to side. "I may go."

She helped Alys climb out of the cart; the girl held Jolie tight, the blanket up over her face. They were at the back of the caravanserai, between the main house and the stables. The boy had run off into the house and now he came back with the innkeeper, a burly Syrian in a turban, his sleeves rolled up above his elbows.

"What is this?" He looked sharply at Sibylla, at the drover, at the cart. He spoke to the drover. "Who are these women?"

The drover gave a snort of laughter. "She says—"

Sibylla said, "I'll talk for myself." She gave him a look that shut him up, although he glowered, and faced the innkeeper. "I wish a room, a private room, for myself and my friend. Has the caravan to Ascalon stopped here yet?"

The innkeeper shook his head; his lips were pursed, his eyes half-closed, surveying her shrewdly. "Later today, or tomorrow." His hand shot out. "Three michaels for the room."

The boy began to speak, and his father glared at him. She guessed three michaels was a lot of money for a room. Opening her purse, she took out six silver pieces and dropped them one by one into his hand.

That did it; the innkeeper's eyes popped, his fist closed over the money, and now he was bowing, and ushering them toward the door, babbling. "The room is very good—if it be not good enough, tell me— I have wine, and wheat bread, for your supper—grapes and honey—" Sibylla put the purse into her sleeve. As long as she had money, she was Queen. She followed the innkeeper into the big stone house, Alys and the baby beside her.

Alys said, "Sibylla, what if they catch us?"

Sibylla shrugged. So far everything was going well. The room was good enough, small, but clean, with a stone floor, a bed and a chest, red and black and white striped rugs of native weaving, a shawl draped over the window, a brass jug for water, a wooden stool. She had plenty of money; when the caravan arrived she would buy them a place in it. "How can they find us? We are away from Jerusalem now; no one will know where we have gone, until we reach Ascalon. These people think we are ordinary folk."

That weighed on her. She felt smaller, lower, plainer than before. It was not the clothes; she rather liked the simple practical dress, the heavy cloth of sleeves and skirt, and the plain coif felt good around her hair.

She could not help but see herself as these country people saw her: not Queen of Jerusalem at all, but just a runaway wife.

They put Jolie down on the bed; the child was fast asleep, her hair stuck to her head, her round cheeks red as apples. She stank. They had been feeding her sops all day and her chin was sticky with dried juice. Sibylla opened her clothes, trying to cool her. "Go find us some water. There's a jug on the chest."

Alys' head came up. "Sibylla, I can't go out there."

Sibylla wheeled on her. "Alys. This is important. Stop snivelling, put your feet under you, and do it, or it will not get done."

Her friend's eyes widened, and she blinked a few times. Her chin quivered. "Sibylla, I cannot believe you have spoken so to me." She got up, went to the chest for the jug, and left the room.

Sibylla drew the child's arms gently from the sleeves of her new dress. She wondered if the little girl were falling sick. With a pang she saw what danger she was bringing Jolie into. And she had just scolded Alys, who had never asked for this, who for all her crying and wailing did everything required of her.

Alys seemed more noble now than Sibylla. Just a woman on the run from her husband. She would be Queen again, as soon as she reached Ascalon. She laid her hand on the sleeping child's face, and Jolie stirred, half-turned her head, and her lips worked busily at nothing. Not sick, just tired.

Alys burst back into the room. "Sibylla. The Templars."

"What?"

"They're riding into the innyard." Alys pushed the door closed, and rushed across the room. "Two of them just came in downstairs! What are we going to do now?"

"Hush! Sssh! Did they see you?"

"I don't know." Alys bit her lip. Her face was dirty, and in the poor peasant clothes, she looked like a country girl. "What are we going to do?"

"Maybe they aren't looking for us," Sibylla said. "Did you recognize any of them?"

Alys blinked at her in wonderment. "I don't know any Templars."

Sibylla grabbed her by the shoulders and shook her. "Think! What did they look like? Their beards—was one red-bearded?"

Alys stammered, "Yes—yes—red."

"Ah," Sibylla said. "That's Mouse. They are looking for us." Then, on the door, there came a heavy knock.

The two women looked at each other. Sibylla licked her lips; she saw, suddenly, one last good chance to win this.

She said, "Answer the door." Standing, she pulled the coif off her head, and shook her hair out.

Alys said, "What are you going to do?"

"Do as I tell you," Sibylla said.

Alys went to the door and opened it, and Rannulf Fitzwilliam came in.

Sibylla stood in the middle of the room. Through the door she saw, behind him, other men. She spoke to him. "Send them all away; I want to talk to you. Alone. Alys, take Jolie and wait outside."

Alys was whey-faced. She went to the bed and gathered up the sleeping child, and went to the door. Sibylla stood where she was, staring at the Templar. The door closed. She took a deep breath, studying him, considering how to attack.

He said, "Why did you run away?"

She went up closer to him. He was looking her in the face, not staring at the floor, his black eyes hard and bright and intent. He had looked at her so in the chapel at Montgisor. She remembered what had happened in the chapel at Montgisor, and her body thrilled.

She said, "De Ridford betrayed me. He handles Guy like a horse in harness, and has turned him against me. I could not stay there to be humiliated. How did you know where to find me?"

"I knew you would go toward Ascalon. That cut down the possibilities." He said, "What did de Ridford do?"

"He told Guy I had sent messages to Saladin."

A grimace crossed his face. "I told you not to do that."

"I am Queen of Jerusalem," she said hotly. "The Kingdom is in my charge. How can I preserve it, save to make peace?" She took another step toward him. His size drew her, his strength. "Who sent you after me?"

He laughed. "De Ridford."

She seized this opening. "Why do you take orders from him? He will ruin us all. Between him and Kerak and Tripoli, there will be nothing left for Saladin to conquer! Come with me to Ascalon. There help me raise my banner. Many will follow me. Many more will follow you—you know not what a name you have in this kingdom. Together we can save Jerusalem." She stood before him; she reached out and put her hands on his chest. "You wanted to kiss me, in Montgisor, Rannulf." Leaning on his chest, she tipped her head back and looked up at him. "Kiss me now."

His hands rose; he gripped her wrists. His face was full of a wild long-ing. His lips parted. He let go of her arms, and his hands slipped into her hair, and held her head. He bent toward her. She shut her eyes, her heart hammering. The first touch of the kiss astonished her, tender as the baby's kiss. His arms encircled her. She lay back in his embrace. His mouth pressed harder on hers. A shock of lust went through her. His tongue pushed on her lips and she opened her mouth and he put his tongue into her throat, and she was bent back, held fast, penetrated, possessed. She felt herself opening like a blossom.

She said, "Rannulf. Make love to me."

He pulled back. His hands slipped away from her. He said, "You want me to fuck you?"

The ugly word repelled her; she stepped back, her hands rising be-tween them. She saw he had done it deliberately. He went across to the stool and sat down on it.

"I want to," he said. "I really do want to. I love you. I've loved you since the first time I ever saw you, on the road to Ramleh. I've dreamt about you a thousand times. Every time I've ever seen you, it's been like burning alive. But I'm not here to do that. I'm here to take you back to Jerusalem."

She wheeled around, in a flash of anger, and spat at him. "You pig, Rannulf! You say you love me, but you'd take me back to them? Back to the men who shamed me? Why would I want to go back there?"

He said, "Because you are Queen of Jerusalem. Where else should you be?"

She lifted her head, shocked. She knew at once he was right. She fought against it a moment, but in her heart something that had been tangled for a long while seemed to straighten and flow free. She put one hand up, shaken, and pushed her hair back. "Damn you." She looked him in the face again. "How can you take me back to my husband?"

"I don't know," he said. "I may kill him. I hate him. But you have to go back to Jerusalem. Nobody but you can hold it, if we must all go fight."

She knew this. She looked away, her hands pressed palm against palm, accepting it. When she turned back to him again, he was still watching her.

"All right," she said. "I'll go."

He got up, wordlessly, and went to the door.

✦ The day was almost gone, but they found a mule-cart for Alys and the child, and a horse for Sibylla, and set off up the road toward

Jerusalem; she saw they meant to travel all night. The Templars went along two by two. There were ten of them, one pair in front of Sibylla and the cart, the rest behind. The two in front of her were strangers to her, very young, their beards half-grown; one kept stealing looks at her over his shoulder.

Rannulf rode behind her. She did not look back. She wondered why she had needed such a one to remind her of her duty, when she was King Amalric's daughter. An ordinary knight, hardly better than a serf. Whenever she thought of kissing him, her body flamed.

She would not let go of him, the next time. She would finish the kiss, and bind him to her forever.

At sundown, two Templar sergeants came galloping up the road toward them. The column halted; Rannulf went up past her, and met the sergeants, and spoke with them. Almost at once he was turning. He said something quickly to Mouse, as he rode by, and reined his horse around beside Sibylla's.

His horse was much taller than hers, so that she could see his face even though he was staring at the ground again. He said, "These brothers here are from Jerusalem. I've been ordered to Sephoria. Saladin is finally moving, and he's coming toward us."

The words jolted her. She felt time running away from her. She wanted to reach out to him, to hold him there. All these other men were watching them. She kept her voice steady. "I will go to Jerusalem. I know what I must do, and I will do it. I shall keep faith with you." He was going to fight. She saw him fed into the teeth of the war. In front of them all she could not even touch him. She said, "God go with you, Rannulf."

He lifted his eyes to her. "I love you," he said. "Remember that." He nodded over his shoulder. "These men will ride with you to Jerusalem."

She stayed where she was, her breath pent, her blood locked in her heart. He turned his horse neatly around on its hocks, and raised his arm. At a trot the other Templars followed him away down the road, two by two, into the deepening night.

The cold air touched her face. The two sergeants were waiting for her; moving seemed hard, useless, uninteresting. She lifted her head, wondering when she would begin to feel this, and started toward Jerusalem.

The King said, "Did you find my wife?"

Hands clasped behind his back, Rannulf stood before him, in the middle of the tent; the red silk of the tent colored the air like wine. "I was taking her back to Jerusalem when the messengers came."

Guy looked haggard, his clean-shaven cheeks stubbled, and his eyes dark. "She is safe. Did you see her? She is safe? And my daughter?"

"By now they are back in Jerusalem, as safe as anybody, Sire."

"You're sure."

"Yes, Sire."

"Very well. Very well, then." The King turned away. The tent was as large as a stone hall. The floor was spread with carpets; off to the right a mail coat hung on a rack. Behind it the King's shield, newly painted. A curtain dangled down across the back of the tent, the tucked edge revealing the cot behind it. Guy would not sleep on the ground. Two pages trotted in, bearing between them a stretcher with casks on it, and a basket that trailed a tangy smell of apricots and lamb. Nor would Guy eat cold bread and drink bad water.

Rannulf said, "Sire, I have ten men with me. Half the armies aren't even here yet. Let me go scout out what the Sultan is doing."

"The Master of the Temple has not arrived," Guy said. "You must wait for your orders until he comes."

"Sire, I can do—"

The King wheeled around, fiery. "No words with me, Fitzserf, I know the Master does not trust you. Stand back; there are better men here."

Rannulf drew off to one side. Past him from the doorway swaggered a short yellow-headed man, a gaudy feather in his cap, and rings all over his hands: Balian d'Ibelin. He had in his train his brother, Baudouin, taller and handsomer and stupider. They greeted the King with cautious words and voices set on edge, being supporters of Tripoli.

Rannulf had already heard reports that Tripoli was coming to Sephoria, and would make his peace with the King, for the sake of the defense of the Kingdom. In among the lordlings crowding after Balian and his brother were other men of Tripoli's, Reginald of Sidon, and young Humphrey de Toron. Guy greeted them one by one, in a high, brittle voice, disdainful.

Balian said, "Sire, for Jerusalem's sake, we shall put aside our differences."

"I am the King, and therefore you will follow me," Guy said. "As for the rest, let it go. You said you brought us some foot soldiers."

Baudouin d'Ibelin stepped forward. "The Genoese sent some men-at-arms for the Crusade—they are coming up the road now from Jaffa. They are green, but well-armed."

"Good," the King said. "We shall have a great power to send against this Mahounder Sultan. Then let him quake and cry in his beard, we'll make him beg for mercy!"

"Where are the Templars?" Balian said, with a glance in Rannulf's direction. "I see some of them here."

"We shall have the whole power of the Temple." The King stepped forward, his voice rising. "The Master de Ridford has gone into the north, to bring back the garrisons of all the castles. By God's eyes, we will have a mighty army here, to make Saladin run like a corncrake."

"God wills it," somebody muttered. Then they got into a discussion of supplies, and who would camp where.

Rannulf stood off to one side, between a lamp standard and a stool. When the pages came around with cups of wine he shook his head. Guy boomed like an empty keg, all words; nothing he said went anywhere. Rannulf thought of Sibylla, married to this nothing, and lowered his gaze to the patterned carpet on the floor, to hide the sudden uproar of his feeling.

He had to stop thinking of her. Even now, just to remember holding her quickened him, she rose up in his mind more real than the men around him. She divided him, double-hearted. Before him her husband strutted like a popinjay, sneering at him, who had held her in his arms. Kissed her, tongue-deep, and her willing and wanting. He had to stop thinking of her.

She stood between him and God. He belonged to God, who had given him everything he had, the revelation that had saved him, the vow that sustained him; in the end, God had even given him Sibylla.

As a test. Another test.

Balian was saying, "We should send out some scouts, Sire. Use this

Templar; that's his work." Rannulf lifted his head, drawn back into this, and saw the lordling nodding at him.

Guy said, "Until the Master comes, I will give no orders to his men. What we must decide—" In through the back of the tent a swarm of newcomers tramped, loud.

This was Kerak, bare-headed, his body like a great boulder inside the cut velvets and embroidered satins of his clothes; in the midst of his knights he rolled into the room, and saw Rannulf. "There he is! By God, I'll halve the son of a bitch!" Wrenching out his sword, he charged.

Rannulf had no room to move; he jumped sideways and got tangled in furniture, grabbed an iron lamp standard and struck off Kerak's blow with that. The lamp went flying. The men around them bellowed. Balian plunged in between them. Someone grabbed Rannulf's sword arm, and another man wrapped an arm around his chest. Kerak's own men dragged the Wolf away.

"Hold," Balian roared, between them, his hands out to keep them apart. "Hold! We can't kill each other, and give Saladin everything he wants!"

Kerak's eyes glittered; his men surrounded him. "He owes me blood. He slew my son; he has admitted it."

Rannulf said, "Let me go. I won't hurt him; he's an old man." Baudouin d'Ibelin had hold of his sword arm. "Let go of me, damn you," Rannulf said, again, and the other knight stepped back.

Balian said, "Stand fast, Saint."

"I said I wouldn't hurt him," Rannulf said. Across the crowded space between them, he looked at Kerak. "I killed Guile, which was a sin, but the sin was against God, not you. God will judge me for it, not you."

Kerak's lips pulled back from his teeth. "I'll drink your blood."

Rannulf sneered at him. "God will judge me, Wolf. You'll just talk."

Balian turned toward him, and struck him on the arm. Kerak was staring at him, and Rannulf stared back, but after a moment Kerak turned heavily away. Someone else was coming into the council.

A page pushed through the mob, squeaking. "My lords, my lord King—" Through the doorflap the Count of Tripoli strode, slight in his threadbare coat, his face sheathed in the little cup of his beard.

Several of his men followed him; they packed the tent. Rannulf backed up to the silken wall to make room and had to stoop to clear the ceiling. Tripoli went straight into the middle of the room, nose to nose with the King. Guy's face reddened. The onlookers fell hushed, and even Kerak gave way, while the two men confronted each other.

At last, Tripoli said, "I am here to fight for the Holy Sepulcher, the True Cross, and my savior Jesus Christ. Will you join me?" He held out his hand.

Guy's throat worked. All the men watched him, he had to answer, and he could make no other answer than to match Tripoli. He said, "Then I make you welcome, my lord," and clasped the outstretched hand.

A low cheer went up. Balian walked up to them, smiling like the father at a wedding. "Well done, my lord Count, my lord King, well done."

"While we are here," Tripoli said, in a high loud voice, "let all men put aside their feuds and hatreds, and face the common enemy as one, as Christians, and as brothers." As he spoke he looked around him, seeing Kerak, and then scanning the rest of the room; when he saw Rannulf he looked past him for someone else. "Where is the Master of the Temple?"

The King said, "He has gone into the north, to gather up the knights from all the castle garrisons, and bring them here."

"Well, then," Tripoli said, "the Temple may need another Master. Because of the treaty I had with Saladin, I allowed some thousands of his men to cross through the Galilee, two days ago, and yesterday, before I left Tiberias, I looked out my window and saw them riding by. On their lances they carried the heads of Christian men by the hundred, and many of those heads had the hair shorn close, and the beards worn long."

Silence met this. Rannulf's hands closed on his sword hilt; he moved up a few steps, standing straight. King Guy's face paled, and Kerak shouted, "Tell us whose side you are really on, Count!"

"It would make things easier," Rannulf said, and in front of him Baudouin d'Ibelin half-turned his head and laughed. The other men were all bursting suddenly into talk. In their midst Tripoli stood motionless, his head high, as if everything he did were King's work. Balian went to Kerak, clasped his arm, spoke in his ear, all the while leaning on him, so that at last Kerak moved back a step. Rannulf pushed up past Baudouin d'Ibelin in his satin-ribboned coat, and spoke to the King.

"If we have no Master, then you give me orders. Let me go scout the Sultan and his army. We have to find out what he means to do."

Tripoli looked at him through the corner of his eye. "I can tell you that. The Sultan has come to Tiberias, I barely escaped from the castle before he drew up his army around it."

Beyond him, Balian grunted. "That will hold him. He cannot take Tiberias."

The King turned, and walked away from Tripoli and the other men, as far as he could. In an undertone, as if to himself, he said, "We must decide what to do."

"If he's at Tiberias," some man of Kerak's shouted, "then we go to Tiberias! Let's strike him!" Half a dozen other voices rose in a eager lustful cheer.

Balian d'Ibelin called, "Between here and Tiberias is waterless desert. Better if he has to cross it to reach us, than the other way around."

Kerak gave a scornful jeer. "Why not just go home, pretty boy, and send your wife out to fight?" Balian's head jerked around, and he cast a fiery look at Kerak, but he said nothing.

The King still had his back to the council. He beat his two fists together in front of him. Rannulf turned to Tripoli. "How strong is Tiberias now?"

The Count gave a quick shake of his head. "Perfect. My wife is there. She can command the garrison, the place is stocked for years, and the walls would withstand Joshua."

Rannulf said, "I am going there with my company, then. I will keep watch on him, and send to you."

Kerak bellowed, "How much does the Sultan pay you, Count, to hold us back?"

Tripoli ignored him. To Rannulf, he said, in a voice that reached through the tent, "Good, you go do that, but be in constant touch with me, and do absolutely nothing without consulting me first."

Pleased, Rannulf said, "Yes, my lord."

The Count looked around at the other men, bringing them into his audience. "Sephoria is as good a place for the rest of us as anywhere. I saw a great horde of foot soldiers on the road here, who should arrive by sundown. We should be here for a while; make your arrangements accordingly."

He had taken over the council. All men were watching him, waiting for his orders, and even the King now turned and faced him, and waited. Tripoli went on in a crisp, dry voice. "We shall gather our forces here. It's the dead of summer, Saladin will quickly eat up all the food around Tiberias, and then he will have to move, and that's when we can hit him."

Rannulf was backing up, sidling away through the other men as they listened. He saw Kerak mark him in the corner of his eye. Tripoli was talking, hard, dry words, making excellent sense. Rannulf reached the door and went out.

✦ Stooping, Bear picked up the horse's foot and cradled the heavy curve of the hoof in his hand. The horse leaned on him, and he rammed his shoulder into it, staggering it back onto its hocks. "I just can't help wondering, is all." The horse's foot was clean; he felt the frog with his thumb and made sure the shoe was on tight.

Mouse came down past the string of horses. There were a lot of Roman ruins in Sephoria and the Templars had tethered their horses up before a row of marble columns. Felx said, "Ask him. He'd know."

Stephen lowered the bucket of water he had brought from the well. "I'd know what?" He spoke to his horse, patting its neck; the horse smelled the corn in his sack, and whickered, and shoved its head against his arm. He scratched its forehead under the forelock.

Bear said, "You'd know about Saint. And the Queen."

Nobody said anything for a while. Mouse opened the sack and held it so that the horse could eat from it. He gave a quick look off down the line of horses—well over two hundred horses already here, and more coming, every hour. More horses grazed down on the wide plain stretching to the west. As far as the road there were camps, most of them just clots of men around a fire, a few with tents and pennants. In the center of it all was the red tent, with the King's banner in front of it, and the Standard of the True Cross.

Mouse crossed himself. Bear said, "Well?"

"Well, what?"

Felx stood up, his eyes glinting. "Back there, at the caravanserai, they were together a long time, in that bedroom. Alone."

Mouse said, "They were talking." He turned back to the work of feeding his horse.

Bear straightened, his hands on his hips. "He doesn't talk to women."

"She came out with her hair down," Felx said, "and looking pretty well handled."

Mouse said, "This is Rannulf you're talking about. And she is Queen of Jerusalem. Whatever you're thinking of, it's wrong." The horse pushed at the sack with its nose, almost knocking it out of his hands.

Bear said, "She's beautiful. A little lean, for my tastes, but pretty as a prayer."

Felx said, "If she'd made him King, instead of Guy, we wouldn't be here now, like this, wondering what the hell is going on."

Bear grunted, agreeing. Stephen said, "If horses had wings, we'd all fly. Where's Saint now?"

"Getting us some orders."

One of the knights who had come with them out of Jerusalem now trudged around the column where Stephen's horse was tied; he was young, downy-bearded, solemn as a drunken judge. He had a bucket of water in either hand, which he set at the foot of the column.

"On the road, the way he looked at her, that wasn't very saintly." His horse stood next to Stephen's, and he watered it.

Stephen said, "I didn't see anything. And he sent her back to Jerusalem."

"What else was he going to do with her?" the boy said. His name was Eudes; he was Burgundian. "Bring her here?"

Stephen grinned at him. "He obeyed orders." He had seen Rannulf coming up along the horse lines from the foot of the hill. "That's good enough for me."

"I still think—" Eudes began, straightening, and Rannulf walked past him, in among them.

"Shut up, Eudes, you talk too much."

Stephen thrust the bucket at him. "Go fetch us some more water, boy." He nodded to Rannulf. "Where have you been, Saint?"

"In the red tent. Trying to get somebody to give me some orders."

Bear stamped up beside Stephen. "Where's de Ridford? Why isn't he here doing what he's supposed to do?"

"He may be dead," Rannulf said. "God willing."

At that, the other men pushed closer, and Stephen said, "What do you mean by that?"

"Tripoli just got here, and he says there's been a big battle, somewhere, and a lot of Templars died. One of them maybe the Master."

"Where?" Bear asked, and Stephen blurted, also, "Where?" A little farther away, someone else called out, and a hoarse voice answered, spreading the news. The rest of the Templars collected around them. Here and there, men crossed themselves. Stephen swallowed, a shiver of panic along his nerves.

"What happened?" a voice called, from the press of men.

"Where? Who was it?" Other voices.

"I don't know," Rannulf said. He was looking systematically around the crowd. "Somewhere in the Galilee. De Ridford commanded them." He was counting men, Stephen realized, getting ready to go do something, and his stomach clenched in a little fist of fear. But he was going to be afraid from now on, and at least they were not staying idle in the camp. Rannulf went on, "Saladin is laying siege to Tiberias. I am taking my company down there, to see if there's anything to do, and then do it if we can. Everybody pack up. Mouse, get us some extra horses. Felx, find me something to carry water in. Be careful. Kerak is here, and all Templars look the same to him."

Mouse said, "When do you want to leave, Saint?"

"By sundown," Rannulf said. "Bear, come with me." He went off again, Bear slouching along after him. Wolf's bane. Mouse took Eudes along with him and went to find some extra horses.

As they were walking down the long slope toward the main camp, Eudes said, "He gets me on edge. I hate him."

Stephen laughed. "You'll get used to him."

All through that day, there were troops of men arriving in the camp; toward midafternoon, a huge swarm of foot soldiers came down the Jaffa road. Their dust hung in the air for hours. Stephen had brought six packhorses up to their camp, and Rannulf was standing in the shade of one of the columns watching some sergeants load them up, when they saw a horsemen riding across the camp toward them, and both recognized him at once.

"De Ridford," Stephen said.

Rannulf folded his arms over his chest. "I was really hoping." Over among the tethered horses Eudes and some of the other knights lifted their heads.

The Master of the Temple rode straight up to them; he wore mail, but a sergeant riding behind him carried his shield and his helmet. His surcoat was smeared with blood and dirt. His left hand and forearm were wrapped in bloody bandages. He sidestepped his horse around toward Rannulf and said, "What did you do with the Queen?"

"I sent her back to Jerusalem," Rannulf said. He straightened, his hands behind his back and his head tipped down. "What happened to you?"

"God punished us for our sins," said de Ridford. "At the Springs of Cresson, I saw a troop of Saracens, and we charged them."

"How many Saracens?" Rannulf said.

"There were a couple of thousand of them." De Ridford stared at him, challenging. "There were two hundred of us." The other men were watching, all around them.

"How many of you made it out?" Stephen asked.

"Two other men and I," de Ridford said.

A groan went up from the men around them. "A pity," Rannulf said.

"Seems as if you could have stayed, and kept our brothers company."

De Ridford grunted at him. He was strung taut, his head back, his nostrils flared; his eyes flickered back and forth, never looking steadily at anything. He turned, and scanned the camp. "What are you doing here?"

"Getting ready to go down to Tiberias and scout Saladin's army."

De Ridford swiveled toward him. "On whose orders?"

Rannulf lifted his head, his eyes hard; he said nothing, and de Ridford leaned over him and shouted, "On whose orders?"

"Tripoli's," Rannulf said, and de Ridford lashed out with his bandaged hand and struck him across the side of the head. Rannulf recoiled from the blow, and de Ridford winced and clutched the hand against his chest.

"Damn you! You are my man, still, mine! You will go nowhere. You will wait until I tell you what to do." De Ridford yanked his horse around, its hoofs sliding on the marble ground, and rode off down the long slope toward the red tent. The sergeant followed him.

Rannulf put his hand up to the side of his head. His eyes were hot and bright and black.

"Two hundred men," Stephen said. "What are we going to do now?"

Rannulf lowered his hand and looked at his fingers; there was no blood. He leaned up against the column again and folded his arms over his chest. "Keep packing, Mouse." He watched de Ridford ride away across the camp.

But they did not move out at sundown; at sundown there was a great council in the King's tent, and Tripoli and de Ridford shouted at each other, and traded accusations, and again Tripoli, with most of the other men now solidly behind him, convinced the King to hold the army at Sephoria and let Saladin break his teeth on Tiberias. After, with Stephen at his heels, Rannulf went up to de Ridford, outside the great tent.

Rannulf said, "Let me go down to Tiberias. I can set fire to the fields along the lakeshore. Maybe raid him a little."

De Ridford gave him a glare white-eyed with accumulated rage. "You go nowhere until I tell you." His left arm was bound up to his side. A pack of sergeants and knights awaited him. The other nobles had gone to their own camps and to bed and the King's camp was quieting down. De Ridford faced him again. "Soon. I promise you." He turned, and went back inside the King's tent.

"That's good enough," Rannulf murmured. He crossed himself.

Stephen followed him over to their horses. "What do you mean?"

Rannulf picked up his reins. "We're leaving at sun-up. Whether he orders it or not. Let's go get some sleep."

✤ Then, halfway through the night, the horns began to blow.

Stephen woke out of a dream of someone calling to him, from far off, just his name in a distant voice. Above him the night sky was white with stars. He sat up, hearing the brasses bellow all over the camp, more and more, as other horns picked up the call.

A sergeant came panting by him. "My lord, my lord, we're all ordered up and to saddle; we're leaving at once for Tiberias."

"What?" Stephen said.

Next to him, Bear rolled out of his blanket. "Tell me this is a dream." He got stiffly to his feet. Stephen got up, looking around; the whole dark camp churned with men struggling to rise and pull themselves together. He sat down and put his boots on. Felx stooped above the fire, poking over the ashes for some live embers, and Rannulf walked out of the dark and pushed him back.

"No, we haven't got time for that; they are already moving out. We're riding rearguard. We have to get some water. I've got everything ready but the water. Hurry." He went on, rousing the men just beyond them.

"What the hell is going on?" Felx went around gathering his cloak, his boots, his belt. Mouse went after Rannulf, to help him fill the waterskins and load them on the horses.

Long before sunrise they were already in the saddle, lined up in a double column on the road, waiting for the rest of the army to pass so that they could take up the rearguard. Mouse was paired with Felx, and Bear with Rannulf; behind them two sergeants led the six packhorses, neck-roped together. The rest of their company were lined up behind the packhorses, and after them came the main body of the Templars, the Jerusalem chapter, and the garrisons of the south, almost three hundred men, under de Ridford's command.

Tripoli had ridden out in the vanguard, his knights making their horses leap and cavort as if they had a ride of only a few miles, and feasting at the end of it. Now the King had gone out, with the Bishop of Saint-George carrying the True Cross before him, and horns blasting and flutes playing. The foot soldiers from Genoa followed, in bad order, already complaining and threatening to stop.

Stephen took his feet out of his stirrups and slouched in his saddle; he had hoarded away part of a loaf of bread from his supper and he got it out and ate it. In front of him Bear was dozing, his head slumped on his chest. The night still held fast but along the edge of the sky some

white daylight began to run. De Ridford galloped up, trailing his re-
tainers.

Turning his horse around before Rannulf's he said, "Don't lead out
until the whole army's past. Give them some room, and stay back, well
behind them; I don't want you running up on their heels."

Rannulf said, "Whose idea was this? Yours, wasn't it."

De Ridford's teeth showed. "Did you think I would let Tripoli take
command? This is my king, I made him, he will do my work." His horse
spun on its hocks, its head tossing, pushing at the bit. "Everybody is being
too cautious here. When we march into view of Tiberias, Saladin will
flee. Then we can attack him, while he's running." He let the horse carry
him magnificently away, down toward the marching army. His retinue
streamed after him.

Beside Stephen, motionless in his saddle, Felx said, "I could have
stayed asleep and done this." Rannulf laughed.

halfway through the morning Rannulf swung his dozen men around to ride at the tail of the column. They were coming into hilly country, tawny in the summer heat. The track of the army they were following lay printed deep into the crusted sand, the thin strands of grass; up ahead, a heavy pall of dust obscured everything.

They passed a few of the Genoese sitting by the side of the road, already finished. At midday, with the sun blazing in the sky like a blob of hot metal, half a hundred Bedouin swooped out of a crease in the hillside and raced down on the tail end of the Templar line.

Screaming and whooping, they charged toward Rannulf and his men, and the knights pulled their shields up; when the Bedouin spun their horses, and tipped their bows into the air, the knights hoisted their shields onto their shoulders. The volley of the Saracen arrows pattered down harmlessly around them, and the Bedouin raced off, shrieking as if at some great victory.

Stephen was cooking inside his mail. He had a white silk scarf over his helmet, to keep his head cool, but his hauberk was so hot it burned his hand to touch it. Some of the newer men coming along after him began to complain, breaking the silence of the march. Then the Bedouin swooped down on them again, squealing like pigs.

Still at a good distance, they wheeled, and fired their arrows in an aimless scatter, and then fled, and behind Stephen, Eudes and two others of the young knights shouted and broke out of their line to chase after them. Stephen roared. He watched Rannulf; he saw Rannulf's head turn, but he gave no order; the column rode straight on after the rest of the army.

The Bedouin on their light fast horses quickly escaped the three young knights, who turned, laughing at this sport, and rode back to the column, and then, as they rejoined the column, Rannulf put his hand up and stopped.

His company drew up, all now in order. The rest of the army trundled off up the road away from them, into the shroud of the dust. Rannulf reined around out of the column, rode back past Stephen, past the six packhorses, to where Eudes and his friends sat grinning on their horses, and going right to Eudes straight-armed him out of his saddle.

"You think you're a Templar, boy? Damn you!" Rannulf reined his horse around; Eudes had hit the ground easily, rolled, and was leaping up, ready to fight back. Rannulf put the horse into him again, shoulder first, and Eudes went down again.

The while Rannulf was shouting at him. "You never break the line of march without my order, baby! If you ever break the line again, I'll cut your beard off at about throat level. Now walk. All of you longspurs. In line." Eudes on hands and knees scrambled across the dusty ground, trying to get away so he could stand, and Rannulf rode over him. The boy went down on his face in the dust. "All three of you can walk. Mouse! Get their horses." Rannulf wheeled around and cantered back up to the front of the column, now a good distance behind the rest of the army. Stephen jogged his horse to the rear of the line, where Eudes' mount stood snorting, its reins trailing.

The two green men who had broken ranks with him were still in their saddles, staring round-eyed after Rannulf. Eudes, streaming dust from his hair and his clothes, tramped up toward them. He looked ready to bite through horseshoes. Stephen reached down and collected his reins, and turned to the other two knights.

"Get off."

"What?" In chorus, they shrilled at him, treble as girls. "We can't walk—we're in full mail—we're knights—"

Stephen smiled at them. Up at the head of the column a yell went up. "Mouse, do you need help?"

"No," he shouted. He turned toward the young men, ready to throw them out of their saddles, and they saw in his face what he intended, and, grumbling, they got down quickly. Stephen gathered their horses; Felx dropped back to ride beside him, and they herded the three men on foot in front of them. Off to the north, now, they could see the Bedouin again, circling in for another harmless, irritating assault.

After a few hours' walk they came to a well, which was dry; the churned ground around it and the broken buckets and knotted bits of rope showed how troop after troop of the passing army had struggled to get some water out of it. Rannulf drew them up around the parched trough and dismounted. "Horses first," he said, and unhooked two of the packed waterskins and emptied them into the trough.

The horses drank; the knights drank; finally they let Eudes and his two friends drink. Eudes' face was grimed with dust, and raw with sunburn; he kept his gaze pinned to the ground, looking at nobody, even when Rannulf came up next to him beside the water trough.

Rannulf grabbed him by the beard and jerked his head around. Eudes was too tired to fight; he only set himself, and stared back at the man confronting him. Rannulf said, "Listen to me, baby. You're stupid. You're too stupid to think. So don't think. Do what I tell you. Nothing else. Now get up on your horse and get in line and ride."

With a yank he let go of the boy's beard. Eudes' head flew back a little, released. He watched Rannulf walk away with a baleful glitter in his eyes but he went wordlessly to his horse and mounted.

They were well behind the rest of the army, now, and the road climbed steadily up through broken country, doubling back along the slopes. The Bedouin wheeled like flocks of birds along their course, sometimes rushing in for a noisy feint, sometimes shooting single arrows from the very edge of their range. The road took them up through a steep pass; on the other side, they came on some Bedouin between them and the rest of the Frankish army, and this time, Rannulf charged.

The Templars drove downhill, and the Bedouin were tired. They set up a hasty shower of arrows and tried to flee away but the Templars rolled over them like an avalanche. Stephen, at the rear of the column with the packhorses, barely got up into the rank before the fighting was over. They reached the bottom of the slope and drew rein. Behind them on the stony hillside lay a score of dead and wounded Saracens and some crippled horses. A wail went up.

"Mercy!" Broken French. "Mercy!"

Rannulf gave the order to re-form and the Templars made columns and rode on, leaving the Bedouin crying behind them.

On the next slope, again, the Saracens attacked. This time in between the first wave of archers there were heavy cavalry, swathed in black robes over their breastplates, and carrying lances. Behind a wave of arrows, they charged in hard, struck a blow, and wheeled away; the Templars took the charge on their shields and struck back when the lancers turned. At the crest of the slope, where the trail was narrow, Stephen and Felx met three such charges, while the rest of the column galloped by at their backs. Under a hail of arrows the two knights broke and ran to catch up.

Felx said, "This is slowing us down considerably. We'll never get to Tiberias by sundown."

They had reached the foot of another short, steep climb, and up ahead, the army was under assault again. Stephen crossed himself.

"Don't think. Just obey orders." He hitched his shield up on his arm; he had carried it now half the day, and the strap had worn a rut into his shoulder and neck. "Let's go."

Late in the day they battered their way through a screen of Bedouin onto a flat dry table of a hill, and came on more fighting. A mass of Saracens, axemen and lancers and archers, had pinned some Franks down on the road ahead of them, and the main body of the Templars, moving along just ahead of Rannulf and his men, were rushing to relieve them. Rannulf ordered a charge. He worked his exhausted horse into another gallop, and with Bear on his right, and the rest of his men strung out in an uneven row beyond Bear he raced up beside the other Templars.

For a moment they met Saracens, axemen, and lancers, whose horses staggered under the weight of the knights' attack, and then scrambled back, while the riders traded blows. Rannulf's shoulder hurt, and he was having trouble keeping the point of his sword up. Bear's shield kept banging into his arm. He hacked and thrust, not seeing what he hit, and then the horse in front of him gave way and they were rushing on, unhindered. Another wave of arrows pelted them. Rannulf drew rein.

The Saracens were flying away into the desert. Behind them on the flat hilltop a cheer went up from the twenty-odd knights and men-at-arms the Sultan's men had been tearing to pieces. The Templars lined up along the road in their orderly columns; in front of them all, de Ridford himself sat his tall sock-footed stallion. A knight not a Templar was riding up to him, a lordling, on a splendid horse, and with a plume on his helmet. His shield made him an Ibelin. They were going to talk. Rannulf turned, and lifting his hand he drew his men quickly around them.

"How far away are we?" Mouse came up to him.

"Too Goddamn far." Rannulf dismounted and went to the string of packhorses. "Come on, hurry; we'll be marching again soon."

The men dismounted, and crowded around him; he unslung two more of the waterskins, and gave out corn for the horses, and bread. The boy Eudes stood before him. One of the waterskins had an arrow stuck in it; suddenly the boy reached out and pulled the arrow out of the skin.

"No!" Several men at once grabbed him, too late; the arrow had been plugging its hole, but coming free it ripped the skin, and the water flooded away onto the ground.

The boy stepped back, white. Two other men dropped down and tried to drink the water as it fell. "I'm sorry," Eudes muttered. "I'm sorry."

Rannulf said, "I told you you were stupid." He gave him a shove. Up there, among the ranks of the other Templars, a horn was blowing. A sergeant jogged down toward him.

"Saint! They want you."

Rannulf turned to Mouse, and nodded at the packhorses. "Make sure this gets buckled up." He walked up after the sergeant, stretching his legs, glad to be out of the saddle for a while. Ahead of him de Ridford lounged on his black horse, his hand on his hip, talking to the lay knight.

This was Balian d'Ibelin, his plume broken, his fine fair hair black with dirt and sweat. Slumped in his saddle, he nodded to Rannulf and turned back to de Ridford, intense. "What do you mean, march on? You look over there; half the Saracens in the world are out there, ready to jump us as soon as we move." His arm swept a flat arc toward the hills east of them.

De Ridford grunted at him. His wounded arm was still strapped to his chest, with his shield looped over it; he had tucked the shield back, while he talked, off the point of his shoulder. He said, "We can get through them." He looked down his nose at Rannulf. "Tell him."

"We can get through anything," Rannulf said. He turned to Balian. "How bad off are your men? Do you have any water?"

"I have a lot of wounded. There's probably a little water left. The horses are good, still, I think. We've been stopped here a while; they've rested."

Rannulf turned to de Ridford. "Let's go."

In the Master's matted beard his lips twitched into a smile. "You first. I want somebody to ride on ahead, catch up with the rest of the army, and make them wait for us."

"Wait. For Christ's sake, they can't stop to wait for us," Rannulf said. "If they don't reach the lake, we're finished. We have to get a foothold at least on the lake."

Balian said, "Damn it, come on. It's almost sundown, and my men are whipped. We can't just keep on fighting our way down the road. They have to hold the way open for us."

De Ridford's eyes gleamed, steady on Rannulf. "Get going. When you reach the King, stop and stand until I reach you."

"Yes, my lord." Rannulf bit the words off, turned, and walked back to his men.

One arm draped across his saddle, Mouse was talking to Eudes; Bear had gone to the steep edge of the hill and was making water off the cliff. Beyond the packhorses, Felx said something and several men laughed.

Rannulf went in among them, to the packhorses, and looked over what he had left.

"One skin of water," Stephen said, coming up beside him. "Two baits of feed for the horses, one for us. What's going on?"

"We are," Rannulf said. He swung around, looking east. Across the next ridge, in the hazy distance, a sharp steep knob of a hill stuck up into sight. "There. You see that little tip of a hill, down there, the rock spur? That's one of the Horns of Hattin. That overlooks Lake Tiberias. We have to catch up with the head of the army, and my guess is that's about where we'll do it. It's Vespers. Say your office."

He put the bit back into his horse's mouth; the horse looked better, too, after the water and food and rest. The sun was deep into the western sky. He was still stinking hot under the mail coat but his face was cooling off. He crossed himself, bowed his head, and said a paternoster. "Deliver us from evil." The night was coming and he always fought better at night. He buckled the bridle again, gathered his reins, and climbed back up into the saddle.

Just at sunset they ran headlong into a pack of Saracens, blocking their path where the road crossed a dry wash. There were a lot of the Saracens; it was hard to tell how many, in the gathering darkness. The Templars charged them. For a moment as they tore along across the sandy flat floor of the wash, it seemed the knights would break through, but at the steep bank of the wadi, the Saracens held, and threw them back.

Then the Saracens attacked, and they went at each other, the knights with their swords, the Saracens with their axes and lances. The thick gloom of the twilight was worse than true darkness; Rannulf could see nothing in front of him, and lunged and hacked and chopped desperately and blindly, while his horse bounded under him, fighting to run. Bear's shield kept banging him on the arm.

Suddenly Bear's shield dropped away, and Bear was down. His horse was down. Rannulf bellowed, and swung around, to close the gap in the line. Two Saracens loomed up in the space where Bear's shield had been, and an axeblade slashed at Rannulf's eyes. The axeman's horse lunged up beside him, crushing his leg against its flank. A lance jabbed at him. He cut awkwardly backward at the shaft and missed and hit the axeman's horse instead. The horse reared up. Blood splattered him in the mouth. Suddenly another shield swung into place, covering him, and the axeman's horse was falling over, its stomach slashed from girth to gelding.

"Bear!" Rannulf twisted in his saddle, looking down where Bear had fallen. The other knight was slumped on the ground, almost under his horse's hoofs. Rannulf bent down, stretching one arm out to him. "Charge!" he shouted, and got Bear by the wrist. He felt the other knight's fingers close around his forearm. "Charge!" he shouted, again, and the rest of the Templars heard him this time, and charged on ahead of him, bulling through the Saracens. In the clear, safe space just behind them, he heaved Bear up behind him on the saddle and went after.

They staggered up the wall of the wadi, scrambling and sliding in the loose sand. He could not keep Bear on the horse. On the top of the bank, Bear slipped, the horse stumbled, and they all went down in a heap in the dark. Rannulf hit on his bad shoulder and skidded. For a frantic moment he could not find his sword. The earth was shaking under him. There were horses charging at him. He stood up and tripped headlong again, over something heavy and yielding and warm. Riders swept in through the dark around him.

"Saint! Here!"

He staggered upright again, and Stephen galloped toward him, leading Rannulf's horse by the reins. "Come on!"

"Bear." Rannulf stooped down, in the dark, and laid his hands on the body he had tripped over. As soon as he tried to lift him he knew that Bear was dead.

"Saint, they're coming after us. Let's go!"

"Te absolvo," he whispered. He made the sign of the Cross over Bear. He straightened, and pulled himself into his saddle, and followed Mouse up the side of the wadi, after the rest of his men.

Felx said, "Bear."

"He was alive when I got him up behind me," Rannulf said, "but he was dead when we fell." They were climbing over a stony ridge, with the moon rising in their eyes. Ahead of them King Guy's army was spread across the barren slope of the Horns of Hattin. The Saracens had pulled back; they seldom fought after dark. He put his hand on his horse's neck, grateful for its strength. All his strength was gone, his legs like water, his arms like lead.

He said, "I was pretty used to Bear."

Felx muttered something. They were passing by groups of the Italian footsoldiers, hanging on each other, so tired they had even stopped whining. Ahead, the slope angled up and away; the moonlight shone silver on the sparse long grass. Against the sky the two rock peaks jutted up that gave the place its name. Out on this open ground, black against the moonlit grass, he could see a troop of men riding, and above them there was a long stick of a standard, hung with pennants and plumes: the True Cross.

"Come on," he said. "There's the King." He lifted his horse up into a weary lope.

There was a well on the slopes of Hattin. When the Templars reached the King, he and Tripoli and the rest of the commanders were clustered around the stone pool, but the well was dry. At the foot of the long gradual slope ahead of them, Lake Tiberias stretched away depthless black into the distance. Between this water and the Frankish army lay the campfires of the Saracens, thousands of them, like fields of wildflowers in the dark. Rannulf drew rein, a little way from the King and his nobles. The strange beauty of it struck him, the countless leaping fires, windstirred and red-gold, against the sweep of the night.

Then someone called to him, ahead, and leaving his men he rode up to the King, in the midst of other lords.

The King's page brought him a flask, which he used, and passed on to the man on his left. "What is it?"

"The Master sent me," Rannulf said. "He and Balian d'Ibelin have fallen behind and they want you to wait for them."

Among the other men Tripoli exploded in an oath. "Are you serious?" His horse pushed up between Rannulf and the King.

"They sent me with orders to say that," Rannulf said. "I say, keep going. We have to get to the lake. Half the army's out of water already."

Kerak said, "Let's go. The Templars can fight their way through."

The King said, suddenly, "We can't fight without the Templars." He lifted his head. His shoulders were slumped; even in the dark Rannulf saw he was exhausted. He reached out uncertainly for the flask and took another pull on it. "We have to wait," he said. "We'll wait here."

Tripoli said, "No. We're going on to Lake Tiberias, if it takes us all night."

The King held the flask out to Kerak. "I'm staying here, until the Templars come." He waved to one of his pages. "We'll camp here tonight."

Tripoli leaned out and grabbed at his arm. "You idiot. We cannot stop. If we don't get water for our horses soon we might as well just give up, they'll drop under us."

"Take your hand off me!" The King thrust Tripoli's arm aside and rode away, across the slope. His servants bustled after him, and one by one the other lords reined around and followed.

Kerak stayed behind, staring at Rannulf. "Are they under attack, back there?"

"We've been fighting all day long," Rannulf said. He waved his arm toward the lake. "Keep marching. You can't stay here."

The Wolf crossed his forearms on the pommel of his saddle and leaned on them, the great block of his head sunk down between his shoulders. Tripoli stared at Rannulf.

"You'll march on?"

Rannulf shrugged one shoulder. "I've got orders to wait here for de Ridford."

Tripoli jerked his attention to Kerak. "Well?"

The Wolf shook his head. "Half the men will stop here with the King, no matter what we do. Do you want to break us up into even smaller pieces?"

Tripoli flung his arms up. He wheeled his horse, and galloped off, shouting, "We're finished! We're finished!" Kerak watched him go, and brought his gaze back to Rannulf.

"You're an evil messenger, monk."

"I think so." Rannulf gave a shake of his head. He reined his horse around and rode away, back to his men, and led them up higher on the grassy slope.

The ground here was hard and slippery, and strewn with chunks of black rock. The winter rains had torn deep gulleys down the hillside. On a level strip of meadow he drew rein.

"We're camping here," he said, to the men around him.

"What?" Felx lifted his head. "What are we doing that for?"

"King's orders," Rannulf said. He swung down from his saddle. "Keep watch on our stores. I don't trust any of these bastards." He loosened the girth on his saddle and took his bridle off the horse's head and hung it around its neck, with the reins tied up, and went off across the hillside, alone.

Away from the other men, he knelt down, and crossed himself, and said his prayers. He thought of Bear, of how he had reached down and gotten hold of Bear's arm, and surely he had been alive then, and swung him up behind him on the horse, and he had been alive then.

Dead now.

For the last time, he let himself think about Sibylla.

She did not belong here; this had nothing to do with her at all. She was behind him now, maybe forever. The fire lay before him; this time, if he were pure enough, he might pass through it, and reach God.

He went back down to his horse, and unsaddled it and rubbed it down with his blanket. The other men were making their camp around him; the ordinariness and routine of it settled him. Mouse came up to him.

"Saint. Shrive me."

Rannulf went off a little way with him, and they knelt down together on the ground and confessed each other. When they were done Rannulf slung his arm around Mouse's neck and they sat together staring down at the Saracen camp in the distance.

Mouse said, "Are we going to get out of this?"

"We've been in worse messes than this."

Felx came up to them, and knelt down with them, and they wound their arms over each other's shoulders. "Ah, Jesus," Felx said. He had been weeping. The three men made a circle, their heads down, and swayed a little. "Jesus," Felx said, again.

"I keep wondering when he died," Rannulf said. "Whether I killed him, pulling him up."

"Poor Bear," Mouse said.

Felx said, "He was the bravest of us. He wasn't afraid of anything."

Rannulf said, "Confused, yes. Scared, never." He remembered Bear standing up for him at chapter meetings, Bear standing next to him in a hundred fights. Bear in Damascus, with two naked girls on his lap.

"We couldn't even bury him," Felx said.

"It doesn't matter," Rannulf said. He crossed himself. "God's got him now."

He clung to the two men, as they clung to him, rocking back and forth on the sandy ground. Felx was crying again, his head down, and under Rannulf's arm Mouse was beginning to shake. Rannulf lifted his head, and looked down the long slope of Hattin, at the countless fires of the Saracens. Off at the edge of the slope, in the dark, he could see men moving: Balian's men, and the main body of the Templars, trudging at last into camp. He tightened his arms around the other two men, holding fast.

e woke before dawn. He had slept in his mail, his blanket under him, and his head on a stone; he stood up, first of his men to get up, and looked out through the grey fading of the night. The Saracen fires had all but gone out. There seemed to be nothing down there but heaps and tangles, like wind-drifted brush, as if he could have walked down through them to the cool clean waters of the lake.

His throat was raw with thirst. His bad shoulder hurt. He went down to where his horse dozed, hipshot, among the other horses, and led it off to one side, and felt over it with his hands. He had liked this horse as soon as it was issued to him, and he liked it even better now; all through the hard riding it had fought on, done whatever he asked, and now it was still sound, still alert, and as he knelt down before it the horse lowered its head and lipped his hair and pulled on him, like a little horse-joke. He straightened up, and patted its neck.

"Keep with me," he said. "The Saracens will hitch you to a cart, if they catch you." The horse snuffled at his hand, hungry.

Now the other men were rising. All across the slope, as the day brightened, the Franks were rolling out of their blankets. The lake was half-drowned in a floating mist; a thick haze banded the eastern horizon, so that the sun rose feebly through it, until the great light reached the top of the haze, and struck out across the world in a sudden brilliance, an instant blaze of heat.

He went down to the packhorses; the men gathered around him, and he unlimbered the water. "Give this all to the horses. If the horses go down, we go down." He filled each man's helmet with water. He divided up the bread among them, and passed out the last of the corn.

When he was done, he took the rest of the water in the skin back to where his horse waited, and let it drink all it wanted; still there was a little left, in the bottom of the skin. He rolled the skin around it and hid it under a rock.

Now he could smell the thin harsh reek of burning grass. Looking down, he saw, all along the edge of the Saracen camp, the rising grey tendrils of smoke. The Saracens were setting fire to the hillside.

Mouse came to him. "We want to say Mass."

"We can't," Rannulf said. "There's no church, we'd have to do it out in the open, and they'd see us." He nodded around, at the vast disorderly army around them.

"For Bear," Mouse said, stubbornly. "And these young ones, they've never had the Sacrament."

"Do you want to get us hanged?" Rannulf crossed himself. "Say your prayers." A horn blew; they were summoning a council. He doubled up his blanket and laid it on his horse's back, and put the saddle on.

A sergeant came and got him; he rode down across the slope to the gathering of the nobles. The King sat on his horse in the middle of them, his face drawn. De Ridford, beside him, seemed bigger, more alive, almost eager. "We need make but one hard charge. Send my men in first, the rest of the knights behind them, and after that, the foot soldiers. The foot soldiers coming close after will keep the Saracens from turning our flank, and the knights will break the line. Saladin will flee. By midmorning we will be to our horses' knees in Lake Tiberias."

While the Master talked, Rannulf looked around him, at the Saracens below him, and at the masses of the Christian army. The foot soldiers were milling around on the lower ground, the knights scattered above them in groups. The Saracens stretched in unbroken ranks from the edge of the lake all the way back around to the west, as far as the road, and beyond. There were very many of them, maybe ten or fifteen for each of the Franks; but a lot of them were Bedouin. He turned to look up at the sheer black peaks of Hattin. There would be no escape that way. They had to go forward, through the Saracens.

God wills it, he thought; he had his helmet on his knee, and he swiped his hand back over his hair and put the helmet on.

Tripoli was saying, "We should arm the first ranks of the knights with lances. De Ridford is right, for once: if we hit them hard, and then push in with the foot soldiers, we can break through."

A few of the other lords spoke up, arguing where each group should ride, and who should go first. The King sat still as a lump in the middle of it all. De Ridford turned to Rannulf.

"What do you think of this?"

Rannulf said, "It's a good idea, but we have to do it quickly. Attack that way." He waved his hand off to the west, where the soldierly ranks of the Sultan's army dissolved into a chaotic swarm of men and horses. "See all those white robes down there? Those are Bedouin. They'll break first."

Kerak nudged his horse forward; his jaw thrust out. "The water's that way." He waved to the east.

"So is the Halka," Rannulf said. "Between those two black banners. Saladin's personal guard."

Kerak sneered at him. "Is that how you got your fearsome reputation? Attacking weaklings?"

"Whenever possible," Rannulf said.

Tripoli said, "Let's get this moving."

Now suddenly the King lifted his head, and spoke. "Yes. I and my men and the Templars will ride in the vanguard, armed with lances. The rest follow. The foot soldiers must stay close in behind us, to keep the Saracens from cutting us off. God be with us. We will charge toward the water." His eyes were sleek with panic, but his voice stiffened as he talked. He scrubbed his chin with his hand. "Now. Let the horns blow."

Rannulf rode back to where his men were waiting, already on their horses, and drawn up in a line. He put Felx on the right end, who had the best stroke, and Stephen next to him. A sergeant with a packhorse brought them lances, and while the men were passing the long shafts along their line he rode around them and talked to them. "You see that water down there? That's where we're heading. Keep going. Stay in line." The muscles of his belly clenched. His horse was walking on tiptoes, snorting with every stride. The horns were blasting incessantly, long brazen rips of noise, and the air was wreathed with drifting smoke. He took the last lance, looped his arm around it, and swung around to take up the left end of the line.

"God wills it," he said, and they all answered him, together.

"God wills it!"

Head to head, shoulder to shoulder, they started down the hill toward the Saracens.

He kept his horse reined tight, watching the slope ahead of him, where the army was forming. At first there was no order to it, a milling mob, but then abruptly the Templars all rode up into their lines, all moving forward, and Rannulf let his horse stretch out into a trot. His company strode out along with him; they came up into the middle of the frontmost line of de Ridford's men, with the Master at the command end, and as they came together, all the Templars broke into a canter.

A harsh yell went up from a thousand throats. Ahead of them lay the long brown slope, and the oceanic mass of the Saracens: beyond that, the lake. Rannulf's hair stood on end. He heard himself bellow, and he swung his lance down level, the haft in the crook of his arm jammed against his side, and then the horns blew again and he charged. By the third stride his horse was at a dead gallop. Rannulf held the lance pinned hard against his side, the tip straight out in front of him; the line of the other lances stretched off on either side of him in a rippling wooden wave. The rumble of the horses' hoofs was like the coming of a thunderstorm. Ahead of them between the two black banners the Saracens held fast, rank on rank of armored men, on heavy horses, in yellow turbans, standing their ground. He saw their black beards, beyond the tip of the lance, he saw their eyes rolling white, and then they were shrinking back, their hands rising, their shields up, and the lances tore into them.

Rannulf felt the tip of his lance strike and slide and strike again, and catch this time, and tear free. His horse shied violently to the right, avoiding a body on the ground, and he forced it back into line. The charge was slowing. A black turban loomed up before him, rolling eyes, an arm with a long scimitar slashing at him, and the lance was useless now and he dropped it, and the first blow of the scimitar rang off the shield on his right. He wrenched out his sword and struck under the shield, and the wild-eyed face yawned open and disappeared.

The horses were stopped. Wedged tight in the line he held his shield up and square so the man on his left could fight behind it, and he fought behind the shield of the man on his right. That man was dealing a steady rain of blows, beating back the Saracens in front of him. Rannulf pushed forward, taking the space they gave up, carrying the rest of the line along with him. Abruptly the man on his left went down under an attack from behind.

Rannulf screamed; he backed his horse up a step, wrenching his shield around, and caught the edge of an axeblade aimed at his back. There were Saracen axemen behind him. He was fighting two ways at once. The line off to his left was bending back, trying to close with him, and then suddenly that line was gone, nothing remaining of it but a few rearing horses, and a surge of black robed Saracens, sweeping in on him.

He flung his shield up to ward off a storm of blows; the Templar next to him adjusted, covering him. A horn blew. They were backing up. Three Saracens at once pressed on him and he beat them back with his sword and his shield, while the man next to him covered him, knee to knee with him. Rannulf flinched back from the assault, and the three Saracens bounded on him. Then with the man beside him he charged forward a few strides and caught the Saracens extended. He struck one on the head and one in the body, and the other whirled and fled.

In that space, he turned, and shouted, "Run! Let's go!" He wheeled his horse back toward the higher ground.

The Templars in line with him streamed after him. Axemen on foot and lancers on horses blocked their way, and now they were fighting uphill. Rannulf pushed his horse sideways, closing the line; he was the right end now, and the man beside him turned up into the lee of his shield and he saw it was Eudes, the Burgundian boy, who was fighting like an archangel. They clawed their way back up the slope. Some of the Saracen axemen tried to stand their ground; they swung their long-handled blades around, to cut the legs out from under the horses, and Rannulf pulled his horse back on its hocks, waited until the moon-shaped blades went by, and rushed in, stabbing and poking with his sword, and felt bone break under the blade, and someone shrieked. An axe struck his shield and stuck and dragged him halfway out of the saddle. Beside him Eudes lashed out, and the axe broke free. They galloped out into the open, back onto the burning slopes of Hattin.

Rannulf reined down. His breath rasped in and out of his lungs, the air gritty with smoke. Under his mail his body was streaming with sweat. The sudden quiet around him made him realize how loud the fighting had been. He swung around, looking back toward the Saracens, and saw their great army unbroken, still there between him and the lake. On the lower slopes lay dead horses and dead men.

Rannulf's men gathered around him. There were horns blowing above him and below him. He looked up, and on the height above him saw the Italian foot soldiers huddled, as far from the Saracens as they could get.

"They never charged," he said.

"They charged," Stephen said, beside him. "They just turned back as soon as the fighting started. Where's Felx?"

Rannulf lowered his eyes to the men around him, searching through them. "Felx," he said. A cold dread clutched him. He lifted his gaze, looking wider. Filled his lungs and shouted. "Felx!"

Beside him, Stephen sighed; he pried off his helmet, and held it on his knee, and wiped his arm over his face. His red beard was plastered to his jaw and throat. Rannulf drew back, and rode around his men, looking all around them.

The charge had thrown the Saracens back, at first, so that if the foot soldiers had charged in behind them the Franks might have broken through. Now they were still trapped, the foot soldiers on the high ground, the knights ranged across the lower slope, in pairs, in little groups, the Templars in their orderly ranks. The horns blew and blew, and gusts of smoke drifted across the lower ground, over the litter of bodies there.

He looked among the living men for Felx, his yellow beard, his high-shouldered sit on a horse, the angle of his head, and did not see him.

He crossed himself. The men around him were silent, slumped in their saddles; he looked through their midst to Stephen, and saw him looking back. The brass screech of the horns raked over his nerves. They were going to charge again. He raised his hand, and his men lined up again. There were only eight of them now. He rode up to Eudes.

"You. You're good. You go ride the far right end. You know what we call that—the dead man's end? Keep that in mind."

The Burgundian nodded; behind the nasal of his helmet his blue eyes were utterly unafraid. He rode off to the right end of the line, and Rannulf took the left end, and they went down through the drifting smoke and the dust to join the rest of the Templars.

The Sultan had taken a position behind his lines, on a low rise where he could see well, with a racing camel close by in case of catastrophe. As usual watching the battle made him sick to his stomach. He had the Franks trapped. This time he should finish them. On the slopes of Hattin everything worked against them. The pitiless sun would make a torment of their armor; even their courage would hurt them. But he had thought before that he had them beaten, and somehow, always, they escaped.

Their first charge had seemed unstoppable, the knights and their horses fresh, packed together in their lines with the slope of the hill behind them and the wedge of lances before, and the crowds of men on foot rushing after them. They seemed about to break through the armies of the faithful as if they were kindling wood.

Then the Frankish foot soldiers quailed. The Sultan had arrayed his armies carefully, putting the best men, the heaviest armed, between the Franks and the lake, and placing squadrons of archers all along the lines. His soldiers gave way, but they fought on, and did not yield utterly, and the archers sent up volleys of arrows to shower the attacking Christians. The knights paid no heed to the arrows, but the foot soldiers shrank back. As the knights launched themselves forward, the Frankish foot soldiers turned tail and ran away, left the knights exposed, so that the Sultan's men could swing in from either side and surround them.

At that, Salah ad-Din shouted, and half-rose from his chair, and his son al-Afdal beside him cried out, "We have won!"

"No," Ali said, steadily, on the Sultan's other hand. "Not yet."

Surrounded, outnumbered, yet the knights were clawing and slashing their way free, scrambling back up the slope below Hattin's spurs. As if by some magic, on the higher ground, the black-and-white lines of the Templars reformed out of chaos. Turned their horses' heads around, and made ready to attack again. Around them the much larger numbers of the ordinary knights seemed much less significant. The Sultan sat down again.

Ali said, "They are coming this way. They know where you are, Uncle. You may need my sword yet."

The Sultan sat back, and took a cup of chilled sherbet from a slave-boy.

"Stay where you are." He had forbidden Ali to fight. The Sultan's favorite brother Turanshah had recently died, and now another brother, Farrukshah, had died also, and he was taking no chances. Before him, on the yellow slope of Hattin, the knights were charging again.

Ali was right: this time they came straight at him. Salah ad-Din sat rigid in his chair, his hands clamped to the arms, watching the wedge of mailed men cleave into the center of his army, grind inexorably toward him, while his own soldiers shrieked and wailed, fired storms of arrows, and lost ground; step by step they yielded. Slower they yielded, and finally stopped, and to his watery-legged relief they flung the Franks back again, onto the slopes of Hattin.

He let his breath out, and folded his hands in his lap. One of his aides said, "Another such charge, and they will surrender." The other men nodded and muttered agreement.

"No," Ali said. "They will never surrender."

The Sultan glanced at him. "You sound as if that's something honorable in them, and not just sheer stupidity."

"You don't understand them," Ali said. "They believe God is choosing them—that the battle tries them. The harder the battle, the greater the trial, the nearer they are to God."

"Let it try them for wormfood," the Sultan said, sharply. His nephew's tone of voice irritated him.

Ali glared at him. "You could at least give them the honor of noticing that they are valiant."

"I notice that they offend God. What, do you believe them, now? Are you become a Templar?"

Ali turned white. He jerked himself forward again. The Sultan pressed his lips together, wondering what evil had infected his nephew.

Down there on the slope, the Templars were lining up again, with the other Frankish knights on either flank. They would charge toward the Sultan again. His guts churned. He tensed himself for the next assault.

✦ Halfway through the day, the Templars and the lay knights mounted one more attack against the center of the Saracen line. Tripoli rode along on the left flank. But when the army charged, Tripoli veered off, and led his men in the other direction, straight at the Bedouin on the western edge of the Sultan's army. The white-robed riders, startled, dodged out of the way, and Tripoli and his forty knights and some dozen other men galloped through the gap, and ran free across the open ground beyond. They never stopped, or even looked back, until they disappeared in the hills to the north.

The rest of the Christians bolted toward this opening, but when they turned, the center of Saladin's army took them in the flank. Ahead of them the hole closed. Trapped again, tired, half-dead of thirst, the Christians drew back onto the slope, where the King's red tent still fluttered, and gathered together again.

De Ridford galloped up to the King, shouting, "I told you he was treacherous! I told you he was treacherous!" He flung one arm out after the vanished Count of Tripoli.

Kerak lifted his head. He was doubled up in his saddle, his breathing rough. He had lost most of his men, some dead, some just finished, quit, lying on the ground, or sitting with vacant looks in their eyes. He said, "It wasn't Tripoli who brought us here to this. It was you, Templar."

De Ridford pried off his helmet; his eyes were burning with sweat, and he rubbed them on the skirt of his surcoat, which did no good. A sergeant ran up to him with a soggy cloth, which did no good either. "We'll win this yet. The likes of this rabble shall not beat us." He scrubbed his face; his cheeks stung.

It was midday. The overhead sun hammered the slope. The Master had not eaten since the day before, and had drunk nothing since daybreak. His bad arm, still lashed to his side, ached from his shoulder to the tips of his fingers.

He would not believe they were defeated. God would not give Jerusalem to the heathen; and if this army fell, Jerusalem was gone.

The slope before him was churned to dust. A dead horse lay only a little way off. Other bodies sprawled across the broad sunbleached hillside, some dead, some wounded, some too worn down even to lift their heads. At the foot of it, the Saracens waited, their rank solid as a wall.

The King said, quietly, "We are beaten. Jerusalem is defenseless. God have mercy on my wife and child."

De Ridford jerked his head around toward him, ready with some scathing words; but the effort seemed unworth the speech. He jogged his horse on past the King, where Rannulf Fitzwilliam had dismounted from his ruined horse and stood, looking away after Tripoli.

"I told you he was treacherous," de Ridford said, and Rannulf walked away without even a glance at him, leading his horse by the reins.

De Ridford laid his hand on the pommel of his saddle. His chest hurt. He looked down the slope at the patient and unyielding wall of the Saracens. He thrust off the wave of fear that rushed over him. He would find a way out of this. He was Gerard de Ridford and he never failed. God would not let him fail. He turned and stared at the Saracens, looking for the thing he had missed, the weakness, the key. His gaze caught on something happening closer by.

On the trampled slope, a little way down from him, Rannulf Fitzwilliam and Stephen de l'Aigle were piling stones into a heap on the ground. The other men were lining up together before this strange altar, and now Rannulf straightened, drew his sword, and set it point-first into the stones, like a cross.

De Ridford lost his breath. They were going to say the Mass. He had only seen this done once; it was not something an officer involved himself in, a heresy, a crime. He turned and looked around him, wondering who else saw this. He realized that Rannulf thought they were going to die, and so didn't care who saw them.

His belly clenched. He went up closer to them. The Templars gathered silently in their communion. Rannulf stood before the altar, his hands raised, his head bowed to the sword, and began to say the Mass. The other men spoke the prayers with him, the Credo, the miserere. Domine, non sum dignus. De Ridford stood like a stone hearing this. The world cracked like an egg, and everything was new to him. He saw he had been wrong. He had thought too small. When he imagined he was spinning grand designs, he was turning and turning in his own little corner. Now the truth yawned in front of him like an abyss.

They were going to lose. He was going to lose. God willed it.

Rannulf lifted up a cup before the inverted sword. "This is my blood." De Ridford was moving forward, up to the end of the last line, next to some young knight watching all this with his mouth open. De Ridford crossed himself. The old words, drilled into him from babyhood, came to him as if he had never known them before. He knew

God was there, that God watched over this battlefield. He had brought God's knights here to this place, to their destruction. The cup came to him, dry. With it a handful of dry grass in place of the bread. He pretended to drink from the cup, nibbled at the straw. Rannulf was coming along the line. "God gives you this." De Ridford's knees shook. He was as afraid as a little child. Rannulf stopped before him. "God gives you this." He kissed de Ridford's mouth. He struck him the blow, impersonal, as if he were any other knight. De Ridford went down to his knees, as if he were any other knight, and prayed to God to forgive him.

Stephen pried himself up off his knees. His mail dragged him down; under it his body ached and throbbed, his skin burning, his lungs sore, his tongue dry and swollen, his belly plastered flat against his backbone. His mind wouldn't work.

He stood looking down at the Saracens, and tried to force himself into a hot righteous hatred, but all he felt was a numb terror. He crossed himself. He thought of Felx, and Bear. He went to his horse, standing with head drooping and eyes glazed a few yards from the altar, and mounted. The horse stiffened, and carried him on down the trampled slope to where Rannulf stood, with Eudes beside him; their horses were a little way off, their necks hanging.

"Come on," Stephen said. "Let's go."

Rannulf looked up. "What?"

"I came here to die for the Cross," Stephen said. "I'm not going to wait for some damned sandpig to come up and slit my throat. Let's go."

Rannulf looked at Eudes, and nodded up at Stephen. "I'm coming." He went over to his horse. Eudes followed him. In their saddles, they went along after Stephen, on across the slope, past the dusty red flutter of the King's tent. Of all the army now only a handful of men kept their saddles, and they moved wearily in to join the Templars, and they turned their horses' heads toward the Saracens, and attacked.

Stephen's horse staggered and stumbled down the hillside. With Rannulf on his right and Eudes on his left, he plunged into the Saracens, who dodged away from them, fleeing from the swords the knights were too tired to lift. Stephen's horse swayed, slowed, its head down to its knees. From the mass of men before him a lance drove at him. He could not lift his shield to meet it. The lance hit him under the arm, where his mail opened, and tore in through his body and burst out the middle of his back.

There was no pain, at first. He sagged, all his strength gone, falling, but lightly, as if he were floating. Someone caught him. He flung one arm out and hung it around Rannulf's neck, and Rannulf heaved him up against him, holding him by the belt, and turned and scrambled back, out of the fighting.

Stephen shut his eyes. Now his chest began to hurt.

His mind was a fog. He knew they carried him back up on the slope and laid him down on the ground. Eudes was there. He had decided, a long time ago, that he would seduce Eudes. When this was over. This was over now. They gathered around him. Rannulf spoke to him, and the voice stirred him, not the words, only the sound of the loved voice. Then Rannulf's cupped hand was to his mouth, and Rannulf was feeding him water.

He groaned. The sweet cool moisture on his tongue was delicious beyond anything he had ever tasted. He lipped at Rannulf's palm. The other knight held him up to drink, one arm around his back. Stephen licked up the last of the water and pressed his face down into Rannulf's hand. Rannulf bent over him, his cheek against Stephen's hair.

"Here they come," Eudes said.

"Leave me," Stephen croaked. There was blood in his mouth and he spat it out, and it kept on gushing out even when he stopped spitting. He lay down on the ground. Rannulf straightened; he heard the metallic snick of a sword being drawn. He shut his eyes, the blood running out of his mouth. Now it hurt a lot. But he wasn't afraid anymore. He would never be afraid again. He began to say his prayers.

❖ Rannulf's horse was done; it stood braced on widespread, wobbling legs, its nose to the ground, its hide rough and dry as wire. He left it where it stood, and on foot, with his sword in his hand, and Eudes beside him, he watched the Saracens rushing up the slope toward them.

Most of the Saracens pounced on the dead and wounded men who covered the hillside. They sheered away from the two knights standing ready to fight. But then several of them gathered in a bunch, and they raised their axes and lances and ran at the two Templars.

Side by side, the two knights beat them back again, and the Saracens drew back. Rannulf was swaying, and could not keep his balance. He said, "God wills it," and could not hear his own voice. The boy beside him stood solid. The Saracens came on again, this time from both sides, and Rannulf stumbled forward. Struck a blow, and went to his knees, and then they were on him.

❖ Saladin watched his army swarm up over the slopes of Hattin; he saw the King's red tent go down, and knew the battle was over. His throat was full of bile. Around him his aides cheered and screamed and embraced one another, but he did not rejoice. He could not be sure, not yet, of this victory. He went to his tent, and gave thanks to God, and changed his clothes. His clothes were as soaked with sweat as if he had himself fought on the field of Hattin. His hands were shaking.

He went out, and sat before his tent, and they brought prisoners before him.

The young King stumbled up and stood there, his face black with sunburn, his eyes brimming with resignation. He said, "God have mercy on us. Sultan, spare my men, who fought for God, not for me."

Saladin said, "You have lost; you have no more power in this matter."

Beside him, pain-wracked, crooked as an ancient, stood the Master of the Temple. Balian d'Ibelin behind him had gone down on one knee; the other Christian lords could scarcely keep their feet. The Sultan knew most of them, but he hardly recognized them now, filthy and beaten, hanging their heads like dogs.

By the King's other hand, at last, there was Kerak, also wounded.

A slave had brought water, and at a nod from Saladin gave water in a cup to the young King. Guy drank, and held the cup out to Kerak. In a sharp voice, Saladin said, "I do not give that to him."

The Wolf lifted his head, and his lip curled. Reaching out his hand he took the water. "I take this for myself, as I ever have taken what I wanted." His voice croaked. He drank the cup empty.

The Sultan laid his hand on the hilt of his sword. "Yes, and because you had no more reck than that, you are an insult to the world, which I will avenge." He drew the sword, and struck Kerak in the chest.

The knight wobbled, but did not fall. The Sultan's guards closed on him and slew him and dragged his body away.

The King was saying, "Oh, my God. Oh, my God." The Master of the Temple only stood, his gaze aimed at the ground.

Saladin said, "Attend to them." He went down to where Ali was waiting with his horse.

After the battle at the Springs of Cresson he had looked among the heads of the Templars killed there and not seeing the one he sought, he had known the job was still before him. Now he went down to see the Templars taken prisoner on Hattin's slope. His nephews rode on either side of him, Taqi ad-Din, on his right hand, Ali on his left.

They had gathered the Christian prisoners on the slopes where they had been taken. The great useless mass of the foot soldiers covered most of the low ground; they sent up a constant wail. Off to one side were the Templar prisoners, chained together in rows. Their armor had been taken, and their hands bound behind them. Half-naked, most of them wounded, all of them slack with fatigue and thirst, they sat quietly, waiting.

In their silence, in their waiting, he sensed the danger still in them, the unbroken will.

Taqi ad-Din said jubilantly, "Surely we have destroyed them now. We have never taken so many of them alive before. What will we do with them?"

The Sultan did not answer him. He rode along, sweeping his eyes up and down the rows of these men, their shorn hair, their long ragged beards. Then across the way he saw the black head he had been looking for.

His chest swelled in an explosive triumph. Now he knew the job was done; he knew he held Jerusalem.

Out there, in the second row, the knight turned and looked back at him. They stared at each other, unblinking, across the bodies of the prisoners, and then, with a massive indifference, the knight turned his gaze away.

Taqi ad-Din said again, "What will you do with them? They won't be ransomed; they would be impossible to break to slavery. We have never made prisoners of so many of them. Usually they fight to the death."

Saladin said, "They fought to the death here. Only it is late in coming."

On his left hand, Ali swung toward him, sharp-eyed. "They are helpless prisoners."

Taqi ad-Din said, "The Koran forbids killing prisoners, Uncle."

"Yet I mean to do it," Saladin said.

Ali's face flared with anger. "They fought nobly, and with valor. Are you going to be less a man than they are?"

"They are the firebrands of the Franks, and I will destroy them utterly, lest they burst alight again from the embers." He nodded at these two younger men, who did not understand the game. "We have those Sufi from Egypt with us. Give each of them a sword and a Templar, and let them all prove their faith."

Ali said, "You are the barbarian, Uncle." On his cheeks the tears glittered like diamonds. He wheeled his horse and rode away.

Rannulf sat with his arms tied behind his back, one of a long line of Templar prisoners; Eudes was on his left, and Mouse on his right, lying on the ground in a spreading pool of blood. Rannulf lifted his head, his eyes on the blazing blue of the sky.

His spirit was soaring. He knew he had won. He had come at last to the end of the test, and he had kept his vow. For the first time he thought God smiled on him. This is my son, who has conquered Heaven.

"Saint," Eudes said. "What are they going to do to us?"

"They're going to kill us."

The boy was silent for a moment. Then his voice erupted from him in a spate of outrage.

"They can't kill me. It's not honorable. This is my first battle. I fought hard, and I fought well. You said so yourself. I don't want to die now. I shouldn't die now, and I shouldn't die like this, with my hands tied behind my back."

Rannulf said nothing. Beside him Mouse was dead already. A slave was coming along the line with a bucket of water, giving each of the knights a drink. The slave stopped before Stephen.

"Don't touch him," Rannulf said, in Arabic. "He's dead." He looked up, and saw Ali.

The Saracen's face was drawn hollow like an old man's, and streaming tears. He turned his cup over, and let the water run down over Stephen's head. Kneeling on one knee, he laid his hand on the redheaded knight's cheek. Then he rose, and came on to Rannulf, and dipped up the water for him, and held the cup while he drank. Rannulf said nothing to him, but drank his fill. Ali went on, and gave water to Eudes.

The boy drank. After, he said, in a steady voice, "Saint. Shrive me."

"Confess, then, brother."

Out there in front of them all, the mullahs were killing them, one at a time. Some of the priests struck cleanly and quickly, some not; the watching Saracen armies jeered the strokes that missed, and cheered the heads that rolled. A Kurdish guard came up the line, stopped at Stephen, and saw that he was dead. Bending, he unhitched Rannulf from the chain. The water had given the knight some strength back. He got to his feet, shaking off the guard's hand on his arm. He had to step across the headless bodies of Templars to reach the killing ground. Like an altar it was puddled with blood. Before him stood a terrified boy in a dirty white turban, holding a scimitar as if he had never held one before. A hand on Rannulf's shoulder pushed on him. He stiffened, and they kicked the backs of his knees until they dropped him down kneeling on the ground. The boy raised the sword.

Rannulf lifted his eyes again to the burning sky. A ruthless joy filled him. He knew himself on the verge of transformation. Like a weight of stones the burden of his life slipped from him. He had not realized before how his life bound him down. He felt light as the air, already rising.

"Bow your head," the Kurdish lancer said.

"No."

The sword swung.

CHAPTER XXXIII

In the citadel of Jerusalem, Sibylla knelt at her priedieu, and Alys came, and told her that all the Templars had died at Hattin.

"All," Sibylla said.

"Not all, my lady. The Master is said to have been spared. The King is spared, my Lady."

"They are worthless men," Sibylla said. "God does not want them."

She lifted her eyes to the Crucifix. It was true, then; she had destroyed them all. Rannulf Fitzwilliam was dead, and they had lost Jerusalem. It seemed to her that her heart split in two, because no single heart could grieve enough for both the city lost, and the knight. She lowered her head, and submitted herself to God.